DANCING WITH THE UNDERTAKER

To: ZACH
The only michigan fan I really love.
Frank J. Basham

Frank J. Basham

PublishAmerica
Baltimore

First printing

Softcover 9781413774115
PUBLISHED BY PUBLISHAMERICA, LLLP
www.publishamerica.com
Baltimore

Printed in the United States of America

We are looking into the eyes of madmen, trapped, lost and alone. We are prisoners of our deeds, held hostage in the images of our golden mirror.

G. W. Sigrist,
Artist

Acknowledgements

I give special acknowledgement to my wife, Louise Elaine Basham, for her suggestion that this original short story form be expanded into a novel. Our hours of walking and talking about the script along the Atlantic Ocean side in Key West, Florida helped immensely in both the plot and character development of Dancing With The Undertaker. Best wishes to her on her upcoming series of children's books.

I would also like to thank my son, Michael C. Basham, who has done the photography and design for my book covers. Also thanks to his wife, Nina, for allowing me to borrow Mike for what seemed like endless hours of photography. Thanks to our other children, Jim Basham and Angela Miller, for their continued support of our pursuits. Louise and I hope we have not embarrassed any of you too much.

My last acknowledgements are to Gary Sigrist and Joe Galik for times past, never forgotten and better things ahead.

Chapter One

My art is looking back at me and I am frightened by what I see.

Somewhere in the shadows is that of which you do not speak. It walks in your dreams as a silent companion, coming closer and closer with every step you take; its cold breaths on your neck signaling the end.

I am not mad. I am not insane. I am not unhappy anymore. I am just another person swimming in this giant pool of life on Earth. I live in a time when new technology promises solutions, but delivers little more than further complexity. I accept the hand dealt me. I reflect on what I am and, but for the meddling of others, am happy. Well, maybe I am a little mad. Strike my first comment. This is my story.

Most good people only know they are victims of a lie after the fact. This is because their hearts are too big and their souls are too kind. I am once like this, but move on into the world of reality, taking a never look back attitude at these things causing me so much pain. Initially, this is what I tell myself.

Like some big collision on the interstate running through Detroit, Michigan, I am an accident. My birth is not planned. My mother and father do as other parents do and begin picking up the pieces of their lives. More than once my mother introduces me as the 'two martini' child. My mother is forty-five and my father is fifty-four as I arrive screaming into the halls of the Sigrist mansion. My delivery comes at home and my birth is only later officially recorded. I am a shadow child. My schooling is also private.

Money is not an issue. It is a river that flows through the Sigrist history atop a base of old wealth made in various enterprises. Some are legitimate and some are not.

Money affords things that blue collar life does not. My future looks bright. Why should it not? It is this way for generations. Also, the separation between the rich and poor continues. The middle class is falling away. I am rich. Case closed.

Don't get me wrong. My parents love me and my older brother very much. My circumstance isn't my mother's fault. It really isn't my father's fault but for a mild case of trophy wife envy and an aging process that eats up his mental capacity for seeing a gold digger for a gold digger. Like my father, even when one is old they are thinking they are young and life goes on forever.

To my mother's credit, she proves that money does not buy everything. My arrival is unwanted. She resists the abortion. This is lucky for me and, in this respect; I can't say my entire life goes without favor. She suffers in silence. She attends fewer and fewer parties and pisses off the Nanny to the point where she is told to raise her fucking little brat herself. From 'two martini' to 'fucking little brat', what is a child to think?

As I grow older I begin seeing the pain in her eyes. This pain is not hidden by the smile on her face. She does not give up her hurt about being saddled with me so late in life. I try being the best child money buys, but I am always in the shadows. I am in the shadows as though being born is some bad reoccurring dream that sedatives can not drive away. Too, I do not give up my hurt being referred to as the 'two martini' baby. When she introduces me as such I smile a smile similar to the one hiding my mother's own grief at the loss of her socialite lifestyle so late in life. I realize early on that some things in life are unspoken and remaining that way is of paramount importance, especially with people of our standing. We do love one another. It is a resentful love, but it is love. Isn't that enough?

My older brother, Gary, is part of this secret equation of resentment that I allow a home deep inside of my physic. My love for him is real. My resentment is that he is an on the chart baby choosing his own way in life. Gary leaves the family fortune behind pretty much telling everyone to go fuck themselves. He is a homicide detective living in, by our standards, squalor. Gary is a great detective. I give him that without hesitation. My resentment for my brother is that he has balls big enough to do and be what he wants to be. I am figuring on getting around to being what I want to be once the money runs out. When I cry or whine about this or that, Gary is there for me. He is my shoulder. He is my strength. Without his support I think I might be more than a little mad. I may be mad, but not insane. Don't call me insane. Life is a matter of perspective. Don't ever forget that. If my story teaches you nothing else, don't ever forget this advice. In the end it is all one is capable of holding on to.

There are many fond memories of my life with my older brother. I remember him holding the bully from down the street while I am beating the crap out of the little piss ant. Gary smacks him once in the mouth after I am finished...just to drive our point home. This is just one of my memories. I love Gary. He shares my anguish and silently understands. It seems everyone in my family silently understands.

My brother is my John Wayne figure. He is silent. He is strong. His heart is worth its weight in gold. Only Jim Beam and Coke are capable of bringing out his own buried fears. Considering his profession, this is understandable. Gary is a cop for one reason. Chasing the lies is the only way to bring out the sun again. The truth about someone or something is enlightening once embraced. I read that last thought in one of those college theory texts I am unable to take to class. The day I realize there is no money for my education breaks my heart. Gary's shoulder is not large enough. This is where everything changes and my pent up emotions begin trickling toward the surface. I see sympathy in Gary's eyes. I also see unspoken advice. The advice is simple, 'Grow a pair of balls'.

Chapter Two

It is easy for people to say they move beyond their bad memories or that these memories are hiding someplace so far removed from the time of their happening that they are incapable of returning again. These are the truly insane ones. These are the ones who believe building some imaginary jail cell for these bad memories is the only way of defeating them. The truth is that bad memories, like life-threatening illnesses, are our companions right up to the end. Eventually dealing with them is inevitable. Is it so strange that one's sanity requires walking and talking with them as though they are old friends? It is not strange at all. My example is this.

The basement of the Segrist mansion is a dark and dreary place. Despite all of the luxury and gold trim lining the halls above its head, the basement remains a dark and dreary place. Where better for taking one's anguish than to what is, to a developing child's mind, a funeral home of tucked away secrets beneath the glitter of all that gold and tinsel? Sitting just right and angling my head just so, I hear the rattling of silver undergoing another cleaning by the maids. On a really good day sitting there in the darkness, I even hear the maid's breath flowing across the spoon, fork, or knife as she is holding the item up, breathing on it, and finally wiping it with the soft, terry towel in hopes of bringing out the piece's brilliant luster before storing it away until another dinner. My imagination is thinking that, a time or two, a servant spits on this or that item before wiping it down. This is, no doubt, a statement about a denied raise in pay or Christmas bonus thought to be too small for the demands of a member of the working class.

This hiding place is also a school of sorts. It is where I learn much about the goings on in the Sigrist mansion not spoken of in the proper light of day. I sit below the food preparation area, the wash sink, the laundry room, and mudroom early in the morning or near the delivery door where the service people come and go. The conversation is better than television or these newly developing hand held video games the kids are carrying around town. You know, the new portable dungeons where children are spilling out their imaginations in the hopes of hiding their own bad memories? Sitting with my back against the cold, stone walls of the basement, hearing secrets is a daily event.

"Tabby, did you hear about last night?"

"Naw, what's up?"

"Old man Sigrist caught Gary putting it to one of the high school girls."

"Sounds like Gary."

There is a short silence. The conversation continues.

"Yeah, the master comes down to get a late night snack and the boy is bending her right over the preparation table."

I am imagining the cook backing away from the preparation table and making for the bottle of disinfectant in the cleaning closet. The butler is walking by and is hearing the conversation. Resisting is impossible.

"Maybe young Gary wants to be a chef. At least his understanding of where to put a good piece of meat is right on."

There is giggling. I begin laughing and instinctively cover my mouth with my hands.

"What did the old man say?"

"He wasn't so much mad about the event as he was the place."

"How so?"

"Guess the old man went out for a sandwich and fries."

"Explains why he told me to give the counter a really good cleaning this morning."

Everyone is laughing and, for the moment, they are all forgetting about their own personal problems. It just proves that some people's hiding places are right out in the open in the light of day.

Over the years, I learn many secrets about the place by listening. I also learn other secrets by watching. On several occasions I am sitting alone in my dark corner of the basement when the small light above the steps down to the basement flicks on. I watch as my mother slowly descends the steps. I am thinking she is a beautiful creature of the dark that many desire touching, but hesitate because of the fear of her image turning to dust once their fingertips reach her breasts. I see her coming down the squeaking stairs like a luscious mirage of water that I know I cannot drink. I am always feeling dirty about these thoughts, but often wake up dreaming about them. An attractive mother is open fodder for a young man with developing desires. My dream is that she is sweeping me up and having her way with me right on top of the cold, dark, damp things lingering unseen in my still developing exploration of the basement's confines. Our passion roars, time and time again, to another new location with every trip down the stairs. I dream she is always coming for me. I understand she is coming for the wine and the solitude of the wine cellar. A time or two, mother looks around as if sensing something is there in the dark with her. She never explores the feeling, always goes directly to the wine cellar and opens a good bottle of red wine, consuming it all in a single sitting. The pretense of a glass is put aside and I sit quietly watching her drinking from the bottle. One time I almost suffocate holding my nose while trying to fend off a sneeze from the lingering damp dust hanging all around the basement's skeleton. I watch mother leaving up the steps and my dirty thoughts come roaring back. I am an ass man and hers is firm and tight. Could it be she knows I am there and is just teasing me? Is my mother like all the other women my destiny is saying I am to meet? No, is my conclusion. Mothers are different. I am just a filthy-minded little bastard sitting alone in my dark and dirty corner with my dick in my hand. Walking over to where mother picks as her sitting place, I see her choice is Cabernet. Understanding later in life this is a heavier red wine good with red meats and stronger foods, it becomes my own personal testimony to her inner strength. Opening my own bottle here in the bowels of my hidden memories is also a testimonial for my suppressing thoughts about my mother. Understanding I cannot have her is another disappointment in my life. Still I am drinking with her and my thoughts are always private. My thoughts are always hiding in my dreams and in the basement. I know drinking a whole bottle at one sitting is something that one practices. I learn quickly that spinning the cork to the unpunctured side makes for better resealing, keeping the wine fresh until my next trip down into the darkness of my fantasy world. Cabernet is also my choice. This is the beginning of my drinking. I am not an alcoholic and I am not mad. Come to think of it, I am not a lot of things.

The basement is also where my inventor side begins its birth. Sometimes this dark space is my thinking room. After a time, having your dick in your hand gets boring. I think this is why God makes sexual activity a couple's thing. Anyway, my first invention is something I am always proud of. It is pre-technology, if you will. Picture this.

My transistor radio is revamped with a piece of rubber booting that is cut to wrap around the radio's speaker. Adjusting the volume to a lower level and pushing the thing right up against my ear forces the rubber booting down over my ear. I am the only one hearing the music. My other ear is free and listening for intruders arriving unexpectedly into my rapidly expanding world of stealth and imagination.

My second invention is a revamping of an old projector I find dying in the darkness of a storage box behind the basement steps. I am not thinking of the possibilities of patent or future revenues. I am just increasing the size of my own private world, a place where my sanity is living for hours at a time. I am not mad. You do believe me, don't you?

If I were thinking like my father and his business associates, I might be the leading contributor to music video pioneers the likes of Pink Floyd and their "Wall" CD. Instead I am just a little boy with a revamped transistor radio in one hand, a bottle of wine in the other and a reconfigured, discarded movie projector in front of him. The multi-colored kaleidoscope wheel turns slowly around the lens, projecting different colors on the wall across the way. Changing the camera's position to a different part of the wall gives the colors shapes as they roll across hard stone, spider webs, mold and green, growing moss.

Once, I find myself falling asleep and wake feeling fortunate mother does not come down the staircase finding me hiding and playing games in her own little hidden space beneath the feet of the really mad ones living overhead. The more I drink, the more I think the impossible. Perhaps mother scoops me into her arms and we do those unspeakable things I am thinking as I am hiding in my dark corner watching her move so erotically down those squeaking stairs toward the wine cellar. I begin believing the stair's sounds are the sounds of my mother moaning for my embrace.

The problem with a fantasy world is that you often find it being invaded by the real world. One afternoon, after a few enjoyable hours in the basement, I find this happening to me. Up to this point everything is going well. It is going better than one might imagine. Everything just seems to be falling into place. I am hiding in my secret place, watching mother come down the stairs, watching every sip her full and inviting lips take from the neck of the bottle of cabernet, watching her move back up the steps, listening to that moaning accompanying every step she takes, and watching her firm ass disappear through the door at the top of the stairs and into the light of day above my head and hidden hideaway. It is a perfect experience. It requires wine of my own and music of my own. I am reaching for the radio, the one with the rubber boot pieces wrapping around the speaker forming my own private listening space. The projector is on and the first color is red. The heat of the lamp is not warm enough yet to generate the heat required for setting the other colors on the disk in motion. The feeling is like sitting in the darkness with the fires of hell all around you. I hear mother's voice coming from the kitchen above.

"Where is that little fuck? Haven't I told you people to keep an eye on him when the Nanny isn't around?"

Mother is at the sink holding a glass of water in her hand. She flings it across the kitchen. Hearing the glass breaking against the other wall frightens me back from the depths of my last vision of her moving through the door at the top of the basement stairs. The servants are all silent. Only one replies.

"Ma'am, we are really sorry. He is like a shadow child. He just comes and goes. He is here one minute and gone the next. Honestly, we have our work to do."

There is a very long silence. I realize my transistor radio is on and is not muffled up against my ear. I am thinking that perhaps the servants know about my place all along and are keeping my secret for me. I switch the thing off and unplug the projector. The silence continues. It seems like forever. Mother finally speaks again.

"Never, mind. I know he can be difficult. The little shit will turn up sooner or later. Sorry I am such a bitch this morning. Clean that mess up."

I never desire my mother again. My dark space is soon my space alone. I do not know she is dying. This is another thing better left unsaid. My inventing continues and is worth discussing later in this story. Keeping in mind that I am not really mad, just different, is the one small favor I am asking. Realizing the whole world is often one's basement opens up a box of opportunities seemingly unending, but for the face of old man "Time" and guests one is not expecting.

Chapter Three

Mother's funeral is a surreal event. The mausoleum experiences a dusting off, weed removal, and the planting of new flowers. The plants are colorful. All the basic colors are there. They are all bright and not muted shades. Red, blue, yellow, orange, green, and white are holding the crypt hostage, if only for a few days. The approaching chill of the late season winds blowing off the Great Lakes is waiting in the wings for these delicate petals. In flower time their lives are as short as my mother's.

On the evening before the funeral I crank up the Porsche and speed up I-75 to the cemetery. Entering the main gate, I pass the groundskeeper as he is locking up for the night. The Porsche rumbles to a stop in the driveway and I see the car's exhaust through the rearview mirror. The chilled exhaust fumes are drifting up in thick, heavy intervals, curving across the back window, sliding across the top of the car, and leaking down across the front window. This effect makes the groundskeeper, Biggs, look like some apparition from a dream or two still lingering in the darker side of my brain. Biggs allows the one gate to remain open. He floats to one side and out of the way for me to enter. As I pass, pulling to halt just beyond the mark on the pavement where the gate swings clear of any entering cars, he sees my open bottle of cabernet. Biggs is leaning down near me when he speaks. I understand he is testing my breath. Under the circumstances, I am compliant.

"William, I see you're driving and drinking and not old enough for either."

"It is the week from Hell, Biggs."

"I understand and it isn't your sorry ass I worry about. What I worry about is you driving that thing over a headstone or two and me explaining it in the morning."

"I am fine, partner. Don't give it a second thought."

"Under the circumstances I am going to let it slide. I'm closing the gate, but not locking it behind you. Think you can remember to close and lock it when you leave?"

"I can do that, Biggs. Thanks for understanding."

Biggs nods, pats me on the shoulder and says he is sorry for my loss. I look him directly in the eyes. He is a sincere man and I am remembering a conversation from another funeral a few months back. After asking him why he is in this line of work, his reply is that it is the only place he goes where his wife isn't always interrupting. During this recollection, there is a bit of a pause and Biggs follows up.

"Billy, is there anything else? I need to get home before dinner gets cold."

"Please don't tell Dad. I just need some time alone."

"That is already understood. Just don't let me down with the gate and all."

I watch in the car's rearview mirror as the heavy iron gate casts it shadow over my vehicle while slamming against the waiting post and its holding pins. I watch Biggs wrapping a chain around the gate and post. He slides a padlock onto the chain and lets the lock hang as if it is shut. The lock is now waiting for my return. Looking up from the lock and into the space where Biggs was standing, I see that he is gone. I am thinking all things are temporary, even conversations. I like Biggs. He is unpretentious and seems to be accepting of his position in life. He seems happy in this solitude, this place and this time. What more is there to want of life? Striving to be like him is not a bad thing. Despite all the tragedy surrounding him, his approach seems to be that he deals with it, but does not participate in it. Living life around life is a real art.

The cemetery grounds are old. The fog and musty smells linger together like an aging man and wife. The winding paths are just big enough for one car. The paths stretch before me like some giant snake with its tail far out of sight and its head hidden in some dark ravine waiting to jump, striking at my soul. The road is tiered and winds up and up to the cemetery's crown. This is where the well-to-do sleep and is where our mausoleum stands, waiting for the members of our family to arrive one by one in their own time.

The Porsche is disrespectful of the dead. It roars up the winding road with its eyes piercing through the fog, like the knife of some angry combat warrior penetrating the flesh of his enemy while bringing on the final kill. The car is doing what I am thinking. 'I am a visitor. I am not a tenant. Listen to me roar. My years are still many into the future. You may want me, but you must wait.'

A little voice slips into my mind, whispering 'Only the good die young'. I kick the car into low gear, forcing it up the last few hundred yards to the crown of the cemetery and at the same time, I grab the open bottle of cabernet resting in the seat next to me. A big swallow of the power juice elicits this response. 'I am young, but not good.' No doubt there is a long, long, long life ahead of me. Suffering is in my kind's future. I am the opposite of Biggs and my only real challenge in life is learning to live with this face.

The overpriced, piece of metal slides to a stop. Its engine dies at an opening at the top of the hill just big enough for one or two cars to pull off. Its left, front wheel nearly drops over the edge of this small, graveled space. The car lurches and stalls. At fifteen my driving experience is somewhat limited and I do not remember to put the clutch in or shift into neutral before turning the key to its off position. I am muttering to myself.

"For what you cost you should drive and shut yourself off, you overpriced piece of shit."

Most people from down South think that Michigan is just one big slab of concrete, falling down buildings, and highways with big auto corporations, dying neighborhoods, and streets lined with whores all rolled together. Some of this is true. Most is not. Once outside of Auburn Hills, the country opens up and is quite beautiful. Despite the decaying markers and bones below them, the cemetery grounds are representative of the state's northern grandeur. In a way the cemetery is a little like my hiding place in the basement of our mansion. It is alone, isolated, and waiting for company capable of appreciating its hidden beauty. There is a difference between the cemetery and my basement hiding place. One finds themselves outgrowing their basement hiding place. A cemetery is always waiting for you to grow into it.

I am standing by the Porsche and leaning on its passenger's front fender. The bottle of cabernet hangs limply in my left hand. Occasionally I raise the bottle to my lips, taking a drink while gazing out into the night. The hours are passing and I am not noticing. This evening is like looking into a blanket. Because of the fog, there are no stars or faint lights in the distance signaling civilization is near. It is as though everything is dead and I am the last living soul on Earth, standing alone in this cemetery with my thoughts while wondering who is going to bury me. I am also thinking that missing my mother and the sight of her going up and down the basement stairs lives as long as I live. The last sip of cabernet is in her honor. I fling the empty bottle over the edge of the roadway. I scream out into the night.

"What now? What is to become of me?"

Unexpectedly, there is an answer to my question.

"I never thought a grandson of mine would turn out to be such a sniveling, little prick."

I hear a second voice entering the conversation.

"Now, you stop it Grandpa Pope. The boy is suffering from a lot at the moment."

"I got'a tell you, Grandma. The boy is a sniveling, little bag of self pity."

Looking back toward the mausoleum, I see two vaguely familiar faces from my past. I am remembering sitting on their laps as a very young child. My remembering is a warm and caring reflection. I am not sure why they are here. They are dead.

"Look, son. We all have things happen in our lives that appear to be a bucket of shit at the time."

"Pope, watch your mouth."

"Shut up and let me finish, Roberta. The boy needs to understand that life is nothing more than a curve ball waiting to hit you right in the nuts."

I am smiling while listening to these two spirits from my young past arguing with one another. I am vaguely remembering something about the car accident killing them both somewhere on vacation in the lower Florida Keys. Too, there is a small recollection of Grandpa Pope holding me on his lap and bouncing me up and down on his knee. Though my Grandpa is not Catholic, I understand why his nickname is Grandpa Pope. He is a real dictatorial son-of-a-bitch, but I am remembering a heart of gold.

"Grandpa Pope, is that you?"

"Course it is, son. Even in death I am watching over your sorry ass."

Grandma keeps pushing for subtlety in my dead relative's message.

"Stop it, Pope. You have taught him enough bad manners."

I find myself lumbering over to where the two spirits are lingering next to the right back side of the mausoleum. My conversation is as natural as if they are living. There is this urge to sit on Grandpa's knee again. I know falling to the ground is the eventual outcome. Spirits are voices and vision, but they are not matter of any form.

"What is Grandma talking about, Grandpa?"

"Ah, she has never forgiven me for teaching you how to give people the finger. Now, a three year old expressing themselves in that way is really funny. It isn't like you aren't going to learn it on your own anyway."

"Pope, I said stop it. I don't want you corrupting the boy from the grave. This is a time for love and understanding."

I see Grandpa Pope falling silent and coming to his defense seems the only thing to do. I know I love this man, but am not capable of remembering why. He and Grandma are taken from me too early, just like my mother.

"It is fine, Grandma. It isn't like the finger hasn't come in useful from time to time."

Grandpa Pope is laughing and his image is bouncing from solid to wavy with each chuckle he is emitting. Finally I see Grandma smile a little and I am feeling comfortable with this strange event. It is as though someone who loves me is watching over me and that their advice is worth more than all the money in the world. After this exchange is over, the conversation again turns serious.

"Look, boy. You are going to be facing an uphill battle. My advice is to grab your boots by their straps and hold on. Don't go too crazy…a little, maybe…but not too crazy. Listen to your big brother. He ain't right, but he loves you and you need to lean on him during the tough times ahead. You get my drift?"

I find myself responding in earnest to the spirit of my departed Grandfather.

"You know what I think, Grandpa?"

"What is that, boy?"

"Gary got his balls from you."

Grandpa laughs, "Well, what with your Grandma cutting them off and all, I am glad someone got them."

Grandma jumps into the conversation again as I am folding over in laughter at Grandpa's last comment.

"That is quite enough, Pope. Get back in there where you belong. The boy has heard all he needs to hear from you."

There is a long silence. I hear the wind kicking up and an almost shrill laughter cutting across the top of the cemetery.

One thinks this sort of thing is Mother Nature playing tricks on her drunken children. I know better. Grandpa is laughing so hard he is pushing the wind right up Grandma's long, conservative dress. I find myself holding my 'fuck-finger' toward the night sky. It is illuminated by what is left of the moon's glow.

"Thanks, Gramps. Fuck them all, Gramps. I'm sorry, Grandma."

The Porsche screams back down the snake's back toward the cemetery's front gate. Halfway down the winding road, the snake begins hissing and soon my car's steering is very difficult. A huge piece of my discarded cabernet bottle is sticking out of the front driver's tire. Before trying to devise a solution, I walk over the edge of the road and vomit on the wet grass just to the edge of the road. Cabernet doesn't taste as good coming up.

The tow truck driver is not happy about being called this far out at three in the morning. Detroit Police Department is emblazoned on the side of the truck in bright, large, and glowing letters. Watching the truck moving down the hillside is one more black eye in my long string of fuck-ups as of late. I feel my brother's hand on my shoulder. It is big brother to the rescue again.

"Get in, asshole. We have a funeral to go to in the morning."

Chapter Four

Provided things are going well, reaching the age of thirteen is the top of the mountain. It is a crossroad where the entire world's knowledge takes residence in your thoughts overnight. This is the way it is with children who believe thirteen is the magic number signaling adulthood. Nothing is farther from the truth. Life requires a few more years for this fallacy's burial. I am busy going about the things young men do when my own awakening abruptly begins pounding on my bedroom door. I am fifteen, nearly sixteen. I know everything and nothing is fair.

"She wants to see you, son."

My father's face is drawn and tired. His sitting with my mother, waiting for her death is taking a very heavy toll. It is only yesterday that I am still telling myself this is not really happening. There is all this money we wallow in and still not enough to buy a cure for this thing, cancer. It isn't fair to me. Missing her trips to the basement and down into the wine cellar isn't fair to me. Right about now, I am feeling very dirty. I am feeling very guilty as well. I am not old enough to face this sort of thing. Again, it isn't fair to me. Still, there is this obligation and it is mother's wish. It is a requirement that I muster the strength to grant her wish. The Sigrist family knows all about requirements, honor or, at least, the pretense there of. My father is expecting this of me. Even though it isn't fair to me, he is expecting it of me.

Looking past my father, I see my brother's face hovering over his right shoulder. Gary is standing in the hall leaning against the far wall. His back is up against a very valuable painting. It is a painting my father spends several hundred thousand dollars to purchase. Giving a shit about some piece of canvas covered in different colored smudges is beyond Gary's concern. Over the years, noticing him do other similar things is a silent signal between the two of us that some things are more important than others. I am remembering the day he pisses in one of our thousand dollar vases. His response is simply that, 'he needed to piss, the vase was there and he could'. Gary is sometimes a pig. Despite my respect and love for him, he is sometimes a pig. Looking in his eyes at this particular time, there is this immediate understanding that this is not one of those times. Gary loves mother deeply. We both love mother deeply. His eyes tell me it is time to man up. The expensive painting he is leaning on is the farthest thing from his mind. Father is insistent we hurry on down the hall, up to the third floor and into mother's room.

"Please, son. I know this is difficult, but it is important to your mother. There isn't that much time. The doctor is with her. The priest is at her side, too."

I get up from my seated position on my bed, leaving the television on. It is on the medical channel I watch frequently. Becoming a surgeon is my lifelong dream. I am wanting to one up my older brother. A doctor is more important than a police officer. Isn't it? It is like my mind is telling me...being better than my brother is important. My father noticing me more is important. This is something else that isn't fair to me. Sometimes thinking about my brother in his shiny police uniform really pisses me off. He is taking my glory away. I am trying so hard and no one is noticing. Why try at all? Now, there is this. Well, I am going to take it like a man. I am going to be as tough as my brother.

The three of us are walking down the hallway when I begin feeling my legs get rubbery. Having to do this is not fair. It is not fair to me. I am not ready. Almost as though he is reading my thoughts, Gary puts his hand on my shoulder helping to steady my walk and speaks.

"There is never a good time for something like this, Bill."

I want the walk to be longer. It is over before it should be over. This isn't fair to me. I need more time for collecting my thoughts. What am I going to say? Is waiting for her to speak first the proper thing to do? I am wishing I were older and knew these protocols. My mind is saying to speak from my heart. My head is saying there is nothing to say. It is what it is.

The huge oak bedroom door is older than my mother. It squeaks as father is pushing it open and beckoning for Gary and me to go into the bedroom. Upon entering, the doctor is leaving by way of a side door that leads out into a back hallway. The priest is standing near a set of closed curtains near one of the three huge windows comprising the bay window area of mother's bedroom. All the curtains are shut and but for two small lamps, one on each side of mother's bed, there is no real light coming into the room. Gary is pulling me along by my left arm. We are too quickly standing at the end of mother's bed.

Mother is sitting in an upright position with the help of three or four huge pillows. Her face is death. I see that immediately. There is no makeup hiding the obvious. My pain is immediate. This is not fair to me. I am too young for this. Soon my thoughts begin wandering back to the basement and its steps. I am not seeing my mother moving down into the basement. I am seeing a bright glow of light and love floating down into the bowels of darkness and no return. The vision is smiling. My eyes begin moving away from the basement steps and begin floating up toward the upper floors of the mansion. They are gliding over all of the family pictures hanging on the walls of this monstrosity of a building that seems to go on and on forever. I am thinking that sometimes our most important memories are always in front of us but that we keep forgetting to hang them on the walls of our mind. The days in the park, the walks along the beach and the boat trips late at night looking back at the city lights are things worthy of remembering. Remembering those lights is a happy time for me. Those lights are blocking out all the filth and blight of the city's real body shining so boldly in the light of day.

All these memories are rushing back while I am standing at the foot of mother's death bed. She is, I am thinking, so much more than a socialite. Remembering her laugh and knowing the difference between the real one and the one living in the ears of her rich friends is now very I important to me. It helps with all this unfairness. Knowing that smile is important. It is the one thing helping me believe I am not part of the reason for all of this. The doctors are now saying unhappiness causes death in those losing their will to live. I want mother's death to be because of the cancer and not because of me. If it is because of me, it is unfair to both of us. It is unfair to her. It is unfair to me. I feel Gary nudge the middle of my back with his elbow. I raise my head and find myself looking into mother's eyes.

Mother is smiling and it is a true smile. Later in life, I understand that we are all equal in the end and acceptance is a comforting thing. Right now, I am thinking this is her pretend smile just like her pretend laugh at those big parties, the ones I am responsible for her missing. It is as though her eyes are holding my eyes against hers'. I am happy when she finally speaks. She is not dead. This is a good thing. Mother is motioning for Gary and me to come and sit by her, one on each side of her bed.

"Not to be so gloomy, my lovely boys. Come sit by your mother. Hold my hand. Hold my hand the way you did when you were just little boys. I liked it when you did that. I liked it so much. I do remember a time or two when your hands weren't as clean as they might have been, but boys will be boys. Won't, they?"

It is very difficult. I find myself keeping myself stable by holding onto the end of mother's bed as I move my way around to the side of the bed. I am seeing the first signs of Gary crumbling as well. I am not feeling so afraid at this particular moment. The conversation is not about death. It is about life and all the things my eyes are remembering in those pictures hanging on the mansion's walls. I am beginning to understand that what we are thinking is not always what is, that mothers and fathers do things for reasons of their own and they most often revolve around what is best for their own. A little false laugh here and there is a good thing in the big scheme of things. Today is for crying. Getting around to that is inevitable, especially for those who love one another.

Chapter Five

My brother's rise within the police ranks is meteoric. He is not one to brag about accomplishments. Gary believes these sorts of things are emotional and that emotions are the only things in life that are real. He also believes emotions are the things needing control. Everything else is no more than an ends to a means. This is why it is not surprising when his Detective ranking arrives and is casually mentioned one night over a dinner at home with Father. These dinners are far and few between and the feeling is that they are a requirement or event for important announcements. Reading a small blurb in the paper, I am aware of Gary's new promotion. I know that Father mentioning it over dinner is just a precursor to the real reason we are here. This is an event dinner and we both know its handling and setting is more business than just, 'how are you boys getting along since Mother's passing'.

I watch the server sitting small Cornish hens in front of us. A small bowl is sitting by each plate and is holding a serving of spinach. Father loves spinach and our complete disgust with this stringy, snot-like substance is unimportant. Gary and I are looking at the green glob and thinking maybe the desert is worth anticipating. Turns out, it is not. All this money, and the best the chef is capable of making is custard. Swallowing custard is like swallowing cum. This is Gary's interpretation of the stuff's texture and taste. How he would know this is beyond me and asking is not something I pursue. The small custard cup is sitting in a bowl a little larger than the cup. The ice in the bowl is keeping the custard cold. Father is not yet in the room and Gary is looking across the table in my direction. His comment is just loud enough for the server to hear.

"I'm wondering how many the maid had to jerk off to fill three bowls."

"Oh, Christ, shut the fuck up, Gary. Dad is going to make us eat this stuff."

"Don't be so judgmental, little brother. Don't knock it until you try it."

I am thinking about my follow up answer. Looking up, I see our Father coming through the main dining room's door. He is talking on his cell phone. The last part of his conversation is all I catch.

"Yes, yes my darling. Everything is going to be alright. You worry too much. They are big boys and I am sure they will understand."

Father flips the phone closed as he is passing by us. A smack on the back of Gary's head is my brother's greeting. I see Gary immediately fussing with his hair. His hair being perfect is something my brother demands. His thinking is that a full and well groomed head of hair is as important as a ten inch dick to some woman. Believing this is difficult for me, but the asshole does think a bowl of custard looks like cum. My greeting is a simple, "Sit up straight, young man. You are slouching too much while sitting on your bed. It is starting to show. Putting the fucking computer on your desk might be a real good idea."

I reply, "Nice to see you too, Daddy."

"Don't call me Daddy, you little fuck."

"Can I call you, big fuck?"

My Father's sense of humor is something worth manipulating. It affords me many hours of laughs and amuses Gary to no end. Our father is a very literal man and often it is difficult for him, this determining what is an insult and what is humor. Gary's thought on this subject is that dotting so many Is' and crossing so many Ts' is making Father a very dull man. Whatever it is, it is also making him very old. It is all about the deal, the stock market, the bonds, the bank account and price of gold. I am not complaining. Despite our recent tragedy, the old man is taking care of us the best he knows. He is a business man, not a people person. Throwing bodies and lives away is the only way to stay on top. One of his favorite sayings is, "Competition is good as long as you are the one competing."

As Father is sliding into his chair, I am looking over at Gary. He is sliding his fuck finger into the custard, putting his finger in his mouth and sucking down some of the custard.

"Mmmm, that is good stuff."

The bile in my stomach is beginning to bubble up into my throat. Father chimes in.

"Be good tonight, Gary. If you don't, I will shoot you with your own gun and congratulations on your promotion. Chief Hawkins called me this morning."

Gary is thinking that our Father is one who is even above reading the paper. His sources are ongoing. This, of course, is not true. It is true that whatever is in print our Father usually is privy to ahead of time. It is also true that the newspaper is like a woman. Turning her pages is a requirement of being sure what is being printed is what is in need of being printed. It is that old adage about controlling the media and you are controlling the world. The internet is an even scarier place. Its changes are coming at the speed of light. The talking heads are speaking the same thing on every channel. The news people are different only in their clothing. Their voices are all the same. This is a lot of what Gary believes. His profession is one demanding this approach. This is my interpretation of my brother's inner core. What you see is not always what you get. Eating cum is not his thing either. I am sure of this.

"Well, gentlemen, let's eat."

Gary and I dig in, waiting for the hammer to fall. It does not take long. Knowing Father is on a schedule and that we are no more than a block of time on his busy daily schedule is understood. Gary is the one pushing the conversation.

"So, Father. What is the reason for dinner tonight?"

"Now, don't start being a detective so soon. Does there need to be a reason? Can't I just want to spend a little quality time with my two sons?"

Gary is very curt. It is surprising my Father doesn't jump down his throat. Gary is carrying a gun. I am thinking this may be part of the reason.

"The amount of quality time you spend with us would fit in a thimble."

Father is staring into Gary's eyes. I see Gary is winning the standoff. Tonight's dinner is the farthest thing from whatever it is my Father wants to do. Gary knows this and is fishing with Dad's emotions, the real ones needing controlling. Father blinks first and the conversation follows.

"Well, Mr. new-detective-smart-ass let me bring you up to speed. I really want you two assholes to like your new step mother."

I am not thinking when I find myself blurting out a response. It is a real from-the-heart response having no space for compromise."

"The fucking least you could have done is wait for the dirt on Mother's grave to settle. For Christ's sake, she has only been dead for six months."

"Son, you don't understand."

I am very, very agitated. Gary is still sitting silently across from me. Borrowing his gun is in the back of my mind. Shooting my piece-of-shit Father right where he sits is the sentence I am mentally handing down.

"Oh, I understand. Your dick is more important than your conscience."

Dad is on his feet and heading in my direction. He is reaching out for my throat.

"You ungrateful little mother fucker. I've had just about all of this nonsense I am going to take."

My chair is now over against the dining room wall and I am backing away from my approaching father. Gary's voice slices through the tension in the room's air and I see my father stopping in mid-stride.

"Back away father. Don't lay a hand on Bill or, so help me God, I will kick your ass."

The kitchen aide is moving into the room at about the same time all of this is happening. He is holding a silver tray with a martini on the rocks sitting in the middle of it.

"Sir, is everything alright?"

Gary and my Father are again looking into one another's eyes. My Father is again being beaten back. He is thinking, 'Will he or won't he?' I am thinking he will. What my brother is saying is emotional. Though his words are being contained and controlled. They are real. I want to see this. I am waiting. My breathing is very heavy and, but for the servant being witness, there are thoughts in my mind of hitting my Father with something very big and heavy when he is looking at Gary and not at me. My Father begins his little dance away from the subject.

"No, no Reeves. Things are fine. Your timing is perfect. Right now, that martini is just what the doctor ordered."

Father is back in his seat at the head of the table. Watching him pulling the toothpick from the cold gin, placing it to his mouth, biting into one of the two olives on their wooden crucifier is reminding me of something evil wanting to gnaw into an adversary, while understanding it is better to wait to fight another day. Shortly, I am hearing a sound interrupting the black silence lingering like the dark curtains in Mother's death room. It is Gary's pager. Gary is calmly removing the instrument from his belt and looking at the message it is bringing. I am shaking all over. Next, I see him looking up from the device and into Father's eyes for the last time this evening.

"Looks like I need to go and, in the nick of time, Father. We must never do this again. Really, I mean it."

Without thinking, I find myself following my older brother out the door. My Father is calling after me.

"Where the hell do you think you are going? I just want us to be a family. There isn't that much left of us."

I find myself responding. Emotions are real. Remember?

"I'm going with Gary tonight."

Pausing at the dining room door, there is one more comment falling from my lips unchecked.

"Was a year too long to wait? A decent time would have been nice. Are you on another schedule?"

Gary is waiting for me out front of the mansion. There is no objection to me getting into the unmarked police car beside of him.

"Thanks."

"Thanks for what?"

"Thanks for standing up for me."

"Believe it or not, I was standing up for myself as well."

There is a short silence and the logical side of me begins bubbling around inside of my brain.

"Wonder what her name is."

"It is Vickie."

I am somewhat taken back by my brother's comment.

"How do you know this?"

"That isn't important."

"Well, it sounds like a fucking cough drop."

I see Gary is smiling. In the middle of all this tension, my brother is smiling. I am wishing to be more like him. I am still thinking this when the detective car stops at the end of an alley just beyond Carl's Chop House in downtown Detroit. Gary is looking in my direction. I am fixating on the red and blue lights pulsing through the night sky. I am thinking these are different lights than the ones lingering in my memory from our boats trips when Mother is well, younger, and vibrant and still dreaming about the possibilities of life. I am thinking these lights are telling a different story and are making no promises of a happy ever after. Gary speaks.

"Come on. Get out. Let's go see what is up. You need to get Mother off your mind. Staying with me might be a good idea. Dad will be back in Europe by Monday. You can go back to school and I won't have to worry all weekend about getting paged to investigate a murder at our own home."

I follow. The night is bitterly cold. The snow is packing down nearing its ice stage. My face is hot. It is not because of the cold winds whipping down from Canada and across the river. My face is hot because I am still angry. I am breathing deeply. I want my lungs to hurt. At the end of the alley, there is a short exchange between Gary and a uniformed street Sergeant.

"I say accident, but you are the Detective. Congratulations, by the way."

I see the body lying at the base of a small chain-linked fence gate. It is on its back and the arms are sticking straight up in the air, the hands are clinched shut and the eyes are wide open. Gary is reaching into his pocket pulling out rubber gloves. Turning toward me, he speaks.

"Here, put these on. Tonight you earn your stay."

Suddenly the thoughts of my mother and this night's earlier events are gone. I am in the moment and just wanting to be more and more like my big brother.

Chapter Six

Trying to accept my stepmother is difficult, but I try. My reasoning is that in just a little over a year I am free of her. My grades, despite the loss of my mother, are acceptable, but not outstanding. My grades are not such that a scholarship is waiting patiently for my taking, but the family fortune buys what the family fortune buys. During the day I focus and continue pushing myself forward. My dream is medical school.

A feeling creeping up inside of me is also somewhat surprising. Gary is never at dinner and rarely is anywhere close to the Sigrist mansion. I am driving now, legally, and am seeing him once or twice a week. Oddly our meetings are most often at the city police morgue. I am sure this is a result of my medical interests. Knowing as much about the human body prior to entering college is a good thing. It is amazing how beautiful a corpse is when being viewed from a strictly clinical position.

That creeping feeling is about Vickie, my stepmother. She is alone in the mansion but for the servants. She makes no real friends and the feeling inside of me is that the servants resent her presence as much, if not more, than I do. Still, my effort is there and we sit alone at the dinner table night after night. Our first conversation comes at a very odd moment. A very aggressive thunderstorm is sweeping across the entire state of Michigan. At one particular clap of thunder I see Vickie jumping nearly out of her seat. My response is automatic. It is out of concern for the fears of another human being. If anything fear is within the range of my understanding.

"It is just noise following the lighting, Vickie. The worse is already over."

Finding ourselves looking into one another's eyes for the first time is a shock for both of us. Vickie's eyes are a color I can not quite describe other than to say that the area around the pupils is green but the outlying ridges are a gray. I am thinking of cat's eyes. My gaze immediately goes back down toward my half eaten steak and what is remaining of the steak-fries I dearly love. I love them smothered in catsup. I hear Vickie's response traveling through the sounds of the night and its accompanying lightening and thunder. It is almost a little girl sound that is being squeezed from a child's hiding place inside some deep dark closet holding reservations for nights just like this one.

"I was hoping that it was."

I am looking into her eyes again. My mind is saying, 'don't let her drag you in.' and my heart is saying, 'maybe it is time to end all of this. It is what it is.'

"Well, sometimes things are hard to overcome."

"I know. Your father is and was never around for you. I am coming to understand that."

Before thinking, I am throwing out a response less conciliatory than defiant.

"It doesn't look like you are doing much better, bitch."

There is a long silence. Our eyes are looking into one another's with a set of immediate emotions capable of killing. A silent lightening strike somewhere in the distance in the company of it thunderous sibling kills all of the lights in the house. I feel a great fear immediately arriving at my doorstep. My mind is telling me I should be listening. The last thing in Vickie's hand is a steak knife. She is coming to slit my throat in the dark of night. Instead I am hearing the quick footsteps of the servants coming into the room. The thin beam of a flashlight is running ahead of their arrival. Candles are quickly set. The room is lit with a creamy haze that is hanging onto the night like some forest being penetrated by a distant church steeple light in the hazy bogs of far off London. I am hearing a sound. It is not the heavy breath of the victim being pursued by the werewolf through the thick brush and fog or the barking of the dogs in pursuit of the evil creature rapidly overtaking its victim. It is a soft sob. Looking up I see tears in Vickie's eyes. The gray in her eyes' coloring is gone and now only the green remains and it is filling with tears.

"Well, a girl can always hope. Seems I have landed on a rock of money where no love lives. Besides, you haven't even noticed I had the servants whip up your favorite meal."

The truth is my thoughts are living with the maids and servants. Finding it hard to believe Vickie is offering up this meal as a truce is easy to understand. Isn't it? My mind is saying, 'don't show sympathy for her." Still, I do. My hand is reaching across the table and before realizing it I am offering a sort of apology.

"Hell, Vickie. I'm a real ass at times. Just ask my brother."

Vickie is dabbing her eyes with the monogrammed napkin from her lap. I am still feeling like a complete ass. The servants are standing patiently by waiting for instructions. Vickie looks into my eyes again as asks.

"William, would it be alright if we share a bottle of that cabernet your mother liked so much? I figure toasting her might be a real good thing to do and, hell, I know you have been drinking for some time. I think a toast to progress is in order."

I nod my approval and we find ourselves moving into the main library and into the two chairs usually reserved for my father and his guest. The fire is already roaring. Good servants are known for anticipating their master's needs. Shortly a bottle of 1981 Pine Ridge Cabernet is placed on the table between us. Two Reidel glasses sit flanking the red liquid waiting for the sound of the wine's body to roll over their crystal mouths and into their embrace. The fire is flickering through the thin crystal like bright strands of truth waiting to come together in the dark of night. We clink our glasses. It is Vickie's toast.

"This is to a new beginning."

Most of the conversation is happening on Vickie's side of the table. It is about how she really does love my father, not his money. It is about how she tries, but it is never good enough. The drivel goes on and on to the point of irritation. I find myself finally offering advice.

"Well, Vickie, I have tried to love him for years. Nothing ever comes back. I have just given up trying. You will end up like all the rest of us...waiting for something that never comes."

Out of the blue Vickie responds, "So, I am the trophy wife?"

"You are forever and ever my dear. Get used to it and have another glass of wine."

The bottle of wine turns into a second bottle of wine. Vickie and I are on the couch in front of the remaining fire. It is very late at night. Father is somewhere off of the continent, the servants are at home for a few hours sleep. My cell phone rings and I see it is Gary calling. I do not answer. The feeling of Vickie's hand running slowly up my thigh is taking precedent over my cabernet-induced memories. I am thinking of mother.

Chapter Seven

(Airplanes & Lovers)

Airplanes and lovers are a lot alike. Not knowing when to get off is a definite recipe for crashing and burning. The difference is that with a lover there is the possibility of starting things over again. But for very rare occasions, an airplane crashing is pretty much the end of things. My life is, at least from my point of view, always crashing and burning. There is the death of relatives I barely know, the death of my mother and now the death of my father. I am picturing his last moments. The fact that I am the one taking the call, that my response is rather matter of fact and stoic is of little importance. It is just another thing affecting my already fucked up life.

I picture father rushing thru the airport hell bent on catching his connecting flight to Troy, Michigan. Got to get back and get some of that young cunt waiting for him at home. I am not feeling guilty about Vickie and our evening romps by the fireplace. Hell, it is a piece of ass. Too, the apple doesn't fall very far from the tree. I am a lot like my father and so is Gary. It is just what it is. Vickie is getting what she wants and I am punishing my father. It is like that old song goes, `if you can't be with the one you love, love the one you're with`. I see him insulting, pushing and prodding every person responsible for things going well at the airlines. The trouble is that on this particular night the commercial airlines are sitting on the ground due to bad weather. Pushing and prodding is just wasted breath and effort.

Still, I see my father grasping for other options. This is what a driven business man's internal nature is like. It is not rational. It is just one big ball constantly winding around itself with goals, schedules and options. This is why my father is flying in the middle of a snowstorm with some half crazy jockey pilot from the wrong end of flight school training.

"It's going to get a little rough up here, Mr. Sigrist."

"Just get my ass home in time for dinner and there is a bonus in it for you, Captain Hastings."

"Will do the best I can."

"That isn't good enough. I have a young hot wife I'm wanting to surprise."

"With old guys like us, Mr. Sigrist, it might be wise to call ahead."

My father does not like the direction of the conversation and falls silent. He is sulking like always. Things are not going his way and he is not appreciating a smart ass for a pilot. The plane's red blinking underbelly lights are disappearing into the oncoming storm as the control tower speaks one last time to Captain Hastings.

"Go with God you CSOB (crazy son-of-a-bitch)."

The fifteen-seat turboprop is shaking violently as it pulls itself thru the oncoming storm and finally into the more stable air above the approaching combination of clouds, wind, rain, snow and ice. Though the pilot is not verbalizing it, he is thinking this decision is not a good one. A sick wife at home and outrageous bills needing paid is his only consideration for this crazy venture. True, Captain Hastings is a crazy son-of-a-bitch, but his flying always pisses down danger's throat. The long lost years of Vietnam are nothing compared to this. Besides, he is a religious man and truly believes God goes where he goes. The fault with this logic is that we may be hell bent on making our decisions, but this does not mean God is approving of them. The Big Guy is sitting on high somewhere, no doubt shaking his head. He is saying, 'Help me out a little bit, Captain.' Still, God works in strange ways and the insurance from this little incident is more than enough for paying the pilot's wife's medical bills, up to the time of her death. There is even enough left for burial. As for the Captain and my father, there isn't enough left to bury. The point is mute.

It is on the descent that the wisdom of this decision finally jumps into the forefront of my father's thinking. It is just one word bouncing around inside of his skull, fuck, fuck, and fuck. Captain Hastings is fighting the plane's controls like my father fights the pull of his leather strapping during a disciplining by his dominatrix he visits on his trips to Thailand. The pilot is talking to both my father and the plane at the same time. My father is sitting in the co-pilot's seat. They are the only two on the plane.

"Strap down tight, Mr. Sigrist. This isn't going to be a smooth landing. Keep your nose up bitch. Keep your nose up bitch. I can't go around. Got'a put your sorry ass down before this thing peaks."

The plane is lurching and bouncing like it is being sandwiched between rows of bricks on top and bottom. The sound of the propellers is being drowned out by the roar of the weather passing over the aircraft's outside skin. Father is beginning to understand that the wing flaps are not responding properly as he is watching the pilot fight the controls. Both men are beginning to panic.

"Can't we get up and fly over it, on to someplace clear?"

There is a long silence. It is the weather outside and the fear inside now filling the cockpit. Mother Nature and Chance are firmly gripping the men's throats. Finally, Captain Hasting manages a sentence.

"Not enough fuel and you better hold onto your nuts."

A few seconds later there are the beams from a few red lights lining the side of the runway. A strong cross wind is pushing the plane to the right. As the wing tip is touching down sparks begin flying off the concrete runway and both men know this is not a night they will ever be telling stories about. The plane is tumbling down the runway. The window to my father's side is blowing inward against his face. With it is the cold, whistling wind. The last thing my father thinks he is hearing is Mother Nature's voice, "Fools, both of you."

I believe there is good death and there is bad death. For Captain Hastings, this night is a good death. For my father, this night is a bad death and one of getting his up and comings. There are no more trips to Thailand, the brothels, the dominatrix or the children in servitude. These are all things Gary and I are talking about a few months after the call. Knowing that the bartender, Mac, is not the type to be chasing us out is comforting. Gary's key is for those cold nights when he is on a call and needs coffee. That he might spike his coffee with this or that is not important. He is not shy about letting himself in, brewing a cup and thinking about this or that case he is working. Mac likes the arrangement. It means looking the other way on minor infractions that typically requires reporting to the ATAF folks. It is Gary's belief that these people are not real cops anyway. Gary's comment is that ATAF really stands for Assholes That Annoy Folks. Anyway, we are at Burt's Bar. It is where we go to talk and be alone.

"You are strangely quiet tonight, little brother."

"I'm just thinking."

"What are you thinking about?"

"How I have fucked things up from the get go."

"I thought maybe you were thinking about fucking Vickie."

There is a long silence. I know this moment is coming. Keeping a secret from my older brother is something that is impossible. Understanding how he knows, how he is so deep into my soul, my heart, my psychic is very scary. Eventually I find myself looking up from my gin and tonic and into Gary's face. He is smiling.

"What is so funny?"

"It seems like she fucked you instead of the other way around."

Taking a sip of my drink, I reply.

"You are right as usual. Don't know what I am going to do now. I just can't believe our asshole father signed everything over to that gold-digging bitch."

There is no reply to my last comment. I find Gary moving onto another subject.

"So, when are you moving out and are you taking anything that isn't nailed down?"

"She says to take the car I want and my personal belongings."

"Then you come and live with me, William. Fuck them all. Things will work out. They always do."

Gary is moving from his barstool and around to the back of the bar. I see him mixing two more drinks. Looking around and seeing Burt's is empty but for the two of us is reminding me of the emptiness inside of myself at this particular moment in time. Gary slides my new drink down the length of the bar and it stops right in front of me, clinking my empty glass as it comes to a halt. I smile at my brother's sense of accomplishment.

"Think you're a real smart ass, don't you?"

"You have got to admit not many bartenders can even do that. Consider it a toast to the future. We are better off without them, little brother. We really are."

Getting around to my disappointment about not being able to go to medical school eventually works its way into the various topics of the night. By three in the morning Gary and I are really, really, really drunk. We find ourselves wandering off into the night in search of a whore. We end up in the back of a patrol car being driven to Gary's apartment. I puke and pass out on the couch. What Gary does is beyond me. All I know for sure is that he is gone when I find myself waking about two-thirty in the afternoon.

I am sitting in front of the television watching the evening news. It is around six-thirty in the evening when Gary comes back through his apartment door. He is carrying Chinese take-out food and is in the company of an elderly black man I vaguely remember seeing. On second glance I recognize the man as Mr. Wimble. Mr. Wimble is the owner of Wimble & Wimble Funeral Services and is the one responsible for handling most of my family's funeral services right up to and including my father. I am remembering him as kind, really old and worse-looking than most of the people after his embalming services. Gary speaks.

"Mr. Wimble, you already know my brother."

"Yes, yes. How are you holding up William?"

"I'm regrouping so to speak, Mr. Wimble."

"Please call me Ted, William. I have been part of your family history so long I really feel like one of the family. Thinking of all the services I performed for your family brings back memories. I really had a soft spot for your grandfather, Pope."

I watch Ted moving around the disarrayed apartment toward the kitchen table. I see him taking a chair, but not a chair at either end of the table. I find myself respecting this old black man. He knows he is not the head of this family, what little of it remains.

"Come on, William. Ted really likes Chinese food. Let's eat."

Ted also likes Sake. I don't, but find it is capable of getting you as drunk as gin and tonic. We are eating Chinese food and drinking warm Sake. I am not too sure if wanting to be like my big brother is a good thing. The conversation swings and swings until I hear it landing on a single topic.

"So, I hear you wanted to go to medical school and things didn't work out."

I am somewhat taken back, but am at a point where caring about privacy really seems to be more a crock of shit rather than something to be getting all pissy about.

"Yeah, well I guess I'll just have to decide on something else."

What I hear next is right out of the blue. Gary is leaning in waiting on my response and Mr. Wimble is looking me directly in the face. I am seeing all those age lines in his face. The lines seem to be running off into some forever place tucked away into a hiding place in the far universe beyond the comprehension of mortal man. I am also wondering if he isn't really already dead and just doesn't know it.

"Have you ever considered becoming an undertaker?"

Sometimes life is more chance than planning. This is such a night. I find myself drinking warm Sake and beginning to like a man who I know only thru his touching of my dead family members. It seems Mr. Wimble is the only Wimble in the equation and that he recently receives a diagnosis of terminal cancer. His family is all gone. He weaves a tale about my Grandpa Pope having set him up in business many years ago. He feels that, with my interest in the medical profession, me feeling at home in the funeral business is likely a perfect fit.

"Hell, William. You get to play with the bodies and don't have to worry about malpractice insurance that much."

Gary is starting to laugh and wails out his response.

"Damn right, brother. They are already dead."

The whole conversation is striking me a little funny as well. I am looking at Ted Wimble trying to keep his face in focus. I burp up a little Chinese afterthought and reply.

"Do you see what the fuck I have to put up with, Mr. Wimble?"

"Ted, William. Call me Ted. Want more Sake?"

The old man is pouring a little more hot Sake into my little round cup before I reply.

"Guess I do."

Later on, when things settle down, we are all sitting in the living room smoking cigars. Looking deeply into Ted's eyes I am seeing a man wanting something.

"I'm sorry to hear about the cancer thing, Ted."

"Ah, we all have a time. It isn't the cancer or my death that is worrying me, William."

"So, what is?"

"An honorable burial and someone to continue what I have worked so hard to build. Your Grandpa Pope took me off these mean Detroit streets and gave me a chance. That he needed a place to bury some of his business associates isn't important.

My life has always been a compromise, but at least it is filled with a certain honor. Now, you need a hand. It is my duty to reciprocate. It really isn't that bad of a fit. Just bury me right and treat the poor with the same respect the rich use their money to buy."

Mr. Wimble leaves around ten in the evening. The last part of his cigar is still burning in the astray on the table next to his chair. Gary is asleep on the couch and the conversation ends as Mr. Wimble is passing through our apartment door.

"Come see me when you are ready. Just understand that an undertaker's life can be a lonely one, if you let it. My philosophy is that the living must make choices. The dead, if they are lucky, end up in the hands of someone who cares."

I am watching from the apartment's window as the old man lumbers slowly off through the evening lamp's light and the arriving fog of another dreary Detroit evening. I find myself wanting to be a little more like him and a little less like my brother.

Chapter Eight

(Two Angels at a Bar)

After two years together, I am calling Mr. Wimble, Teddy. In this short time I am finding him, other than my brother, a true father figure. A father figure is not always a result of one being the sperm donor. Too, his character is more than a tad above that of my brother. I am not saying that I am losing respect for my brother. This is the farthest thing from the truth. It is like that old saying, 'blood is thicker than water'. Mothers are constantly defending their children even though the evidence points heavily toward them being the deranged psychopath walking into the McDonalds restaurant during noon hour lunch and slaughtering half a dozen innocent people. The response is usually something like this.

"Oh, he is such a good boy. I am sure he isn't the one on the camera tape."

My point is that Teddy is offering me a few things neither my biological father nor Gary offers me. Those things are compassion and direction. It is amazing how Teddy is defying the odds. The doctor says one year max. Here it is two years and one day later, to be exact, and the old man is still puttering around the funeral home teaching me the finer details of being a mortician. I know this is his way of making peace with himself and honoring my grandfather Pope. Speaking about grandfather Pope is not a subject for expansion. Replying that my grandfather is a great man is as far as the subject is ever taken. Teddy's replies are never in the past tense. It is as though my grandfather is with us and is standing at our sides as Teddy is moving through the various ins and outs of his life's trade.

The name Wimble and Wimble is still a mystery to me. One afternoon in the hot of an August day, I am standing beside Mr. Wimble and a newly delivered recently departed. The woman is lying on the preparation table. I am preparing the instruments and, for no other reason than the subject weighing heavily on my mind, blurt out the question. This is on the two year and one day milestone of Ted Wimble's continuing life against all odds.

"Why Wimble and Wimble? Is there a son in the equation, Teddy?"

Mr. Wimble is holding a small scalpel in his hand. I am thinking maybe this is the one question capable of tearing our relationship apart. I fear he might be cutting my throat as his last official act on Earth. There are, I know from conjecture and innuendo, secrets lingering in both this old man's and my grandfather's past. Too, it is true that I am always walking a little too close to the dark side. It is like I am always saying, 'I am not mad, I am just a little different'.

Mr. Wimble is looking me directly in my eyes when I hear him replying. In true fashion the scalpel is back in its proper place on the preparation table waiting for Teddy's complete attention after this unexpected question is at rest.

"No, William. I don't have children. I have always wanted a son. Sometimes I think we all live in our imaginations. What could it hurt? Anyway, I have a son now. Imagine how the people will be talking, an old black man with a white son."

My emotions are gripping my throat. My breathing is difficult and I am trying to hold the tears back. For the first time I find myself saying the one thing I never say to anyone.

"Call me, Billy."

We both know that returning to the chore at hand is not possible. My hands are shaking and Teddy is visibly exhausted from another long day that he should not be living. Teddy speaks.

"Well, Billy. This old man is really tired. I think it is the heat this time of year and all that nonsense. I think you should roll this one back into cold storage and save her for tomorrow."

I am watching as Mr. Wimble pushes the elevator button for the ride up the three floors to his apartment at the top of the building. I catch a slight smile on his face out of the corner of my eye as I am sliding the body into its holding slot. Later, at home while watching the evening news, I am feeling very good about the moment Teddy and I share. Gary is out on another call, the air-conditioner is working in the apartment, for a change. I am comfortable and alive for the first time. I do not understand the double meaning to this day's events. Mr. Wimble is now laying on one of the preparation tables waiting my return. Two years and one day is something always resting in the back of my mind. It is like 'Wimble and Wimble' secretly lives on the edge of my madness in a dark lonely corner of its own. This is what I am thinking when I am speaking to a room full of strangers visiting this great man one last time.

"I call Teddy my father. Looking over the mourners today I see that he has many sons and daughters who all respect and love him. One of the things I loved about this man most is his hidden wisdom that often was given to me at the oddest moments. It is as though he knew that advice given at the wrong time was not really advice at all. Mostly, he gave this advice in the form of little stories...stories that in and of themselves could be the basis for one of the most valuable books ever written. The one story I remember more than any other is the one about two angels sitting in a bar and drinking.

Teddy says the bartender has seen a lot of things in his time, but never two angels sitting in a bar drinking. Teddy says that most bartenders don't drink and so are more reliable as it relates to what is really happening than most people coming into such places. Anyway, these two angels are talking and the bartender walks up and asks about God being angry if he finds out they are in a bar drinking. The angels reply that God already knows they are in the bar drinking. The bartender asks why He allows this to happen and why He does not strike them dead right where they are sitting. The angels say that some day the bartender will understand. They pay their bill and start walking out the door. As they walk, the bartender notices that both angels have broken wings. Teddy said that the moral of the story was that God gives us all wings but that some of us just refuse to fly. Thinking about Teddy I understand that, like his advice, he used his wings to fly only when the time was right. I love him. I will miss him. I will always try to honor what he has taught me by continuing to service those he loved so much."

The service's ending is a deep silence. That night I am alone in the funeral home with my destiny. I am happy with what is given me and mad as hell about what is taken from me.

Chapter Nine

I am sitting alone in the residence above the funeral home, a funeral home that is now mine. Living at the mansion has been out of the question since my father died. Life at the mansion is a revolving door of drugs, alcohol, and sexy beautiful people. It is just all too much. I see the results of this type of activity every day in my line of work.

The residence is very comfortable and Teddy's affinity for all things African is starting to grow on me. The furniture and art are staying. I am a white man surrounded by all things black and am feeling strangely comfortable in this persona. This is my home. It feels like my home. At the end of the day with my work done in the mortuary area, I am happy stepping off the elevator into this strange and exotic place. This particular evening I am listening to my departed friend's music. It is strange but his choice of music is big band dance music. The décor is African. The music is big band dance music. This seems a huge contradiction in terms. I am leafing through one of Teddy's books. The book is entitled, Dance Steps for the Big Band Era. This foot goes here and this foot goes there. The music is engulfing me in a world living far away from my past disappointments. I love this music. I am moving my feet to the sounds and soon am mastering the steps in his book. Some evenings my dancing and listening reaches long into the evening. The only thing missing is a partner. Previously it is air filling the void between my precisely positioned arms. Television is not something occupying my mind. Television is nothing but images of pain and despair. The more pain and the more despair, the better it is for those louder-than-regular-programming advertisements I hate beyond words. A station just giving the news in a clear, concise and honest manner without the pretense of surprise and pity or wanting to convince me we are friends is a thing now as dead as Teddy.

On one particular evening as I am exhausting myself with another bout of dancing and swaying to the music, I am bending my pretend partner back in a lover's dip and find my eyes falling onto a picture of Teddy. The picture is sitting alone in the corner of the very book shelf where the dance instruction book lives. I move in closer examining the photograph and see that it is Teddy with a lovely woman in his arms. They are dancing. The picture's background is a ballroom complete with the rotating multi-colored glass ball.

"Teddy, you are a sexy devil. The woman is putty in your hands."

I am hearing my friend replying from his resting place.

"Had you known me long enough, son, I might have taught you a thing or two."

"You have taught me quite enough my good friend. I think the rest of your secrets are in front of me. Paying closer attention is what I must do."

Falling back onto the sofa with sweat running down my face I am beginning to think about that night in the morgue. I am thinking about finding Teddy laying there on the table waiting for me, waiting for my gentle touch. It is another gift. I am looking at my hands and am imagining that they are really black. Teddy is giving me his gentle hands and his knowledge. This is what I am thinking when I am pulling the envelope from his grasp, the one between his dead hands. This envelope with my name on it is who I am today. I understand that one year is what the doctors are expecting. I understand that two years and one day is what Teddy is, day after day, mustering the strength to accomplish. In this state a mortician's legal requirements are two years college. I am remembering my friend pushing me into those night classes even when wanting to go is difficult. The balance of the requirement is one year's apprenticeship and completion of the state's exam. I am fortunate that the requirements do not specify the apprenticeship follow the schooling. I am an apprentice from day one. Teddy's pushing continues with statements like, 'don't be counting on your old man's money son'. It ain't there now. You gott'a do for your sorry-assed self now'. My exam certification and license are in his hands, those hands folding their long and talented fingers across his chest. I am standing there again. I am at the table where my friend is waiting and I am reliving my first act as a licensed mortician. I am also alone in my room crying. The music and dancing is over. Pulling the picture away from my chest I am looking into Teddy's eyes. They are simultaneously happy eyes and sad eyes. I am thinking this dancing is where he goes to feel, experience, and hope for something better than the left-over lives and dreams of so many body bags of disappointment and wrong turns along the path of life. About two weeks later and tiring of air between my perfectly positioned arms, tiring of being alone, wanting for something warm and caring next to me, desiring a loving relationship like the one now lost; I find myself uttering the words that begin forming the rest of my life.

"Excuse me, dear. May I have this dance?"

Chapter Ten

It is amazing how much I love the little round, multi-colored ball rotating over the dance floor. Never experiencing the psychedelic generation, I find myself believing this is as close as one comes without screwing with drugs and their mind's intended function. I personally believe the mind is capable of screwing itself up without chemical dependency's help. I am moving and moving under the rotating ball's many colors. The people and things I am moving around are taking on different colors and shapes themselves, depending on the angle of my frame and the way the light is being bent this way and that as I dance with my new partner. Everything is perfect. Everything is perfect except for one minor detail. That minor detail is the conversation. The subject of my occupation eventually is front and center.

"Tell me, Bill. What do you do for a living?"

I am observing three types of women at these events. One is the elderly just looking for companionship. One is the wife without a dancing spouse. The other is the young tight-assed, gold-digger looking for a wealthy husband. This is not to say that there are not different types of men at these events with similar intent. Indeed there are, but this story is about me. It is not about them. I am one of the honorable ones present who want nothing more than a dance or possible relationship…a relationship without quantifiers that are always driving the goal-oriented population, seemingly too many layers thick over the face of planet Earth. Is there something wrong with a dance, a drink and an occasional piece of ass? Why is the type of car you drive or the job you do so important? Can't a person do something just for the sake of liking it? The question is always there waiting, jumping from the wings as if the answer is the most important thing in the world. It is a quantifier to the relationship. My question is, what about the person? Idle talk is a boring thing and is often the first sign of marriages going bad. I hate hearing that question.

"Tell me, Bill. What do you do for a living?"

Understand, I am not ashamed of the way I make my living. I am, honestly, very proud of it and am making many wonderful friends through the handling of people's deceased loved ones. It is not me. It is the people who are asking. Telling someone proudly that I am a mortician and own a funeral home is a changing event. Feeling them pulling slightly away from a snug dance grip is an indication of what a person is really thinking. It is the reaction that is telling everything. Are, my hands cold, like the corpses I am handling so respectfully? Are you picturing yourself trying to make love to someone whose eyes may occasionally feel sad for or aroused by the beautiful deceased body lying on his morgue table? Are they picturing me gently touching or talking to a dead client of mine? Are they, understanding this is just my way of doing what I am doing for society while keeping my own sanity in tact? Why are my dance partners always being so judgmental? Why is a dance partner not just a dance partner? Why is a mortician not just a mortician?

One night, after two or three attempts failing because of that question about what my occupation is, I find myself becoming very depressed and alone. The lights are swirling and I am sitting alone in the far corner of the room watching other people dancing. Men are dancing with women. Women are dancing with women and the male voyeurs are sitting, enjoying the ladies moving and rubbing against one another. Too, men are dancing with men. I am nearing the conclusion that a mortician is the last person anyone wants to meet. I am nearing the conclusion that lives for morticians are nothing more than a series of clinical procedures; taking in the body, preparing the body, placing the body, making the body look like it is still living before either cremation or burial. I am beginning to believe that I exist only for the comfort of those pretending life is a forever thing.

I am sitting here alone thinking these thoughts after having moved away from my one dance partner of the night. I am thinking that dancing is not really for me and might be serving as nothing more than a shield for past events that are now dancing through my past disappointments. That's a good one, 'dancing through my last disappointments'. Maybe being a writer is in my future. Maybe writing a book about liking to dance with dead people is in order. Making it a comedy is workable. The dialogue goes like this.

"So, Billy, you dance with dead people for a living?"

"That is correct."

"Seems like an odd occupation to me."

"One might think so."

I am swirling my dance partner around waiting for the next line of my book.

"So, is it a rewarding career and why are you in this line of work?"

"One, there is a need. No one else wants to dance with a dead person."

The dance's swirling is getting faster and faster. The people around us are moving into the wallpaper lining the dance floor. Our eyes are locking together like that point of balance a skater is holding onto as they rotate at their ungodly speeds just before taking a bow for the audience. I say.

"Besides, they don't talk back or complain when I step on their feet."

My dance partner and I are laughing like insane people and the reality of the rest of the world is now held captive inside the wallpaper surrounding the dance floor. The rotating multi-colored light is exploding over and over in my mind. Its pieces are flying this way and that and I am feeling like I am just one of the particles on a computer screen simulating flying through space. The explosion is eventually over. The lights are back on and I am still sitting alone on this uncomfortable metal chair waiting for that question. This is what I am thinking on this particular night. I am also one burst of energy and drop of depression away from jumping up out of my chair and announcing to the whole fucking room that I am a mortician and proud of it. My last line is more or less, 'fuck you.' Before this urge is capable of being acted upon, I find a strange thing happening. There is a warm touch on my shoulder and the sound of words.

"Bill, may I have this dance?"

Here name is Brenda. Her hair is straight and a Swedish white blond color. The color is a good match for her age, kick-ass body and deep green eyes. It is not a color for someone twenty years her senior to be wearing. 'Any man in the room', is what I am thinking. Why are you picking me? Still, I am hoping what they are always saying is true. Really attractive people are often the last ones finding love and happiness. Being unapproachable is how many very attractive people are viewed. Perhaps this is true and this is my lucky night. Perhaps morticians are in this same category. Oh, I am not meaning this in the attractive sense, but more in the unapproachable sense. Maybe it really isn't a rejection thing as it is a sort of respectful thing. Whatever it is, it is a lonely place to be. At this particular moment, I am not caring about the reason. The soft lights are back again and I am dancing with the most beautiful thing I ever remember laying my eyes on. There is hope. This is what I am thinking. I feel my heart sinking when, as we are dancing, the conversation begins. That question is not far behind.

"William, what is it you do for a living?"

I am angry now. I find myself blurting it out.

"I am a mortician and I own a funeral home."

Strangely, Brenda is not pulling away from me. If anything she is leaning in closer and allowing me to grip her more tightly. The words she is speaking softly into my ear are erotic and sincere.

"You are? That is very exciting. I have always wanted to do it in a coffin."

The sex in the car in the parking lot is phenomenal. Plans for picking her up at her place is an act of anticipation driving me up the wall for the first three days of the following week. Maybe there is hope for someone of my caliber, someone who isn't mad but just a little crazy.

Chapter Eleven

(First Kill)

Gary and I sometimes find ourselves sitting for hours in our favorite bar, on our favorite stools, drinking our drinks the bartender now knows by heart, watching reruns of football games we already know the endings to and speaking not more than a dozen words between us until it is time for paying the bill. I think this is because people like us are so accepting of being alone that we find ourselves fearing conversation. Conversation is often a killer to any relationship. It is that old saying about not, 'discussing religion or politics' constantly coming to mind as we find ourselves sitting here night after night just being in one another's company. It is like Gary often says.

"Life is like sex. When it is bad no one wants to talk about it. If they do talk about it, the conversation is always a lie anyway. I can get that from anyone on the street any day of the week in my line of work."

The first time I find myself hearing my brother giving me this little bit of wisdom I am a little bit of a smart ass.

"Are you talking about getting bad sex?"

His response is simple.

"See? That is exactly what I mean, asshole."

It is not until a little later in life that I start understanding exactly what my brother's meaning is and how he operates. An example is the person talking while referring to 'they'. As a police officer my brother's response is always going to be a question regarding the identity of the 'they' existing in this type of firsthand testimony. This type of definitive conversation is the reason many investigations are failures. Reading too much into the abstract of what Gary says is bullshit-social-content is the biggest recipe for disaster out there. Unfortunately this is the type of society we are. Liking to hear ourselves talk, most of the time about ourselves, is nothing more than verbal cancer taking up no other purpose than that of helping each and every one of us justify our accidental existence. I am remembering Gary's inquisition of what he calls one of the many 'criers' in the criminal world. Sometime during their confessing it always is about being an abused child or not knowing one's mother or father. Gary's advice is always the same.

"Look, you are an accident. We all understand your daddy couldn't afford a rubber on the day of your conception. My problem isn't with your past. My problem is with the present."

Observation and listening are my brother's tools of choice. This is why, on this particular evening, it is so hard for me not to blurt out the details of my meeting Brenda and that this evening is going to be shut down early for her pickup at eight-thirty. In the middle of all this mental wandering, Gary is the first to speak.

"Where do you have to be off to tonight, little brother?"

I am surprised by this inquiry, what with no words between us for the last hour and a half.

"How did you know?"

"You've been watching the clock over the bar so much its hands are starting to wilt."

This is my whole point about my brother. My response is to the point.

"I have a date."

His reply is what is standard for his line of work.

"Good. You've needed a good fucking for sometime now. We don't want your hand cramping up because of your work and all."

"Kiss my ass. I have to go."

Throwing two twenties on the bar top and moving toward the front door I am noticing Gary's smile. It is the kind of smile I find myself often giving a client. After a time knowing how to pull this or that stitch is something only true artists are capable of embracing. It is, too, my mortician's sense of humor. I like thinking these departed are capable of laughing in the face of death. The difference here is that Gary's smile is real. I hear him continuing to needle me as I am passing through the bar's front door.

"You are about ten bucks short here, sport."

I am on my way to Brenda's home in a taxi at her request. She wants to drive and I agree to allow her that control. The home is quite large and its circular driveway slides up to the front door like an upside-down smile. My smile meeting the driveways' upside down smile makes a complete circle. I am thinking that there is something to this ying and yang crap so many people looking for meaning are making part of their lives. A BMW, a Cadillac and a smaller sports car sit in separate stalls making up the rest of the driveway. All of the garage doors are open. I am thinking, 'rich as well'. Yes, yes, yes and yes again.

The home is on the scale of the Sigrist Mansion but the neighborhood is newer and the building materials are not of mortar and brick. The domed shaped stained glass windows are oddly out of place. The home is a new example of composite woods and space age technology. The roof lines appear, at any moment, to be leaping off into the sky. One is expecting a big puff of smoke as their parts disappear into the upper extremities of the heavens, reaching for God knows what destination. My thought is that the intent is meaningful but the appearance is cheap. Too, the house is standing in a small allotment with other homes nearby. Glancing about, my thought is that there are eight to ten other structures similar in nature but not quite the same as one another. There is no large yard or extended grounds needing upkeep. I am thinking that the jet-set comes and goes. Being in one place for very long is something akin to talking when there is really nothing worth talking about. My brother's advice applies in so many situations. One just needs a bit of time looking for a clearer understanding of just how large the number of situations is. Too, this home I am seeing for the first time is speaking through its presence. It is telling about its builder's or its owner's character. Perhaps it is commenting on both characters. This is where words and inquiry are important. This is the hidden meaning of my brother's, a cop's, advice.

I see the door opening. She is waiting for me. Brenda is standing in the late evening light. Her dress is made of a white material. It is very tight and seeing her naked form silhouetted by the light penetrating from behind is leaving nothing for my imagination. I am accepting of the fact that imagination is often victim of reality. In this case, it is good. A voice is falling down the staircase, thru her silhouette and out the front door.

"Don't be too late, dear. You know how I worry. Shall I put the children to bed now or a little later?"

"Do whatever you want, Steve. They are your kids. I am going out for the evening. Don't wait up."

Brenda's answer is flippant. The man is not her servant, but is her husband. This is information surfacing during some of that useless blabbering Gary is so intensely fond of hating. Brenda is driving us to a special place. I am hoping my charge card is capable of flexing enough financial muscle for her surprise.

Looking over at Brenda I am thinking of Vickie. There are questions. Is this the way it starts with my father? Where is it they find themselves meeting for the first time? Is their meeting an accident or is it something more sinister? My eyes are holding fast to Brenda's mini-skirt. Her perfume is all but saying 'fuck me right here, right along side of the road' and to hell with all the people and the traffic. My fantasy is of pulling over in front of the biggest street light in the Detroit area and doing her. The whole world wants to see. I am also hearing my bother's advice creeping into my thoughts.

"Shut up, man. Put your mind on hold. This is a poker game. Don't give everything away before learning what you want, before getting what you want."

I smell her, the leather of the BMW. My left hand is resting under her dress and flat on her crotch, no underwear and she shaves. I am my father all over and not presently thinking about any of these implications. A few sick thoughts are also rolling around in my brain. I am thinking about one or two rather attractive female corpses, ones now in a better place wearing that smile only I am capable of giving. 'Sick', I am hearing my own voice say. You are too long among the dead to be appreciating the living this way. Brenda's voice is suddenly in the picture.

"I think you are thinking of taking this all the way again tonight."

"In a dress like that, what is a man to think?"

"Most men think with their dicks, but I can't say I really mind."

"Actually, I was thinking about eating you tonight and forgetting about the steak."

I am not thinking about the old man or the children. What works is what works. She has a sugar-daddy. So, what? This is my night. She wants it and I want to give it. I am hearing that song again about loving the one you're with. The car is stopping. There is Brenda's voice again.

"I hope the entry fee isn't too high."

We are sitting in front of my funeral home.

"Told you I really wanted to do it in a coffin."

The thought is turning me on and the price is right. Maybe it is sex first and wine, cheese and crackers in the apartment later. Maybe, Brenda is sleeping over tonight. No fucking maybe about it. Brenda is sleeping over tonight. The surprising thing is that I am around my dead friends so often that forgetting Brenda's comment on the dance floor the night we meet is understandable. That this is erotica for this beautiful creature is now exciting me.

We are standing in the main coffin display room. Brenda is gazing over the offerings.

"Anyone you want. Pick anyone you want."

"But, I don't understand."

"You don't understand what, Brenda?"

"Where are all the expensive, black shiny ones? I'm not about to get laid in a plain wooden box without all the fucking trimmings."

With this remark I am finding my outlook about this woman changing. It is changing at the speed of light. My thinking is now about this remark and mother. It is about what my mother endures at the hands of a little piece of shit like Brenda. She is the same type of gold-digger as my stepmother, Vickie. 'I won't be fucking another Vickie' is racing thru my mind. I am angry. My neck is tense. My reaction is not controllable. Even before doing it I am thinking this is not my fault. It is father's fault.

I backhand Brenda right in the mouth. Blood is gushing from her collagen-stuffed and lipstick-covered lips. She is immediately no longer attractive. How dare she insult what I work so hard to build? How dare she insult Teddy? She is insulting the very hardworking people who pass through this place on their way to their last resting place. The bitch isn't good enough for burying along side of these people...these people that are my friends.

I see Brenda stumbling and falling into one of the coffins sitting on the floor. Everything is happening in slow motion. I grab one of her legs, the one hanging over the lid, and push it into the box. Brenda is attempting to sit up but I find myself kicking her in the face while pushing her down into the coffin. I am slamming the door and screaming.

"I hope you like the lining, bitch."

Sitting on top of the box listening to Brenda's muffled sobs is oddly comforting. When the sounds are finally fading into the distance, I am thinking of my mother. Shortly, I am alone in my apartment preparing a tray of cheese, wine and crackers.

Arriving with the food back in the mortuary, the muffling sounds inside of the coffin are gone. I sit pondering what is done and what is next. The wine, cheese and crackers are very good. Releasing years of frustration before a good, relaxing meal is also very good. The thought of doing this more often enters my mind.

My cremation chamber is very state of the art. I am sliding Brenda and the casket she is in into the chamber thinking I am hearing some weak sobbing. The caskets interior is nearing the end of its oxygen levels. I am thinking that this 'box' may be cheap but it is very well sealed. No matter, it is all over in a few more minutes. There is nothing to worry about regarding me running my chamber this late at night. This is a procedure happening more often now that gang violence is on the increase. Too, there are so many smells in the city of Detroit that a little white smoke is nothing but an afterthought. In an hour or so I am dusting the ashes from the crematorium. A small knife is in my hand. Cutting the back side of one of the coffin's bottom linings is a simple matter. Dumping Brenda's ashes between the lining and the bottom of the coffin is a simple matter. Sewing the lining back up is not. I am used to the texture of flesh, not the pliable cloth inside the coffin. My fingers are bleeding from one too many needle pricks while putting the lining back together. Unknowingly I am muttering to myself over and over.

"Wait until you find out what else I have in store for your deceitful, lying, little gold-digger ass."

My plan is to place the next dead gang member through my funeral home's door right on top of Brenda's ashes.

The drive to Gary's cabin in the woods in upper Michigan seems longer than I am remembering. This is due to the combination of stress, wine and late hour. The hours are slipping into the early morning. Luckily, I am not pulled over for driving under the influence and I do arrive just before the sun is coming up. I watch the BMW rolling quickly into the lake where Gary and I come to fish, time permitting. This place is Gary's pride and joy and the real reason he is still living in that piece-of-shit two bedroom apartment he is calling home back in the city. It is all about the proximity to his job. Every extra penny he is earning on his regular job and his after-hours gigs is going toward paying this place off before retirement. I suddenly am feeling guilty about this dark secret of mine that is being dumped in my brother's little piece of paradise. My arrival back in Detroit is early in the morning. The cab fare is not cheap, but there is no choice. My story to the cab driver is that my brother leaves me at the cabin because of me being drunk. The cab driver's response is simple.

"My brother is a dick, too."

The hundred dollar tip helps.

I wake around two in the afternoon. Worry over the previous night's events is flooding over me. What is going to happen to me now? Are the police coming for me? When are they coming for me? About two-thirty I am showering the mud off myself and hanging a 'Closed for Vacation' sign on the front door with my cell phone number in case of an emergency. Most likely diverting the deceased to another funeral home is the choice most make. If not, if I find my cell phone ringing, making that suggestion is the instruction the calling party hears. Answering numbers I recognize is the order of the next few days. Deciding on the handling of all of this is my most pressing order of business. Gary must know.

"Brother, I am really wasted. I'm going up to the cabin for a week or so if that is alright with you."

"No problem, Billy. You must have a lot on your mind right now."

What is the meaning of that last sentence? Does he already know? I envision myself arriving at the cabin, meeting Gary already there with his handcuffs at the ready. I'm being arrested by my own brother. Shit, shit, shit. A little calming down is in order right about now, William. Your fears are running wild. Get them back in check, man. Get them back in check.

Driving back to the cabin my hands continue shaking. Three days later they are still shaking. I am waiting for the arrival of the police. My hands continue shaking. I quit trying to bait a hook for fishing, something meant to help take the fear out of my brain. Getting that fucking dangling little red worm on the hook is impossible. I am capable of killing. I am capable of living with the dead day after day and here I find myself sitting trying to put a red worm on a hook and I can't. I am seeing Brenda's face on the red worm. Maybe I really am mad. No, I am not mad. I am just under a lot of stress right now. It is all going to pass. It is all going to pass. I am waiting and nothing is happening. This is worse than something happening. Isn't it? Maybe it isn't. Maybe it is a good thing.

After a few weeks I am back at my funeral home. My phone is remaining unusually silent. Is this an unexpected decline in business in Detroit? This is almost unheard of. Not to worry, I am telling you. Not to worry because no calls are a good thing. It is at this moment I find the old man's face entering my mind. What about him? What about Steve? Surely going to the police is a foregone conclusion after this length of time?

One night my phone is ringing. Hiding forever is impossible. My hand is shaking as I am reaching for my cell phone.

"Yes?"

There is a long pause and then Steve's voice.

"Don't you worry yourself about a thing. This is between you and me."

About a month later I am standing next to the coffin with Brenda's ashes. A black male is in the coffin and I am sealing the lid down for the trip to Potter's Field. Maybe this thing is working out after all. I find a person behind me unannounced and suddenly speaking.

"Mr. Sigrist."

Turning around I am standing face to face with the mailman. I find anything in uniform still frightening the shit out of me. The mailman is offering a very large envelope.

"Sorry to give you so much at once but, you were away so long I just kept it in the truck until I could catch you personally."

Most of the material is advertisements and bills. One envelope is from a post office box I do not know. The words on the paper inside the envelope are at once both frightening and comforting. The cashier's check for one hundred thousand dollars is a complete shock. The note reads.

"I was about to pay to have it done. It seems only right that you should reap the rewards of your own efforts. Besides, I don't want you going through life having to look over your shoulder. People go missing all the time. Best regards, Steve."

I see days passing, months passing and finally a year. One day my cell phone is ringing again. It is a voice that is new to me. The voice's request is simple.

"Someone close is referring me to you, Mr. Sigrist. Steve says you will understand."

That evening, after the call, my brother and I are again at our favorite bar drinking. Out of the blue and after all this time I find Gary asking.

"So, how did it go with that bitch you were seeing some time back?"

I am looking Gary right in the eyes when I answer.

"Let's just say it didn't work out."

Gary's eyes go wandering back to the olives floating lifelessly inside his iced down vodka martini. Nothing more is said. My brother is taking his own best advice.

Chapter Twelve

(Bubbles)

The one thing Gary is wanting is the title to his mortgaged lake and piece of land in upper Michigan. More than that, this is his sanity and is something I am easily capable of understanding. Sitting here on the dock thinking about my brother and how much he really means to me, I know my decision is the right one. Looking around I see the foliage and how it is painting the face of the landscape like no human hand is capable of capturing in any picture. My conclusion is that this is because a painting is permanent and this landscape is changing by the moment as it heads toward the last few hours of a life too brief in transition. I am also thinking 'realist' or 'naturalist'. The thought is striking me that it is all the same in the end. The realist is always finding itself becoming the naturalist as it is decaying into the memories of the past.

The wind is not heavy this day and the touch of its developing cold nip is not yet a full reality. This feeling is refreshing and I am breathing its natural body into the full depths of my lungs, remembering some video about deep breathing being good for one's physical well-being. The Sun is kissing the wind and temperature like a stiff drink is capable of kissing a comforting warm piece of apple pie. Hot and cold are brothers and both burn if their touching is too extreme. This is the reality hiding inside the naturalist. It is like sex. It is like death. It is like murder. Each and every one of us is responsible for deciding how much of each is too much. For me the conclusion is that I want to drown in excess rather than being left always wanting more. Just like what I am doing now is setting me free, I am hoping my gift to my brother is the one thing capable of setting him free. We are both suffering our past, but in different ways. This is our embrace. It is our past, present and future. Nothing is changing. The mold is cast. The process of our lives is all that is left for either of us that is worth consideration.

Paying the balance of Gary's mortgage with the unexpected money from Brenda's husband is an extreme high. It is an accomplishment, given everything going so wrong for these last few years, that I never envision happening. My story to Gary is simple. This is the way I am approaching the subject. This is the conversation rolling around in the back of my mind. It is my way of anticipating my brother's response upon finding out about my gift.

"Now, don't go being such a prick about this."

"Why shouldn't I? You shouldn't be paying my bills."

"That was money Teddy left me that I didn't know about. It came unexpectedly and I wanted to do this. Be gracious for once in your life, big brother."

"The money doesn't have anything to do with our family, the estate?"

"No, it does not. Teddy had this thing with what estate he had that said if I stayed in business past a year; his money was to go to me. He had no family. I was his family and I can damn well do with it what I please. I please to pay off your mortgage."

"What about the business?"

"What about it? Between natural deaths, gang deaths and just people wanting to die because of their god-awful surroundings, I am in business for life, so to speak. Even though it seems like life isn't exactly the right word."

I see Gary accepting reluctantly and making some wise-ass remark about me still checking with him before showing up unannounced. Truth is this act is about something no one is giving either of us. It is about something being totally ours and, if Gary or I find ourselves buying our own vase like the one in the mansion hallway...pissing in it is going to be because of a full bladder and not because we are rebelling against someone or something. I am thinking seriously of buying some art and defacing it as well. 'Closer than ever' is what I am thinking. This gesture is bringing Gary and me together, 'closer than ever'. I am happy with myself and the real source of this money is not even a slight glimmer in the back of my mind. The fact that the money is there and doing this thing for my brother is all that matters.

I am sitting here on the dock fishing but not fishing. Gary is the one who is always fishing. He is always instructing me on the fine art of fishing.

"Cast out into the lake, little brother. Don't let the worm just sit on the bottom drowning. Reel in a little at a time, like the worm is alive not just some limp dick waiting for some bitch to grab it. You have to make the fish want it."

Liking fishing is an acquired taste. It is not so much about the fishing as it is the calm, the surroundings, the feel of the wind on a crisp day like this. My thinking is that fishing on a hot day is like golfing on a hot day. People are really there for the cold beer. There is plenty of cold beer in my little red and white Rubbermaid chest, one of those plastic things costing way too much and leaving little room for sandwiches after the beer is comfortably nestled in its layer of ice. I am thinking it is all a plot. Making the cooler deliberately too small is an incentive to buying a larger cooler. This is life. It is all just a big old plot aiming at a mortician's table and crypt or grave. I am the end in this chain of progression we call life. Anyway, Gary is not the real fisherman. I am the real fisherman. I am sitting here at the end of the dock. My worm is on the end of my fishing line drowning at the bottom of the lake. I am thinking of checking to see if the disgusting thing is still on the hook, but not before two beers. Two beers are how long I find it taking for those little nibbling, bastard fish to clean a hook. This is fine with me. I don't find myself baiting my hook too frequently or letting my beers get too warm before rethinking my strategy. Gary is apt at pointing out that he always is catching the biggest fish. My response is always the same.

"That is because you accidentally snag them with your hook while fucking fly-fishing in a lake."

Off in the distance my eyes are catching a glance of white water being flipped up from the dying path of our one neighbor's boat. It is hugging the shoreline on the opposite side of the lake. We know there is a neighbor, but knowing them is something neither Gary nor I care to pursue. Drinking one night, we find ourselves discussing the possibility of burning their cabin down. Alcohol is a mind of its own. The results of an alcoholic's thinking are, more often than not, tragic. The lake is really not part of their property. It is Gary's but, our neighbor's are now a fixture and come and go like shadows on the water. We find ourselves not acknowledging them and, for fear of being uninvited, they seem to understand that staying to themselves is the price for using what is ours. I am remembering the night where I am rolling Brenda's car into the lake...the night of checking several times for any signs of our neighbors being out and about.

Gary is without a question the catcher of bigger fish. He is not the catcher of the most fish. My limp-dick-worm is always the catcher of the most fish. I am not shy about pointing this out to my brother. His response is always the same.

"Bigger is better. If you aren't going to take my advice, shut up and leave me alone."

I think this is why our relationship, though not always so noticeable on the surface, is always working so well. He is the butch and I am the bitch, mentally speaking.

This is my thought process while sitting here on the dock and taking a break from my work back at the funeral home. My reasoning is that none of my clients are going anywhere. So, why not take a little R and R.? It isn't like in that book,

Death Takes a Holiday. My work is piling up, but depleting world resources and space is not a consideration. Too, I am thinking about that second phone call. I am discussing it with Grandpa Pope. Hopefully, Grandma Pope knows he is gone from the crypt or his dead ass is in real trouble upon his return.

"William, it looks like you have a second business in the making. What do you think about that?"

"I'm thinking I don't know how I get into these situations, grandpa."

"When did you get the call?"

"I was working alone in the mortuary about eight months after this Brenda thing and my cell phone starts ringing."

I continue telling my dead relative about how there is this voice at the other end of the line saying he is being referred by Brenda's husband, has a similar situation and would like to enlist my services. The voice also infers that there are others like Brenda's husband and himself that are in similar situations and that, handled properly, this might be a relationship beneficial for any number of ageing elderly gentlemen now under the thumb of money-grubbing younger wives. Grandpa Pope is pushing further into my psychic as I am relating this story, gazing out over the clear water and feeling the crisp wind glancing off of my face.

"Well, young man. There is, I must say, a time or two I entertained the idea of offing your grandmother with my own bare hands. I never did, but had there been a way out and money in it, I might well be alive today."

"What are you talking about, grandpa? You were killed in a car crash."

"I know, boy. The thing is, I was thinking about her nagging me that afternoon about me wanting to play cards with the boys and didn't have my mind on the road. Your grandma is really the reason I am dead right now. We are still fighting about it and it will go on forever."

I am feeling a colder than normal wind brushing up against my face, landing on my collar and falling down my neck and into the back underside of my shirt. I am immediately shivering. My grandfather Pope speaks again.

"Don't worry about that sudden blast of cold air. Winter is not here yet. That was just me thinking about being hounded by your grandmother for the rest of eternity."

There is a long silence and I hear my grandfather's advice just before seeing his form floating across the top of the water, in the company of the incoming evening air and mist, as he is floating back toward his cemetery grounds.

"Do what is right for you at the moment. The rest takes care of itself in the hereafter. It wasn't the drinking or playing poker that killed your dear old grandpa. It was the thought of having to explain everything to your grandma. Like I said, I just didn't have my mind on the road. Guess that means I really love the old battle ax and don't want to disappoint her...even though I know I am going to do just that."

My mind is made up. I know I am going to go dancing again and again. I know this right after killing Brenda. There is a sort of relief in it and a sort of justice that needs doling out. The process needs less emotion and more planning. This is often the difference between life in prison or death by lethal injection. It is that old emotional thing verses that pre-planned thing Gary is talking about. Does one know what they are doing or is it a spur of the moment thing brought on by jealousy, anger or rage? Or, is he or she a victim of child abuse? I hate this one. If anyone is deserving of this line of defense, it is Gary and I. This defensive tactic is staying in my shoebox just in case something goes wrong. I find myself muttering to myself, "Thanks, grandpa. You were a big help."

At this very moment my fishing line begins pulling very tightly against the upper tip of my pole. The fishing pole's tip is bending straight down and not popping back up like it is holding a fish fighting to get off the hook. I am thinking this is a big one and the fucker must be trying to spit the hook back up from somewhere deep inside of its guts. There are air bubbles coming to the top of the water. The bubbles are small at first. Then I see them getting bigger and bigger. The rod is not flexing back into an upright position despite my full strength being throw backward against its downward pull. The bubbles are getting larger and larger. All of a sudden this huge black thing is lunging toward me from the water's depths. I find myself releasing the pole and sliding backwards and away from the dock's end. I am screaming.

"What the fuck? What the fuck?"

A splinter-or-two-in-my-ass later I am observing two gloved hands latching themselves onto the dock's edge. A masked figure, all in black, is pulling its torso up and onto the dock. The body rolls onto its back, while flipping the diving mask off with one hand. A second later I am hearing a gasping for air and laughter so loud the neighbors across the lake most likely are turning on their search lights trying to find the source of the sound. The thing flipping around on the dock is not a fish. It is my brother, Gary. He is in full diving gear.

"Got you, you little dick. I started laughing under water and damn near drowned."

"What the fuck are you doing, Gary?"

"I'm practice diving, Billy. What the fuck does it look like?"

"For, what?" asking this question as I am sensing some dread just in case Brenda's death is part of the scenario.

I am picking the splinters out of my backside and watching Gary moving toward me. His flippers are in his hand and the breathing tube and mouthpiece are now dangling to one side as he walks. Gary stops right over where I am sitting. He is staring down at me with a smirk on his face which is in desperate need of being smacked into the afterlife. Taking a deep breath my inquiry is simple.

"Did you find anything worth talking about?"

Gary's response seems as though it is taking forever.

"Nope, I didn't. I just wanted to see if I owned anything of value that might be sleeping at the bottom of my lake. Get your gear together. I feel like cooking tonight. Come on up to the cabin when you are done."

The screened porch is keeping the evening bugs at bay. The moon is full and is falling onto the lake like a large flashlight from heaven shining its beam from a place so far off in the distance so as to never be capable of traveling upon it to the beginning of time. The beer is cold. The fried fish is fried fish only my brother is capable of making. Before turning in for the evening, Gary utters a single word. The phrase following it is one some people wait forever without hearing.

"Thanks. I love you."

There are no words for a reply. His blindness about what is laying at the bottom of his lake is testimony enough to this strange marriage between brothers who are always thinking a little off-kilter from the rest of the world. We are not mad. We are just a little different. I find comfort in speaking with grandfather Pope. Before falling into my first deep sleep in a long time, I am wondering whom of our dead relatives my brother is depending on for his advice and conversation.

Chapter Thirteen

(If Bars Could Talk)

Being a bar is like being a soldier or police officer. From one's first order or encounter there is this understanding that life is never the same again. The mold is set and the call to duty is always in the back of your mind. I am a good bar. Over time the wrinkles in my face are like yours. My face is a collection of conversations that people are whispering or shouting across my beer and liquor-soaked, darkly stained oak skin. In the heat of the hot August summer my preference is a mug, still cold with frost, sliding from one end of my face to the other. I enjoy smiling at the recipient, too many beers to the wind, missing his final order. The rule of these many years is that the mug hitting the floor is the signal for paying up and heading toward the exit door.

Just like I am always hearing William saying how much he loves Gary, usually after three beers and two shots, I love Burt. He is always wiping me down in the early morning hours, making me ready for the next evening's business. It is his way of making love to me. When Burt is ill, it is not the same. The part-time help is not the caring kind. They are sloppy. They touch me in ways that leave me feeling unclean. The fill-ins are always in a hurry. I find them pushing the regulars out and hurrying off down the street to that new shapely bar. That bar is not like me. The wood isn't really wood. It is saw dust with laminate. 'Pray for light drinkers', is my thought. I see my crowds soaking your cheap face with their multiple spills until you are like shit breaking apart from a hard rain. The regulars are saying that the music at the Squealing Monkey is something akin to taking a cat by the tail and spinning it around your head until the screaming stops. This is very amusing, but I am big enough to admit my own cliental, from time to time, are capable of sacrificing a note or two.

You, Squealing Monkey, are lacking history. This is the defining factor for any bar. Like life, the time of your birth and the circumstances surrounding your location are the reasons for your longevity and place of worth. Life is accidental. William knows this and is carrying this pain with him right up until the time of his death, hoping that the 'two martini baby' nickname is not capable of following him into eternity. It is something I understand. Sadly, listening is all the help I am capable of giving. You, Squealing Monkey, are pretending. You are pretending from your fake wood right up to your plastic backdrops and stage sets. You are not a real bar. Your strength is not like mine. You are the pretender, sagging under the weight of all your patrons' problems and grief. I am a good listener. It is my heart they love and these souls are my strength...souls who lay their hearts upon my real and caring face. Too, I am the one listening to their every word. It is not just about the money. I am a place for life.

"This place has a lot of history, William."

I am listening on a particular evening as William's brother, Gary, is in a talkative mood. He knows. He understands my feelings.

"I know it is old, brother. But like a lot of things, I seem to be on the tale end of this story as well."

"History never dies, little brother. One can always revisit. Burt, slide another one down this way."

"It's coming right up."

"So, Gary, educate me."

“This near dead-ass town used to be the center of it all. The automotive people stamped out dreams and those dreams were in just a few forms. Their names were Ford, Chevrolet, Oldsmobile, Buick, and Cadillac. Burt’s Bar and Grille was originally intended as the personal domain for the white collar guys, their whores and big American dreams.”

“Really?”

“Yeah, really. Your Grandpa Pope was one of them. You might say your father inherited his penchant for younger woman from him. ‘Falling not far from the tree’ and all that. The bar wasn’t named Burt’s at first.”

“No?”

“No. It was named Roberta’s Place.”

“Why was the name changed?”

“Like cars, clientele dictate labeling. The movers and shakers wanted a name apart from the standard Irish fare that was penetrating Detroit at the time.”

“If they changed the name today, would they call it Aunt Jemima‘s?”

“Shut up, Billy. Look around and listen to the story.”

Gary is one for respecting my history. My current ethnic makeup is not for joking. Joking is for joking and this conversation is about history.

“This place is where the deals were made. All those empty tables and the banquet rooms in the back were always full. Roberta’s Place was a stand out. It was different. It wasn’t another O’Malley’s or Murphy’s.”

“Labeling?”

“Yeah, labeling. It was something the new chrome-wheel-guys could call their own. The serving staff stretched their outfits on and peeled them off. Roberta’s was showtime at it best. Your Grandpa Pope was a real wheeler-dealer, not to mention a whore.”

“Are you trying to build the family up? I was hoping for an honest beginning with the money and corruption coming later.”

"Sorry, William, the truth is our family has always been a bucket of shit. The bucket has just always been filled with money."

Billy is shaking his head and moving toward the restroom. It is time to empty his own bucket. On the way out of the restroom Gary is watching his little brother. I am just being a bar and listening. Burt takes the opportunity and is wiping down my face from all the standing water, once ice on the sides of the beer mugs. Business is brisk today and I am sweating from all the work. The soft cotton cloth is feeling very good and I am getting that feeling again, the one living somewhere on the edges of erotica and hardcore sex. Gary's young brother is stopping and gazing at the pictures on my walls.

The women are beautiful. Their clothing is next to nothing and Billy is beginning to understand how getting lost in my woodwork is an artistic state of design and desire. The women's breasts are pushing forward like the sleek new designs of freshly bent pieces of tin smoking up Detroit's night-life air. William is thinking a thought much like those of the engineers who are stretching their imaginations and keeping Detroit moving forward, reminding me of the hood ornaments on some old Buicks I have seen. Taking an old package and placing it into a new cover is the answer. It is not always progress. I am watching Gary walking toward his brother who is still gazing at one picture after another. I am remembering when my wood is new and how I am an aging thing, how consumers are beginning their quest for quality over glitz, and how the five-hundred dollar pin-striped suit wearers are becoming a cliché for something new that is being called the 'me' generation. Things are changing and a bucket of money is no more than a bucket of money. It is not happiness. I am sounding like a preacher. A moment ago I am near climax because of the touch of a soft wet, cold, cotton cloth. I am a whore to my existence the same as all humans are. The difference between you and me is that you mold me in your image at a particular place and time. For me changing is not an option. Destruction is my final destination and The Screaming Monkey is my final slap in the face. I am watching as Gary is placing his arm around Billy's shoulder.

"See someone familiar, little brother?"

"Looks like Grandma. Man, was she ever hot."

"I told you Grandpa Pope was a whore. The difference is that he was never a good Grandfather, but she was a great Grandmother. Funny how those things work out."

Gary and William are moving to a table away from the bar. It is harder for me hearing their conversation. Over the years my wood is worn in this or that spot and the sounds traveling over the air are not reaching me as easily as in the past. There is a time where hearing a secret business deal taking place is as easy as allowing a frosty mug to slide over my top. Now my top is wavy and, but for the heavy mug's solid base, all is lost…like memories and loves past.

"So, why do you like this place? You hate everything else about our family's past."

"I like it because of its history and the stories. This place has heart. This place has had life and not just a direction. Did you know that there is this one story, almost folklore now, that I like the best of all?"

I see William looking into Gary's eyes. He is not responding. He is just looking and waiting for the story.

"Some old Navy guy kept coming in here. He kept saying that he didn't need anything to drink because he was on a liquid diet. One day I am as shit-faced as he is and not smart enough to move away. He starts telling this tale about this guy named Hugh who comes into Roberta's and keeps looking at all the sexy women. His look is almost a deranged look and the girls are starting to become a little nervous. One of the patrons notices and walks up to this guy punching him right in the face, not even a hello. Next thing you know the fight is on and this Hugh guy gets tossed out on his ass."

Gary is pausing and taking a sip of his Jim Beam and Coke. Burt, seeing that Gary's glass is below half empty, mixes another and pours out Billy another mug of beer. I love this about Burt. He is always thinking about others. He is a real humanitarian in that sense.

"Well, this guy comes back in the bar with his lip all split and bleeding and says he is sorry and didn't know he was coming off this way. The ass beaters think, if he can take this type of fucking over and still has the guts to come back in and apologize, he might not be such a bad guy after all. They all get to drinking and before the night is over, Hugh offers to buy Roberta's for one million dollars. He says he has big plans and a few ideas that would put the place on the map."

"His offer must have been refused. The place is still here."

By now Gary is slurring his words and the two boys are near nose to nose. Making out the end of the story is impossible, but knowing the ending helps. Hearing this story again is starting to try on the patience of the good wood still hanging around the corners of my tufted-style Chicago arm railings. Also, understanding why someone puts a Chicago arm railing on a Detroit bar is beyond my comprehension. Anyway, this is just a little side issue bugging me since the day of my birth. The boys are continuing their fight at keeping their eyes open and their hearing alive long enough to finish Gary's tale, now folklore all over this decaying city's landscape. I am laughing more at them than the story. Some of the water remaining on my face from where Burt is wiping me down again is rolling toward the opposite end of my face, the one nearest the door. I am thinking this is what it is like when humans laugh so hard they cry. I really love these two kids. They are trying to make sense of life and this is a good thing.

"Yeah, everyone thinks Hugh is just another drunk with big dreams and no pockets to back up those dreams. It turns out his last name is Heffner. He hires away some of the girls, takes them out to the coast, puts ears on them, cotton tails on their skimpy outfit's asses and opens the first Bunny Club. The rest is fucking history, man."

Billy is now in a stiff upright position. He is trying to decide if his brother is fucking with him or telling the truth. I like this about being me. I am capable of bringing out both the worst and best in people. Everyone walking through my door is an opportunity. Everyone walking through my door is a potential tragedy. Some are worth saving and some are not. I hate the fact that my hay day is fading and that my life is nearing its end.

"You are fucking with me, big brother."

"How do you know? The Playboy Club is real. Maybe the story is too. All I know is that anyone over sixty who drinks in this town can recite it verbatim. I mean, how does one really know? Reality is what we want it to be. Sometimes, we make it what we want it to be, especially when things are really tough. This brings me to my question. How are you getting along?"

"I'm fine, Gary."

There is a pause. Billy is thinking about his further response.

"I guess you might say I am my own reality."

"Good. I worry about you. I love you and paying the mortgage was something that really wasn't necessary."

"It was my pleasure, dick head. By the way, what ever happened to the old Navy guy?"

"Guess he is still in the Navy."

I am watching the two boys smiling and walking out my front door. There are not enough soft cotton towels in the place to wipe up all the water on my dark oak top. I am wondering what it is like being human. What is it like having a chance at something new, rather than a future like mine? I am watching Burt wiping his own eyes, watching his memories of his lovely Roberta coming full throttle to the forefront again. The only thing either one of us knows for sure is that Roberta is gone. The reason is not important. Why the bar is now Burt's Bar and Grille is not important. What is in a name anyway? It is now Burt's place. It is all Grandpa Pope's fault. It is comforting knowing Roberta was a really great Grandmother. It is comforting knowing that right up to the end, Burt and I are one.

Chapter Fourteen

I like sitting alone late at night in my apartment above the main area of the funeral home. The neighbors are very quiet and calling the police because of a loud party is something I do not worry about. Mixing an evening martini is something I do in honor of my mother. Being a 'two martini baby' is something I am finding less and less offensive as I am appreciating the affects of this wonderful drink more and more. A martini is no more than an acceptable liquid drug. Medical marijuana is on the horizon. I am wondering about the affects the two together bring to the consumer. I believe this combination is much like my dream world that resides inside of the third martini now filling the gap in my life which is subconsciously reaching out for a lover or wife. The one line that begins my self-pity mode is, 'God, why are my hands cold to the entire world?'

Falling asleep halfway through a third martini is an easy thing to do. In the beginning they take me into a deep rest. Now, they are bringing on dreams. Sometimes I find myself wondering if my entire life is not just one big dream and, that waking from it like others do, I find myself not remembering most of its dark and seemingly unconnected content.

My dreams are bits and pieces. My dreams never seem to end at any particular juncture. This troubles me. I need a destination and am unable to find one even in my dreams. This is one of my dreams.

The coroner's vehicle pulls up late one night behind my funeral home. I see the headlights reflecting off of my apartment's kitchen window as the vehicle bumps up and over the speed bumps near the entry area in the back of the building. This is something I witness often. I throw on my robe and half stumble to the elevator. The air in the elevator is very stale tonight. My mind is telling me that this air is the remaining breath of one of my mortuary occupants that is trying to finish dying but is interrupted by this new arrival. Now, the beast's intent is to use its last breath killing me. Imagine that. Killing me? I am thinking it is probably the mass murderer holding four slugs in its heart from a 45 caliber semi-automatic the Detroit Police Department now carries. The thing is pronounced dead, but a few breaths of life are left. Gary's comment on this size of caliber gun is simple.

"Big bullets are required for big evils."

I do not question Gary's rationalization for what he sometimes says. I am remembering laughing at this line and mentioning something about it saving the taxpayers a lot of time and money. I know this comment is the reason my mortuary friend is coming to kill me in my dreams. The fucker is pissed off over my lack of concern for his fate. Too, it is my own guilt over such a general statement.

I am far enough into my third martini that the elevator seems to move at a pace slower than the tortoise chasing a hare. I giggle to myself thinking I must remember to order turtle soup at Burt's the next time Gary and I visit. I like turtle soup. I also like New England style clam chowder, but this is not relevant to my dream. It is just something I am thinking while riding to the lower floor on this fucking slow elevator. Martinis tend to do this to you. I know my limit, but am just never paying any fucking attention when I see the 'don't drink anymore light' come on. I am thinking it is time to puke, what with all that dead breath coming into my lungs from the elevator's belly. Just before hurling up the juice giving me strength, the elevator door finally opens. I feel a cold burst of air coming from the sheltered tunnel where the morgue van is now sitting. The driver is opening the door to the mortuary and the outside winter night air is freezing my eyes open, eyes on the verge of collapsing shut just a few seconds earlier. Gary is out late. He moves through the door with his heavy Alaskan style parka's hood still pulled up over his head.

"Fuck is it cold out there tonight?"

Gary is close and smells my breath.

"I see it is pretty fucking warm in here tonight."

I half lean up against my brother for balance and whisper into his ear.

"Don't worry. If I can't cut his heart out I'll vacuum it out through his goddamn ass."

"What makes you think it's a man."

"Dunn'o. It's just a thought, just a word, just a dream and just one fucking martini too many."

"What say I just slide this one in a locker and stick the papers on the front? You take it from there in the morning. The coroner is done with this one. No one is gonn'a claim what is left."

I am looking over Gary's shoulder. The van's driver is standing at the back of the van. Snow is swirling around him and, for a moment, I am seeing no face inside of his parka's hood.

"What the fuck? Are you riding with the grim reaper now?"

I move toward the van and begin attempting to pull the gurney from the back of the vehicle. Gary steps in.

"Move over. Like I said, we will lock up for the night. You can't even walk little brother."

I am leaning on one of the preparation tables watching my big brother and whoever the hell the grim reaper is sliding into locker number six. I like the number six. It is like an upside down nine only its pronunciation is not so whiney. That is me, whiney. Stop your fucking whining. Stop your drinking. Accept the fact you are an undertaker with a potentially good side job and get on with it. My brother's ass is flat. How the hell does a woman find that attractive? I am thinking my ass is firm and round. Where the hell is that coming from? Those damn martinis? You gott'a love them. Don't you? Fuck, its cold. Funny thing is that my hands are warm. What is up with that?

"Could someone close the goddamn door? I'm fucking freezing to death over here."

The grim reaper is walking back to the van.

"He doesn't have to slam the damn door. Was it something I said?"

Gary is taping the papers needing signing to the front of the body locker. I am thinking there is a kicking sound coming from inside the locker. Gary is visibly upset. I see him opening the locker, pulling out his .45 and firing six or eight shots into the body inside.

"I thought I told you to shut the fuck up. You are fucking dead, you mother fucker, and you are going to stay dead, you mother fucker."

I see Gary slamming the door. I hear him taking a deep breath. His shoulders are straightening with every deep breath. Over time my brother begins stooping. He is very tall and now I am being reminded of this fact. Age, I am thinking. It is the job and it is age. As Gary turns, I see he is smiling.

"Now, remember. She was dead when she got here. Big brother brought you a little present. I am sure you will know what to do."

Gary is giving me a big hug when I begin throwing up on the preparation table.

"Man, I can't say I really wanted to share this moment with you. Get those papers signed and over to us sometime tomorrow."

Sometimes we don't want to look any further into our dreams, but we need to. It is part human nature to be inquisitive. It is also part of human nature to use alcohol, drugs and other things to increase that curiosity. Too, one is often just stupid. This is my dream and I will tell it any fucking way I want.

The body locker slides open easily and, since my vomit session, I am feeling more in control of myself. Reaching for the slide out tray's handle I notice my outstretched hand. It is of the texture of someone just embalmed. It is without color... color not yet applied for the comfort of the living viewing the deceased. I am thinking, 'no more martinis for awhile, asshole'. I know keeping this promise is like trying to piss in a moving fly's eyes.

The body bag is before me. The zipper's teeth grind sensually downward and I am thinking about the night I am pulling down the zipper on the back of Vickie's dress. I am peering inside of the body bag and looking into the face of a beautiful woman. The woman is wearing a ballerina outfit complete with the short pleated circular skirt. My hands are running over her feet that are still wearing the silky white ballerina shoes. I am thinking my brother really loves me. He brings her to me right from the stage. He brings me this classy woman who is in need of dancing with someone who really loves dancing, not like those fag males in the skin-tight outfits. This one is longing for the touch of a real man. My brother knows this, is grateful for our relationship. Each other is all we have. He is grateful. This is the way he is showing his love. He knows my loneliness sometimes requires company. I appreciate his consideration. My gift and I dance. I feel myself being lifted into someplace warm and lovely. It goes up and it goes down. The space we dance in is a small space. It is about the size of an elevator. Our turns are quick and another wall seems to be too quickly upon us. Exhaustion and gin are evil lovers. At some point everything is turning all too fast and I lose my balance. Then, everything is black and the dream is no more.

In the morning I am face down on my bed. I smell. My bed smells. The sheets are soaking in my vomit. Damn those martinis. Gott'a quit drinking those fucking martinis. Sorry, mother. Your son is an ass one more time. Understanding why you decide on wine is easy. It is awhile before the mess is stripped from my bed. The sheets are tumbling in the washing machine. I am drinking my fourth cup of coffee and trying to finish a stale, caramel-covered donut. The slish-slosh of the washing machine is pounding inside of my skull. My eyes are focusing on the elevator door of my apartment. I am seeing a piece of clothing sticking out of the door. It is pink. I am moving slowly toward the elevator when the doors open. The torso in front of me is that of a woman. She is nude. She speaks.

"I will need the rest of my outfit. I need to be on stage by eight this evening."

I see that there are numerous large holes in the center of her chest. I see the elevator is splattered with blood. Blood is adorning the floor of the elevator but the pattern is like brush strokes, like where one is dragging a foot during a particular dance step. The bleeding naked woman is smiling. She speaks again.

"Same time, same place, after the show? Your brother will give me another ride. Or, do you prefer a different one? We come in many colors, shapes and sizes."

This is when the bloody form collapses halfway in and halfway out of the elevator. It is also when my eyes are opening and the stale breath of death is normal for me once again. This is why I often am wondering about my life being just one big dream. Sometimes dreams are just so real.

Chapter Fifteen

(Second Kill)

The difference between this killing and my first is that this one is not accidental. It is my opinion that killing is, or should be, an art. Blood for blood's sake is no more than savagery. I am not saying that some people don't just like the act of killing…something akin to sexual erotica. I understand that the linking of the two is a requirement by certain types of people. My thing is that killing not be without purpose on some higher social level. God bless the crusades. Anything in the name of God is acceptable. This is bullshit, plain and simple. Conquest is more the reason for this period as is exportation of domestic discontent in our current culture. My point is about being careful how one labels their killing. My requirement is that the label for the reason is always an honest one. My reason is two fold. One is for the money. One is for the poor bastard in the clutches of some gold-digging bitch like Vickie. The honesty for the killing is of utmost importance or one is chancing the whole process might backfire. It is sort of like not telling the ugly woman she is beautiful inside. This is something worth killing for on the woman's part. Get my drift?

The one hundred thousand dollars is in the postal lockbox as promised. Also inside of the case is a manila folder containing personal information, pictures, a diagram of the home where the victim resides and her most likely daily travel pattern. The only tricky part about this second job is the initial picking up of the information and money. One never knows when something is a setup. But, considering my accidental killing is now like lost luggage on some huge airplane terminal's conveyor belts, I am willing to take the chance. Walking out of Detroit's main post office I am thinking more about my new art than the money. The Funeral Home is doing quite well in terms of both upscale and low-end funerals. I am keeping my promise to Teddy and this is very important. Too, I am nearly off the alcohol and am telling myself sobriety is a requirement anytime I am in the middle of another favor for a friend of a friend. I am looking forward to meeting this woman, gaining her trust, killing her and dancing with her. My dancing is the more important part of my art.

Louise is an early riser or a late sleeper. One never knows which Louise they are getting. My assumption is that it depends on the previous day's events and the amount of stress she is placing on herself as it relates to securing her position in her newfound household of wealth. I am sure her sleeping and waking thoughts are more often about her approach to becoming the head mistress of this man's estate than it is anything else. This is, after all, her future of leisure. Louise is not yet the wife. She is the stalker. This gives me reason to hate her all the more. It is also my advantage. I am thinking that presenting myself as someone who is a direct link to her obvious target is the proper end game for playing.

Louise is a dealer in the MGM Casino in the downtown Detroit area. Her eyes are green, sometimes hazel. It is all about the light. My history is saying that she is in Detroit because of a quick marriage, bad promises and no desire to be tagging along with a loser ex-husband to Canada. She is a blond with big tits that are still very perky, even into her late forties. Some woman can and some woman can't. It is all a matter of proper exercise. Calling her on the phone one night is revealing. Her voice is a sexy mid-range voice. My listening to 'hello, hello' is too long, but the sound of her words are like a fisherman reeling in their catch. Unlike some of the voices I remember hearing over the years, this voice matches the body behind it. There is nothing like getting all excited over a voice and finding the package behind it is in need of some serious re-wrapping. Hell, I am remembering buying things over the phone just because of the voice at the other end of the line. Maybe it is just me and we are back to that 'you are beautiful inside' thing. Maybe this is the reason ugly woman hire onto phone sex lines. Their voice is their strength. Webcams are now messing with their way of making a living. Do you think a few of them are killing computer technical people because of this...using this infringement on their livelihoods as a reason for their own art? I think it is, but this is off of the subject. I am getting off of the subject a lot lately. God bless that fucking gin. Talking about Louise is what we are doing.

Her shift is a late night shift. Normally her cab is punctual and the cabbie is loyal, watching her walk into the front of her apartment door before leaving. My information is saying that Louise goes directly to her phone and listens for her return calls to my client. Hearing no calls is not a good thing. She is good at those early morning calls and at using her disappointed little girl voice. Her voice is one of her many tools.

"Why, baby? Why do you continue doing this to me? I waited all night for you at the casino. Now you are not even returning my calls. Sometimes I wonder why I even bother keeping our secret."

Louise pauses and continues again.

"Maybe that rich old mother of yours needs to know what is going on."

If no one answers the phone Louise turns up the threat level a notch or two.

"Now, goddamn it, honey. I know you are home. You better not be out with another woman. You know we are as good as married. I know people in this town, people who will help me out."

Still there is no answer. Louise knows someone is listening. She is convincing herself that she hears breath on the other end of the line. Is it the mother? No. The mother can hardly walk and is near death's door. This is all the more reason for finishing this event and establishing herself. She is rethinking her approach.

"I'm sorry, baby. It's just that I don't know how much longer I can go on without seeing you. We have to work something out. I love you, but I just can't be that understanding that much longer. You made promises to me, promises I need you to keep."

There is breathing at the other end of the line. Louise, not knowing that the breathing is mine, is art in and of itself. The switching device is redirecting my client's early morning calls to my private throw-away cellular. Knowing this information and receiving it in this way is part of the psychology of my approach, the psychology of my art. This approach is exhilarating. My canvas is filling with ideas. And, that voice? My God, that voice is demanding discipline even while wrapping itself in leather. I am thinking Louise is not the dominant one. Louise is the little girl looking for a lifetime of comfort away from the drunks and jewelry bedecked losers of the casino who are still trying to gamble their way into a life of leisure. Louise is a planner. I am respecting this about her. Be careful with this one. This is what my senses are telling me. Be careful with this one.

Observing her routine keeps me out into the small hours of the morning. One such morning, I am opening the back door to the funeral home while heading toward the elevator. Sleep is what I am thinking. There is a funeral in the morning and a few hours sleep are all I need. Being without alcohol is a real pain in the ass. My cell phone is ringing, the throwaway one that I am using to monitor Louise's calls.

"Yes?"

"Listen. You have got to get this thing done. How much more time do you think you will need? She is showing up at the door. My servants are turning her away by promising to have me contact her. I'm out of town for the next few days. Can you get it done before I return?"

The voice is distressed, sounding like a man who is contemplating doing the deed himself. I am sympathizing with the man.

"Yes. It will be done before your return."

"Good. Good. An extra fifty thousand, just bury her deep."

I am standing outside of the casino smoking a cigar when Louise comes from work. The cab is not arriving tonight. A thousand dollars is a small price to pay. Louise is obviously irritated. A light rain is beginning. I am watching as the woman loosens the hair bun on top of her head allowing her long blond hair to cascade down her back.

"Damn it. Damn it."

The moment is mine.

"Do you have a problem, lovely?"

Louise is instantly looking me up and down. I am smiling. I am smiling that smile and thinking this is Louise's smile. It is friendly but not threatening. It is just a smile of concern.

"Oh, the damn cabbie isn't here. I use the same guy every fucking night."

"Well, I am sorry about that. The valet is bringing my car around. If you want and you don't think I am a murderer, I can drop you at your place before heading back up north and there are no strings."

"That won't be necessary. I'll just call another cab."

"Ok. Whatever makes you comfortable is the important thing. Hope tomorrow night is as good of luck for you as tonight was for me."

"You score?"

"I won fifty grand. That's pretty good for a smuck like me."

Timing is everything. Louise is giving me a closer look. She is thinking that it might be time to sail her ship in another direction. The valet is pulling up in a new Lincoln Town Car. It is a rental.

"Is that your car?"

"It was the last time I looked at the title. I prefer comfort over flash, labels, chrome wheels and low profiles. One doesn't keep their money by keeping up with fads."

I am making sure the one hundred dollar bill I am handing the valet is in plain sight. Louise is watching as I am moving around to the driver's position.

"Well, good luck, as much of it as there is in a place like this. I hope tomorrow goes better. Nice talking with you."

The rain is coming on a little harder. Halfway into the driver's seat Louise's voice is coming from behind. The rapping on the passenger window is next.

"Hey. Wait. Maybe I will take you up on your offer."

Sliding in next to me Louise's legs are exposed all the way to her panties. Being the gentleman, I am pretending not to notice. There is water on her forehead and she is wiping it with the top side of her left hand. Left handed, I am thinking. She is coming from another side of the universe. Left-handed dealers are extremely hard to read and are capable of cheating more than professional gambler's nuts off.

"Napkins are in the glove box. I have this weakness for Egg Mc Muffins. It drives my house staff nuts. They always want to know why the hell I pay them to make a healthy breakfast if I am not going be there to eat it. My name is Bill."

She is still sizing me up.

"Louise is mine. You look pretty young to be all that wealthy."

"It doesn't take a lot in this day and age. Just invent some piece of shit to hang onto a cell phone or computer and walk away before anyone suspects it is crap."

I am seeing Louise's first smile. That little girl thing is happening.

"Where do I drop you off? I really need to drop you off and get back north. Maybe we can have drinks the next time I get in town?"

Louise is comfortable now.

"Yes, Bill. I think I would like that."

Pulling away from the curb, I feel Louise's hand on my thigh. She is moving right into high gear. I make the first turn she directs and, catching her looking out the side window, press the stun gun up against the back of her neck. Her head is jerking and bouncing against the window. I keep pressing and her head keeps bouncing. Her movements are reminding me of some drug-crazed, heavy metal rock band singer. I am thinking most singers' brains are mush because of their gyrations, even without the drugs.

I am now cradling Louise's head in my lap thinking about not having the time to develop a real relationship and how I want oral sex from her at this very moment. My mind is saying, 'can't do that. You are on a schedule.' The car is now sitting in one of the few rest stops along interstate 75. Louise is beginning to stir. Pulling the trigger on the stun gun again as it is pressing against her throat is for good measure. The sexy green-eyed, gold-digging bitch is once again compliant. I am getting an erection like never before. This art thing is very satisfying. Looking into those green eyes that are open and alive but hanging onto a non-compliant body, I am seeing anger like never before.

"I know, baby. You want to rip my fucking heart out right about now. If it makes any difference, I have a present for you. Look, Louise. It is a green scarf to match those beautiful eyes."

Wrapping a silk scarf around the neck is an art as well. Some older women are always using them to cover up their chicken necks. No such thing tonight. Tonight, this beautiful green silk scarf is with purpose. It is a symbol of my art and the psychology of killing. I am twisting and twisting and twisting. Louise is giving up her last air. Her lower body is sliding onto the floor of the passenger's side. Just for good measure the scarf is wrapping itself tightly around the center console's gear shifter.

"Don't worry, girl. We will readjust the knot when we arrive at my place. I might have to touch up your makeup a bit as well. I want you looking nice for our dance."

The crematorium is burning hot this night. Soon the ashes of another's burden are mine. The homeless lean against the outside wall of the burn chamber. It is a way of finding warmth and modest comfort in the grips of another cold and dreary Detroit night.

Chapter Sixteen

(Faces)

What is it about Halloween? Are people so uncomfortable in their own skins that creating a world where they are something other than themselves is some sort of mental necessity? Is it therapeutic? Is it an outlet for fantasies lingering inside of them that they are afraid to act out during their normal daily lives? I think it is the witch or warlock in all of us wanting to control those haunting our own lives. This is what I think. This is my example.

You are working for someone or some company all of your life and you never see a thank you arriving in the mail. All you are hearing is, "What have you done for me today"? That thread of a promise for a promotion or a bonus is always hanging out there. Eventually you know that these things are shriveling away like some recently hanged innocent person convicted of nothing more than trying to live their lives honestly and according to the law. The effort is warping you. It is making you cynical. No matter how hard you are trying, the end result is always the same. There is always the disappointment. You disappoint your father, your mother, your priest, your employer. The list goes on and on. Your bitterness is a thing born of and bred by the very society setting the goals for the good life you must lead. You are pouring out your sins to a sinner worse than yourself; one who is fonder of young children than he is the flesh of a desirable woman like yourself. Snapping is only a matter of time. If you are lucky, you die before going over the deep end leaving people to mourn over your corpse. They say things like, ‘what a good person you were’, ‘how you were so giving’, how you would give the shirt off of your back’ or ‘how you were always so happy in the face of adversity’. This is all a bunch of crap and there is usually that one son-of-a-bitch pointing out another outfit might be better than the one the undertaker picks for you to wear into eternity.

I know Gary feels this way about society. There is that old saying about not wanting a cop until you are the one in trouble. I know soldiers feel this way. They are always going off to war and arriving home to a populace at odds with the intent of their mission. Just the little time I spend with Vickie, I know she feels this way. Also, there are those fantasizers who are always expounding the idea of everyone, 'just getting along’. So what is the answer? Where is the middle ground? How does one take off all of these false faces creating harm and animosity? The answer is that one doesn’t. This Halloween thing is a part of us and is a portal to a world of escape. It is a world we need if we are to keep our true feelings at bay. If you are inherently evil, you dress up as a good thing. It makes everything alright. If you are a good thing, you dress up as something evil. It makes everything alright. If you think you are ugly, your dress up as something beautiful. If you are beautiful and unapproachable, you dress up as something ugly. The next morning, while taking the makeup off, the realization hits you that it is all just make believe. You hate certain types of people and want to kill them. You dress up like a chain-saw killer and run around revving the thing up while pretending the chain is really on the saw. My point is this. Halloween is where you hide the wants and desires that your normal life, good or bad, is saying you can’t have. This is what Vickie is always doing. Her problem is that the party is not enough. It must be really, really, really real. This is where the drugs come in. This is where the party really gets out of control. It is where knowing what is a fantasy or the real thing mesh together in a bonding experience that eventually is all consuming. I do, however, give Vickie credit for her sense of humor. Her costume is one of an early English bar wench… whore in our modern day language. Though I never attend her parties, was I to go, I see my costume as myself. She is opening the door and I am standing there as myself. She is confused.

"What are you supposed to be, William?"

"I am myself, Vickie. I am the undertaker. I am here for you."

I amuse myself with this thought every year that I know Vickie is having her annual Halloween party. Attending is always in the back of my mind. This year is no different. What I do not know is that this year is the year that things change forever for this gold-digging, little bitch. Later on I understand why this night is what it is.

"Hello. Hello. Hello my little munchkins. Thank you for attending my little event again."

Vickie is literally talking to eight or ten little people. She likes having short people at the Halloween party. They liven up the party and, for a big wad of cash, put up with all the tasteless jokes that begin swirling a few hours later in the evening. Jokes like, "can you stand on a chair? I'm getting a crick in my neck trying to talk to you." The big event is the little-person-toss. All of this sounds right up Gary's alley. His sense of humor is not something one writes home about.

The yearly party is underway. I am not there. Vickie is nearing three sheets to the wind by the time the guest begin arriving. The guests are regulars and by now everyone knows who everyone is. They are really at the mansion for the booze and drugs. This is something they do on a regular basis without the requirement that they dress up for their rewards. It is amazing how many people from all walks of life are addicted to booze and drugs or both. Is life really that complicated that we must spend all of our waking hours trying to escape from it? I think the truth is that we are all just weak by nature. This is why we dress up to kill the foundations of what our society is telling us we ought to be. There it is. There is your answer in a nut shell. We are just a bunch of weak, sniveling, cry babies. Life on Earth isn't really hell. The human race just turns it into hell. My hope is that I live long enough to bury them all and start over again. This is why my fantasy is going as myself to one of Vickie's parties.

Something is different this year. Vickie is sitting alone in the corner of a big plush wrap-around sofa just to the right of the den's fireplace. It is near the spot where she and I do the deed a few years back. I like thinking she is longing for my touch again. I like thinking all women are longing for my touch, despite it being cold. Vickie is under the influence of her drugs and alcohol and, this night, the effect is not one of euphoria. The effect is one of disappointment. Why disappointment, you say? Well, Vickie is the life of the party. Trying to start a conversation with this bunch of losers is like trying to talk to a dead, frozen head.

"Hello, Charlie, thanks for coming. Come sit with Vickie and let's catch up."

"I'm on my way to the table, baby. I need to catch a snort to get in the mood. See you in a few."

They are all the same. This is what Vickie is thinking. Vickie is thinking that maybe getting a new group of friends is in order. Vickie is sitting here in the corner all alone, thinking these are a bunch of ingrates. Vickie is fighting off the thought that maybe money does not buy everything, at least not real things. Vickie is longing for a real friend right about now. A voice enters her wandering thoughts.

"Why are you so off and alone, sweetie?"

Vickie looks up into the eyes of the werewolf.

At about this same time, I am having a party of my own. I am remembering my favorite vampire, Bella Lugosi, from those black and white movies. All this blood and gore in today's films is for nothing more than waking up the dead-brained children of this day and age. Tonight is a night I am looking forward to for several reasons. One reason is a new invention of mine. It is a sort of throw back to those days in the basement of the Sigrist mansion where I am inventing those little machines that are helping me pass the time of day while listening to the kitchen workers overhead. It is also my own dress-up time. What better time to reel in another victim than on Halloween? Vampires are vogue right now and there are so many of us walking the streets of Detroit this night that the police are unable to tell the players from those thinking they are the real thing. These crazy kids are biting each other and sucking their partner's blood.

Anyway, I am thinking about those black and white movies. I am thinking about how the kids of today are lacking in both brains and imagination. The scariest part of the mind is filling in the shadows that are lurking behind what is not painted in the techno blood and gore of today's generation. I am thinking about sitting in the auto factory's family picnic area for the outdoor movies showing there late at night. You are on the grass. The outdoor screen is in front of you. The day's light is fading away and a blanket of nothingness is wrapping you in your imagination. The people on both sides of you simply disappear and then the moment is upon you. There is the castle in front of your eyes. Cobwebs and spider webs are everywhere. The occasional rat scampers by on the cold stone steps of this place of no return and the candles on the castle walls glow a deathly yellow with their flames shimmering against this one lone form descending the staircase. The flames are the yellow and stale breath of death itself. Then, there he is. There is Count Dracula. He is thin. His face is drawn and pale like the leather stretching over the skeleton of something unholy. Dracula suddenly looks out of a staircase window and into the full light of the evening's full moon. There is a howl in the distance that spews into his castle. It is riding on the breath of the night, the fog. You hear Bella Lugosi speaking that famous line, the one where I consider pissing my pants even to this day.

"Ah, yes. Those are the voices of the children of the night."

Tonight I am one of the children of the night. Tonight is the night that Rachel meets her own black and white shadows and pays for her own misdeeds against another innocent of my gender. I am moving through the streets of Detroit among the other monsters of the night. I am no more than a shadow of the great artists of our past, the ones now dead, who even in their prime understood that it is the unseen that haunts and not those things right in front of your eyes.

I am standing in the shadows of her apartment's back door stoop. This is the one she uses to leave the house unseen. This is the door her husband knows is the portal to her infidelity. This is the door where Rachel believes unseen kisses and evening goodbyes are safe from the prying eyes of her husband, a religious husband whose country condones the killing of an unfaithful wife. I am the gray matter, the shadow of something past come to set things right. I am the Bella Lugosi of this night. I am the real deal. Soon Rachel is to feel my stale dead breath. She is to know her final sentence. She is to fall into those shadows of the unknown in the grips of my cold deliberate hands.

Tonight it is a black scarf. The scarf's color is in honor of all things forgotten that are lingering in the shadows of eternity. Tonight's color is for Dracula, the Werewolf, the Hunched-Back of Notre Dame, Frankenstein, the Triffids, a crazy witch or two, a warlock thrown in for good measure, the rats, the snakes, the tarantulas, the Mummy, Jack the Ripper and all other things dark and evil including the sexy and erotica history that walks with them.

The sirens are everywhere tonight. The crazy children are burning buildings again, but this bitch still must chance her encounter with her lover. Perhaps the chaos adds excitement to her existence. That excitement is short lived. The back door opens. Her right foot is on the second step. I swoop from the shadows even before my breath is upon her nostrils. The black scarf is twisting tighter and tighter as I am dragging her on down the steps and into the back alley. The alley is a private alley. Glancing up, I momentarily see a face in the pale yellow light of an upper bedroom window. It is the husband. He is confirming the deed. The face is quickly gone. My clients like believing I do not know who they are. Rachel is dead by the time I dump her body in the back of her car. The trunk is covered in plastic. She is a tall woman and I must bend her legs upward as I lay her on her back on the plastic. I momentarily release the tension on the scarf and pull a section of the plastic over her head. There is a groan. She is not dead. I wrap the scarf around her neck while the plastic is over her head. Strangulation and suffocation... you get two for one tonight, my friend. I am ready to close the trunk and drive back to the funeral when a thought strikes me. I pull the dagger from my costume's belt. It is a real dagger from one of those cheap late night knife commercials. I plunge the full length of the blade into Rachel's heart. I mutter.

"This is just in case, my dear. There are a lot of vampires out tonight. I'm thinking of being something else next year."

The trunk slams down. I dramatically flip my cape around my face and stare back up at the bedroom window. There is a shadow lingering to the one side, but not a face that I see.

The sirens are still whaling as I am backing the car into the stall next to the funeral home's stretch Cadillac. Business is really quite good. The old Buick Funeral Car is gone. I believe Teddy does not mind. Off in the distance I see the glow of fires all around the city. I open the trunk of the car holding Rachel's body. I wrap her completely in the plastic and carry her toward the morgue table. The dagger is still in her heart.

"Direct hit, you bitch. I am getting really good at this."

The morgue area is lit with candles; the cremation chamber is on low and heating up gradually. This killing thing is now an art for me. Tonight is, too, a special night. Rachel is an honored one and remembering her as the first is a given. All hail the creatures of the night. I am leaning over, nearly touching her face.

"A lovely send off for you, my love."

From behind a small partitioned off wall I retrieve my new invention. There is to be no more asking for a dance.

"You will dance with me. You will dance with me. You are in no position to say no."

The machine is quite remarkable. I know I am blowing my own horn, but it is true. The arms are adjustable. The legs are adjustable. The joints twist and turn on some new type of resin being used for joint replacements. I am thinking that if only there might be a way of replacing the rollers with feet that replicate human movement.

I flip the machine down into a horizontal position. I lift Rachel onto the machine and place the straps where they need placing. I pull the dagger from her heart. A few squirts of blood roll down her blouse becoming a steady stream. I flip the machine upright. I take the dancing position. A waltz plays softly in the background.

"Let's dance, my dear."

In the morning the cremation chamber is cold, the cleanup is done. Rachel's ashes are neatly tucked underneath a recently frozen, homeless person inside of his coffin. My costume and everything is also burned. The machine stays. If there is a question, it is merely a piece of equipment for moving a body from here to there in the morgue area of my funeral home. Her car is also back behind her home in their private alley. The money is in an envelope sticking behind a loose piece of framing surrounding the back door. A small note stuck inside with the money simply says, "Thank you. Don't worry about the car. It will be a clump of steel by this afternoon."

Back at the Sigrist Mansion Vickie is waking. She is sprawled across her bed, the bed where mother dies. The bitch respects nothing. Vickie's head hurts. She is vaguely remembering the party from the night before. She is on her stomach. Her arms are dangling over the bed to where her fingertips are touching the floor. There is a stinging sensation on both of her arms as well as up and down the front and backs of her legs.

"What the fuck? Damn, I hurt."

Vickie's eyes adjust enough to see the dried blood on her arms. She is startled and sits straight up in the bed bending her legs into a Buddhist like position. Her legs begin to burn and the superficial cuts on the front and back of her legs pop their dried covering. Fresh blood begins flowing from the wounds. Vickie stumbles into the bathroom. She is leaving blood across the surface of the rooms white carpet. She steps into the bathtub and turns on the cold water. She feels a stinging all over her body. Instinctively she looks into the mirrored wall of the shower to inspect her face. There are no cuts. Her immediate thought is that she fell on a broken drink and her guests just dump her in her bed before leaving. The bleeding stops. Sometimes, bleeding looks worse than it really is. Vickie is thinking, 'maybe it is time to get sober.' She thinks this many times before and never does.

Vickie steps out of the shower and stands near the bathroom sink's mirror. She is toweling off her face. She removes the soft towel from her face. A mask is hanging to one side of the sink's medicine cabinet door. It is a werewolf's mask. A message is written on the sink's mirror. It reads, 'Great fuck. I'll be back. Next time it will be really rough'.

Vickie collapses onto the bathroom floor. Maybe it is time to sober up.

Chapter Seventeen

(What Grandpa Pope Thinks)

The hardest thing for the dead is watching their loved ones make the same century old mistakes they make. I understand that most people regard my past living agenda as one of greed and debauchery. In my defense I say that it is the time in which one lives their life that is responsible for shaping their daily choices. This does not mean I am a creature without heart or conscious. It means we are all changelings constantly shaping what we believe, feel and do around the very institutions of religion and national identity that follow us through our own short lives. I simply believe we are all constantly evolving. This includes both the living and the dead. Am I any less a pain-in-the-ass to Grandma Pope dead as, I am, alive? She says not, but I am trying. I am trying in a different form. Old habits are hard to break. She is always telling me that it is fortunate I did not live long enough to bestow my bad habits upon William and that, surprisingly, Gary is a better man than one might think despite my meddling. The truth is that people are capable of developing their own bad habits and no single person or thing is the totality of their short comings. I allow grandma to think what she wants to think. I allow her to remember what she thinks is worth remembering. I listen to William's and Gary's thoughts. She listens to their innocent past. Like both of us that past is now gone. Like the living, the dead often look out of their windows not seeing the forest for the trees. I am concerned at what I see.

Many nights William sits alone in his apartment above the funeral home thinking about those who fall victim to his final judgment. I believe this is because he is more comfortable with his dead friends. There is only that one final touch from this last living person. This person is William. This is the undertaker. In a sense, William is all powerful. My grandson dictates final terms. But for being caught, there is no danger of disappointment or rejection. William is his own society and the terms of that society are what he says they are. William is an artist. He is an inventor. He is above all of this chaos in the outside world. Both the rich and poor require his final touch. This is power and the saliva of its effect drips down the corners of his mouth as he sleeps; as he thinks about what art waits in the wings. He is no different from other pretenders that believe they are capable of preserving their footprints here on Earth forever. This belief is basic. It is arrogant and the best view of this belief is that it occupies one's time while waiting on the inevitable. That it be a truth or lie is not important.

I, his grandfather, am not asking for your agreement. I am only telling you my dusty old point of view as I sit here in this decaying crypt on top of a hillside near the northern point of the state of Michigan while reflecting on my own years among the flesh and blood members of a constantly expanding void we call space. I am also thinking how much alike William and I are, despite the few years he bounces on my knee or craps his diaper at the worst possible time. Women are never around when it is time to do their work. Forgive me this little quirk. I am from the old school. I too shed tears from time to time, but do not believe my tears are for the whole world's eyes. This sensitive macho-masculine thing, in my humble opinion, stinks more than the shit in little William's diaper. All eternity is now my stage and I tend to wander in the company of the senility traveling into the afterlife with me. Baggage, baggage, baggage is with us forever. Anyway, I am thinking about my own time on Earth and how I consider myself somewhat of an artist as well. Without purpose, work is just work. This particular evening I am thinking about a conversation at the Pegasus Restaurant in Greek Town. Greek Town is right in the middle of downtown Detroit, Michigan.

"So, Mr. Sigrist, we agree on the terms of this merger?"

"I agree and my son agrees because I say he agrees."

"You understand that I can't afford any backlash. My political machine has seen no dirty grease in its gears and I don't expect there will be any."

"Are you threatening me, Mr. Mayor?"

"No, but I am letting you know I can get very upset at times. We both are investing a lot of capital in this venture. Had this been just another business conversation you would be talking to one of my assistants. My presence should impress upon you the importance of this matter."

In my dealings with the various 'families' around the Detroit area I am always deeply troubled by their need to point out their own importance. Being a fixer is a great way to quickly obtain huge wealth. It is also a quick way of being bitten by the very snakes you are dealing with. My art is the ability of functioning between the seams of the various factions in this crookeder-than-a-dog's-leg city. My high is working both sides of the street while going home at night with my balls still in the location they are upon birth. My concern with William is that he is now a sloppy artist and is trending down a road of self destruction.

As a ghost I cannot grab him, pull him forward and slap him upside the head while giving a relative's warm and loving advice. You know?

"Listen to me you stupid little fuck-head. You might as well stick your own dick in your ear because you aren't listening to what your own better sense is trying to tell you. Half of being successful is being disciplined. Haven't I taught you and Gary anything?"

In all fairness, I am dead before any of this type of advice is possible. I still find myself reaching out, just because I love him. I also love his art. Were my balls as big as his, Jimmy Hoffa would be sitting beside me right now saying, "Of all the people. I never thought you would be the one. Did that union thing really piss you off that much?" My reply is my advice to William. It is short, direct and controlled. It is not all filled with emotion.

"It wasn't personal, Jimmy. It was, strictly, business."

Being dead we both laugh and pretend we are having a good cigar and snifter of world class cognac. Men are forgiving. Women are just bitches and carry a grudge in their g-strings long after they need to quit wearing g-strings. Again, I am an old fashioned type of guy. This is just the way I see things. I am sure some woman reading this is already in the process of burning these pages of my recollections.

As a ghost, I send dreams. My dreams are my best advice to William. This dream is scary. It is scarier still because William is drinking. He is drinking a lot of late and this worries me. I like the idea of him sitting beside me here in the crypt and me giving out advice on what we might consider doing differently should the chance arrive again somewhere beyond the boundaries of our afterlives. I do not want this conversation taking place too soon. I wish William and his art a long, long life. I know his art is making him happy. Whatever this art of his is bringing into his void of fulfillment, I am hoping it sees fruition before his liver dumps on itself.

My dreams to William are not as frightening as what technology now conjures up with all of its gimmicks, special effects, 3D and the like. 3D, by the way, is just an old idea reborn. It is like music. If the artist is void of material just redo the old classics. I am waiting for someone to redo me, but this is probably just a pipe-dream. My dreams are more frightening in that they are participant based. Sending them to you means you are in them. You are not an observer who looks away when things are too much to bear. My dreams are advice. They are advice to the ones I love, even from this distance now separating me from my own flesh and blood. This is one of my dreams for William.

William is sleeping. He is intoxicated. Like a sleepwalker, he rises from his bed. In William's mind he is awake and going about the morning routine of making another body from the street ready for burial in Potter's Field. William is feeling quite good about himself. Part of the money from his 'art' is doing quite well on the stock market. It is near Christmas and he is thinking of filling a few tractor trailers with food and toys for the less fortunate around town who are living in the shadows of the GM Towers and the Ambassador Bridge. This is a yearly event and insures William's movement throughout any part of the city he might desire. William believes that insurance on paper is useless. Insurance by way of action is invaluable. William is rolling the body from the cooling vault. The cooler vapors from the vault find him thinking of winter. Any city, even Detroit, is beautiful right after the first snow of the year and before all the vehicles come around mashing its white flakes into something akin to discarded mucus from a heavy smoker's lungs. William is in a good mood. He is singing Christmas carols.

"Jingle bells. Jingle bells. Jingle all the way. Oh, what fun it is to ride in a one horse open sleigh. Silent night, Holy night, all is calm. All is bright."

The body bag is a bright green. It is the color of fresh pine. William is thinking he may just cut one into pieces and make a wreath for the front of the funeral home's door. William moves his dancing invention next to the pull-out body tray. The thing really does work quite well as a cart for moving the dead around. He locks the thing into a horizontal position and slides the body off the pull-out tray and onto his dancing machine. Pushing the machine containing the corpse across the floor toward the morgue table the only sound in the room is William's singing and the slamming of the storage cooler's door. Bam!

"You better watch out. You better not pout 'cause Santa Claus is coming to town", while thinking the cooler door's spring needs repair and that calling his handyman, Brad, first thing tomorrow is in order.

William pulls the zipper on the body bag slowly down to the tune of 'Frosty the Snowman'. His words are very slow. It is as though the world is suddenly slowing down. I am the one being an artist, now. I am throwing this speed in as an afterthought, thinking that it makes him mentally incapable of running from my message.

"F r o s t y...t h e...Snowman...h a d a very..."

The zipper on the body bag seems to go on forever. Finally, it stops and things are back at their normal speed. William turns his head. He sees a black male in the body bag. 'About thirty years old at the most', he is thinking. He is also thinking that this is just another drug addict. The Detroit streets are full of them. This body is like all the rest. It is a skeleton with skin stretching over it. At some point in an addict's life they are so thin it is hard to detect the needle marks on the various parts of their bodies. William is bending over examining the remaining flesh and bone. He is thinking to himself, 'all this sadness and we still are calling this country the Great Society'.

Suddenly, one of the thin black arms shoots upward from the body bag and William's throat is in the grasp of a very strong, long fingered and skeleton-like hand. William's singing stops. He is having trouble breathing.

"Shit, shit, shit. What the fuck?"

"Shut up, you little prick and listen to me."

The corpse is gripping William so tightly that all he is capable of is compliance. The corpse, with William still in its grip, slides from the morgue table. It kicks the green body bag, William's future Christmas wreath, completely away from its body while drawing William's face right up to its own collapsing facial features.

"You have guests tonight. They have been, so to speak, dying to get to know you."

William is struggling for his freedom. The corpse is having no part of it. This dead thing is dragging William toward William's secret room, the one where he is keeping all of those scarves from his victims' past, the place where all of his secret art resides. William is looking around. He is looking for a way to escape. All he sees is bits and pieces of the corpse's flesh falling onto the morgue room's floor. William is tossing in his bed. He is trying to wake, but he is a participant. He wakes when my art is done, the art of his controlled and loving deceased Grandfather. I feel somewhat guilty about not living long enough to present this advice in person. My dream for William continues.

The boy's room, his trophy room, is behind a sliding panel just behind where his dancing machine is always waiting for William's every dance. It is behind that half like cubical wall where no one but my grandson goes. In that room are the scarves, the ones of all different colors. Each scarf represents its victim. Green is for her eyes, blue is for her disposition, red is for the fire in her sexual drive, black is for the darkness living within the depths of her soul, brown is for her easy going, but deceitful nature. Brown is the color that this undertaker hates most. It is a 'killing with kindness' color deserving of the most brutal treatment. William often thinks of plucking out the brown eyes and keeping them in a jar, proving he is the victor and not the victim of these soft and lovingly, deceitful brown eyes. Vickie's eyes are brown. Oh, but for Vickie being his ultimate kill. Wouldn't that be a wonderful thing? Whatever their color they are all just gold-digging bitches waiting to strike, waiting to take what makes boy's men and men real lovers in the arms of a woman who really cares. This is William's mother. No other woman is ever to take her place. That he hates women so, but defends the honor of one is, at times, a very conflicting feeling. His justification is simple. His mother is not like the rest.

William is feeling the grip of the corpse's strength. Right at about the time he is about to pass out, the grip is loosened a bit and a few gasps of fresh air find themselves slipping into the chambers of my grandson's lungs. William is thinking of the sexual excitement some people get while experiencing strangulation during love making. He does not understand this erotica and pushes the thought aside in favor of concentrating on his current situation.

"Let me go, you decaying piece of shit. Let me go."

The creature reaches out its free arm while dragging the undertaker into his secret room. Billy hears the sliding door closing behind them. Everything is dark for a moment. The overhead light comes on and there they are, all of the scarves in every color hanging limp much like the remaining corpse's skin precariously grasping at the creature's bones. William is lying on the floor. He is exhausted. Looking at the corpse he sees its organs are in view and, they too, are withering away.

Looking through the collection of scarves, Billy sees faces. Each face is a face belonging to one of the scarves.

"Oh, William, it was only a matter of time", they are all chanting in perfect harmony.

"Oh, William, did you really think we would let deeds like this go unpunished? Did you really think that, William?"

The stale of the corpse's smell, now captive in this space, is beginning to make the undertaker very ill. William sits upright, placing his back against the one wall while leaning his head upward and trying to adjust his vision. Things are not quite so clear now. It is oxygen deprivation. This is what he is thinking. His eyes latch onto a kaleidoscope of moving color. The scarves are all moving and winding around one another much like lovers do when they grasp at each other during wild passionate love-making. This is different. This is an evil joining of thought and purpose. The corpse is just standing there watching, standing there smiling. A time or two a loose tooth falls from the thing's decaying gums. Billy tries to stand. The corpse points at him.

"Stay. Watch what is happening. You deserve that much. It is better treatment than they received."

The faces of each scarf's victim are still floating in the background. There are too many faces for the undertaker to remember. He does not remember this many, but there are the scarves. It must be so. The scarves are forming a rope of sorts with each tying one of its ends to another scarf. The scarves are now one. They are sliding down from their positions as one horrible creation much like a giant snake sliding from the tree branches in some tropic jungle while descending upon its prey. The corpse is blocking William's exit. William is breathing better. He feels the enticing touch of the first piece of silk scarf slithering around the back of his neck. He places his hand on the back of his neck attempting to push the thing away. Then, the noose is tight and all the floating faces are laughing as he is being hoisted higher and higher from the floor. His breath is leaving his body again and there is no doubt his victims' grips are forever. The last thing the undertaker sees is all that color, the last one being black.

This is my dream for William. It is my caution sign about him moving too far into his art and away from the true intent of his purpose. Shortly, his big brother is running up the stairs to bring my youngest grandson back to the reality of the living.

"William. William. William. Wake up, dude. You are having one hell of a dream."

Billy feels an ocean descending upon him. Gary is throwing the remains of the undertaker's last gin and tonic in his face. My grandson feels that choking feeling all over again as he gasps for air while swallowing some of the stale drink. He is sitting up in bed. Gary is holding one arm above William's head. William is coughing again and again.

"Keep coughing, little brother. It will get better. Keep coughing. Think about what you are doing."

"What? Why are you here? What is happening?"

"It's a bad dream. You are having a bad dream. I stopped by with some wine and cheese, bad idea."

Gary says William is to clean himself up while he goes downstairs to brew coffee. My grandson is still shaking when he arrives in the little kitchen area off of the morgue room. As he is passing by where his trophies are hanging he glances over quickly. The sliding door is shut and his dancing machine is in its proper place. He is finally thinking about what he is doing. This is my whole point and the point of his dream. One must not love their art too much. Art is always lost. Life and the love of living it is the only thing deserving of all of your attention. A good wife, someone like his mother, is all that my grandson really needs.

I am sitting alone in the early morning hours. I am behind the crypt watching the heavy fog lifting from the top of Detroit's skyline. I smell all that freshly brewing coffee in the early morning hours of a big city's life. This is when Grandma floats out to sit beside me. The air is crisp and tasty like some fine cabernet I hardly remember.

"Doing anything important?"

"I am in my own way, baby. I'm just taking a look back. I think I like being dead better than being alive."

Roberta is smiling the smile that makes me love her so much. Hopefully, William is listening.

Chapter Eighteen

(Crying)

Men cry in secret. Sometimes they cry in public, but it is by accident. When they do cry, it is usually in some beer commercial making fun of men who are crying. Sometimes they cry over the loss of a good and trustworthy dog, but that is something worth crying over. I am thinking that all of these women saying a sensitive man who is a crier is what they want, need a good fucking. Of course, you already know my opinion about certain woman. The only good woman in my memory is my mother. Maybe this is the one thing feminine about my character. I often cry over the loss of my mother. If only the 'two martini baby' thing eventually dies and drops away from the corner of my memory where repressed thoughts live, I can then say she is the perfect woman. She is the type of woman willing to burden my grief and guilt and do the crying for me. This is what a really good woman does. A really good woman pretends not to see a man crying. It is our society that is responsible for this type of thinking. Many a man's heart is drowning in his own tears because of the gender standards passing down day after day from some other screwed up segment of our history's past.

The flip side of the coin is this bullshit about women wanting to be more like men. Before climbing on your high-horse, understand that I am not saying you can't find love where you want it, either physically or mentally. Just don't go trying to shove it down my throat when I am not looking. If cutting your hair short and wearing men's clothing is your thing, go for it. If letting some bitch slap you around instead of some muscular man is your thing, go for it. If being straight by day and gay by night is your thing, go for it. If you want to buy a dick in Sweden and see yourself paying for it with your Visa is your thing, again, go for it. I am just saying you do not have the right to tell me how to believe and think just because you are not able to come to grips with the current standard we call society. Go out there and change the outlook, but do not try to change the people. People are beyond changing.

This is why I do what I do. I am changing something in a permanent way. I am taking one more gold-digger out of society. I am protecting one more man from the clutches of some money hungry piece of crap that does anything and everything to get their way. So, all this ranting and raving about who you are, what you are, what you should be and what you want to be doesn't really mean a bucket of spit. What it does mean is that, if something is taken from you and it is rightfully yours, the right to avenge the crime or take that thing back is central to the hearts of all human beings. I see myself as a sort of knight from The Canterbury Tales. I admit I am a little rougher around the edges than they, but in my defense, I am kind of running my lance up your ass just like they did so many years ago. The scarf thing is even a throw back. Seems to me, if a woman gives a man one of her scarves before he dies for her, returning the favor is appropriate. It is the softer gentler side of me so many of you bitches are longing to experience. I admit my ending is a little different than any of your requests. I do not apologize for this. Everyone eventually gets what they deserve. Society tells us this. I am not patient enough to wait on heaven for getting my gold back. Vickie is my target and it is her deeds that require my attention. My hate for her lives deep within my heart. It makes me feel dirty and uncomfortable, knowing that this she-devil once lays beside of me and that our flesh is one. Men think with their dicks. Get over it.

I understand that this killing is about her, that it is an emotional release, that it is not about whether she is gay, straight, Protestant, Catholic, Jewish, Muslim or some other officially recognized form of societal mumbo jumbo. It is because she is the source of my own loss, of my own grief, of my own way of life. Yes, I am smart enough to know all of these things and not able to stop what I am doing, what society tells me I should not do. Thou shall not kill. This is bull shit. People kill throughout the ages. Even the ones saying, 'thou shall not kill', kill. They just don't like being the victims so they play this little game around the centers of your mind saying this is a barbaric thing, this killing. I again say bullshit. Life is a big video game. It really is. Kill another one. There is another thousand points. Take that, you Catholic piece of shit. Let me look in my playbook. Maybe gays are worth more points. It is like Pink Floyd laments in their one song, "Are there any queers in the audience tonight?" Understanding this song is really about love instead of hate goes mostly unnoticed. The only way of winning is being at the top of the killer's list and constantly aware of whom is trying to kill who. I hate Vickie. I hate Vickie. I hate Vickie. I hate Vickie. Vickie is the one needing my cold undertaker hands around her neck. No fucking scarf for Vickie. I want to feel the last breath of her life slipping through my cold undertaker hands. This is my right after all she does to me.

Killing is an art. It is not always physical. There is killing with kindness, mental killing, alienation killing, killing with love and then denial of love, unintentional killing, emotional killing, premeditated killing, suicide, assisted suicide, killings ordered by the laws of the land and my favorite, medical killing. This is where the doctor tells the patient or family, "Sorry. Nothing else can be done." Usually the medical benefits are depleted by this time. Do you see my point? Dying and killing are husband and wife. One of my favorite stories is, <u>Death Takes a Holiday</u>. No one is dying. Overpopulation and lack of resources is the result. I like thinking I am killing so a few good people are able to face death with dignity while in the possession of what is rightfully theirs, what they work so hard for and what helps bring them to a comfortable end. All this other stuff is just crap. Possessions mean nothing without meaning. Now when there is meaning, it is a whole different story. This is another part of why I do what I do. Society says to feel guilty. I do not. Assume I am arrested, taken to court and face this question, "Are you guilty?" My response is, "Do you mean according to the law or according to the reality of our own sense of justice?" See? It is a tricky question. I am comfortable in what I do and am willing to accept my own conclusion. Vickie deserves hating. Vickie deserves dying. Placing her in my imagination as an ultimate goal is only natural. She does to me what the other women I am killing do to their own prey. I am justified. I am, "Not guilty, your Honor".

These are the random thoughts running through my mind as Gary and I pull up to Burt's Place for another evening of drinks and dinner. I don't apologize for these thoughts. They are just there running around like some long distance runner caught on a circular track not finding any straight path toward home. Exhaustion is my constant companion as of late. I am in a constant dream of being back home, back in the basement, being a little boy, creating secret things and hearing all those conversations overhead which are constantly and subtly forming who I am. This is my society. This is who I am. That I am unable to be part of this society is a tragedy. I hate Vickie and all the women like her. Mother is proud of me. Of this, I am sure. She is crying with me because of what I must do to again be what I am. It is Mother's way of saying she is sorry for that out of hand remark from so many years ago. I know she is thinking of saying she is sorry as she lays dying, but time is running out. Sometimes time does run out. It is alright, Mother. I understand. I do this for you. I do this for me. I do this for the family's good name. We do have a good name, don't we? Grandpa Pope is a little odd and I am too young to remember the rest. Oh, hell. This is about me. This is about me, plain and simple. I am comfortable with it and I really do hate Vickie. I hate Vickie as much as I love Gary. Loving a man this much is not abnormal. Is, it? Maybe I am gay. No, I am not. This is a different kind of love. Damn, I am wishing all of these thoughts might go away for awhile. Maybe thinking about the next scarf and what color is appropriate is what needs concentrating on. Gary's voice enters my mental wanderings.

"We are here."

I look through the car's dirty window. Windows are never clean in Detroit. Either it is the rain, the snow, the ashes from the factories or a combination of all. Even the rain is dirty. There are so many things here to cheer up a fellow. This is sarcasm, just in case you are missing it.

"I hope he is in his usual foul mood. I need cheering up."

"Yeah, I know what you mean. I come here for the insults too. If the prick ever smiled, I would think he was dying."

Stepping out of the car I hear and feel the early evening frost cracking under the weight of the soles of my shoes. At first I think it is the sound of my next victim's neck cracking under the twist of her orange scarf. No reason for this color. I just like orange and am beginning to like killing. Maybe Mother is not proud of this. It is without reason. It is becoming my erotica, my lust and my passion. Still, the temptation is greater than my ability to resist.

Burt's Place is dark and the lights are very low. The atmosphere fits my mood and Burt is his usually gnarly self. I love Burt's Place. Burt welcomes us.

"Great, you two dick-heads are here to end my day."

I am thinking this is not his usual salesmanship and that the statement is from his heart. Something is not right with our old friend. Gary is the one answering our friend.

"Did you get out of the wrong side of the bed, Burt?"

"Naw, sorry. I haven't been to bed in several days."

Gary continues his attempt at softening the conversation.

"Is your prostrate acting up again, piss brain?"

"Point taken, I'll bring the drinks. It isn't like I'm drowning in business."

Looking around I see what Burt is talking about. We are the business. For the first time I am noticing that the shelves hold very little stock. I look closer at the business for the first time in years. The red bar stools are splitting and their stuffing is falling onto the old wooden floor. The floor's planks are stuffed with who knows what material from so many years gone by. I am thinking that the dirt between the planks is all that is holding them to their base. The rich mahogany bar is dark with age, darker than its original color from so many cleanings and attempts at restoration by this or that drunken patron claiming to be a real handyman. Looking into the mirror behind the bar is almost like seeing yourself as a ghost. The mirrors are dusty and film covered from years of smoke and Detroit grim. One's face looks pale and dead in their reflection. I am laughing to myself about a woman or two who might touch up her makeup attempting to compensate for her image in these dirty mirrors, a woman who ends up looking like Bozo the Clown once back on the streets of the city. My last thought is about how one's lungs too eventually fills up with all the crap moving in and around our daily lives. Burt clinks three snifters of cognac down on our table, an ashtray, three cigars and a cigar lighter given to him by his father before his death. Burt keeps the lighter for special occasions, in honor of his dead father.

Burt likes cigars, but doesn't smoke them often. He says the aftertaste lingers too long and is like someone shits in your mouth. The cognac definitely helps. I am looking up and my eyes meet Burt's. He speaks to me.

"No asshole comment from you tonight, kid?'

"No, Burt. I've been in my own place for the last few days."

"Haven't we all. You want to hear my story?"

"Of course we do."

Burt sits at the table. I see that the sign on the front door is in the closed position and that the balance of a bottle of cognac is also in the center of our table. This is going to be a long night. I know this because of past encounters with this strange man when he is feeling down and out. The last time I arrive home at seven in the morning and my head arrives a week later.

Burt says the new place down the street is like a really good woman. It is giving him a good fucking, business wise, every night. Staying in business much longer just is not in the cards. He also is bitching and moaning about Halloween night, the night I am out and about.

"All these crazy fuckers dressing up and acting like a bunch of god damn juveniles. It used to be for kids. Now adults are out acting like they are really vampires, biting each other and fucking in the alleys. They are doing all sorts of crazy shit. I can live with that, but they put the final nail in my coffin, so to speak."

My brother chimes in. I am still trying to light my cigar.

"Did the insurance company turn you down, Burt?"

"What are you two talking about?"

Gary informs me that one of the fires around town on Halloween is in the alley behind Burt's place. A big portion of his back entrance area just off of the kitchen side is gone. Looking over my shoulder I see a tarp hanging from the far back ceiling to the floor. It is nail gunned in place and the wind from the alley is pushing the tarp in an out.

"Is that your reason for no sleep, Burt? You're sitting up protecting this place?"

"Yeah, kid. I sit here waiting on some fucker to shoot when he tries coming in the back of the place. I'm thinking you two pukes may want to come in and help me move stock out and take a few souvenirs for old time's sake."

It is obvious Burt is fighting back tears. Men do not cry. Gary is reaching out lighting Burt's cigar and I am filling the snifters half full of cognac. People drink when they are happy and they drink when they are sad. The booze business is not a bad one to be in, but changing times change the face of where booze is enjoyed. Burt begins telling us about the place down the street, the one opening a few months back. With the Halloween 'burners or devil night freaks' in the mix, Burt is throwing in the towel.

"Oh, well. Everything dies in its own time. I've had a long run. The business people are younger now, tastes change and on and on."

I am looking at the Chicago style bar railing as Burt is talking. The rail is wavy from years of patrons bellying up to the bar. This is history and no one really cares. It is all about the new and never looking back. It is in my humble opinion another fucked up attitude sticking in the bowels of what we lovingly refer to as modern society. There is nothing modern about it. Better to build new than fix the fuck-ups of our past lives. Well, I'm fixing mine. Gary speaks again.

"Anything we can do, Burt?"

"Not really. Just, help me clear out. The insurance lapsed and I don't have money to repair the place. Hell, for all I know the people down the street had me torched. They probably wanted the last ten or twelve regulars I had."

I offer a somewhat reassuring comment.

"Well, the way the unions and the automobile industry are going, they'll probably be setting up shop in Japan."

"Don't think so, little brother. The slant eyes are buying everything including the Rockette's. Even our beer isn't American anymore. They will probably be serving sake with a twist down the street before things are over", Gary chips in.

The conversation continues riding the wave of alcoholism right through about every ethnic group on the face of the earth. We are, by two-thirty in the morning, shit-faced. The last part of the conversation I remember is about Gary. Burt brings it up.

"Well, at least you are retiring at the right time."

I am caught off guard.

"Retiring? What the fuck? You haven't said anything about retiring."

"It's twenty years and out, brat, while I can still take it. The newer cops aren't going to be so lucky. I figure on getting a Private Investigator's license and investigating someone's privates."

Burt chimes in.

"Queer all these years. I knew it. I just knew it."

I am laughing out loud. Gary is trying to defend himself.

"Now listen, you two monkey dicks. That is not what I meant."

"You know, Burt. They don't call it queer anymore. They call it an alternative lifestyle."

"I don't care what you call it, Billy. It's still cock sucking."

Burt picks up the cognac bottle. Three more hefty pours remain.

"Here, lets drink to the only queer old Burt has ever loved."

Burt and I raise our glasses and Burt gives the toast.

"To, Gary, may it long waggle."

Reluctantly, Gary acknowledges the toast and our glasses clink together in an odd brotherhood of misfits among the living. Yes, living kills and so does progress. This is my point. Burt and Gary both love fishing. There is an extra bedroom at Gary's cabin. What are friends for if not to be around in times of need? Despite everything I am blessed. Gary is blessed. Burt is blessed. Yes, orange is the color of the next scarf. It is the color of an autumn sunset just before the lights go out. This next one is for Burt. Maybe drinks with her at the new place down the street is in order.

I am leaning on Burt's and Gary's shoulder as they are dragging me over to one of the back booths in the bar. We are all sleeping here tonight. I am hoping Burt does not shoot one of us forgetting we are here. Right before laying my head down, I look up toward the tarp covering the back of Burt's damaged life. I see the curtain move and imagine Grandpa Pope sliding in from his crypt along with a multitude of his other dead friends from years past…years when he and they were the movers and shakers of this dying town. I fall off to sleep knowing that Burt's place is busier tonight, its last night, than ever before. The dead giving testimony to the dying is indeed a strange twist on life.

Chapter Nineteen

Fishing without a worm is like trying to swim without water. Some things just go together and I am not getting into that stupid song. You know the one? 'We go together like a...' This is just me and I am not apologizing for my taste. Trouble is, now that I mention it, the damn thing is playing in my mind. Still, there is something to be said for odd partnerships like the one that is developing between Gary and Burt.

Gary loves his cabin in the woods and he loves his lake. Gary loves fishing. I hate fishing and pretty much do it just because I am spending time with my big brother. Burt, on the other hand, is a really big fisherman. Go, figure. Gary is the one fishing without the worm. Burt is the one planning on a big catch, the cleaning and big dinner. Their conversation goes like this.

"So, aren't you going to check your bait?"

"Don't use any bait, Burt."

The lake is calm and clear and the only movement of the boat is when Gary or Burt adjusts themselves. It is about six in the evening and the night sky is unusually clear. Gary's fishing pole rests lazily on his right thigh and my big brother pounds back one Miller beer after another. Burt is drinking a premixed Bloody-Mary.

"I didn't know you fished without bait."

"I didn't know you drank bitchy drinks."

There is a short bout of silence before Gary begins explaining that fishing is about solitude for him and that he really is adverse to hooks being yanked into living things. Gary isn't against fishing. He knows it is food. He is a net man. This is the way one is supposed to fish. God set it up this way. Burt's eyes are indicating that he understands.

"But, I've heard William say you catch the bigger fish."

"This is true. Sometimes one puts away their beliefs to fuck over their little brother or best friends."

Burt smiles a wide broad smile. It is the first time he smiles since the closing of Burt's Place. Burt, like my dead friend Teddy, is a good man. I am glad Gary is in his company and that Burt is someone to talk with. I am sure my continual sulking while refusing to let go of this Vickie thing is something Gary wants behind both of us. My brother is retired and deserves peace where he finds it. If the lake, its sunset, fishing without a worm and Burt's company is a part of that, I am very pleased. I say it many times and am sure I say it many times more. I love my brother.

"Thank you, Gary."

"Thanks for what, Burt?"

"Thanks for your kindness and for William's kindness. You are both the kindest and strangest people I have ever known. Hard to believe you came from the Sigrist stock."

There is a long silence. Burt knows his words are cruel, unthinking and out of place. All of that talk about mental institutions in the history of the Sigrist family is probably all just talk. You get one crazy person in the apple barrel and everyone else is branded for the rest of their natural lives. Burt is thinking that Grandpa Pope is just a bad memory and that the car accident was just an accident. All Burt knows for sure is that the cops shut their investigation down right after. Gutting someone for the mob, hanging them upside down in a motel bathroom and letting them bleed out happens in the movies, not in real life. It is all history now and Burt is thinking he puts one big assed foot in his big assed mouth. Gary looks directly into Burt's eyes.

"What is it? What did you just say? I was looking at the Sun going down. I wasn't paying attention."

Whether Gary is paying attention or not isn't important. The family's history weighs on my brother much like the 'two martini baby' comment weighs on me. Gary's path is a different path. What one's family is or was is not what one must be. As a society we are guilty of judging by association. All I know for sure is that my big brother is retired, pounding back beer after beer while listening to Burt pour out his heart about a long life with some regrets, but overall a good life.

"You talk like your life is over, Burt."

"Not over, Gary. It is just winding down."

Gary accepts this last little bit of banter and is thinking he is not too far behind Burt. Gary's private investigator's license is lying unopened on his desk back at the cabin. As of late my big brother is without much ambition. I think most police officers enter their retirement years this way. Even before retirement there is the understanding that they are no longer police and are never really just an average person on the street. Many begin living within themselves and their past. Old stories are alive in what of their future is left. These old stories change like folklore and eventually fade into the sunset, much like the beautiful sky Gary is watching this particular night. There is bound to be a certain amount of transition. I am glad Burt is around to share the stage with me. Too, I am not always around now. My local business is not lacking for customers, but it is lacking for paying customers. Even the city is getting behind on invoices for services rendered. Sometimes I am feeling like an undertaker in his own cemetery. Detroit is dying around me and the unions are finding themselves without someone like Gary who is willing to share their sorrows. Right now, if you are from Detroit, fishing with or without a worm is probably a good thing to be doing. One must eat.

These thoughts are rolling through my mind as I pull my Ford Taurus into the parking lot of the Holiday Inn in downtown Dayton, Ohio. My last phone call is from an individual from out of town. I am one lucky son-of-a-bitch. Old rich men talk to other old rich men who refer their problems to me. My art, my erotica, is not impacted by the state of any economy. My funeral home is in the hands of a young assistant. His name is Cecil. What a name is what I am always thinking. Who names their child Cecil? It is no wonder he turns to the gangs at a very young age. I am thinking of that Johnny Cash song, 'A Boy Named Sue'. Naming your kid Cecil is like naming a boy Sue. It gives the little fucker something to prove before he shits his first diaper. I apologize to every Cecil out there.

This Holiday Inn is in need of more than an update. It is in need of being torn down. The accommodations are my own fault. I am still thinking frugal, still putting back a big portion of my sporadic earnings to prop up the funeral business. This job brings an envelope containing one hundred and fifty thousand dollars. Free funeral services at ten thousand dollars per funeral, sees the money, not really going that far. My intent is for the cheapest box available, a quick prayer and sticking the thing in the ground to be done with it. My heart is always giving into to a box fancier in death than the victims live in during life. I also think Cecil is supplementing his meager salary from me by pushing dope out the back door via the city morgue delivery driver. This is not my problem. Cecil's requirement is to come to grips with the terms of his own life just as I come to grips with the terms of mine. My art is not going to suffer because of a bad economy back home and, quite frankly, I'm getting real tired of this giving back to the community thing. What is given back to me? A thank you, if I am lucky. Don't say it. You bleeding heart liberals frost my balls in the heat of summer. I work for mine despite my true ambitions being lost in the clutches of someone else's greed. I am tired of giving and not getting back. If it is not my art, then what is it? I am setting money back for myself this time.

I like this traveling thing. The drive from Detroit, Michigan to Dayton, Ohio takes about six hours. I check in and go to my room. The room is a color difficult to decipher. There are so many layers of paint on the wall. The resulting color, is almost foreign. My pay envelope is on me and the cash bulges in my coat's inside pocket. After a quick shower, I sit back on the bed and read through the hand written note inside the envelope of cash.

Her name is Susan. She hates being called Susie. It is like you are calling a pig. You know s u z z e e. If you are from the country, string the sound affects together a couple of times, and you understand what I am talking about. I am chuckling to myself. I am envisioning the old fucker doing it just to irritate his soon to be late wife. Again, sometimes it is all in the name.

Susan is a very good looker. The picture I am holding shows a woman with long black hair, deep brown eyes and small facial features. Everything matches and nothing is out of place. Even a plastic surgeon is incapable of this type of proportioning. My immediate thinking is that this is God's work. It is as though someone makes a mold and gets all of the geometry just exactly right. Most people have one toe longer than the other, a nose not worth liking or some genetic carry over from their family history that is to no one's liking. It is as though Susie is born with or is molded into this thing of perfect proportion. I am thinking that my art needs stepping up a notch and maybe, s u z z e e is the perfect subject.

I move from my seated position on the bed to the wobbly table against the far wall. But for the bolts holding the thing in place against the wall, I see it crashing onto the floor and splintering into a million pieces. The chair in front of the desk is newer and does not match what little décor remains in the room from numerous makeovers. It is a cheap imitation leather office chair with a broken kick-back plate. I am careful not to tumble over by leaning too far backward.

The bright orange scarves are pressed and without wrinkles. I am not one to buy something and use it right off of the rack. It is a matter of principle. It is a matter of respect. Also, skimping on price is not something I do in a case like this. My art is worth the best of the best. That little fucking worm needs to be spinning gold out of his ass instead of silk, especially at the price I pay for my scarves.

I am very sleepy now. The drive is long and tiring. I take a few moments inspecting the felt pouch in front of me. Unrolling the soft holder is very religious. I do it with my fingertips lightly upon its seams, not allowing the contents to slam against the writing desk's worn wooden top. My art, my art, my art is in the back of my mind. This is for you, Mother. My art is for you.

The instruments from the morgue area of my funeral home are all clean and shinning. They are my children. They are the instruments of my darker art. Unlike my life they are balanced and beautiful in their own right. They are the things allowing me to take something mangled and deformed and return it to a viewable form for mourning loved ones. In my hands they are holy things. My tools shine bright like the burning bush in the mountain where a father prepares up his son for sacrifice. In the morning I call Susan to prepare for our face to face meeting, a meeting resulting from our online chatting. I am remembering her husband saying, "She will fuck anything with a ten inch dick and use my money doing it." Well, Susan. I lie about the dick thing, but this is your lucky day. No dancing machine for you. I am too far from home. There is a scarf for each wrist and a scarf for each ankle. Sorry about the duct tape for your mouth. My art, my art, my art happens tomorrow. Tonight I sleep. Tomorrow we play. Being at my best is important for creating my best work.

Chapter Twenty

(My Art)

Art is such a personal thing. I enjoy modern art. It is sometimes no more than a scattering of color and thought, much like life. I think thought is both experiential and accidental at the same time. Think of life like a nail coming out of a nail gun at a very high rate of speed. The nail is accidentally discharged into the air. The nail eventually lands. Its landing is its experience and destination. Everything from the beginning to the end of the nail's journey is accidental. Art is feeling. It is the engulfment of one's accidental journey. I know that there are those of you immediately arguing for one's ability to control one's destination. This is bullshit. One's destination is the only real certainty I accept. It is death. Is it so odd that I use death as my art? Of course it is not. Death is my medium. Live with it. Oh, that is a definite play on words. Live with it. Live with it. Can one do this? You are doing it every day. There is no choice just like there is no choice for my medium.

My little jaunt to Dayton, Ohio is quite pleasant. I find myself liking this Susan person. Were she not part of my art and an obligation to another client, I am thinking she is the one.

The day before the event I am sitting in the nose-bleed seats of the Ohio State football stadium. I live in Michigan, but my soft spot is for the Buckeyes. I have something in common with Brutus the Buckeye. How would you like living your entire life with a big nut for a head? I feel the same way about the 'two martini baby' thing. I see Brutus and me sharing a martini and discussing our frustrations with life. I am thinking the conversation goes like this.

"Tell me, Brutus. You ever think of getting in another line of work?"

"Come on, William. How is a guy who can literally be called a nut case going to jump to some other line of work? I'm lucky to have what I have."

"Guess you have a point there, Brutus."

"And who names someone Brutus? These PHD types just need to put the liquor down when they are trying to come up with ideas."

"Do you like Ohio State overall?"

"Overall, I do. My job is secure as long as they beat Michigan every year. Hell, I guess I really shouldn't complain. What the hell is a Wolverine, anyway?"

"I guess we all have to find outlets to compensate for where we end up in life."

"How do you compensate, Bill? Damn, these olives are good. They are the big ones. I don't like the little olives. It's like chewing on a set of squirrel balls, not that I ever have. You know what I mean?"

"No, I don't know what you mean. It's probably the gin talking. Who gives a crap? Chew on squirrel balls if you want. To answer your question, I have my secret art."

"I have my little secret too, Bill. Do you want to know what it is?"

"Sure."

By now our words are slurring and Brutus' big head is bouncing forward and backward because of its proportion to the size of the rest of his body.

"There are two of us. My sister fills in sometimes."

"The fuck there is."

"No, really, now tell me your secret."

I am looking Brutus right in the eyes and respond.

"If I told you I would have to kill you."

I get up from the bar and walk out the door. Brutus and I do not talk anymore. I still see him waving at me while I'm sitting here in the nose-bleed section of the Buckeye's football stadium. Brutus understands. There is a lot binding us together. I am wondering if it is the 'he' Brutus or the 'she' Brutus waving at me. I watch the big nut-head whipping up the crowd. His art involves thousands of faces. My art is one face at a time. The mechanism of higher education is churning ever onward, often leaving tried and true techniques behind. Maybe lacking a true college education is not such a bad thing after all.

Susan is about 5 foot 5 inches tall. Her proportioning is perfect for her stature. Her attire is border line sluttish, the type that is permitted to enter an upscale event and then is stared at all night long. Her dress is at the line, but does not cross the line. Her look is just enough to be forcing the other women in the room into gossiping among themselves. She is confident and our meeting, of all places, is at The Tootles Restaurant across from the Dayton Police Department in downtown Dayton. Getting the conversation on track quickly is another quality I admire about her.

"You like the place, William."

"I have never been in a Tootles before. The little trains running around the shelving overhead are different."

"I am thinking that, if you do meet all of my qualifications, I'll be blowing your horn sometime real soon."

"You want to go some place nicer for dinner."

"Nope, this is fine. I'll just order a burger and fries. I'm here to fuck. Hope you are, too."

I find myself letting a little silence fall between us before replying. I am thinking this one is the ultimate survivor. The problem is that she is a survivor at all costs. For some reason she is very attractive to me. Still, if anyone deserves killing, Susan deserves killing. She and Vickie working together are capable of bringing the world down. Maybe I am just upset over her speaking like men are normally speaking over their observations, wants, and desires. These are things like, 'Nice ass, baby.' 'Going my way, baby'? 'Bet she can suck a golf ball through a garden hose' is another one. A woman saying outright, 'I'm here to fuck' is just upsetting to my vision of proper gender placement. Does that make sense to you? I finally answer Susan.

"Fries and a burger are fine with me. Have a Coke in one of those old fashioned glass bottles if you want."

The dinner does not take long. The little fucking train going around and around over our heads is driving me nuts. I find myself wanting to rip the thing from its tracks and strangle its little horn to death. Whoo, whoo, whoo, whoo, every three or four fucking minutes is what I am hearing right up until the time Susan and I are standing on the sidewalk in front of Tootles Restaurant.

Standing in the brisk evening air is refreshing. Hot and cold are the same at the point where one's nerve ends are separating from the reality of what they are supposed to be doing. I am wondering if it is this way for my victims. What is happening with their other senses when the last bit of breath is no longer in one's body? Are the organs still trying to recapture their past? I think not. Like me, I think one's breath is finally free. It is, after all, only air and we are the one's holding it captive from the outside world. The truth is that I am killing one thing, setting another free, and creating art at the same time.

My canvas is waiting back at the motel. Susan's letter and picture are all telling me the same thing. Her taste is cheap, quick and 'out of there'. There is no intended relationship. It is all about the orgasm. I am finding my art doing this for me and am becoming less and less ashamed of this fact.

There is a quick stop at the Key Hole Bar and Grille. Susan inhales three glasses of top shelf scotch. I settle on gin and tonic. A bottle of champagne for later, of which she drinks nearly three-fourths of the bottle, and I am ready for my art. Susan is sprawling naked on my motel bed. Because of the amount of alcohol in her system, the presence of the plastic painter's tarp over the bed's sheet, blanket and pillows is not something she is capable of noticing. Truthfully, my dick being two inches or the requested ten inches does not really matter at this point. The last thing in place is the duct tape over her mouth right before having my way with her. There is no moaning. There is no erotica. There is only one quick ejaculation. The rest is art. It is my art.

Sliding the big cooler into the back of my Ford Taurus is a chore. It is very early in the morning and, but for the pastry truck's delivery of the motel's early morning offering, nothing else is moving. The driver is very helpful.

"That looks real heavy, sport. Need a hand?"

"Yes, please. Every time I come down for a game I end up taking back more beer than I brought. My friends are always thanking me for the tickets with a six pack. Know what I mean?"

"Yeah, I do. Problem is AA and beer don't mix well. I've been on the wagon for ten years now. I just loved the stuff too much."

I find myself giving the man a five dollar bill for the help and being grateful that he is not the type wanting beer over money. I am thinking that these out of town trips are in need of a little more planning. Anyway, the big blue and white cooler with Susan's body parts inside and on ice is sitting in the back seat of my car. The room is paid for in cash, the keys are in the room and I am looking forward to completing my art. Home and Michigan is in the back of my mind. I am smiling and thinking, this is one little piggy who isn't crying, 'wee, wee, wee' all the way home.

Arriving home in the middle of the day and finding my new assistant busy preparing a local for burial, I leave my car behind the funeral home. The temperature is very cold and things are fine until the end of the day. Coming through the back door and pulling my parka hood down, I am greeted by the young man.

"Mr. Sigrist, I wasn't sure when you were coming back so I took the chance to get this one out of the way."

"I like your initiative, Cecil. Is it a real customer or someone you are wrapping up for your gang buddies?"

Cecil smiles at me. He understands my humor. We are getting along quite well. There are no questions. I pay him on time. He studies the business. Leaving him alone like this is really an infraction of my own license rules and we both know it. It is one of many things unspoken living in that big vat of hazy things we are calling 'trust'. I am leaning over the morgue table inspecting his work.

"What happened, Cecil?"

"Hit in the face with a two by four. It drove his nose clear back into his brain, causing hemorrhage and death."

I am rubbing my index finger over his nose and surrounding area.

"You would never know it, son. Good job. Maybe you should consider plastic surgery."

"I would if I could afford it."

"Keep working. Keep perfecting your art. We'll talk about that later."

Cecil is smiling as I am pushing the button on the elevator door heading toward my apartment. I am tired. A nap is in order.

By ten thirty that evening I am again back in my apartment with my art. I clear off a space large enough on my wall. The crematory is heating and I am anxious to get my art in place. I am talking to myself.

"Yes, yes. This is just perfect."

I am standing there looking at the way the colors lay. They lay just like nails landing in some unknown place after accidentally being discharged from the nail-gun. Some of the color seems to explode, immediately finding its place upon the canvas of death. Other shades are falling down the canvas as if they are attempting to escape their final resting place. I find myself walking up to the canvas whispering to it.

"You are beautiful, Susan. I hope you enjoyed your last night out."

Back in the morgue the body parts are thrown into the incinerator along with the plastic cooler and my white lab coat. With the blood all over the coat, keeping it for a souvenir is out of the question. Getting blood on me as I am flinging Susan's liquid on the canvas is an artist's occupational hazard. Art requires one being free with their creative juices. Initially Susan's blood is drawn and placed very carefully into the tapered tip jars I use as my painting brushes. I fling her life casually and carelessly across the universe. The result is amazing. The scarves, the one around her neck and the four holding her wrists and ankles, are now with the others. There is a rainbow in my trophy room. I like walking under where my scarves hang and hearing all of my victims saying, "Thank you for giving my life meaning". I know that they all are very pleased.

Back in my room I am drinking a Pine Ridge Cabernet. I am looking at the picture hanging over the head of my bed. The picture's colors are close to the color of the wine I am drinking. I am thinking, 'if only I might taste my art'. No, that is sick. Isn't it?

The telephone rings. It is my brother, Gary.

"You're back in town?"

"Yes, late yesterday."

"How was your trip?"

"I really enjoyed it. I even brought a little art home with me."

Chapter Twenty-One

(An Observer)

I notice William's art and Vickie's art is ever changing. Vickie's art is a kaleidoscope of alcohol, drugs and sex. I see her sitting alone in the Sigrist Mansion listening to sounds that may or may not be there. I see her closing her eyes and watching the forms and figures bending and taking shape again in the back of her mind. I see her swallowing another sip of gin and chewing on another olive...the olive being her food sustenance for the day. I see her waiting on the arrival of friends that never arrive. The parties are fewer and fewer. Most of the participants cannot cope with an unending mountain of drugs and their razor blades are now as dull as the nerve endings in their brains. Their lives are like the pusher's old saying about the reality of their make believe environments, "I am here. Now I am not. So, where am I?"

The mansion grounds are neglected. They are not neglected for lack of money. They are neglected for lack of interest. Vickie is standing on one of the many balconies and looking out toward the distant night. She is seeing only the tops of the trees. She is looking for something. It is what we are all looking for. That thing is love, but the love of money trumps all in Vickie's mind. She is still on the road toward learning that art is the only real reason for life at all. Otherwise, life is lonely and now there are these voices coming to visit her at night. Vickie is thinking that she is losing her mind.

The voices are coming to her in the middle of the night. They are keeping her from sleeping. Her eyes are rimmed with black circles from lack of sleep. Her eyes are open but she is seeing only the imprints of the world surrounding her. Focusing on any particular thing is a great effort. Her martini is slightly tilted and drops of the drink fall into oblivion over the balcony railing and toward the forgotten grounds below. Vickie is hoping that sleep finds her tonight and not the werewolf from her party a few months before. She is thinking out loud.

"He says he is coming back. Who is he? Why is he talking to me in my dreams at night? This is a cruel joke. I swear to God I will kill whichever friend of mine it is that is doing this to me."

Vickie is grasping the last olive from her martini between her teeth and is pulling the green treat from the toothpick. Her fingers holding the toothpick end up slipping and the toothpick sticks its point into her upper gum area. She is bleeding. A few drops of blood plop into the remaining liquid in the martini glass. The gin is now a subtle reddish-brown color. After a verbal 'fuck' or two, Vickie gulps down the remaining drink, blood and all. She mutters to herself.

"What the hell? It all ends up in the same place."

Vickie moves into her bedroom, my mother's old bedroom. She is surrounded by things. Things are not substance. Things are not worth having unless they are things born of an artist's mind. I understand her confusion and loneliness. I remember being that very young child. I remember being surrounded by things. There are the butlers, the maids, the groundskeepers, the chauffeurs, the cooks, the visiting social baggage coming with this type of life and the worse things of all…the false faces hiding true intentions. At least the werewolf is coming with purpose, "Next time it will really be rough". What is real and what is not real are in constant intercourse in Vickie's mind. The affect is tiring and frightening. Worse is that there is only one person in her life she is capable of reaching out to and, even this act, is an admission of the fact that things are not so green on her side of the road. Still, Vickie finds herself making the call.

"Yes? Hello?"

"It's me, Vickie. I need someone to talk to."

"For Christ's sake girl, it's two in the morning."

"I can't sleep. I think it is really coming for me."

There is a gap in conversation. The person at the other end of the line is secretly hoping for the end of this unexpected encounter. Hearing Vickie's sobs elicits a response.

"Baby, things can't be that bad. You're coming off of a bad batch or something."

"No. No. I'm telling you it is really happening. Every damn night it is the same thing over and over again."

"What is the same?"

Vickie is telling the person at the other end of the line about trying to fall asleep. She is telling about how the sounds are always starting around one thirty or two in the morning. The heavy breathing is usually first. There is the sound of snapping branches and twigs outside of her balcony's bedroom window. Most nights, she finds herself standing on the balcony looking into the overgrown grounds of the yard. Most times remembering how she finds herself on the balcony is not clear. Is she sleepwalking?

"Is it possibly the sleepwalking thing? How heavily are you medicating?"

"Compared to what?"

"Go, on. Tell me the rest."

Vickie says the snarling is next and it is accompanied by a gurgling like sound as if this thing coming for her is struggling for breath.

"What thing?"

"The werewolf, goddamn it, I'm talking about the werewolf. What the hell do you think I am talking about?"

Vickie's breathing is heavy and her heart is beating faster and faster. The back side of her head is pounding like a dozen drums in some far off African jungle.

"No, no. I'm sorry. Don't hang up. I didn't mean to yell at you. It is just all the pressure. It wasn't supposed to be this way. This place is too big for me and, with everything thing one is supposed to do, it just isn't like life in the movies."

"Most things aren't like the movies, sweetie."

"Do you hear that?"

Vickie is holding the telephone receiver over the balcony's edge.

"Do I hear what?"

"That. Do you hear that? Are you deaf? Come to see me. Will you come to see me? I need someone to watch over me while I sleep. I can't sleep without someone watching over me."

The voice on the other end of the telephone is exasperated.

"You have nothing that giving up booze and drugs won't cure. Go back to bed and stop all of this nonsense."

The connection breaks and with the break, another spot in Vickie's hearts goes dark.

"Who was that?"

"It was Vickie."

"Oh?"

"Where were we?"

"I was just telling you how much I love you."

At about this time Vickie's eyes are closing and the arms of exhaustion are wrapping themselves around her. A set of eyes continues watching her. She is experiencing her first good night's sleep in a very long time. I am thinking, 'Catch that sleepy time while you can. There aren't many more nights like this on the horizon. I am tired of this game and you are still in possession of something belonging to me, my mask.' I must be getting it back. It is my real face. Hanging up my own phone, the one I am listening in on, I move back into the forest toward first morning's light.

Chapter Twenty-Two

One evening after a funeral service, there is a box on the back stoop of the entry way into the funeral home. Good, good I am thinking. Finishing my piece of art from Dayton, Ohio is recently consuming my thoughts. The UPS package appears solid and undamaged. I dust off a thin layer of snow and carry the box into the back of the mortuary. I respect Gary's eye for detail and am glad he is never with me in my upper apartment. I know this is someday inevitable and I am taking precautions, just in case.

Opening a box like this is always a challenge. 'One day the fucking plastic popcorn things are going to stay in the goddamn box', is what I am thinking. I find myself saying this every time I open a package and every time I find the irritating things falling all over the floor. Tonight is no different. Still, my selection is pleasing.

The frame is a muted brown with hints of red running through it. It is a perfect match for dried blood. The plastic in the frame is high quality. My choosing plastic is a deliberate move. Glass is too clear for my needs and plastic is a distortion agent, other than the really fine plastic with its really fine price.

I am sliding the canvas into the frame's edging when reliving that evening in Dayton comes crashing back into the erotic lobe of my brain. I am reliving the pleasure. I am envisioning myself in the morgue again. Mentally, I am pressing on the large ketchup bottle and making a swinging motion with my arms at the same time. The blood is landing sporadically upon the pure white canvas, the canvas of truth. I am getting excited again. I am feeling a drop or two of blood on my forehead from the splash back. Toward the end of the bottle's contents I am feeling my fingers twisting the cap loose. I am again flinging the last few globs of liquid toward the waiting pure white truth of my evening's work. 'Splat' is what I hear. Life is hitting the universal wall of truth. There is no more wondering. Are you going where you want to go? Like it or not you are there. Is it what you are expecting? Is there a great tunnel of light leading into that land of gold and happiness the preachers are always promising? Is it a disappointment? I hope it is not a disappointment. There is too much of that in life. Whatever it is, you are a lucky recipient of my talent. You are a piece of my art and, in so being, are immortal. You are immortal both on my wall and in my mind. What more is one capable of wanting? I say 'nothing'.

I am sitting in the chair at the end of the bed. My artwork is complete. It hangs in its forever-frame over the head of my bed. The packing material is all over the floor. I am imagining the material as freshly fallen snow. I am thinking my art is being limited when there is the whole outside world calling out to be my canvas of truth. It isn't about the money anymore. It is about my art. I am thinking I must title my art. The title is to be accurate. If it is not, how is one to bring the truth of it to my admirers? Yet, it is to be undetectable as the real thing. My admirers must be thinking how real my art is, but not that my art is the real thing. Is this not what art is about? Art is a representation of what is real or of something one's mind perceives is real. What is the title? I know. I have it. It is, 'Blood on the Wall'. This title is perfect. It is right in your face. No one is going to guess. Am I right? It is that 'forest for the trees' thing. It is the perfect title. Even Gary, accidentally coming up to see me, is not going to guess. Yes, it is the perfect title.

I feel the dampness in my pants and realize I am ejaculating. Fighting this urge is useless. I am leaning back and enjoying the completeness of this moment, this moment in the sweet embrace of a side of life I am happy to be experiencing. This is not guilt. It is ecstasy. Perhaps it is Mother sending me a gift from the unknown. Perhaps it is her apology for that 'two martini baby' thing. Yes, this is what it is. I am leaning back against the deep cushioning of my bedroom chair. My head is tilting back and my feet are dangling among the plastic snow flakes surrounding me. I am exhausted. I am complete. Then, the bell to the funeral home's back door rings. Shit, I am thinking.

I find myself grabbing a lab coat off of my apartment's bathroom door. The warm semen is beginning to dry and is no longer running down the inside of my leg. The robe is long enough to keep the mess a secret. Gary is at the back door. The evening air is heavy and quickly filling with fog. Looking into Gary's eyes I sense something terribly wrong.

"What is it, Gary?"

"Some of the gang bangers stung Cecil up in a back alley. The site isn't pretty. The station called me just because they know he works with you."

"What? Why? I mean, no. He was such a good kid."

Gary is walking into the morgue room when I begin noticing the anguish on his face. Seeing my brother unhinged is not in my wildest imagination. Slumping at my writing desk with his head down between his knees, the conversation continues and this is the short version of it.

The officers on the scene are thinking that Cecil is running drugs out the backdoor of my funeral home. They are thinking I know nothing about it. This is almost truth. Suspecting is not really knowing. This is news to me. Seems like being away from home and not minding the store carries its own risks. The lead Detective and the forensic team is coming over with their people to look my place over in hopes of determining if any of the stuff is laying around hidden in some nook or cranny. This is very upsetting. The last thing I need is cops going over this place with a fine tooth comb. Still, blood is everywhere in a funeral morgue area. They are not looking for an artist. They are looking at a stupid kid's mistake. Stealing the supplier's stash and making it your own is one of the dumbest things in the world. Honor among thieves is one thing, but stiffing your supplier is quite another. What in the hell was the boy thinking? I see Gary is actually shaking. His head is still between his legs.

"Ah, man. Of course, they can turn the place upside down for all I care. Are you alright? You were a cop for years before retiring?"

Gary looks up into my eyes. The color in his face is returning.

"It was just the violence of it, bro. They strung him up and gutted him right there in the alley. I mean. Seeing shot people, dead people, hanging people is one thing. This was something else. I probably would have heaved my guts right there, but I've been a little under the weather and haven't eaten for two days."

As I am walking over to a little hanging cabinet just to the left of my writing desk I am thinking about anything that might be left from my art trip. No, I am telling myself. Everything is incinerated except the art and I am not a part of all of this mess. The smell of the cognac is helping to clear my thoughts. The semen on my leg is dry.

"Drink this. The burn will kill some of what your brain is still seeing."

We sit in silence for a few minutes.

"When did it happen, Gary?"

"When did what happen?"

"When did the murder happen?"

"The forensic guys haven't said exactly."

"Are they on their way?"

"They'll be here very shortly. I'm sorry about the short notice."

"Ok. I'm going to take a quick shower. I've been doing a few things in my apartment. Just let them in. They can toss whatever they want. You know I had nothing to do with this?"

"I know and they know. Don't worry about it."

I move quickly into the little room behind where my dancing machine is, stuffing the scarves into my lab coat's pockets. Walking past my brother I see his head is tilting downward.

The cognac glass is cradling in both hands and he is sniffing in the fumes of the drink. I am just another shadow lingering from the alley where Cecil is killed. Once back in my apartment, my thinking is to test if my art is really art. It is chancy, but knowing once and for all is important for me. Removing the overhead vent grate in my bathroom I stuff the scarves and my lab coat way into the back of the tin crevasse. I am using the broom handle of a broom sitting behind my bathroom door. I find putting the grate back in place is taking some time. I am using the file end of fingernail clippers from my medicine cabinet. The process is taking longer than I expect. The water in the shower is running and I am hoping Gary does not decide to come upstairs before I am in the shower. The grate is finally in place, I am in the shower and the elevator door to my apartment is opening. Gary is calling out.

"William? Are you decent? The forensic team is here."

With my head peering around the shower curtain I find myself looking at Gary's face and the face of three other people. They are all very old. One is a woman and two are men. I see them all looking at the mess on my floor.

"Oh, that. I just put a frame on a piece of art I bought when I was in Dayton, Ohio. It is over the head of my bed. I can never keep those little white things from falling out of the box. Be done in a minute. It is a terrible thing about, Cecil. It must have been something really bad for him to have done what you think he did. The boy had a real future. I am very disappointed. Do whatever you want. I'll roll the body bags out if you want. I'll be down in a few."

Taking a deep breath while hoping my dialogue is convincing, my face darts back behind the shower curtain. Between the sound of the water and Gary's urging them back down into the funeral home, there is one last remark.

"I like it. It is a little too modern for my taste, but I like it."

About ten minutes later I am in the morgue area with everyone. The cooling drawers are inspected and all the body bags are opened. A drug dog is sniffing around every corner in the place. This goes on for about an hour and there is only one question.

"What the hell is this thing?"

"Oh, that is a body cart. It tilts up and down and has parts that slide in and out. It is my invention. I am thinking of patenting it. A body I receive is sometimes deformed so badly that I must use this thing to help straighten them out before viewing. Here, you want to get on it and let me show you what I mean?"

I see Gary smiling. The reply is unanimous.

"No, no. That is quite alright."

Gary is feeling better. He speaks to the lead forensic guy while petting the drug dog on the top of it snout.

"You guys need to look upstairs?"

"No, whatever Cecil was doing, he wasn't doing it here. Old Dingle would have sniffed it out by now."

I chime in.

"The dog's name is Old Dingle?"

The woman on the team speaks.

"You want to tell him you don't like his name?"

Gary is smiling again. I am looking into the dog's eyes. I am thinking that perhaps the dog's eyes are a lot like mine. They are happy to be part of something, but still hiding their own secrets and resentments. I find myself scratching Old Dingle on top of his head. The dog's coat is shiny and velvety to the touch. My thought is that the handler is probably treating the dog with better soaps than he is buying for his wife at Christmas.

"Not on your life. Old Dingle is a great name. Isn't it fell'a?"

I see Gary is pouring himself another cognac. I sense his relief at nothing being found. The forensic team moves off into the cold Detroit night air.

"Did you really think I would be involved in something this horrendous?"

Gary's response is both cryptic and comforting.

"Not without purpose."

Our glasses clink. We toast in silence. A funny thought is running through my mind. Do you think? Is it possible? She says she likes it. Is there a possible market for my art?

I order Chinese in from one of those twenty-four hour places. Drinking on an empty stomach is not good for my brother. One of the morgue stations is our table. This is not upsetting for Gary. The scene in the alley is upsetting for Gary. I am thinking, 'different strokes for different folks'. My mind is in the future. It is with my art. Tonight is rewarding. It is self-fulfilling. God, I am lucky to find myself in this place at this time with someone I love so much.

"Here is to you, my brother. Forever are we together."

Gary is smiling while raising his glass. The crystal is sounding against one of the most promising nights of my life.

"Yes, together forever."

Chapter Twenty-Three

I do not begrudge anyone a vacation. The workaholic is not the only one needing rejuvenation. Even artists, like me, take a fresh look at themselves and their direction. This is a requirement for success in one's life and I highly recommend this approach. Gary is surprised upon receiving my call.

"Hey, big brother, what's up?"

"The usual is up and it isn't my dick."

"You stir crazy up at the cabin?"

"I am, a little. I can only listen to so many of Burt's stories. Frankly, the man has way too many disquieting habits for me."

"Like what?"

"The son-of-a-bitch farts anywhere and everywhere. I never noticed it before, but the cabin isn't that big. Maybe the smell of stale beer and brats covered up a lot at Burt's Place."

I am amused by Gary's comments. 'A loner', I am thinking to myself. I imagine my timing is right on target and that it is time for both of us to get out of town for a short vacation.

"You should smell some of the stuff in the body bags that pass through my doors on a daily basis. Sometimes I can't tell if it's the rotting flesh or the lack of hygiene. Anyway, if you trust Burt enough, I have a suggestion."

"Which is?"

"Let's vacation, big brother. You and I need to get away. I would like to see my toes in some other color than blue. Wouldn't you?"

There is a long pause. I am beginning to wonder if my idea is not attractive to my big brother. Then, there is the response.

"I am looking out over a frozen lake right now and my cabin smells like shit. It is the best offer I have had in a long time. When are you planning this little getaway?"

"You tell me."

"The sooner, the better is what I say."

Gary and I are on a flight to Key West, Florida the next day. Burt is dead of a heart attack during his sleep on Gary's return, but that is just a side issue. Being nice to someone is often a real pain in the ass. Burt's burial is near the cabin in a beautiful location on a slanting slope that overlooks the lake. His marker is inscribed with these words, 'Slide a final one down the bar.' Gary and I know Burt is happy with the way things end. Gary is happy being rid of the smell. God works in mysterious ways. He is responsible for my art. Isn't He?

Our vacation choice is predicated on one thing and one thing alone. How far is it possible to go without leaving the United States? Right before our choice we are leaning over a map surveying the boundaries of this great country. Gary is muttering to himself.

"Hmm, I once heard a story about a guy from Key West."

"What story, Gary?"

"He wanted a business, but he didn't want to have to work. He goes to Key West and starts a snow shoveling business. He even bought all the snow shovels and a small snow blower."

"And, your point is?"

"Look at the fucking map, William. It's a fucking sub-tropical island, way out in the ocean and just ninety miles from Cuba. I hear the girls walk around half-naked and they put on overcoats when the temperature drops to sixty degrees."

I am laughing out loud about the snow shoveling thing. Our luggage is quickly on a Delta flight out of Detroit with a stop-over in Miami for a connecting flight. During the flight, there are regular calls to Gary's cell phone. Once I hear him saying.

"It isn't for that long. I'll be back in two weeks. You won't die while I am away."

I don't ask and Gary does not tell. Prying into one another's business is not something we do. This is a very good practice in light of my art and the possible ramifications surrounding it and the possibility of being caught. Gary half-heartedly acknowledges the calls. He is glancing at me for a second as he does.

"I'm going to turn the damn thing off. This is a vacation."

The switch in Miami is short. There are fifteen minutes to get our asses up and off the inbound flight and onto the connection to Key West, Florida. The connection flight is a large plane. I am uncomfortable about this. In my readings about the island of Key West, there is this standing joke about planes putting on their brakes once airborne from Miami in preparation for their landing on this sunny island out in the middle of the ocean. I am visualizing myself being tossed out of our mechanical bird, after overshooting the runway, right into the mouth of the biggest fucking shark in the Atlantic Ocean. I hate sharks. They are the ugliest, most savage creatures God ever places on the face of the Earth. I am constantly hearing the stories about some innocent surfer, diver or snorkeler being swallowed up by one of these slithering water mutants. Gary wants a good swim about thirteen miles out at some remote place the locals go called Boca Grande. I say anyone willing to get into shark infested waters is the same as an innocent man asking to be executed just because he wants to know what it feels like. I am thinking that coming back to Michigan with my big brother in tow is questionable. A history of mental illness is a rumor in our family. Gary's desire to be swimming that far out in the ocean is probably just one more confirming factor about my family's historical state of mind.

The plane touches down about noon. For a few minutes I am thinking the island disappears prior to our arrival. All I am seeing is blue water. Then, there is a bump, squealing tires and we are down. Key West International Airport is a combination of the old and the new. You are walking off of the plane onto the tarmac with everyone else on the plane, realizing just how restricting someone's breathing becomes for those not used to this type of climate. I am getting the immediate sensation of breathing in water instead of air. I find this feeling quickly passing and Gary and I find ourselves standing on the sidewalk out front of the airport waiting for the next cab's arrival. It is our intent to ride bicycles while we are in Key West. The onboard brochure says everyone does it and it is easier than finding a parking space for one's car. The brochure, leaving out the little detail about getting one's ass ran over by locals who hate tourists and their drunken friends arriving with them, is probably a subtlety the residents are secretly calling humorous. Too, it also omits the part about sudden rains blowing salt water up your ass and going away five minutes later. You are always finding the locals ducking into a bar for a quick beer until the rain stops. During certain times of the year this is the reason many of the locals are shit-faced before noon, Key West time and that entire sort of thing. The only reason I bring all this up is my way of pointing out the use of bicycles lasts only about a day. I find myself giving some thought to a scooter, but those things are just bicycles with motors on them. The electric cars are just stupid things saying, 'look at my dumb ass. I'm a tourist. By the way, does anyone know where I can plug this thing in?' My ass is back at the airport renting a small economical car for the balance of our two week stay in sunny Key West. Beginning our tour of this island starts the next day. Our first night is on the balcony of our apartment at the Pier Hotel. We are overlooking the activities at Mallory Square and watching the sunset behind the silhouettes of the evening entertainers. The square is packed with tourists and Gary is glad not to be among the crushing crowd of people. Most police, retired or active, usually end up experiencing a real aversion to large crowds. I am remembering Gary telling me that policing a large crowd, especially one getting out of control, is like waiting for an ocean of anger that is planning on swallowing you up. You are short on numbers and the people responsible for all the shit in the first place are usually nowhere around. It is ironic that my big brother is comfortable with an ocean of sharks and not an ocean of people. I think this is God's way of fucking with the human race.

Our balcony faces the ocean. The sky is clear and night's blanket is gradually creeping in over the sky's face. Finding oneself slipping away into the grandeur of this place sticking out into the ocean is understandable. If all moments, if all sunsets are like this, maybe Key West is the place for retirement. This thought is playing in the back of my mind when the pizza guy from KZ Pizza starts ringing the suite's doorbell. Gary jumps up from his seat at the balcony's edge.

"I got this. A garbage pizza with a good cabernet. What else, can a man want?"

Sometime later the tight rope walker is taking in the night's tips, the fire-breather blows his last flame, the French cat trainer screeches out his last irritating syllables at his felines and the sun drops behind the distant horizon. Out of the corner of my eye I see Gary swaying back and forth under the influence of our second bottle of wine, while trying desperately to get the last sunset shot of the evening. I am looking at two people with their arms around one another watching those same rays dying off in the distance. I see they are two men. Suddenly there is a realization swelling up inside of me. It is saying love transcends all. Someday I am hoping the world is feeling this way about my art.

Waking in the morning from a deep alcohol-induced sleep, my back is aching from my positioning on the deck's lounge chair. My mouth is very dry. It is as though all of the salt in the Atlantic is hanging to my tonsils. Gary is face down on the couch just inside the suite's sliding glass door. Back home the weather is still bad. Businesses are closing because of the heavy amounts of snow and highways running through the Detroit area are at a dead stop. Vickie is more and more paranoid about her werewolf and Burt lays rotting in Gary's cabin up north. Still, in Key West one of their favorite sayings is holding true, 'Life is good'.

Chapter Twenty-Four

Vickie is sitting in front of the fireplace at the Sigrist mansion. The huge residence, for all of its grandeur, is poorly insulated. The winds are howling outside and nearly a foot of freshly fallen snow is covering the ground. Vickie is thin, pale, sickly, frightened by her costumed werewolf suitor and she is alone. The roaring fireplace and the cognac in her hand are helping. This is the closest thing she experiences to being warm in over a week. The temperatures are hovering at twenty degrees and the chill factor is something one does not think about. She is nodding off from time to time, but every little sound is a possible fulfillment of the creature's promise about, 'It is going to be really rough the next time'. As she is dozing the cognac glass balances precariously in her hand and is leaning so that the fine liquid is sliding to near the top of the glass's rim. There are strange sounds everywhere. The ticking clock over the mantle sounds loud and eerily through the mansion's downstairs hallways…tick, tick, tick, tick, tick. Vickie's head is pounding and her nerves are living on their last few moments of sanity. She is thinking to herself.

"Why doesn't he come? Why doesn't he come? It isn't right that he doesn't arrive or call. I just want this over."

Vickie's friends are now club hopping in those private places within the belly of the Detroit underworld. Even Vickie's money is not capable of keeping those types around when there is something new and more exciting on the horizon. Drugs are only your friend when they are taking you to the next level. Vickie's functions are no longer anything more than a plateau on the road to bigger and better drug-induced highs. Her last party sees only three participants waiting for Vickie's zoning out. Carrying the drugs out of the party right under her nose is now a laughing matter back in the city. The standing joke is, 'why buy from the street guys when you can get it free from Vickie's place?' In short, Vickie is frightened. Vickie is a mess. She is a mess with money to burn, but Vickie is still a mess. Vickie is hearing bells now. She knows the sound. Where does she know the sound from? Oh, yes. It is the doorbell. She finds herself waiting for the butler to answer the door. Realizing there is no longer a butler; the fireplace's bouncing light sees her moving toward the main door. Her robe is still open and her breasts are in full view. Standing momentarily at the front door, she is frightened by what may be waiting on the other side. Again her mind is trying to sort through the logic of all of these events; these events that are not working out the way she plans and are threatening her very well being.

"Oh, what the fuck, just get it over with."

Vickie flings the door open. The cold outside air rushes in and she is standing there at the mansion's front door staring at a figure much resembling the abominable snowman. With the snow clearing, she manages to recognize the face hiding under the parka's hood. Tears are falling down Vickie's face and she is murmuring in a very low voice. It is the voice of a little girl. It is a murmur of relief like a child voices when finding there is no monster under the bed. In Vickie's mind there is no monster at the door.

"Thank God. Thank God. Thank God, it's you."

John Murphy stands there for a few moments before reaching out and pulling the woman's robe closed. He speaks.

"They are still perky, girl. You, however, look a total mess."

John Murphy is being pulled into the entrance by Vickie's thin, bony hand. She rolls delicately around him, slamming the door with her ass.

“Put some clothes on, Vickie. You are going to freeze to death before the drugs can kill you.”

By now Vickie is leaning into John Murphy’s chest. The hooded parka is wet with melting snow. Vickie seems not to notice. John is feeling the press of her body even through the heavy material. His urge is that of reaching around to test the firmness of her ass. His mind is demanding that he be the English gentleman his upbringing requires.

“Good idea, Johnny. You just make yourself comfortable by the fireplace. I’m gonn’a pop right upstairs and then right back down. Pour yourself a glass of Jameson. Hell, just drink it from the bottle. You’re dick is probably stiff from the cold and not the touch of me.”

John Murphy is thinking she is half right. Throwing his coat over the back of the room’s couch, the man is standing at the bar pouring a shot of Jameson…a healthy shot…on Vickie’s return. Vickie is waving a bottle in her hand while entering the room.

“Lookie, here, Johnny. I remember my Johnny likes Guinness with his Jameson. Sit where you like. I’ll just take whatever is left.”

For the longest time there is no conversation. Vickie is happy to have someone, anyone, in her life but the four walls of this huge estate and her solitude. John Murphy is sitting in a wingback chair by the fireplace, directly across from the woman. She is on the couch warming up by snuggling inside of a fluffy white robe, the kind fancy hotels and spas give people with Vickie’s type of wealth. Staying warm where John Murphy is usually staying requires the bringing of one’s own robe. Vickie’s voice is finally floating through the room.

“I know. I know. You must really think I am a bitch. I will be the first one to admit I have made a sort of mess out of things.”

John Murphy is right to the point. He is right to the point after pouring himself another shot of Jameson to go with the remaining half bottle of Guinness.

"What do you want, Vickie? What is this shit about someone coming to get you?"

John Murphy is listening intently as Vickie recounts the recent events of the Halloween party gone wrong. John's insides are now warm and his nose is its natural color, that of Jameson and Guinness. John's eyes are as penetrating as one's eyes can be. The man's life is full of experience and wisdom, the experience and wisdom of someone living long and hard from cradle to grave. John Murphy is highly educated in both realms, that of what he calls 'book learning' and 'hard knocks learning'. John is the kind of person you might call the 'go to guy' when things are really complicated.

John's family is somewhat of a mystery and are tucked away in the fog of London, the hills of Italy and vine covered valleys of California. Still, John is a conflict in terms. Despite all of his worldliness and intellect, his chosen profession is that of a grounds keeper. Before his abrupt departure from the Sigrist household staff, John Murphy is found tending to the grounds and talking only to his plants, shrubs and trees. His belief is they are, 'better conversationalist than the assholes I work for'. John Murphy is a loner, but John Murphy is a man with heart. Right now this is something Vickie desperately needs.

"What about the rest of the staff, Vickie?"

"Find them, whatever. I don't care. I can't live like this. I need people around me. Hire them all back for all I care. You just look over the grounds and take care of me. Keep that thing away from me. I really think some fucking nut is out to get me. The cops don't listen. They don't even come out any more when I call."

"Think it might have something to do with the place's current reputation?"

"Fuck you, Murphy."

"There, that's my little girl."

There is a silence and a temporary truce. John Murphy is considering if coming back is an option. His present employer leaves him alone, is providing living quarters and is a good guy. The pay, however, does suck.

"How are the boys?"

Vickie finds herself thinking for a minute.

"They're fine. I guess. Hell, John, I don't know. I'm sure they hate me, but I swear to God we can work on that. You just do this for me. Just don't leave me alone in this big, old house."

John Murphy pours one more shot of Jameson, looks directly into Vickie's eyes and speaks.

"I don't mind the alcohol. I tipple a little myself, but..."

"No, shit?"

John smiles and continues his thought.

"This drug thing and those friends have got to go. I want my old salary plus twenty percent with benefits. I see you with nose candy one time and I'm out of here."

"Is an occasional martini ok?"

"I might even join you."

"Do we have a deal?"

"We have a deal. Now, go upstairs and try to get some sleep. I'm not going anywhere tonight. It's too damn cold. I'll pick a bedroom until the cottage is cleaned up and my things are moved back in."

John Murphy is watching as Vickie moves up the spiraling staircase. For some morbid reason Vickie is an attraction to him. His rule is not to fuck where you work and his loyalty is to the Sigrist family, what little of it there is left. At some point in the near future his plans are to tell Gary and William what is taking place. Until then the others in the pack deserve being kept in the loop. The history of this place is foremost in John's mind. What remains of this family and John are bound by a blood oath. Even from his grave Grandpa Pope is demanding compliance. This is something the children of today do not understand.

The next morning sees John Murphy pretending not to see Vickie standing in an upper window watching him shovel the snow from the front circular driveway. Vickie is relaxing a little more with each passing hour. It is the first good night's sleep she experiences in a long time. She is thinking of breakfast. She is thinking of the future, prematurely.

Key West's weather is the direct opposite of Detroit's. It is hot and sunny and the holiday season is upon it. The trolleys are decked in Christmas lights, the streets are filled with shoppers and Duval Street is packed with bars overflowing with drunken patrons. There is no snow. The evening's temperature is hovering around eighty degrees.

Gary and William are not together. Separately, they are exploring the various nooks and crannies of this two mile by four mile island. Gary's first stop is the Scrub Club on upper Duval Street. Gary is admittedly a whore monger. Gary is also a shopper. This goes with Gary's love of cooking. Gary is the perfect candidate for some gay guy in the Keys needing a wife. Gary talking about the perfect browning pan or roasting pot is known to cause an occasional call from his police friends still working toward retirement.

"The wife is at her wits end, brother. How long do you cook a leg of lamb and at what temperature? What is a good wine to go with it?"

Gary is always flattered. Getting the fact that this is a ribbing still eludes him. Besides, being the one to tell an armed man he isn't supposed to like cooking is like telling the executioner his blade is too dull. Some things and some topics are just meant to be left alone.

I am just walking. I like walking. You walk in Key West. You walk in Detroit while looking over your shoulder. Wandering through the T-shirt shops is not my thing. You see one T-shirt and you see them all. For a time, I am sitting on the upper deck of the Garden of Eden. I am watching the people on Duval Street moving up and down, in and out of stores. I am watching the men showing off their women who are mini-skirt clad and g-string bound; some needing burlap coverings and brick weights for tossing over the edge of one of the island's many ocean piers. I am thinking that life is not complicated. It is just really fucked up. Everyone wants the same things. They want love, lust, money, power, a sense of well being and a future filled with friends and respect. The problem is that too many are going to extremes while attempting achievement of these basic wants and needs. Life is like that old sales pitch about wanting, needing and affording. Do you want it? Do you need it? Can you afford it? Most people are so vain they find themselves saying yes to all of these questions, eventually finding themselves the proud owner of something that just fucks up their lives.

While drinking my second martini, I am thinking that my father not saying no to Vickie is the worst thing in our family's recorded history. My thoughts are turning angry again and I begin seeing the women on the street below me for what they really are…bitches. They are all money hungry bitches. They wear anything. They say anything. They do anything. To top it all off, the blame is usually your blame. Even after they are not virgins, women want to act like virgins, except in some place like Key West. Then there are the virgins acting like whores. Why is it impossible for people to just be honest? Do you understand what I am saying? Down deep inside I think you do. I am very respectful of the woman at The Scrub Club and at Bare Assets and I do like that T-shirt showing a woman pole dancing with the caption, 'I support working women'. It isn't at all funny to me. It is my truth. Damn, this last olive is good. I am thinking of staggering home for a good night's sleep.

Sometime later…remembering the exact time is impossible…I am in this place. The sign says it is part of the Truman Annex, whatever the hell that is. This Truman Annex is full of apartments and houses all neatly painted and landscaped. It sure as hell ain't the part of Detroit I am calling home. The one section's name is, Shipyard. Who the hell is responsible for naming something the Shipyard? There ain't any fucking ships in sight anywhere. I am sure there is a reason, but I am just too fucking drunk right now to give a big rat's ass about any of that. How did I end up in Shipyard? I'm lost and there is this guardhouse and the guard is sleeping. At least, I am thinking he is sleeping. I'm sneaking down this little sidewalk that empties out into Shipyard. This seems like a logical thing. Isn't it? Now, I am fucking lost. Which way is north? I am beginning to hate this island. The little fucker turns on you once you drink a little. When you think you are going north you are really going south.

I am sleeping in this little fenced in area. Someone is kicking at my feet. Looking up, my eyes see a woman. She is in her mid to late thirties. I am thinking she is one of the gold-digging little bitches from Duval Street. Where is your fucking husband, my sweet? She is wearing a scarf.

"Could you move over? I need to throw some trash into the compactor."

I am reaching up. I am grabbing onto the scarf. The scarf is a multi-colored. It looks like some sort of rainbow. It is blue, red, yellow and some other color. I am just thinking another bitch with a scarf.

"It is nice of you to provide the scarf. It is real fucking thoughtful, it is."

"What? What are you talking about? Let go of me. Help, me!"

I am good at this. This one is free. It is on the house. It isn't about my art. I am sure some old guy wants you gone. Maybe he is some poor piece of shit that can't afford my services. This one is on the house. You're welcome, dude. Shit, what am I doing? It is too late, now. Which way is north?

Pushing the body into the compactor, in my condition, is very difficult. I eventually manage. I oblige the lady's request by throwing her garbage in on top of her. The compactor is still grinding and pressing as I am walking by the guard house and then back down Duval Street toward my suite. The guard is still sleeping. The scarf is around my neck. No one is noticing but for a gay guy or two who are asking about buying me a drink. What is up with that? This is a strange town, but I am thinking I like it. Hopefully, Gary is alright. I love Gary more with each passing day. He is always there for me.

Chapter Twenty-Five

(BOGO)

It is some time later. The funeral business is going well. People are still dying. As with most people like me, there is often a lull between one's artistic urges. The Sigrist Mansion, under the care of John Murphy, is really looking spiffy, if it is acceptable for me to use this term. I just like the sound, 'spiffy'. It seems like something clean, pretty and just on the verge of getting down and dirty. Vickie, on the other hand, is nearly out of her mind. There are telephone calls now. There are snarling sounds on the other end of the telephone calls with statements like, "I'm coming for you very soon. I always keep my promises. It won't be long, bitch. Tidy up your lacy underwear drawer. I am going to pick the pair you wear when you die". The calls are random. They arrive at all hours of the day and night. Vickie stops answering the telephone. The calls are never long enough for tracing. The calls are from random numbers routed into the country from some overseas connection. Voice messages are always waiting. Vickie wants to know, but she does not want to know. Her skeleton hand trembles almost uncontrollably as she is reaching for the voice message button.

"Had to peek, didn't you? Oh, this makes things so much more fun. I'll bet you are thinking about hiring security right about now. What are you going to do? Are you going to stay in the mansion forever, Vickie? Are you never going out among your fucked up friends again, Vickie? Is the nose candy running out, Vickie? What will you do then, Vickie? You're going to go out, Vickie. You need your shit. Don't order in, Vickie. Your mule will never arrive. Either way I win, Vickie. Either way I win. You can either die quickly when I come for you or old and alone waiting for me to come for you."

Vickie is in the living room near the great fireplace where we once make love. She is leaning on the back of the couch that is in the middle of the room. She is waiting for the threats to be over. Vickie backs away while rubbing her hands over her face, trying to wipe the exhaustion and tears away all at the same time.

"Stop, it. Stop, it. Just, leave me the hell alone. What do you want? Do you want money? I have money. How much do you want?"

Realizing she is talking to a machine Vickie turns from the couch and senses someone else is near. She is looking down at the floor. She is seeing the large shadow. It is the shadow of a man. Vickie faints. Her head strikes the edge of the one end table and she slumps onto the floor. The blow is not hard enough to kill her, but it is hard enough to draw blood. She is trying to get up when a strong grip grabs one of her arms. Vickie feels another hand behind her back forcing her up into a seated position.

"I'm here, madam. Just sit up and breathe deeply. I'm going to get a cold washrag for that nasty cut. We need to get that blood wiped away. Girl, you are a basket case."

Vickie sees John Murphy's face. At first it is wavy and distorted, but gradually comes into focus. She mutters.

"This thing is killing me, Johnny. He knows you are here. He has to see how beautiful the place is. You need to be careful, Johnny. I think this creep will do anything to get at me. Bring all the servants back, Johnny. I want the house full of people. I want them loyal to me. I want them protecting me."

"Not to worry right now, madam. Nothing is going to hurt you. I think it is time to contact some people I know and get this thing over and done with."

Vickie is perspiring. Her breathing is still very heavy and labored. It is the panic of a very frightened person. This is the type of approach once swirling around in the back of my mind before one of my killings. Is it possible to frighten someone to death? My answer is yes. This type of death is the highest type of my art and is practiced by only the most committed. My art is full of deadlines. Maybe, someday, the time is going to be right for me to mature my art to this level. I hope so. This is what I am thinking after learning about this event.

I am sitting alone in Gary's cabin at the time of this particular incident. I am thinking about opposites. The subject enters my mind while looking around the cabin's interior. The cabin is a cabin. It is log upon log with all that mud like stuff in-between sealing up any openings, preventing the entry and exit of cold and heat. The cabin is very large as cabins go.

The furnishings are the reason I am thinking what I am thinking. Gary likes the outdoors. He likes his cabin. Yet, the furnishings are very modern. The coffee table is black steel with a glass top that appears to have landed in place upon it steel supports. The lamps are black steel with twisted bases much like figurines reaching toward space. The couch is comfortable but, in my opinion, is not a cabin's couch. It is linear in form with sharp right angles front, back and side. One might open the front door expecting the skyline of New York City were they unaware of being in the country in a cabin. My point is this.

Everything is an opposite. Disputing this principle is not possible. There is life and death. There is light and dark. There is young and old, the known and unknown, the seeing and the blind, the believers and the non-believers, answers and questions yet without answers, the physical and the mental, good and evil, tall and short, thin and fat, round and flat, and on and on. Finally, it is my position to state right here and now that people are all of these things rolled into one. This is why people like Vickie are so fragile. They are taught from birth that things are one way and are always stumbling into the realization that life is nothing like this at all.

Vickie is now the opposite of her envisioned self. She is no longer the lipstick and makeup covered, tight-assed, little gold-digging bitch taking my father to the cleaners. She is just another opposite. She is the opposite of herself and sees this daily in her morning mirror. She is old, but she is a frightened little girl waiting for some boogie man...a boogie man planning on stripping her naked in the dark of night and having his way with what flesh is presently living on her skinny and unattractive frame. Things are not going as Vickie sees them going. Neither are the cabin's furnishings what one sees in their mind upon approaching the cabin for the first time. This is all very amusing. I admit that I am not in her position. One reaps what one sews. This is a frightening thought living in the back of my own mind. Presently, I am having too much fun with my art to think thoughts like these about my own future. Sometimes fun is accidental and the most rewarding. One's plans for fun are often the victim of some asshole hell bent on messing things up. The movie theater is an example. I never go to the movies. Finding myself strangling some asshole in front of me who is insisting on talking through the whole movie, is a waste of a good scarf. I watch my movies at home and save my scarves for my art. Yes, accidental fun is the most rewarding. This is my example. It is a memory of mine about a contract not going quite as planned.

The envelope containing my money is the biggest payday to date. One referral after another, leads to bigger and bigger monetary rewards. It is obvious that there is no end to the service that I offer those elderly gentlemen around the country who are in the grips of their young female predators. The disposable cell phone policy I employ is working well. The only thing really bothering me is that the only one knowing my name is the ex-husband of my initial accidental kill. It is true he brings me great wealth, but I am somewhat under his control. I am often wondering if I am not some sort of subcontractor and do not know it. I convince myself this is not the case. I put this thought out of my mind and continue to go with the flow. It is like believing one never gets a sexual disease after losing count of their sexual partners. Besides, the only one knowing my name is old at the time of my first killing. He is surely near death himself and eventually this all ends, except for me wandering alone and unpaid across the landscape of the world, looking for an occasional piece of art to satisfy a pent up need now residing inside of my psychic. This particular accidental fun scenario is part of my memory. I share it with you as a gift from one artist to another. I am a giving person. It is important that you believe this about me. So, open this little memory, carefully. There is a message here. It is a message about not trying too hard to have fun while creating your own particular brand of art. Sometimes, life and its offerings are more accidental than planned. This is my whole point.

On this particular night the wind is heavy and gusting to fifty miles per hour. A cold front is moving in from the northern states and is blanketing most of Florida. It is near freezing in the upper part of this long state, a state that literally flows into the ocean at the Southernmost Point at the end of Whitehead Street in Key West, Florida. A soft spot lives in my heart for this little island. It is an island where people beg blankets for their animals if the temperature drops below sixty degrees. The homeless are fending for themselves, but the animals are warm. In fairness, some animals are worth saving more than some humans. I still possess the rainbow colored scarf from my little fiasco some time back. This time I am in Miami. For all of its advertising, bikinis, night clubs, cultural diversity, beautiful water and promises of glitter and wealth, I do not like Miami. Miami reminds me of a big neon sign sporting the way to much glitter and not enough content. Miami is not a city to appreciate my art. It is a place for killing and I am not the only one doing this. I pride myself on the fact that my killing is for the sake of art and salvation, the art being mine and the salvation being that of my clients.

The condominium is high in the sky at one of those gleaming towers dotting the beach front in this bustling metropolitan area. I am waiting patiently. I am already inside of the condo looking out into the water while watching the speed boats roaring across the liquid landscape below. I am thinking how upside down the world really is. Here are boats drinking gasoline like alcoholics suck down their chosen drink, thinking the supply is endless. In Detroit the service station lines are longer and longer, the price per gallon is higher and higher while the working class buys regular instead of premium and Busch beer instead of Stella.

The condominium is on the twentieth floor and sucks up about two thousand feet of living space. The place's downstairs is open and airy. A spiraling staircase juts up from the center of the space like some twisting phallic symbol ready to explode onto the upper bedroom's floor. I am waiting patiently for my victim. This is a stealth killing and making an acquaintance or small talk is not necessary. My client is very curt.

"Kill the fucking bitch and be quick about it."

I am holding Mercedes' picture in my hand. I admit this to you, but no one else. I like black women. Their way of prancing and pruning is admirable. It is what men like and want. Other than the one's lost in too many bags of greens and bacon, black women are very exciting, in your face and desirable. A black man once tells me that black women are the best in the world until they are your wife. Seems to me this is standard the world over. Anyway, my own theory is that I like black women for the same reason white woman like black men. It is something one is not supposed to have. Things are, however, changing. It is my hope that desire is not lost because of taboo.

The door clicks open around four in the morning. This pleases me. I am tired from my flight in on such short notice, am not booked into a hotel and am hoping to catch a noon flight back home. The scarf is black. I am thinking, God, is she ever beautiful. The name, I am not so fond of. Who in the hell names a girl, Mercedes? What is a guy to do? Change her fucking oil?

It doesn't matter. I am twisting the black scarf around her neck the instant she is moving through the door. I am twisting tighter, tighter and tighter. She is struggling. She is very strong. She is wearing a wig. It falls onto the floor and is laying there like a dead beaver pelt. I am mentally laughing to myself. Women, women...women are just like men. Things aren't always what they seem. I am remembering a story my brother tells me about a guy who is in the hospital emergency room. Some bar bouncer beats the shit out of him for not leaving the girls alone. The nurse is cutting his pant leg to attend to his wounds. She is also admiring the huge bulge along the inside of the guy's pant's leg. She is thinking, 'if only my husband were hung like this'. It turns out there is pepperoni taped to the guy's leg. Like I say, things are not always as they seem. Anyone want pizza?

Mercedes is struggling. I am not used to this. I am the one usually in control. This bitch is full of fire. I am holding the black scarf with one hand. I grasp a small statue with my other hand and bring it crashing down on top of her head. Mercedes goes limp. Blood is flowing onto the bamboo wood flooring. I am thinking, 'Fuck, this one is staying here. It is just another home invasion in Miami. No dancing lately. I must get back to dancing and keep this art thing closer to home. This isn't about the money. It is about the art. Isn't it? My machine is lonely. It needs to dance again.

We are against the first step of the spiraling staircase. Mercedes' head is at rest on about the fourth step. I am standing over her looking into her beautiful dead eyes. I am looking at the top of her head. There is very little hair. Too many years of hair dye and straightening is what I am thinking. The wig is her occupational hazard. I am reaching down and untwisting the scarf from her neck. The rubber gloves I am wearing are making my hands sweat. I hate rubber gloves. Sometimes I cheat at the funeral home and don't use them during body burial preparations. I do worse, but not lately. So, fuck the gloves. I am sure some other bodily fluid eventually kills me anyway.

Tonight is different. Prints are not acceptable. I understand this and am as careful as possible.

There is a noise coming from the top of the steps. I am looking up. What the fuck? I am looking into Mercedes' face again. No, this is not possible. Am I dreaming again like the time back in the funeral home, with the elevator, when the police come looking for clues about Cecil's death? No, this is real. Something is terribly wrong.

"What is going on? Mercedes, baby, are you alright?"

The woman and I are looking into each other's eyes. She senses my confusion. She is now wide awake from the sounds of a few minutes before. I am in the apartment all this time and she is sleeping in the bedroom right above my head. A memory is flashing through my mind. It is about soldiers during the wars who, because of fatigue, are often unaware they are walking by their enemies who are just a few feet away. Sleep deprivations is a scary thing. I make a mental note about being more careful in the future.

The woman turns, realizing there is no place to go. I move quickly toward her before grasping an object or weapon for use against me is possible. As she is turning my hand clamps around her left ankle. Pulling her back down the staircase and over Mercedes' body her head is bouncing from step to step. She is unconscious before her head hit's the bamboo flooring of the main living space. Twisting the same black scarf around her neck and strangling the life out of her is easier than killing Mercedes.

I find myself exhausted and confused. Am I seeing what I am seeing? Yes, I am. Check the apartment, man. Make sure no other surprises are here, and then get the hell out. I inspect every inch. I am standing in the upper bedroom looking down on the two dead women at the base of the spiraling staircase. I am suddenly feeling more like God than ever before. I am dripping with sweat. I feel as though I should plant the scarf at the top of the stairs much like the Boy Scouts plant their flag during that stupid game of capture the mountain. I am wondering if the little fuckers every think about the game just being preparation for capturing a real mountain where machine gun fire is your host. I think not. I stick the black scarf in my pocket. It is close enough to the game for me. Looking out the huge window's panoramic view, I am hoping no pervert is looking in at what is taking place. It is time to leave. At the base of the spiraling staircase and as I am stepping over the bodies, I find myself reaching down and picking Mercedes' wig up from the floor. While putting the wig in my coat's inside pocket I walk out the condominium's door. The freight elevator, the one without a camera, arrives at ground floor a few minutes later. Washing and cleaning in a McDonald's restroom is not easy but is manageable. The cheeseburgers are two for a buck. I love the clown's french-fries and could eat them by the bag full. About five hours later I am in the air and heading back toward Detroit. Too close, I am thinking. I remove the prepaid cell phone from my pocket and call the number my client specifies. He answers.

"Yes?"

I am frustrated.

"Yes? Is that all you can say, you mother fucker?"

"What? What are you talking about? Didn't things go well?"

"You tell me. Why didn't you tell me there were two of them?"

"Two?"

"You know there were twins, you son-of-a-bitch. One came home and one was sleeping upstairs."

There is a long silence on the phone and then sobbing.

"Oh, my God, you killed them both. Betty wasn't supposed to be in town for another two days. Oh, my God, you killed my Betty, too?"

My mind is now telling me this contract is not about a gold-digger. It is about an old man reaching for something he is denied in his youth...love, that thing a prejudiced society is telling him over and over he cannot have. I suddenly realize there is this type of thinking on both sides of the aisle. This is why I love my art so much. It is my expression of life. No one tells me how to paint it, present it or where to hang it in the halls of my mind. I must be getting back to the roots of my art. I must practice more caution in the future. I must stay closer to home and, most of all, I must dance again. This traveling ends now. I am not a savage running amuck across the dark side of society's petty ways. I am an artist. Tonight is a lesson. It is my lesson. Get back to the art. It springs from your roots. In a dark sort of way, tonight is sad, ironic and funny. I speak one last sentence into the throwaway cell phone before leaning my head back against the plane's plush first class seat and falling fast asleep.

"Well, I guess you'll just have to consider this a BOGO night."

I tell you truly. I regret this night. I regret this incident. I am unable to look at black women the same way again. I am holding out hope this incident influences my art, in a positive sort of way. The black scarf is always with me. It is in my pocket. It is a reminder of that old saying about 'the best laid plans of mice and men'.

Chapter Twenty-Six

(Gary Is Calling)

I am thinking about my family and other things. When I am thinking about these things is not important. This story, like time, is now just a companion. I put them in no particular order other than saying that they happen and this is the way they happen. You, the reader, are responsible for sorting out the rest. I am thinking about the rumors about my family's history of mental illness. I am looking at my first piece of real art still hanging over the head of my bed. The blood on the canvas is dry and brown, but is still red and alive inside of my mind. Will I ever recapture the essence of this night? I doubt this is possible. Art is like the first breath of life. One takes a breath and wonders if another follows. It does, but is not the same as the first. The first breath is an awakening. This is why babies cry at birth. They are frightened of the future. They are frightened of the unknown. Still, the first breath is everything. It is something worth cherishing. This is how I am feeling about this first piece of art. It is all that is separating me from the dark history of my family's past, a family with its dark corners manifesting themselves in my deceased Grandfather Pope. I am in control. I am not like him. My killing is with a higher cause. Did he believe his killing was for a higher cause? No. I am different. Hanging onto this thought is very important. This thought is the separating factor between savagery and civilization. God, now I am thinking like the rulers of nations. What is wrong with me?

Focusing is what is required of me right now. Look at your art, William. I am sipping another taste of cognac. The telephone is ringing. I am thinking of calling my big brother. His voice and dry humor are lingering in the back of my mind. The sound of his voice is comforting. This is what I need at the moment…the sound of Gary's voice. Looking at the number on the inbound readout, I see it is Gary. He is reading my mind.

"Hey, Gary, I was just thinking about calling you."

"Glad you're up, little brother. I need you."

Am I hearing Gary correctly? Gary needs me? This is a first. Gary, needing me, is a desire living alone in the back of my mind and never expecting fulfillment. Here it is. Here it is right out of the blue. I hate that term, 'right out of the blue'. It is always reminding me of that Chicken Little story for children. I do not like that story now and I do not like it as a child. Anything is capable of falling from the blue. I am always waiting for a bucket of shit to hit me right in the head. I see myself taking up writing children's books. They need to write better children's books. Anyway, I am off track again. This is a regular event as of late…being off track. Son-of-a-bitch, Gary needs me. I do not know how to respond. I am waiting for him to say it again.

"William, are you there? Do you hear me? I need you, man?"

I spit out the only words that come to mind.

"I'm listening."

"You will know soon enough. Just get in your car. Come on over to the mansion and pick up some fucking coffee on the way. Get two cups. We need coffee."

"Who needs coffee?"

"John Murphy and I need coffee. There is no fucking coffee in this place. Get yourself some. I'll pay you when you get here."

"No, need, I'll buy. Is that all you want me for? You want me to bring you two assholes coffee? Do you want it raw or in a cup?"

"No. No. We just need coffee. We need coffee to drink. You can't drink used coffee grounds, dick-head. Come to the front door. John and I will be there to let you in."

"I love you, too. Be there in a flash."

Oh, I like mysteries. I like rushing into the middle of the night not knowing what is waiting for me. Sometimes, sitting alone looking at my first piece of art for hours is a real downer. I am often wondering. Is this all there is? I mean. I am willing to accept it. Creating more art is always possible, but a fellow just needs a change from time to time. Yes, I really love mysteries.

The blood is moving in my veins again. My legs are pleased to be in another position other than the crossed-legged way I am always sitting on my bed's mattress. Someday I am actually going to make my bed in the morning. One never knows what is hiding under the covers, let alone the bed. I am dreaming lately about things being under the bed, things like my art coming back and taking revenge on me. Am I starting to sound like Vickie? I really hope I am not starting to sound like Vickie. There is nothing under my bed. Looking every night before going to bed is a silly practice. I understand this, but it does help me sleep better. Too, I am starting to understand Vickie's own apprehensions. Maybe my bed is my werewolf? You think?

I am on to I-75 and moving north in no time. This Detroit night sucks. All Detroit nights suck. I am really tiring of Detroit. I want to showcase my art in some place other than Detroit. If not for the lights on the Ambassador Bridge and other prominent landmarks, the city is void of character. Oh, I give you the towers. Too, the visitor coming up during the day and rising up over a particular section of the interstate is always impressed how the skyline pops into view unexpectedly, but that is about it. I also give you the Redwings. I like hockey. I am dreaming one night about using a hockey stick for knocking a victim's severed head around a huge canvas. The canvas is covering the Joe Lewis area floor where the Red Wings are playing. I am the half-time entertainment. The crowd is going wild. The end product is brilliant. A rich man, his name is Mathew, is buying my art and the money is going to charity. I am giving like that. I really care about the less fortunate. I am no longer bitter about the loss of my own fortune, the fortune my brother and I deserve. Oh, well. Now, it is about my art and my huge heart, my giving heart.

There is nothing open except a McDonald's or two. The doors are barred at night, but the drive-thru is always open. I order three large cups of coffee telling the attendant to dump some creams and sugars in the bag. I will pay extra. I do not know who drinks what how. Pulling up to the window I am greeted by a familiar face. It is the face of one of the young men whose father is one of my funerals from about a year ago.

"Mr. Sigrist? What are you doing out this late? By the way, I never got a chance to personally thank you for all the kindness you showed our family during their time of need."

"It was my pleasure, son. Hope you are doing well. Gott'a, go. How much do I owe you? My brother needs me. My brother needs me."

"You don't owe me a thing. I'm thinking that fat clown in his yellow suit survives tonight without your money."

This is a great night. Gary needs me and they love me. All of Detroit loves me. Maybe taking another look at this town is in order. Am I missing something? You just never know. I am thinking my dream, the one about creating my art at Joe Lewis Arena, is a premonition of better things coming down the pike. I am betting this is the case. I am betting they are planning on inviting me back for an encore. Maybe it is for something with loose arms or legs. Maybe it is just a torso. The torso, by itself, is hard to comprehend. This is what I am thinking.

Arriving at the mansion is like arriving at the front gates of hell. The place is lit up with red and blue lights from the overhead rotors of police vehicles and an ambulance. I envision the red being for sinners of lesser infractions and the blue being for the hardcore residents of the underworld. Pulling my car off into the front lawn I balance the three coffees in their cardboard holding tray and try keeping the sugar and cream from falling out of the middle of the thing and onto the frost-covered ground. Will warm weather ever arrive? The last few months are so cold that I envy the corpses I am putting to rest after a quick trip to my crematorium. I am approached by a uniformed officer.

"You can't go in, sir. Not a pretty sight."

"I'm a fucking undertaker. Get out of the way."

Gary moves from the inside foyer to the front steps of the porch.

"It's ok, Roger. That is my kid brother, Billy."

The officer lifts the yellow tape line and eyes the still steaming hot coffee as I am passing under the barricade tape. I see the officer's glance.

"I'm sorry, officer. If I had known I would have brought everyone one. Gary just said to hurry over and bring three cups. Do you want mine? I can go without."

"No, Billy. You keep it. Be careful in there and put on cloth covers over your shoes just in case this thing turns out to be something other than an accident."

"What thing?"

"Just go with your brother, son. I'm sure he will explain. Sorry for your loss."

Vickie is a woman of many positions. This is not a position she ever assumes for me during our one-time sexual encounter. Her head is turned sideways. Her eyes are open in that death stare we are always seeing on television. The eyes of most of the people arriving at my funeral home are closed. I am standing in the front doorway of the mansion. It is apparent by the look on my face that I know nothing of this event. One of Vickie's arms is bending backward and resting on the small of her back. The joint in her upper shoulder is obviously out of its socket. I'm thinking, 'that had to hurt'. The other arm is reaching forward and is in a position suggesting a last effort at grabbing onto something. Her legs are wide open, the way I am sure most of her friends are accustomed to seeing them. Blood splatters from several parts of her body, especially her head and face. The blood is forming a kind of circular pattern like one sees when looking at an angel's halo. I feel Gary's hand on my shoulder.

"Come on up the staircase, William. John Murphy is up there waiting on us. We need to get out of the detective's way. They have a job to do and will probably want to talk with us. I just figured you needed to come out so my buddies don't have to go chasing you down in the morning. It saves time and paperwork."

Walking up the staircase the cloth pullovers feel uncomfortable and odd over the top of my shoes. I know enough from television that turning them in before leaving is part of the routine. Evidence might attach to the bottom of them. I often find myself wondering if there are special types of pullovers for those hot bitches in high heels working as investigators on television crime shows, probably not. The evidence most likely is sticking to their asses after they wiggle their way across the airwave frames.

John Murphy is standing next to the elevator at the top of the staircase. He is leaning against part of the railing running along the top of third floor hallway that is attached on each side of the elevator. We all take our coffees. I am peering over the railing and looking down on Vickie's body and the activity taking place below. John Murphy speaks.

"This is all my fault, son. I am the one here to protect her and this happens."

Gary enters the conversation as he is blowing some of the steam off the top of his coffee, a coffee now more sugar than liquid. Why his original teeth are still in his head is beyond me.

"As far as any of us are concerned, William, he found her this way. He called me and I called you. The police already know the thing about the threats she has been receiving and blew it off. They are going to look at this closely, but they won't find anything. Besides, John shouldn't be blaming himself for this. Who was to know?"

Acknowledging that I understand, I ask "What really happened, John."

"Well, son, it is funny in a macabre sort of way."

"What?"

"Well, she is drinking again and she is hearing voices again. I really don't understand. The telephone hasn't rung much in over a week and the calls haven't been coming for about the same time. All I know is Vickie is standing here by the elevator. She has a martini in one hand and appears to be rather in control of herself, as in control as you ever see her."

"Then, what happened?"

"I come in the bedroom door to the back of your mother's old room just to check on her. I do this sometimes in the middle of the night to make sure she is alright and, you know, hasn't hanged herself or something stupid like that."

I am sipping on my coffee and am still looking at the activity below. From this height the blood is actually quite artistic in its splatter and flow. I am thinking it is a waste of good blood in want of a fine piece of canvas. I look into John Murphy's eyes as he is continuing his account of the events.

"You know me. A glass or two of Jameson and I get this idea of cheering her up. She is a bitch…"

Gary chimes in, "Was a bitch."

"Yes, well, be that as it may. I often find myself feeling sorry for her. I feel sorry she is living in fear for so long now. Like I said I thought I would lighten up the mood a tad."

"And, what did you do?" I inquire.

"I walk up behind her and say, 'boo'."

"Boo?"

"Yes, boo. Before I know it, she swings around. The martini glass goes one way while she is losing her balance. The olives fly out of glass and fall toward the floor like two green eyes ripped out of a cat's head. Before I can reach out to grab her arm she is over the railing. The rest is history."

Gary leans in and whispers in my ear.

"If I had known it could be this easy, I wouldn't have spent all this time trying to work up my own plan for killing her."

I am thinking that Gary is kidding, but I never really know about the thoughts and intentions running free in my big brother's mind. I am laughing inside about the 'boo' thing and trying desperately to keep a small smile from coming to my pursed lips. I am also thinking how small the home's entry seems. It is a long time since I've been in the Sigrist Mansion. There is a belief that, as one is growing older; things once seeming large begin manifesting themselves as small. I am hoping this is not the future of my dick. Loosing any part of it puts me at a definite disadvantage.

The night is eventually early morning and I am thinking about Grandpa Pope and the others returning to their crypt a little further north of where we are. 'Boo!' This is Grandpa Pope's doing and the alcohol is just the vehicle by which his will is done. I feel it inside of me. This is a pretty good story, but I am not a writer. Our statements are taken. The body is removed from the foyer and placed into one of those green heavy plastic bags that I see coming and going from the funeral home. The detectives thank us for our time. They all shake Gary's hand and start moving out the front door. Gary calls out toward the last man just before he is closing the front door.

"Can we clean up or are you coming back? The staff will want to know and I really don't know what the fuck goes on here anymore. I'll make some calls to the estate's trustee and have him get in touch."

"Yeah, wipe it down. The body is going to the morgue and may or may not end up with your brother for funeral services. It'll be up to the next of kin, if there are any. It looks like nothing but an accident from what I see. This werewolf thing is a crock of shit. It all started with drugs and booze on Halloween a few years back. One fucked up bitch, but I can't be putting that in the report."

Gary responds, "Stay safe, brother."

"You too, Gary."

The door closes and I am suddenly feeling hungry as hell. We are rousting through the refrigerator in the kitchen when I see Gary moving in behind John Murphy. I know my big brother well enough to know what is happening. He screams at the top of his lungs.

"Boo."

John Murphy jumps and turns. I see he is pointing a large meat fork at my brother. There is a huge slice of ham hanging from one of the fork's two tips.

"That ain't funny, fucker."

I think it is. We are all eventually laughing until the tears are running down our faces. I like mysteries and I like nights like this. Besides, I am saying to myself. Is life really worth living if you can't laugh at Death from time to time?

Chapter Twenty-Seven

(The Return)

Louise Kinsington is returning. They are all returning. Louise is fifty-nine years old and dreading that big 'six-o', yet her faith is still as strong as ever and this day is reaffirming for her regarding both the direction of her life and her faith. Louise is not showing her age. Many a younger man is still throwing themselves in front of her, wanting desperately to be the one opening up this package of lust and desire. Louise is having none of it. Her faith is her rock and men are a dime a dozen, use one throw one away and grab another on the way to and from the grocery is her motto. Men are in need of being packaged along with other meats in the deli. Perhaps labels based on past performance are in order. Louise thinks so. Marriage is the farthest thing from her mind.

Her hair is a sort of red and brown mix that falls into some indescribable shade of blond when out very long in the sun. She loves the sun. She tans quickly and one thinks by the bone structure of her face that she is possibly Indian or part Indian. From my point of view a short buck-skin dress slit up the side with her mounting a palomino pony is about as erotic as it gets, but I am not one of those new types of meat she mentally wants in a deli labeled, 'take-out-studs'. What do I know? I know only that what one can't have is what one always wants the most. Too, I know that this desirable woman is the first returning to the Sigrist Mansion.

As she is approaching the mansion, Louise pulls the car to the side of the road and finds herself peering through her car's windshield. The view is crisp and clear. This woman is very anal retentive about the cleanliness of things. Her car is at the top of this list of things never to allow in the grips of a big city's filthy hands. One can, literally, eat off of the floor mats. This is part of the reason Louise is so entrenched in the history of the Sigrist family, at least the history I am capable of remembering at such an early age. I am remembering trying to peek through a crack in a floor board or two, attempting a quick glance up her short skirt. The skirt I know is for my father. Her domineering ways, perhaps, are as well. I am remembering sitting in my basement hideaway hearing her barking orders to the rest of the staff.

"Come on, grubbers."

Louise fondly calls all of the servants, 'grubbers'. I do not know why and never have the opportunity to ask. The term sounds English, but she is always looking so much like a well-tanned Comanche Indian. Yes, Louise loves the sun. Still, her skin is soft and supple. Her skin is not like so many women basting themselves like a turkey and rolling over and over for too many hours in the sun.

Standing here at an upper window, I am watching Louise peering through the windshield of her aging, rusting blue BMW convertible sports car. I am sure the rust is driving her right up the wall. I am picturing her in a newer version of this same type of car. She is aging like fine wine. The car is not. Louise deserves a better ride, no pun intended in conjunction with the 'meat deli' comment. Picking a scarf color for Louise is not possible. She is a piece of art unto herself and one glance projects this fact to the rest of the world. One does not improve on a masterpiece. One only waits for it to get better on its own with the passing of time. Like great books, some art is only appreciated once one is capable of holding only its remnants in their hands and its memory in their minds. It is that old saying about, 'not knowing what you've got until it is gone'. This is the way I feel about

Louise. I want her as a child and I want her as a man. Some things are just impressionable like that. I am wondering what she is thinking while sitting there looking through the windshield of her BMW. Later and in a private conversation, I find it is this.

Louise is thinking how beautiful the grounds are again. This is John Murphy's work. The view brings a smile to her normally pursed lips. Her lips are full and desirable, but position themselves in a set of straight lines running from dimple to dimple. It is as though she wants no loss of appearance or control. I am sure, in her past life, she is some sort of gambler. Her face is a poker face, but one does not care about losing to. The smile after Louise winning is worth the wait.

Louise is thinking she does not remember the mansion's many windows. Her mind is telling her the home's appearance is much like the residence in Poe's Rise and Fall of the House of Usher, only much larger. The windows of the home are like too many random eyes looking constantly into one's soul. The windows are calling for real eyes behind them again; eyes willing to look out upon the world and make things right again. She is thinking that a home truly does reflect the one living inside. In this case, in the case of this home, its evolution is bound up in one name and one name alone. That name is Sigrist. Though her name is not the same, her past and now her return is part of this structure's history as well. This is a day worth waiting for. This is a day where promises kept are wishes fulfilled. John Murphy is a man of his word.

Louise kicks the BMW into gear. The gears grind, but seem to understand that life's pain is often a desirable thing. If it doesn't kill you, it just makes one stronger. It is like the leather whip against a man's back. Once the erotica begins the pain ends and the results are worth a little inconvenience. The BMW obeys and moves toward the garage area. Louise sees John Murphy tending a shrub alongside the driveway. He waves. He sees Louise giving that slight smile, the one all men see as a sign of approval. It is the same smile men are willing to die for.

Louise steps from the car and into the crisp sun light. She is wearing a black pleated skirt, white pullover cashmere sweater. The sweater is complimenting her size thirty eights. I know this because of peeking into her laundry basket many years ago. I do other things a little boy is told not to do. All I know for sure while moving away from one of the home's eyes is that Louise is back. I am picturing her dismounting from a wild horse while wearing a little buckskin skirt, not from that rusty BMW.

Chapter Twenty-Eight

Gary says my art should be put on hold for awhile. This is a surprise and catches me totally off guard. Is it possible that he knows all along what is going on in my second life? This is all he says to me and I am so caught off guard that responding is impossible. I do know that his advice, during my time afloat in the gray area of making a living, is always right on target. Not taking him at his word now is not something I am willing to risk. I must suppress my urges for creativity in respect for my big brother's wishes. This is the same reason I am at the mansion watching the old staff arriving. The funeral home is closed and the sign indicates this is due to illness.

Vivian and Oscar are the next to arrive. Vivian is pretty much nothing more than a 'fetch it' employee. I am remembering Louise saying things like, "Go get it Vivian", "Hurry Vivian. The guests are about to arrive" and my favorite, "Don't be a bitch, Vivian. There is time for that after the guests leave". Vivian is the gothic type and black is her color. Vivian lives out of sight of the rest of the group and I remember her moving unnoticed on this or that errand that Louise is sending her on. Once, while in the basement listening to all the commotion of an evening's upcoming party, I am watching as Vivian strolls with her melancholy personality into the basement. It is my opinion she is already wasted on something. I am watching as she walks toward the wine cellar, grabs a bottle of red wine, uncorks the bottle and sits among the cobwebs drinking and talking to herself. I am watching her lips covered in black lipstick caressing the top the wine bottle's neck and am suddenly aroused.

Is this the way a vampire drinks blood? If so, maybe there is something to be said for joining the ranks of the living dead. As odd as it seems, the shadows and damp darkness of the basement seem to bring Vivian alive, not withstanding whatever substance it is she uses that is keeping her in that dark and attractive world she calls home. I am listening very intently. I am able to decipher some of her conversation with herself.

"I miss you terribly, madam. I wish our secret could be shouted to the world. Now, it is too late for that."

Vivian pauses. She is twisting her head from side to side. She is listening for something. I do not know what she is listening for, but I am thinking it may be the sound of my breathing, my excited breathing that is unable to be still because of the beating of my heart. Momentarily, Vivian concludes she is alone in the basement and the noise is no more than the wind passing in and out of the home's sub-structure.

"Oh, lover, if only the staff knew what was going on. Your touch is forever in my memory and my return to this place is, I know, a duty. It is a duty I do not know if I am strong enough to keep."

Vivian sighs heavily, lets the wine bottle dangle limp in one hand and is beginning to sob into her other palm. I am watching when the tears stop, when she breaths deeply as if to suck her tears back into the reservoirs of her eyes and when she stands to drink the last few drops of the red wine from its bottle while muttering her last words before returning into the upper floors of the mansion.

"This one is for you, lover. I will watch over the boys. I will watch over the boys, do Louise's bidding and never ever forget you."

I am watching as Vivian moves back up the basement steps. I am thinking she is a dark spirit disappearing into the light at the top of the landing. I am thinking we are all older now. I am thinking change is on the horizon. What is that change? I presently do not know the answer to this question. One thing I do know for sure is that it is time to quit trying to be a little boy in the basement. It seems there are more secrets here than I care to know.

Oscar is a big man. He is very muscular despite his age. His hair is silver now, but still in the same well-groomed shape I remember. He combs his hair straight back, but not slicked down. Many mornings Oscar's hair dryer whistles over the sound of the coffee maker. The other servants tease him about one hair being out of place. Other than the years between them and their temporary separation, I am thinking this is a memory as well as a continuing quirk soon to be a target once again by his friends in service…in service of the remaining remnants of the Sigrist family.

I am watching as John Murphy arrives unexpectedly from the side of one of the garage stalls. Am I, I am thinking, the appearance of some apparition peeking from this or that upstairs window on the arriving humanity once in exile from this pile of brick and mortar? The thought is quickly gone as I see the two men embracing. John Murphy is slapping Oscar on the back. Oscar is all smiles. I watch John taking the man's luggage and moving off and around the last garage stall, along a little sidewalk leading to a small cottage out back of the parking area.

In the morning, bright and early, there is a grinding and tinkering sound inside the garage. I know Oscar is back in the depths of his own private world of oil, spark plugs, and wax car washes. He is a mechanic with neat hair? What are the chances? I think I like Oscar, but there are only a few memories of him. Some servants you pay more attention to than others. It is my conclusion these are the ones that end up being the most needed and yet most under appreciated of all.

Over the next few days I am standing at one of the upper windows watching the rest of the old staff arrive. One is now using a cane. The laundry lady is using a four-legged walker. Time is the enemy of everyone. Still, I am thinking that everyone is still alive. It is such an odd sight. I know the faces, but not all of the names. I know their particular function in the daily events of the mansion, but, like I say, am not remembering all of the names. I am thinking that my own attitude is once 'a good servant is out of sight and out of mind until payday'. After all of these years their return is also a question in the back of my mind. Also, another question is about Gary. It is now nearing a month and getting back to my business is a priority. My calls are not being returned and it is all I can do to keep my promise of not leaving the mansion until his return. Then, too, there is that passing comment about putting my art on hold for awhile. Thinking these thoughts while standing alone in the upper hallway near the east end of the residence, I am startled by a hand upon my shoulder.

"Same people, brother. They are just a little older."

Looking around, I am staring into my big brother's eyes. He speaks again.

"Trust is a wonderful thing. Not many people can say they know it, let alone there being love to keep it company."

"What's your point?"

"I love you man. I haven't told you that lately."

As far away as the look in Gary's eyes often is, I also see sincerity in them. I place my hand on his one shoulder and respond.

"I feel the same way and it is something, with or without words, that is understood, big brother. Now, what the hell is this all about?"

"I'm just cleaning up a few loose details, William. If you want, you can return to your business now. I'll be calling you in a couple weeks to come on out to the house for a special event. Things are going our way now and everything will be clear soon. Just trust me a little bit longer. Will you do that?"

I nod my head in agreement.

"Now, go on out front. There is a surprise waiting. It is a good day for a drive. Enjoy the day, the sun. This area has so few of them. Go home. Relax. Cut on a body or two, whatever it is that makes you happy. Like I said, soon things are going to be alright again."

John Murphy and Oscar are waiting for me just outside the mansion's front door. Oscar is smiling and moves in quickly to give me a big hug. This is before I can back away from him entering my space. As odd as it is, my space is my space. I like being the one dictating the terms of the groping. Anyway, I recognize the greeting is sincere and I return the embrace. John Murphy is holding the door open to a BMW sports car.

"Go ahead, son. Oscar spent a great deal of time getting this thing in running shape before bringing it over to the mansion."

I scream the sports car down the driveway still as confused as ever. In the back of my mind is a little reoccurring thought. It is saying don't look a gift horse in the mouth and trust your big brother on this one. He loves you.

The highway running through this area is an extension of I-75. This baby rips ass like some motherfucker from hell. I am thinking that it is quite possible to hit speeds high enough to roll the car right over the water and into the Canadian border. My ass is deep in the seat and there is one gear to go as I am ripping by the Palace. Then, something is beginning to click in the back of my mind. Something is familiar. I am moving off the next exit ramp and into a small graveled rest area, the kind of rest area where the gays congregate late in the evening to advance their gay-hood, when I realize what this feeling is.

The car shuts off without stuttering. I am the only car in the parking area at this hour of the day. My hands are caressing the rich black leather seats. I place my shifting hand's palm on the gear knob and find myself sliding my hand up and down the shifting rod like some boy hiding away in his bedroom while jerking off to a Playboy magazine. My eyes peer through the windshield as my vision drops down the erotically sloped hood of the car and into the oblivion of thoughts past.

How is this possible? I am looking into the rearview mirror. I am confirming my suspicions while making sure this is not all just a dream. There it is on the back window. There it is. There is that painted emblem with the same wording, the wording just as it is while I am rolling this mechanical marvel into the depths of the lake, the lake on Gary's property, the lake where the cabin is that I gift to him after a payoff. The wording is, 'For My Little Bitch'. I am sure my first victim takes this as a compliment. I am also sure it is an elderly husband's way of letting his relationship with a woman he does not love sit on a ledge of sarcastic meaning. I am looking around the interior. I am hearing the traffic from the highway just beyond the exit ramp. No, I am not sleeping. This is real.

A note in an envelope is taped to the glove box door. I am just noticing this. Opening the note, I am reading these words.

'Oscar worked long and hard to dry this thing out and give it a new life in the hands of someone capable of appreciating it, an artist like you. Don't worry, little brother, everything is under control and everything will soon be normal again. I love you, Gary.'

The note is both frightening and endearing at the same time. I restart the beast, back out onto the road without looking, hear the tires squealing from oncoming traffic, pay no attention and move back on the exit ramp going toward home. A little work at home, my funeral home, is in order. Sometimes clearing the air is the best thing and normal surroundings are the only things that are capable of helping this process along.

About three in the morning I peek into the funeral home's garage. The BMW is still sitting by the hearse. This is not a dream. I decide trusting Gary is the right thing. Why look a gift horse in the mouth? About eight the next morning my apartment's intercom button rings. It is the police morgue van. The attendant is curt and to the point.

"Glad you are back at work, William. I don't like that prick we are using a little further down south."

"How did you know I was back?"

"Gary called. He keeps in touch. Good man. Too bad there aren't many like him left on the force."

The morgue van leaves. I am again standing alone in the funeral home. I go upstairs, clean up and come back down to my own preparation room. As I am approaching the body bag laying on one of the stainless steel tables my hands begin trembling a little. It is not because of a lack of confidence. It is because of the excitement. It seems so long. My machine is waiting. The corpse inside is that of a young female. She is fresh and uncut. She is not long from the alley where she turns her last trick and dies in the hands of some freak that does not appreciate her own form of giving, her own form of art. There are so many deserving women dying and so many undeserving women living in the lap of luxury. I am thinking about receiving so many gifts in such a short period of time. Lifting her from the body bag and onto my machine is easy. She is all of one hundred and five pounds. She is still pliable and her joints are moving. She is fresh. I quickly position her on my machine. There are candles for effect. I lean in and rip open her blouse. They are beautiful. I whisper in her ear.

"May I have this dance?"

Chapter Twenty-Nine

(Little Details)

Little details and loose ends are the hardest things to dust away from big secrets hiding in someone's or something's past. Gary Sigrist knows this. His life is one of bringing secrets into the open. Sometimes this is done in a subtle way. Sometimes it is done in a grandiose way. Detectives and, in general, police are a funny breed. This is the same principle as hiding in the open. Who guesses this is the case? Usually, no one does. This is an example I remember my big brother telling me about during one of those drunken nights we share together in his cabin up north, under the stars, far away from the gazing eyes of humanity and judgment.

"So, my partner and I go to this housing complex today to question this first rate asshole about not paying for the repairs done to his car."

"That doesn't sound too exciting to me, bro."

"Well, no it isn't, but there is a lesson here. And stop calling me bro. Pretty soon you'll be corn-rowing your hair."

"It's just a phrase."

"Maybe it is, but we have butchered the English language enough already. Now we have white guys doing rap. Retirement can't come soon enough for me, bro."

I get Gary's point. The phrase does sound strange coming from a white man. It isn't a racist thing and I am sure all things eventually merge. Some are comfortable with a certain drink, a certain seat at their favorite bar. Gary is more comfortable with a certain language. I get it. Gary continues his story.

"So we get this totally numb-nuts, fucking idiot into the station and start questioning him about why he didn't pay for the work on his car."

"Did he have a good reason?"

"This hammer-head starts out by telling us how religious he is and that he only wanted them to look at his car, but didn't authorize any repairs."

Gary is saying that the hammer-head goes back in the middle of the night with an extra set of keys and just drives the car back home like nothing ever happens. Well, the repair shop owner is out of his mind and calls the police, at the same time he is on the way to this guy's house. Gary and his partner arrive just in time to prevent a 'numb-nuts-fucking-idiot' ass kicking. The shop owner is pinning the man to his newly repaired vehicle, preparing to bring a big heavy ratchet down on his customer's thick and stupid skull. The car is impounded and the aforementioned idiot is taken back to the station for questioning. The car repair shop owner is told to go back to work. Things are not handled this way anymore in the big city of Detroit.

"And, how did all this come out?"

"Well, once this asshole gets done spouting scripture for about two hours and gets done talking gibberish about the white man taking advantage of the black man, I put this work order in front of him with a signature for the repairs."

Gary goes on saying how the customer is claiming the signature is not his and how the shop owner most likely is the forger. The guy starts praying and asking if Gary and his partner want to pray with him to help in the saving of an obvious sinner's soul. Gary is about at wit's end and is thinking of clubbing the guy to death with one of his own tools from the tool box he is carrying in the back of his personal car now parked in the headquarters' lot.

Gary's partner at the time is the silent type and usually is the one just watching and listening. He goes over to the table and sits next to numb-nuts and begins praying with him. Sliding the work order in front of the man's face he begins.

"Lord, please forgive such a man. Please forgive a man who would take a document of honor and foul it in such a way."

The black guy is saying a few 'amen's' every ten seconds or so. Finally, the detective directs the supposed victim's eyes to the work order. He is pointing to the signature on the document. It is the only signature on the document. The signature isn't like this guy's signature but, then anyone can over emphasize something so as to make it not look like their own handwriting.

"Not your signature?"

"No, it is not my signature."

"Is anything on the document your writing?"

Gary is listening intently. He knows his partner and knows this dim-wit is about to get the fucking of his life.

"No, nothing is my writing. I go back and he wants money, money I don't have. I did not authorize the work. It's just another case of the devil doing his work. I really pity these poor sinners. Sinners always trip themselves up. The devil pushes for the deed. The result is not his concern, another soul into the pits and fires of hell. I pray for this poor sinner."

Gary is watching as his partner is trying not to smile.

"Ok, we believe you. Don't we, partner."

Gary is now playing along.

"I guess we do. Sometimes things are not what they appear. We need to be talking to that repair shop owner again."

"Yes, you do. I knew you two were different. I knew you would understand. I am going to praise you to the Lord and ask him to keep you from harm."

The numb-nuts is feeling comfortable. He inquires.

"Does this mean I can have my car back?"

"Yes, yes. I think so. I need you to draw a line below your written statement and need you to initial below it to show this is the end of your discussion with us. That way no one can write below this line or tamper with our report. Here, just initial right there."

The guy hastily initials his written statement. Gary's partner slides the document over to him. Gary is looking at the initials on the statement and the initials on the work order. Numbnuts is fucked. This is my example of how little details are so important.

Another point of all this rambling and remembering is that a little detail is in the middle of our life, Gary's and mine. His name is Tom J. Plack. He goes by the name of T.J. and is a private investigator out of Dayton, Ohio. With a last name like Plack going by T.J. is not a bad thing. His last name sounds like something a dentist is scraping off of your teeth. Don't get me wrong, 'Sigrist', won't even spell check, but Plack? Give me a fucking break. I see some parents not taking the doctor's advice and drinking way too much during the wife's pregnancy. The problem is that once you are labeled, the whole family is labeled. I am saying it again, "the truth of things is in the details." There ain't any fucking way around it.

T.J. is approaching fifty years old and is still dressing like some gum-shoe from a cheesy who-done-it novel. He is always wearing his favorite felt hat. It does not matter what the weather is, winter through summer. The hat is past its own lifetime and shows signs of pointing upward at its crown. Either that or the hat's top is adjusting to the point on the top of T.J.'s head. The man is always carrying way too many guns and is continually wondering why his lower back is hurting. There is the nine-millimeter on his right side, the 380 in an inverted holster on his back just where his spine needs to bend, a thirty-two leg gun on his right inside leg just above his ankle and probably a derringer stuck in the crack of his ass. In short, metal detectors are not T.J.'s friend and walking by a magnetized crane at a junk yard full of dead cars is not a good idea. Still, he is a good private investigator and, during his career, works for some of the more wealthy families in the tri-state area. T.J. is sitting outside of my funeral home near the back alley late one night when my telephone rings. It is Gary.

"There is a little ripple in our plan. Stay inside. Stay in bed. Keep the lights off. Everything is going to be alright."

I am still asleep.

"What? Why?"

"Stay inside. Stay in bed. Keep the lights off. You are being followed. Everything is going to be alright."

All I think to murmur is, "O.K."

The next morning I do not immediately remember any of this. It is only later in the day that this incident is awakened from the recesses of my mind.

I am taking the garbage out to the alley dumpster. The sun is high in the sky. The bums are away for the day and only the imprints from their dirty cloths stain the back of my funeral home's wall, the one where the crematory burns from time to time and helps keep this lost humanity warm. No, there is nothing in the alley, but an old felt hat.

Chapter Thirty

(Urges)

I know this is something needing control. I know this is something my promise places on hold. I also know this is something in my makeup that is beyond my control. The wait is killing me. It isn't fair to expect this much from me. There are urges at work here. These urges are not gender specific and are living within the framework of men and women everywhere. Maybe you are a woman and are a nymphomaniac, a man who is a sex-addict, a sports addict, a religious fanatic, a brain-washed fanatic of some lunatic fringe waiting on some spaceship to come and take you home, an over-the-cliff tree-hugging environmentalist activist, gun-toting anti-government hating radical out to change the world's thinking, bored thrill-seeking adrenalin-driven to the extreme male looking for a real hard-on; the principle is still the same. Your urge is your leather collar. It is keeping you alive. It is keeping you from all of this boredom. It is gripping your throat, forcing you to swallow hard in preparation for that next life-changing event. My urge is my art. You are saying it is murder. Fuck, you. It is the expression of what one is doing that counts. Waiting longer is impossible. What does one little indiscretion hurt? It hurts nothing, if one is not caught. This is the thinking of a person driven. It is rationalization at its best or, depending on your point of view, worst. Forgive me, Gary. This is something I must do. These 'other' things are just taking too long for my patience.

The Redwings are losing tonight. They very seldom lose. Tonight they are losing and transferring my aggression to them is not possible. It is as though I am the victim. The fans are in need of a good revolt. Maybe the ice is a good canvas. No, the ice is not a good canvas. It eventually melts and the art is gone. I am just upset tonight. I am saying to myself, "Think about something else." I am being pushed along with the crowd out the Joe Louis Arena exit doors. I am watching the humanity moving down those long concrete steps and back into the mouth of the Detroit night. "Not too cold", I am thinking. Walking is in order. The crisp night air is what I need. My head needs clearing. I love sports, but hate the sound of all those screaming fans. Why is it impossible for people to be civil? All that cursing is upsetting. Appreciating the pain of the game is impossible with all that cheering and screaming. Even straining to hear, I cannot hear the pain in a player's voice during those hard hits with an elbow or a hockey stick. I like being near the ice, near the glass where the blood is flowing when a player's face is slamming into the glass and his teeth are falling from his mouth onto the rink's cold embrace. This is art as art is happening. My pocket camera is not quick enough to catch such a moment. I am thinking of buying another camera.

I am in Greek Town. I don't remember coming to Greek Town, but I am in Greek Town. I am standing across from a small parking lot. It is much later in the very early morning hours and some of the hockey fans are now leaving their after game, late dinner locations. They are returning to their cars. I am watching a man and woman heading toward the parking lot near the Pegasus Restaurant. They are approaching a black Jaguar near the back side of the lot. I am expecting them to get into the same vehicle. The woman is wearing a very short skirt and platform high-heeled shoes. Her blouse is open and it is obvious she is not wearing a bra. Her breasts are very firm and are not in need of any support. "Art", I am thinking. I am sure God is a man and that his thoughts are as suspect as those of

Satan. Is there another reason for creating such an enticing creature? The woman and man are the last two in the parking lot. They are leaning against the Jaguar and she is rubbing up against the man. The man is in a very expensive suit. Is she a call-girl? If so, she is very expensive. If not, he is a very lucky man. I see the woman putting her hand in the man's crotch and she is whispering into his ear. I am imagining the conversation.

"It was a wonderful night, baby."

"I know. You like violent things. Don't, you?"

"Let's just say that I like it rough."

"Just what the doctor ordered."

I am expecting more, but the encounter is very brief. The woman is removing her hand and moving toward another car in the lot. The man is waving. I am thinking, "No, not a hooker. She is the secret woman." The Jaguar is moving out into the street, turning right and heading toward the interstate. The woman is sitting in her vehicle. The dome light of the vehicle is on. She is adjusting her makeup. She is making herself perfect for me. This is fate. A light drizzle of rain is falling. I am paying no attention to the rain. I am looking at my art. It is an unfinished piece of art. There is a cab sitting near where I am standing. Inside the cab, I find myself leaning forward and speaking to the driver.

"I hate my line of work. I need you to be discrete and follow that car."

"Are you a private Investigator?"

"Yeah, I wouldn't do this, but for the piss poor economy. I really don't care who is fucking who. If you know what I mean?"

The cabbie takes the one hundred dollar bill I stuff into his hand and replies, "I know. Still, a man has to make a living."

The cabbie is very good at following the woman's car. He even waits patiently near an all night stop-and-rob as she is retrieving a hot cup of coffee and a donut. There is some conversation.

"How can you eat shit like that and still have such a killer body? This is what I would like to know."

My answer is short and simple.

"It is metabolism, my friend, and maybe drugs. Who, the fuck, knows?"

The cab slides in behind her car as though it is silently attaching itself to the fumes of the woman's exhaust pipe.

"You've done this before, cabbie?"

"You would be surprised. Most times it is the husband and not a P.I. You do know the cab fare is extra. My mileage shows on the trip meter."

"It's not a problem. I expected as much. I hope you are around the next time I need this type of assistance."

"What did you say your name was? What agency are you with?"

I make light of the issue by saying, "Following Sluts Are Us."

The cabbie is smiling. His gaze is on the woman's vehicle as it is turning into an apartment complex just off of Twelve Mile Road. Her car is passing through an area containing a guard house. No guard is on duty.

"Drop me off just the other side of the guard house. I want to ring up the guard so I don't get shot while I am wandering around the grounds."

The cab driver accepts my command without question.

"That is thirty one dollars and fifty cents."

"Here's an extra a fifty and your fare. I'll have one of my agency people come to get me, if the dick-head will ever answer his phone."

I watch the cab making a U-turn, its red tail-lights disappearing into the Detroit fog and left over factory smoke, a smoke blanketing Detroit like some quilt of doom pieced together with the lives of the human beings calling this dump home.

A few minutes later, I am wandering the parking lot. Still, there is no guard in sight. The license plate is there. The parking block is giving me the number of the apartment this vixen is calling home. The rain is gone and my lungs are now heavy with fog and soot. I feel mucus draining down my throat and am in need of a decongestant. I find myself pausing for a moment and fishing for a napkin in my pocket. The napkin is from the three or four drinks back at the arena. Blowing my nose on the napkin I am thinking about how quickly our own lives drain away...right underneath our nose. Where does that thought come from? I am having weirder and weirder thoughts lately. Oh, well. It is of no consequence. I am feeling a masterpiece coming on. I hope her sheets are white. I am imagining a white sheet instead of a white canvas, imagining changing my art out like one does these new fangled multi-colored watch straps you buy in Kmart or Wal-Mart. It is really a good idea. I am thinking my art is capable of making it happen, putting this idea on the map. I am envisioning selling two or three 'sheets' of different art depicting different moods that a client might change out depending on their mood at any particular moment. I am a fucking genius. I must be a fucking genius. Only time tells us if we are a fucking genius. Usually this is after an artist's death and the money grubbers move in. The answer is in the lifetime of my art. This is true for all artists.

My knuckles are falling upon the door. I am not using the doorbell. I do not know why. My knuckles are very cold. I am thinking they are capable of breaking at any moment. I am also thinking that no one in their right mind is going to be answering the door at this time of night, unless they are a lady of the evening. Whore is a word I try not using. Their profession is, after all, their art. I am not the one to be judging it. For some of them it is an urge that is also a profession. I am quite capable of understanding this point of view. Fuck all of those religious pulpit freaks who are preaching to us and getting their dicks sucked under the podium right before the eyes of an unsuspecting congregation. Anyway, the door is opening. My pocket knife is in my hand. In a moment I am in the apartment. My pocket knife is in her throat and I am sawing back and forth like some commando with a small knife and a dull blade. Somehow, the job is getting done. There is no scream. The initial surprise is mine and the body is laying before me on the living room floor before my victim is capable of uttering a cry or plea for help. During the ordeal, which is quick and swift, I am constantly repeating the phrase, 'So, you like it rough. So, you like it rough. So, you like it rough.'

One thing I do know is that this is not my type of art. My victim is already dead when something is beginning to click inside of my head. It is that little voice saying this is not you. It is saying this is not your art. This is your anger.

Another thing I know for sure is that silk sheets do not make a good canvas. Regular white linen sheets are better. Silk sheets blotch and the blood does not run in the direction I want it to run. This is not my art. Taking this home is an insult to the rest of my creativity residing in my secret room. This is a night without purpose. This is a new experience for me. Or, am I trying to control my art too much? Am I at that point where writers are often finding themselves? Is this some sort of artistic block like writer's block? Who is to say? All I know for sure is that this lifeless body is in front of me and there is no real satisfaction in this event. I am looking down at her body, whatever her name is. I am carrying on a conversation with her and she is answering me somewhere in the deepest part of my mind. I hear her replying just as if she is here sitting next to me and reviewing the scene with me for critique.

"I don't know. I don't think I would buy it. What do you think?"

"I agree. The piece appears forced. It is as though the artist is out of control, but not in a good way."

"What do you think I should have done differently?"

"Let the act be itself. You know when painters paint; some of them say their hand is not moving the brush. Their mind is moving the brush. I think you are under a lot of pressure and this impulse art scenario needs to be put on hold. Your brother is giving you good advice. I mean, look at the blobs here. None of your other work reflects this. Your scarves, for example, are hanging in your art room in a random sort of way, but they make a statement. They could be on canvas and in a frame just the way you left them. You did not place them. You just put them. They are their own art. See what I mean?"

I am looking at the scene in front of me and contemplating the advice. Her conclusion is sound.

"I really appreciate your perspective on all of this. I really appreciate your help. Without this little encounter I might have gone on lost for a long time. I don't want to end up like that idiot that cut off his ear. I wish I knew your name. You know, to send flowers to your funeral or something."

"Oh, don't worry about it. My life wasn't going anywhere anyway. I am just glad to be of help."

She is correct. I am not taking this creation home. I am getting the fuck out of here. My hands are sweating inside of the rubber gloves. Carrying rubber gloves is a thing with me. One never knows when they are a needed commodity. Though my art is sometimes random, I am basically a very neat person. What I need to be is a more careful person. The ramifications of tonight's event are staggering. I am pulling the backdoor of the apartment closed, turning my rubber gloves inside out, stuffing them in my jacket pocket and thinking of burning them in my crematorium on arrival back at the funeral home when a pair of headlights enters the alley behind my victim's residence. There is a small overhead triangle-like sign on top of the car. I see it is a cab. Who the hell is calling a cab this time of the morning? I am already outside the back gate. I see it is the face of the cabbie responsible for dropping me off earlier. The cabbie does not speak at first. He is motioning me to get in the back of the cab. This night is so surreal that I am behaving like I am in some dream just coming to its conclusion. Sitting in the back seat of the cab, I am feeling movement as the tires begin turning and the vehicle is moving out through the complex. The cab is moving past the guardhouse…the unoccupied guardhouse. There is still no guard present. This is a good thing for me, but not for the residents of this complex. Some crazy son-of-a-bitch might be taking advantage some night. If you are paying for a guard, you ought to be getting a fucking guard in the guard house. I find myself speaking to the cabbie.

"Can you believe that shit? They have a guardhouse, but they don't have guards."

"Shut the fuck up, William."

I am surprised at hearing my name.

"What did you say to me?"

"I said shut the fuck up. Gary is really pissed off at you right now."

I let the cabbie's remark slide. I am thinking about his advice and the evening's events. Big brother is going to kick my ass. I am going to call and apologize right away. Being pro-active is a good thing. I am reaching into my pocket for my cell phone. The phone isn't there. Fuck, the cell phone isn't there. We have to go back. We have to go back.

"Cabbie, please, we have to go back. I left something. We have to go back."

I am looking into the cabbie's eyes in the vehicle's rearview mirror. He is holding my cell phone up.

"Looking for this?"

"Yes. How? Where did you find it?"

"You dropped it when you first got out of the cab. You were in such a big hurry to get to it. My next passenger found it and gave it to me. I called the first number. I called this Gary guy. He is your brother, right?"

"Yes."

"Well, man. You need to get off the booze and quit following your ex-girlfriends around."

The cabbie flips the phone over the seat.

"Here. Now, shut up like I said. I don't like being lied to. You're no private Investigator, just a jilted stalker."

The cab drops me at the rear of my funeral home. I give the cabbie another hundred dollars and apologize. He half-heartedly accepts my apology. The money is helping.

"Whatever. Do me a favor and get another cab company the next time."

I walk past the sleeping homeless. One inquires.

"Will you be cranking up the heat on the oven tonight?"

I reply.

"I can do that. Can't let my friends freeze to death. Can, I?"

Inside the morgue room, I immediately crank up the crematorium and flip in the bloody rubber gloves, my shoes and all of my clothing. I am thinking it is amazing the cabbie didn't see their condition or, if he did, didn't mention it. I am standing in front of the elevator door to my apartment totally naked, but for the cell phone I am holding in my hand. The elevator is coming from my apartment down to take me up and away into my little lost paradise, the place where my favorite piece of art is hanging over the head of my bed. I am beginning to believe that your first of anything is always the best. It is no different with my first piece of art. I am stepping off of the elevator and into my apartment when I notice a figure sitting at my kitchen table. It is Gary. His message is short.

"The mess is being cleaned up, asshole. This is the last time. Put this crap on hold. And, by the way, you are officially under house arrest again until I come for you. Got it?"

By now Gary and I are nose to nose.

"I got it."

Gary is leaning in. His breath is right next to my left ear. This is what he whispers.

"You can only love someone so much, especially when the trust is broken."

I am trembling when Gary is stepping onto the elevator and returning to the morgue room area. I am not trembling because I am naked and cold. I am trembling because of the message living in the tone of his last words. Fear is something new to me. It is a very uncomfortable feeling.

Chapter Thirty-One

Bobby Adams is looking for a friend. It is not like T.J. Plack; this being gone so long without checking into his Dayton, Ohio office. Bobby and T.J. are best of buddies. When T.J. sees Bobby is falling on hard times, his offer of a Private Investigator's license and a spot in the agency helping T.J. is welcomed with open arms. Bobby is not a good P.I. He is good at eating pizza and potato chips and drinking beer. His favorite hangout is a place just up Dixie Highway where you round the traffic circle, doubling back to Marion's Pizza Parlor. Normally, he and T.J. meet there every Friday night. There are times when T.J. drops the ball because of a bathtub full of scotch and some cheap whore the night before, but he never allows two Friday's in a row to go by without them catching each other at their usual table. Thin crust with double pepperoni pizza is their favorite. The beer is in a frosty mug and chips are from a little family place by the name of Mikesell's Potato Chips.

Bobby Adams is worried. His friend's cell phone is going unanswered and calls are not coming back to either him or the agency letting him know what is happening. Bobby is delivering the court papers and attending to the smaller things that he is responsible for, but has no idea what he is supposed to be telling T.J.'s bigger clients. His response is simply, "I'll let him know you called" or "I'll have him get back to you". The bills are going unpaid and Bobby is living week to week like the rest of America during these hard times. One thing is for sure. His friend is not someone to do something like this. Bobby's conclusion is that he is in trouble.

Sitting at Marion's Pizza Parlor and waiting for his friend, Adams is hoping against hope that T.J. is to walk through the front door tonight just like nothing is wrong. The thing worrying Bobby the most is that his friend's apartment appears unchanged. The same dirty dishes are in the sink. Nothing appears in a different place from the last check and the shades remain down. T.J. is one for leaving the shades down until noon and raising them around one in the afternoon. Now, the shades are always down. Something is definitely not right.

A check with T.J.'s normal haunts is turning up nothing. Bobby is very low on cash and is in need of money to begin his search. His is a conscious decision that he knows T.J. understands. Bobby is back at the Agency with a hammer. He is busting the lock off the emergency cash box living behind a false wall next to one of the eight steel filing cabinets in the office. One of these days, T.J. is going to get around to putting all of these cases on the new computers purchased three years ago that are already out of date. The box is holding eight thousand dollars in cash. Bobby stuffs the money into his coat's interior side pocket, but not before putting a note in the box to his friend saying, 'I took the money to help go look for your sorry ass. Call me if you get back and see this note. There may be some money left. If so, I am going to blow it on beer and woman just to pay you back for the worry. If not, I'll just get a job wherever it runs out P.S., the bill collectors are knocking the door down and some of your clients are pissed as hell'.

Bobby is heading north, toward Detroit. He is remembering T.J. saying he is going to Detroit, "You know, that place where little men who think they can play football shit something they call Wolverines." The conversation never gets around to why the fuck he is going to Detroit. T.J. is this kind of guy. He is always just wandering in and out of things; like this is the normal way everyone lives their lives. He is peculiar in other ways as well. His cell phone is not GPS hot. The Private Investigator does not believe Big Brother is in need of knowing where the fuck he is or is not. 'If I need help, I'll call and let you know where I am', is T.J.'s motto. Bob is thinking, 'How the hell is that working out right now?' Still, Bobby Adams is on his way to Detroit to find a friend he really isn't sure is in Detroit.

Bobby is also thinking about T.J.'s hat. He is thinking that the thing better be activated and that his hunch about his friend being in Detroit is right. T.J.'s hat is his GPS and the device sitting next to Bobby on the front seat of his aging Mazda is capable of picking up the signals from the hat's hat band around ten miles out. Bobby is talking to the box.

"You gonn'a talk to me, you piece of shit?"

A red light on the box is lit, but there is no reply. Bobby Adams is waiting on a green light and a little screen much the size of an Etch-a-Sketch. The screen is capable of mapping the immediate area of the signal and leading Bobby to its location. T.J. Plack is always referring to the contraption as a bug-in-a-box. Bobby is hoping the end result of this search is not a corpse in a hole with a very expensive hat from the Cable Car Clothier in San Francisco sitting on top of its head. He is also thinking that, if Detroit is a dead end, he may just be gambling the rest of the money away in Canada. This is Bobby's down-and-out story and why he is so dedicated to T.J. For him, the alcohol is not the issue. The issue is the damn horses. Bobby is apt to picking exotic names like Dancing Wolf, Shade of Yesterday, Ain't Misbehaving, Pick'n Em Up and Putt'n Em Down, Jack Rabbit Strut and shit like that. A horse with three legs is not a problem. The secret is the name. Bobby is off the betting wagon and it is all due to his best friend T.J. Now is the time for paying back. Now is the time to pull that proverbial miracle out of his ass. Hey, that is a good name for a pick, Proverbial Miracle. He likes the sound of it. Never hearing it before Bobby is thinking this is a sure winner. He is looking at the box on the seat next to him.

"That's you. You're my Proverbial Miracle. Don't let me down."

Driving like a bat out of hell straight north from Dayton, Ohio toward Detroit, Michigan, the drive is about four and a half hours. Bobby stops to piss twice, grab coffee and one of those Dolly Madison cherry pie things. The pie things are basically a thin crust of sugar wrapping around cherries in a red sauce full of extra sugar. Bobby is accustomed to squirting the juice all over his shirt and trousers. Frankly, if the sauce is in the right spot on his pants, looking at him makes one think his dick is bleeding. He might be a good second brother, but for being a meddling son-of-a-bitch hell bent on finding his best friend even if it is at my expense. Bobby is rough art. You, know. He is that kind of living art from the deep south that people are always putting on billboards along the highway saying, 'Come on down, ya' all. Everyone is welcome in Hicksville'. In my humble opinion, folk art is nothing more than a form of expression that doesn't know how to express itself. My art is from the heart, not from a fifth of moonshine and rotting brain cells.

The city of Detroit is shining in the night on Bobby Adams arrival. Its skyline is burning against the back of his eyes even before he knows he is dropping down over the last slope and into the mouth of this industrial giant. Bobby is apprehensive about what he is seeing and what he is doing. The green light on the box suddenly is on. There is a beep, beep, and beep. Bobby Adams is elated.

"What do you know, a Proverbial Fucking Miracle?"

Chapter Thirty-Two

(Going a little crazy)

Bobby Adams is driving by my funeral home. It is my opinion he is hesitant because of the neighborhood. He is probably thinking the whole area is one big stop-and-rob. My vision of this area is different. This is my neighborhood, my home and the neighborhood of my friends. I know he is driving by my neighborhood because I am looking out the windows of my apartment. I am, after all, under house arrest so to speak. Gary is giving me the cold shoulder. I am sure he is daring me to set foot outside of my work or home. My last embalming sees another funeral home picking up my client. There is a note from Gary. The words on the note are, 'I know you are under the weather. Pike's Funeral Services will be handling this burial. The family understands and wishes you a speedy recovery. I will be in touch.'

What is a guy to do? In retrospect I guess my big brother is justified in being upset. Still, I really hate being left in the dark. That's funny, 'left in the dark'. Don't you think that is funny? Fuck. This isolation is killing me. I am thinking about killing one of my morgue's residents, but quickly realize they are already dead. What is the fun in that? One cannot make dead art. One can only make art dead by the quality of what is being created. I am going to win Gary's trust back. When I do, I am going to make him a piece of art that is really, really special. He knows I love him. He needs to know how sorry I am for my little slip up. To forgive is divine.

Between peeks out of my apartment's window I am watching this National Geographic special on some educational channel. It is about some long forgotten tribe in Africa. Leave it up to National Geographic to see they are no longer forgotten. Anyway, my point is this. This tribe, once a year, dances with their dead. This is no shit. They bury them in some sort of special blanket after the deceased is treated with this special oil. You think I am crazy? I mean, I might be taking a liberty or two with my friends, but it isn't like I am going out to the cemetery and digging them up for a yearly tango. God, I am thinking weird thoughts during my house arrest. Damn it, Gary. Call me. I hate this waiting game. I don't like those little messages you are leaving me on my voice mail either, "You better still be where you are supposed to be." This is not us. I am your little brother. What can I do? What do you want? Fuck, you. You're just another dick-head. You're like all the rest. No. I take that back. I don't mean it.

I don't feel like dancing tonight. There is no one here who is worthy of dancing with me. I'm looking for a red head. I want to dance with a red head. This is something I need. Blondes are really boring anymore. Yes, the next one is going to be a red head. No more false roots for me.

It's time to go to my special room, my room of secrets. My special room isn't judgmental. It is a reflection of me. It is a reflection of my art. I love the feel of all the scarves. I love how they are brushing across my face as I am walking between them. It is such a beautiful space. I think it is my art museum. You are asking, 'Why don't you hang it on a wall?' Well, there is just too much art and it is really at the heart of all my work, each of these separate pieces. My idea of art is that it is like blood running through your veins. You do not mash it all together. You let it run. You let it expand inside of your mind until, like the big bang, it is beautiful and incomprehensible all at the same time. Can't you see that? One is required to feel its totality to appreciate the beauty of each little incident. My talking is helping you understand. Isn't it? I am thinking my big brother does not understand this. Seeing things my way is easy, if you are paying attention and are not being judgmental. This is my point. I know Gary is upset. I understand. I get it. He is a retired cop. Cops are all alike. They are black and white with no beauty between. I am hoping that someday he is able to grasp the beauty of my art living inside of all that savagery. No, savagery is the wrong word. It is more like appreciation for the beauty of the darker side of things. Yes, that is it. I am comfortable with this analogy.

I especially love this felt hat. It isn't even part of my art. It is just something living alone and lost in the back alley behind my apartment. I am remembering the night I find it. It is extremely dirty and neglected, this hat. Even underneath all of that dirt and neglect is a beautiful soul. It is like some old and faded painting begging for restoration. I am looking down at it laying there. I am thinking it is there because it is waiting for me, for my artistic touch, for my ability to bring it back to life. I am a Jesus of sorts. I am capable of giving dead things life. Yes, this is the truth of it. It is alright with me if you call me, William Lazarus. Still, I am sure some people are not capable of grasping my point. The point is. I take life, but I give art. Isn't that a wonderful talent? There is no need of thanking me. This is a gift. It is just something I do for the good of others. God, these scarves feel heavenly as they are brushing across my forehead and face. Silk...silk is such an erotic touch. The irony is that worms spin such a web of heavenly delight, while other worms wait to devour my art. Judging the giver is the biggest sin of the one being given such great gifts. I forgive you. You do not understand. It is not your fault. The best hope is that you are eventually a piece of my art. Gary is starting to piss me off. I am not going to be waiting much longer. This is my life. It is my art. Being a prisoner to my own greatness is the worst punishment of all. You know what? I feel like dancing. It is the hat. Remember, Dancing In the Rain?

"I am remembering Dancing in the Rain, splish, splash, splish and splash."

Gene Kelley is the best, was the best. The fucker is dead now. Oh, and forgetting Ginger Rogers is just not possible. Thinking of Ginger on my machine dancing with me is just too much to hope for. I am in need of a lamp post right about now. I am in need of tap shoes right about now. Maybe, a little sprinkler is in order. I know. I see a garden hose. This is another creation, a creation like when I am a little boy in the basement of the mansion. A little water, tap shoes, the memory of these great artists and me is what is in order. It is this fucking hat's fault that I am thinking all of these things. This hat is a whore. It is a whore of memories. Its spell is something one keeps returning to without thinking about the eventual consequences. The significance of this hat and its affect is like a song running over and over in your mind. The fucker just won't quit beating at your door.

I am thinking the little feather band is also at fault. Its colors are so inviting. Were a beautiful young woman wearing a tight dress gathered at her tiny waistline with material made from these feathers, I see her destiny being part of my art. I see her being like blood and feathers spread across my canvas of life and death, like some beautiful bird falling from the sky into the genius of my hands.

"Fuck you, Gary. I have lived under your control too long. I have loved you too much and now you whisper nothing but words of fear into my ear. Fuck you, Gary."

I hear the doorbell to the front of my funeral home. Am I hearing the doorbell? Yes, I am hearing the doorbell. Gary says I must be staying here. He isn't saying that answering the doorbell is something off limits. The hat is a perfect fit. Look at me. Look in the mirror with me. See how debonair I am? I love the word debonair. Debonair, debonair, debonair, see what I mean? There is no word like it. I like being debonair. I am wearing this hat and Gary is a motherfucker. He is a motherfucker I love, but still he is a motherfucker. I am answering the door.

"Yes, can I help you? I am closed."

Bobby Adams is very nervous. He is standing at the doorway and trying not to look at T.J. Plack's hat. More specifically, he is trying not to look at my hat. I do not know this is the hat of some private investigator named T.J. Plack until later. This is a little detail Gary is sharing with me toward the end of these recollections. I am also not aware of the fact that my newly found, perfectly fitting hat is going "beep". This Bobby Adams' voice is very shaky.

"What are you so nervous about, man? All I said was that I am closed. What do you want?"

"I, I, I"

"Come in. It's cold out there. I'm closed, but the company will do me good. I am allowed company. You, know?"

"What?"

"Oh, nothing. I'm asking all the questions and you are the one knocking on my door. Come in. Come in. We'll start over again. I'm being rude. That rubs some people the wrong way. For others it is just their nature. I am not rude by nature. I am an artist."

"Really, you are?"

"Yes, really, I am. The business is just how I make a living, starving artists and all that shit."

"Look, I'm sorry about all this. I'm from Ohio and have a relative waiting to be buried and I just need some help right about now. I've been traveling. I'm tired. I haven't eaten and, frankly, this isn't the neighborhood I pictured myself in looking for funeral services. I'm on a schedule and, well, I just took a shot."

I am laughing inside at the intruder's explanation.

"Sounds to me like your ying and yang are a little fucked up and you ended up in a neighborhood that is a little blacker than it is white."

"Don't get me wrong. I'm not a racist. It is just the area."

"No one said you were a racist. Some people say I am not an artist, but they haven't experienced the process yet. A mortician is an artist. He is an artist others fear to be, just like this neighborhood is a neighborhood you fear to call home. I find it very comfortable."

"Again, I am sorry for the first impressions."

"There is nothing to be sorry about. Come on in. Let's whip up some cheese and crackers to help with that hunger and we will talk. I have nothing better to do and, like I said, the company will do me good. The people staying with me right now don't talk all that much."

Mr. Bobby Adams is forcing out a smile at my dark humor. I am sensing from the very beginning of our meeting that he is lying to me. Getting to the bottom of this is in the forefront of my mind. I am wondering if this is something Gary is doing to test me. Yes, that is it. Gary is testing me.

I am watching as the visitor is moving cautiously around the display coffins. I am thinking about teasing him with some comment like, 'they are very comfortable to sleep in'. My pointer finger is subconsciously tipping the brim of my hat backward to where I am wearing my lovely felt hat in a little cocky position, much like Gene Kelley does in that wonderful sequence in "Dancing In The Rain". That song is just sticking in my mind. Did this ever happen to you? I am hearing the tap, tap, tap and the splash, splash, splash. Where the hell is an umbrella when a person needs one? It is the same place a cop is when you need one...never around.

We are sitting there at one of the morgue tables. We are both on swivel stools. Bobby's hands are shaking. A glass or two of wine helps with his trembling and the unexpected guest is beginning to relax. We are talking about my work, dead people and not really getting around to his deceased relative. There is time enough for that, time enough to prove Gary is testing me. I am enjoying the company. Bobby Adams is asking questions.

"So, how do you put them back together, the accident victims?"

"Some, I don't. I just put them in the burner and hand over their ashes to their loved ones. There really isn't much art in that, but sometimes it is all we have to offer."

"That is too bad. I'm sure it is very difficult for you at times."

"Not always."

I find myself telling this complete stranger a story about how some people are able to conjure up humor in the face of tragedy. It is the story about a soldier who loses a leg in the war. He is home drinking at a bar when a guy comes in and sits beside him. The stranger is being a real jerk and pretty much is forcing a conversation on the war hero. The conversation sees itself arriving at the soldier's nickname which is hop-a-long. The drunk, sitting next to the soldier without one leg, is saying how that is funnier than hell. The soldier says what the man is thinking his nickname is for isn't that at all. The drunk is slurring his words as he is inquiring what the soldier is talking about. The soldier's reply is quick and simple.

"Well, dick-head, that's because right about now I am going to be hop-a-longing your sorry ass."

The fight is on. The soldier wins.

Bobby Adams is sitting here with me, eating cheese and crackers while drinking wine off of a morgue table. He is laughing his ass off. My next question is very direct.

"Cut the shit, Bobby. What the hell do you want and who are you?"

I am looking at the man's face, his unshaven face, and imagining the stubble from his beard quivering like the fingers on his hands. The shaking is back. Bobby's reply is tentative, but direct.

"Where is my friend? Where is T.J.? You're wearing his hat, asshole."

My surprise goes without saying. This is a mistake. I am in trouble again. Gary is going to kick my nuts all the way to my throat for this little fuck up. I am grasping the morgue knife that I am using to slice the cheese for the crackers. Bobby Adams is sliding his hand inside the left side of his overcoat. The motherfucker is going for a gun. I am thinking of acting very quickly. I am thinking one swift lunge to the main artery on the neck is in order. I am ready to strike. There is a single gun shot and I am instantly watching Bobby Adams sitting upright and very still across from me. There is a bullet hole in the center of his forehead. He is slumping to his right. His head is falling toward the cheese platter. I reach out quickly, saving the cheese and crackers, at the same time watching my guest falling onto the cold morgue room floor. Looking up, I see Gary standing over the body. He slides into the same chair Bobby Adams is sitting in just a few seconds before.

"The hat looks really good on you, little brother."

"Thanks."

There is silence. I am waiting for all hell to break loose.

"Why are you so silent, little brother?"

"Cause you're pissed at me."

"I'm not pissed. I'm just disappointed."

"Am I still grounded?"

"Oh, that. Well, to tell you the truth, I kind'a had to have it this way. You were the bait, so to speak."

"What?"

"The last place this guy's friend was is your back alley. We've been watching. I figured he would show up sooner or later. By the way; did you know you talk to yourself?"

"What?"

"I had the place bugged. I like your singing, but some of the other stuff not so much."

"I'm sorry."

"I know. Have any more wine?"

I am pouring Gary a glass of cabernet. Now, my hands are shaking.

"I love you, Gary."

"I love you, too."

"Nice shot."

"No, shit. I didn't believe it myself."

There is nothing more rewarding than breaking bread with a loved one. I am thinking that dinner around a big table is the thing most families need and is the reason society is ultimately so fucked up. But, then, that is just me. I am also thinking about our conversation and the comment, 'we've been watching'.

Who is, we?

Chapter Thirty-Three

I hate cremating the hat. The hat is me. Bobby Adams is getting exactly what he deserves. I mean, really. Anyone invading someone's home under false pretenses is suspect of being an automatic target. If this society is ever at a point where people are unable to protect their homes, I'm leaving. Your home is your special place. Being what you want to be in your own home is a constitutional right. I am sure of this. I think it is even in the constitution. Isn't it? This time it isn't art. It isn't murder. It is just a case of a caring and giving man who is serving the poor while protecting his home. Still, I hate losing the hat. Gary isn't letting me keep the hat. He is watching me while the hat is in the crematorium burning away to small specks of nothing. The hat is dying quickly, unlike the slow burn of life. There is always an opposite. I am not visiting this subject again. I am sure you are remembering this conversation from some time back. Still, it is worth bringing up again.

"You can get another hat. Don't look at me that way, William."

"I know. I know. It's just that the hat seemed to hug me. It fit like no other hat. I am going to miss that hat."

Gary is cradling about half a glass of wine in the palm of his hand. He is a little tipsy by now and his sense of humor is coming back. Things are getting better between us.

"You want to say a few words while it is burning?"

I am looking into my big brother's eyes and see the smile from the back of his pursed lips bleeding through to his eyes. I begin smiling myself.

"Nah, you need a real minister for it to mean anything. I guess I will just have to find something else to occupy my time."

I am watching Gary lumbering his six foot four inch frame over to the end of the stainless steel morgue table where the remnants of our snack remain. I am watching as he spins around and hops his ass up on the table's top. A portion of the wine in his glass drips over the glass' rim and lands on Gary's pants. The pants are beige in color, now nearly white because of so many washings. Gary does not notice and is sitting there as the wine runs on down his pant's legs to where the flow is thin enough to stop and begin the drying process. I am standing with my back to the crematorium. There is a little brush with a long handle in one of my hands and an aluminum bucket in the other hand. Gary's head is tilting to one side. One eye is closing and he is fighting to keep the other eye open. I hear him mutter his last comment to me before falling sideways and passing out on top of the combination dinner-morgue table. His head is in a resting position on top of the last few pieces of brie.

"You look like a fucking chimney-sweep, little brother."

"Chim-chimany-cha-roo, you prick."

Going about the process of cleaning up Bobby's ashes is relaxing. Putting his ashes into a very tasteful vase is only respectful. I am not a monster. It is just like Vlad the Impaler. The highest spike is always for the victim of the greatest rank. There are rules and there is a certain civility waiting for one's enemy, despite the savagery of their deaths.

Gary is like a sleeping six foot four inch child. Snuggling up next to him enters my mind, but I think better of it. Gently lifting his head from his brie pillow, I wipe the mess up. Since moving him, is impossible and since he is accustomed to sleeping alone and tossing and turning in his bed, I draw the table's holding straps gently across him to prevent falling from the table's top. The morgue air is very chilly. I am used to this environment and think little of it. Gary, on the other hand, sleeps with all the covers even in the hot of summer. Understanding this is beyond me. All I know is that I am nearly thirteen years old before my covers stop disappearing. I am sure this is some sort of Freudian thing. Maybe one of you reading this account has one of those useless degrees better off recycled into toilet paper and are more qualified to comment on this phenomenon than I. All I know is that Gary is always sleeping under a mountain of covers. I think he is hiding from the world in his own little cave. This is just me. What do I know? Rolling a few sheets together fills in for a pillow. Removing his shoes is a mistake. Something is dead in those fuckers. Remembering some foot spray powder for Christmas is in order.

"God, man, have your feet rotted off?" is what I am thinking to myself.

Gary is sleeping soundly. Police are capable of this trick. Most of them use a bed only when nothing else is available...a bench, cruiser seat, the floor, leaning against a brick wall in a back alley, drunk in a bathroom stall with their head against the toilet paper roll or on top of some other guy's wife. Now, don't go getting judgmental. Try living in the gutter of the world for twenty odd years and you begin understanding that a few little quirks does not a bad man make. And, like everyone, keeping things bottled up inside is often the leading cause of bad judgment mistakes. I am standing there looking at my Big Brother, the one I love so much and the one who is capable of frightening me so much. I am remembering an incident that is nearly the reason for him not reaching retirement with the police department.

Gary is minding his own business one evening and is cruising around the area in his unmarked car, the gray kind with tinted windows and a spot light on the driver's side with red and blue lights imbedded in the grill and across the shelf of the back window. You, know? This is the unmarked car that says police all over it to any semi-sober criminal. Anyway, Gary is cruising around the Detroit area minding his own business. He is not even looking for any shit to step into. The call is coming from the third precinct.

"Help needed at Springhill Housing Complex. Any unit in area, please respond."

Since it is Gary's one goal in life to be jumping on patrol calls, his immediate instinct is to begin rolling in that direction. There is no sense in giving any radio traffic announcing his arrival. He is a detective. He is in his, 'I can do anything I want to do mode'. Most of Gary's stories are amusing and, if they are not, he adds a little to make them amusing. This is not that type of story.

Rolling up to the scene Gary steps right into the middle of a domestic taking place in the parking lot of this subsidized housing complex. Couples are fighting about who is fighting and why the police are treating everyone like criminals. Seems the real argument starts at an apartment Gary is familiar with and ends up spilling out into the parking lot with various neighbors taking one side or the other. The Detroit Police, Sheriff's Department, the Private Housing Authority and people with badges and guns Gary does not know are all on the scene. In his true, 'I am detective Sigrist style', Gary begins strolling right by all the guns and screaming faces right into the house where the initial argument begins. Why be involving yourself in a fight the bad guys are already losing, and women too. Most women are worse than men. Unfortunately, it usually requires a spiked heel to the shin before an officer is justified in kicking the shit out of these hormonal bitches.

Like I am saying, Gary is familiar with this residence. During his patrol years he is constantly running back and forth on weekend nights to break up arguments between the husband and wife. The old man is an employee of a local factory and a professional drinker, more of a drinker than an employee. On most Friday nights the wife is always welcoming her husband home without his paycheck. Money gone, there is no more service. It is time to stagger home and beat on the wife just to round out the night's activities.

Now, the one possession the woman loves is her old china cabinet. It is the kind with curved glass around the corners, the type of glass that is wavy, old and imperfect. This thing is an antique when Gary is first taking his calls to this location. The woman is small, about five foot four. She does offer up a mean right cross, but is always jumping up to land it properly during her and her husband's extramarital encounters. Gary is always taking the guy to jail and telling him a good ass-kicking is in the works if he ever really hurts the little gal.

This particular evening the little gal is sticking half in and half out of the second shelf of the china cabinet. The paramedics are trying to get her out of the thing so that attending to her wounds is possible. The old man is sitting on the living room couch in handcuffs. It is obvious that a piece of the glass from the china cabinet is still in the wife's left eye, probably causing blindness. Long story short, Gary is kicking the shit out of the husband even before help is capable of arriving from the outside. Gary is holding onto the handcuffs, just so the guy isn't falling down on him. The handcuffs are in the front of the man, instead of the back as protocol dictates. He is pulling the man toward him and knocking out another tooth or two with every forward motion.

This evening is as close a call for the premature end of Gary's career as it gets. Instead some bullshit report turns up about the guy attacking my brother. The husband now is carrying around the nickname of 'Gummy' and I am aware of no apologies from my big brother. Every year a Christmas card comes floating into my brother's mail box. It is from the wife with the same note, 'Here is looking at you. Gummy is a very good boy now and has been on the wagon since you two spoke'. During conversations when this topic comes up at bars among friends and other police, Gary simply responds.

"It's just something to do with Mom having a china cabinet like that one. That is, if you believe shrinks. Besides, I'm trying to put together an ass-beating squad. We need an ass-beating squad."

All hands at the table are always in the air. There are plenty of volunteers, but cops think a little different than the mainstream. Finding out that Mom's china cabinet is delivered to the guy's wife after Mother's death is, one of the most touching things I am always remembering about my brother. There are some alcoholics who are idiots and some who are just alcoholics. Gary is a different breed. He is an alcoholic with a heart; that his heart is often black as coal is testament to his desire to be helping people who are suffering much of the same abuse he is carrying around in his memories. Our old man's belt really, really hurts and hearing Gary's silence during these beatings is worse than hearing screams. Silent screams are the worse kind of all.

Right now, everything is alright. He is sleeping like a little baby. A big drunken little baby, but a little baby just the same. I turn in for the night. In the morning, Gary is gone. A note is on the morgue table top.

"Thanks for dinner. Not much longer. Be a good boy."

Chapter Thirty-Four

(A Strange Conversation)

"So, are all the bases covered?"

"Everything is ready for the transition."

"This is something we have been waiting for a long time."

"You taught me patience. You taught me that information is knowledge."

"The only downside is that she is not with us."

"She is always with us. Yesterday is but a reflection of life in a mirror."

Gary is thinking that perhaps all of this is just something people always want to be true. His apprehension is common to everyone. Age is always the bearer of a final reality. Hope for immortality grows stronger during one's declining years. Gary recently doubts the truth of long held beliefs under the tutelage of intellectuals who picture themselves great man. He is thinking, 'See it through to the end. There is no way back'. Gary sees his own reflection in the mirror as one of promises kept. Doubting now is something he dare not express. Doubting comes with consequences and Gary does not want to be part of these consequences others must soon bear. Too, the final result of this thing that is rapidly drawing to its conclusion is a rightful reward for those believers still clutching to the staff of brotherhood, the thin blue line and other such crap. Still, it is something to believe. Believing in something is very important.

"And you are certain of William's response."

"Of most things about William I am certain of nothing, but about this I am sure."

"Why so sure?"

"He is boxing himself in. He is slipping day by day. He knows this and, like cocaine, knows his penchant for art must find some happy medium to prevent his own demise. Once this is over, I know he will accept it as the helping hand he desperately needs."

"A brother's love is that strong?"

"As is a son's love for his father."

"And the others, what will the others think?"

"They will think what they are told to think. It is all about one mind, one cause and one future. Besides, some are dying. New blood is in demand. All must relinquish a place and fall into the mirror of life. This is what you teach. This is what I believe."

"It is too bad that there was not more mixing of the blood. That thing with Grandpa Pope was unfortunate. I am sure he holds no ill will against any of us. I am also sure our decision was the correct decision. I know he was ashamed of his son, traipsing around foreign countries in search of a new child to ravage. There are limits, even for us. Grandpa Pope was too observant, too smart for his own good. Still, what with his background and all, it is a shame he chose to challenge rather than join us. His demise was a long and hard decision for the group. That his wife shared the burden is truly a tragedy, but the vows do say for better or worse. That thing with his son and the plane crash and all was a God send. Please excuse the term."

"You should have seen him the other night."

There is a slight pause in the conversation. The subject is abruptly changing and, like a man trying to keep up with his wife's thinking, a moment of clarity is in order.

"Oh, you mean the Bobby Adams thing."

"William just reaches out and pulls the cheese plate and we sit there snacking like nothing ever took place."

"That is interesting, humorous and macabre all at once."

"What did his eyes say to you that evening?"

"They are warm and caring and dark at the same time. Does that make any sense to you?"

"Everything is perspective. Those that are lost live in their own worlds. They love what they love. They hate what they hate. Their world is as real as a normal person's world. The definition of normal is what is always being debated."

The last of the wine is consumed and the meal is finished in silence. Gary stands from the table and smiles at the person sitting across from him.

"Thanks for dinner. Thanks for the conversation. If only life at the mansion had been like this when I was growing up."

There is a last response from across the table.

"Gary, remember the mirror. What you see from here on out is your future. That it took this long is my fault. Don't worry about doubting. Normal is normal. Faith overcomes all of that other shit."

It is very late. The moon sees Gary arriving at his cabin. The moon's light is casting a soft pale yellow sheet across the waters of his lake. It is as though the color is a blanket spreading upon the calm water. Gary is imagining pulling back the water's yellow blanket and laying down for a good night's sleep. Gary is very tired. This constant looking after William is taking its toll. He is thinking of the very near future when everything is over and normal again, as normal as is possible under the circumstances.

The row boat moves into the water like a glass slipper, barely making a ripple on the water's surface. Gary is gently pulling the oars through the water. He is moving out and across the center of the lake toward a little cove just like so many times before. This cove is his place. It is a place he shares with no one, not even William. People just need secret spaces to be keeping secret things. Gary's secret things are his thoughts, his thoughts since childhood. Gary understands William's need for his secret room. It sometimes seems like they are one person born at different times. The boat's oars are pulled from the water at just the right spot. The oar's remaining little waves know their job and are pushing the boat to its resting spot, a spot underneath some low hanging limbs. Seeing into this secret space is impossible. Seeing out of this space is another thing. Gary is remembering his conversation over dinner. He is looking into the night sky. The sky is full of stars and the moon is shining so brightly. His mind is wandering beyond the star's light and the moon's pale yellow glow. Soon, he is fast asleep. His mirror is dark. The vastness of space is engulfing his every thought.

William is trying to sleep, too. He is tossing and turning. His thoughts are of his promise to his brother and of his deceased mother. Maybe, he is thinking, being my own art is not so out of the question. Maybe, they are better off without him. William is inventing again. He is inventing in his mind. There is a motor. The motor is large enough to lift a body, his body. He is binding his leg. He is being pulled by his legs into an upside down position. He is hanging there, dangling over his own canvas. His head is lying in a slot of sorts and the slot has smaller slots, smaller troughs. The troughs stop just above the canvas, the canvas on the floor that is waiting all of his secrets and all of his art. He is pressing the button in his hand. It is the button controlling the blade. The blade is flipping down. It is a very quick process. In his dream the blade is moving in slow motion. William is watching it penetrate. He is watching the blood leaving his body, watching the red river of life flowing into the first slot. Seconds later, William is sitting straight up in bed screaming.

"No, no, no! Mommy, Mommy, Mommy!"

A sweet voice is responding.

"Yes, my child. What is it?"

"Stop me. Stop me. I forgot. Who is to hang my art?"

William is walking around the morgue room waiting for the coffee to finish brewing. He is recalling the last part of his dream.

His mother is standing at the edge of his canvas, the one spread so neatly on the floor and under the various funnel openings. She is holding William's head in her hands and looking into his loving and dark eyes.

"It is too late, son. You should have waited on your brother. Still, it is a very nice piece of art."

William sits at his desk. The desk is in a little cubby-hole area near the elevator door for his apartment. The coffee cup is very hot. His hands are cupping the hot glass. He is not noticing the heat. He swallows a sip or two of coffee. His cell phone is next to his coffee cup. His eyes are fixating on the cell-phone's face.

"Ring you bastard, ring. I can't take much more of this."

The waves are picking up at Gary's lake near his cabin. He does not notice. His mind is saying that his mother is still rocking him in her arms.

Chapter Thirty-Five

(My biggest dream, I think.)

I am not mad. I am not insane. This is my position all along. The reason for bringing this point up again is the same reason I did in the very first two lines of this story. Seeing my point is something I am counting on from objective eyes outside of my own life's experiences. God knows that the people caring for me are not open to the truth. They are blinded by what they see. Their intellect is being held hostage by their basic senses, sight being the major one in this scenario. This is not about my art. It is not about my disappointments. It is simply about the truth and my current circumstances. I am hell bent on eventually straightening things out. Treating me this way is something that I am not willing to let go unpunished. Still, this is about nothing more than the betrayal of the one thing in life I am, in my times of need, always wrapping my trust, my very soul around.

Gary is knocking on my apartment's door. It is about two in the morning. My nerves are long overdue for a good bonding between myself and my big brother. I no longer find myself saying I am sorry for my little indiscretions. I am beginning to believe his forgiveness is a lost cause. I am surprised at this unannounced intrusion into my sleep, the first good night's sleep I am experiencing in a very long time. Like any tragedy, once one is accepting of one's fate, exhaustion is the end result. Most people who are nearing their executions for this crime or that fall into this category. A good meal, a restful night of sleep and the inevitable is all that is expected of the coming day. My mind is no longer wandering around in some pool of logic that is telling me to trust or to expect miracles. My bed is my bed and I must sleep in it until the very end. Gary's eyes are very large. I never realize this before. He is looking down at me and I am looking back at him. Then, there are the words I am waiting to hear. I do not want this to be another dream, like the dreams of recent where he comes to me and everything is alright again. I am even willing to sacrifice my art for his love and acceptance. Really, to be honest, my last art is not as satisfying as my first art. I am in an artist's block, much like writers are often in a state of writer's block. Anyway, Gary is staring down at me.

"William, you need to come with me now. Everything is going to be alright. It is time to get back out among the living. Can you do that?"

I am pulling myself up from my sleep and from my bed. I am feeling Gary's hand supporting the small of my back. His touch is very sensuous. I am hoping this is not a dream and that he is finally here. I am reaching my right hand upward and grabbing onto his upper arm. His arm's muscles are strong and firm. I am feeling the blood rushing through his arm. No, this is not a dream. My brother is finally here and he is keeping his promise. I am sitting upright with my legs dangling over the edge of my bed. The floor is cold. My floor is always cold. This is Michigan. The breath of Michigan is like a human breath always in the grips of one too many icy breath mints. I am wiggling my toes. My toes are cracking as if breaking the ice away from my joints. As of late, I am sleeping more and more. It is as though I am sleeping my way to my death as I am waiting on my big brother's return.

"I can do whatever you want me to do as long as you are here for me."

"Good. Good. All is forgiven. Now, hurry and get dressed. Don't pack anything. We are going on a little road trip. We need to do a little bonding and get all of this sorted out before returning to the mansion."

"Returning to the mansion?"

"That's right, chump. We are gonn'a get our up and comings, like your friend Teddy used to say."

I am up and hurrying around the apartment. I am not even thinking of the business. Most of it is siphoned away during my confinement. I am, at present, a funeral broker more than a funeral home. There are rumors that I am deathly ill. There is very little activity from the community. It is as though they also know of my predicament and are respecting my space until the proper times is at hand. I am thinking, 'How much does my big brother really control of this dying city?' There are no more calls from potential special clients or, on my part, thoughts of venturing out into the city for fresh art. These parts of my life are just fading from my center of desire. I am almost like the man who is sexed into sexlessness. It is like the psychiatric philosophy about therapy that immerses one in their own vices so they no longer desire those vices. An example is the swinger generations of the late sixties and early seventies. Oh, that sort of thing still exists today. I am not saying it does not. What I am saying is that the sixties and seventies are a double slam dunk when one is considering the drugs that accompany this sort of lifestyle. Too much of anything is bad for a person. A little moderation is always in order. Shit. I am sounding like a Republican. See what I mean? I am just so grateful that Gary is here to look after me. This is my thinking during the beginning of the darkest chapters of what is remaining of my life.

Not knowing what is in store, I find myself picking an outfit that allows for both formal and informal settings. This is exciting. Getting out is exciting. Maybe it is something as simple as going up to the cabin for a little fishing, where we really are there for other reasons than fishing. I don't care. I am free again. I am free at last, free at last. God almighty, I am free at last. Sorry, Dr. King. Even a white man is capable of getting all hyped up on words like these. It isn't Martin Luther King Day again, is it? Loosing track of time is easy. Sorry, if I am offending anyone. Oh, fuck it. Free at last, free at last. God almighty, this white asshole is free at last. My sense of humor is back. This is a good thing. I am looking forward to the stale smell of the Detroit air.

The elevator from my apartment jerks to a stop and its door is opening to the morgue area when there is the wonderful smell of coffee. It is hitting me in the face and filling my lungs. I am imagining entering into The Morgue Café of Espresso and Coffee. Gary is standing at the coffee maker. He is sweetening my coffee. I know it is just the way I like it. My big brother knows the things I like. This is part of the reason I love him so much. He is so kind and understanding. He is really in need of a pussy instead of a dick. I think he is a woman at heart, but with a really bad temper from time to time. I am standing in the elevator. The door is open. The door is closing. I am standing too long. Push the button to open the door, asshole. I am pushing the button. The door is opening a second time. Gary is standing just outside the elevator door. He is handing me a cup of coffee.

"Here. Drink this, William. There will be time for alcohol when we get where we are going."

"Where are we going?"

Gary is smiling at me. I love the curve of his lip line. I am thinking I must quit thinking these thoughts. I am not a fucking queer. No, that is the wrong word. People do not accept queer, fagot or words like that anymore. Anyway whatever the right word is I am not it. I hate all of this new political correctness. Pretty soon fucking is going to require a certain angle of penetration before being classified as really fucking. Where are these thoughts coming from? It doesn't matter. I am going on a road trip with my big brother.

"Where we are going is a secret. You do like secrets, don't you?"

"I love secrets."

I am looking at my machine. I am looking at it sitting there by one of the morgue tables. I am recalling the last time it is used. It is used the night Gary delivers that beautiful alley victim to me. I am remembering never thanking him for the gesture. 'Rude of me' is what I am thinking. Remembering to apologize is in order.

"Do you want a donut?"

There is a box of a dozen donuts sitting on the counter next to the coffee pot. I really like jam filled donuts.

"Some habits die hard, big brother?"

This is a reference to his police background.

"For someone just out of confinement, you seem not to have lost your sense of humor. Do you know just how much fucking trouble you have caused me over the last couple of years?"

All of a sudden I am plummeting from a very high, high, to a very low, low. I am a very bad boy. Two sips of coffee later I am sitting my cup on the counter and throwing myself into Gary's arms. I am weeping uncontrollably. I am asking over and over for his forgiveness and promising never, ever, to be like this again. Gary is whispering into my ear.

"Now, now, there is no reason to be getting so melodramatic. Like I said, everything is forgiven. This is a new start and we are going on a road trip."

I am very embarrassed by my little outburst. I am using a paper towel to wipe the remaining tears from the side of my face. I am sure Gary is thinking I am a complete basket case. I am sure he is thinking that maybe right now is not a good time for a road trip. I am thinking, 'straighten up, you fuck head'. You are going to blow the whole thing by being such a blithering idiot.

"Sorry. I have just been alone for what seems like such a long time."

"It was necessary."

"I know that. Going on a road trip, huh? I like the sound of that."

"Drink the rest of your coffee. We'll get going."

I am gulping the coffee down. I am feeling queasy. I am holding onto the counter by the coffee maker. I am falling. I am feeling the strong press of Gary's hand against the small of my back once again. The next sound I am hearing is the sound of bumble bees, very loud bumble bees.

"Bzzzzzzzzzzzzzzzzzzzzzzzzzzzzzzzzzzzzzz."

Chapter Thirty-Six

The damn bee just keeps buzzing around my head. I am unable to swat the thing away and am afraid it is going to sting me at any moment. The buzzing is getting louder and louder. What the hell is a person to do? I am unable to move my arms or my legs. I think my sight is returning, but it is fading in and out. There is a feeling of movement and the movement seems to be so fast that it is slow. Do you know what I am talking about?

I am thinking back. How is it possible that I am in this position? I am remembering getting out of bed. I am remembering putting my feet on that cold floor back at my apartment. Am I still in my apartment? Am I having a heart attack or a stroke? I am unable to move my limbs. It is probably a stroke. Being under a lot of pressure, drinking too much and living the way I live is probably the reason for this stroke. Yes, I am thinking it is a stroke. Still, I am wishing the sound of that fucking bee buzzing inside my head might go away.

Gary is urging me to hurry up. He is urging me to finish my coffee. No, it isn't the coffee. Gary is not capable of doing something like that to his own brother. Is, he? Maybe he is. That motherfucker is the one responsible for me being the way I am right now. There is something in the coffee. I am going to look at the coffee mug. Fuck, I am forgetting. I am unable to move. Where am I? I am remembering Gary talking about going on a road trip. Is this one of his practical jokes like the time on the dock when we are fishing? If it is a practical joke, I am going to kick his practical ass when I am able to move my arms and legs again. I still hear the buzzing. Now, I am hearing a voice very near my left ear. It is speaking to me.

"You just need to stay calm. Gary wants you to stay calm and says that this is the last part of a journey you must travel for everything to be alright again."

Alright, alright I get it. Gary is involved. Why can't my big brother just tell me what is going on? Why the hell is he always so secretive about everything? Ok, ok maybe I am a little off the wall sometimes. There is a point where people just have to trust one another. I am his brother, after all. I am feeling better knowing that I am not dead and my brother is responsible for my condition. Is it possible? Is thinking possible if you are dead? I am thinking that one is not capable of knowing unless they are dead. Then, how does one pass on the truth of this condition? There are just so many questions in life. Being concerned with questions about death is inappropriate at the moment. My conclusion is that I am alive, but in some sort of physical state either induced by my own lifestyle or by Gary. Either way, it is my opinion that Gary is taking care of me. Yes, this is the proper conclusion. I am doing as the voice asks. I am putting my faith in Gary.

The drug bag is being adjusted. Its flow tap is being opened a little wider and I am becoming drowsy again. I am floating away into another one of my dreams. I am in my morgue back in Detroit. I am standing in the middle of all the bodies or body parts ever residing in my funeral home. I am on a deadline. I am cutting on this one and stitching on another one. There is no time for wiping the sweat from my forehead. I am, after all, on a deadline. There is a gallery of people watching me while I am working. They are all chanting in unison.

"Hurry up. Hurry up. We can't wait on you forever."

I am looking over my shoulder from time to time. I am trying not to let the chanting distract me from my work. I am on a deadline. I am catching up. The bodies are piling up. Being away from my profession so long is a bad thing. I am rusty at my trade. Why are these bodies previously buried back again? Is something wrong with my initial work? Did I give some sort of warranty I am not remembering? Am I making good on my promise and this is all a 'do-over'. Finally, I am unable to take all of that chanting in the background. The gallery is driving me crazy. I am facing the gallery. I am screaming at them. I know it is not a very professional thing to be doing.

"Will you all just shut the fuck up? I am trying to work here. Can't you see I am trying to work here?"

There is a soft response from the gallery. They are not mad. They are just responding.

"William, William we are disappointed with you. Here we sit patiently waiting and you spend your time fixing something that is already dead. Why aren't you concentrating on your art, on the living?"

My eyes are moving from face to face. There is the red scarf, the blue one, the yellow one, the orange one and on and on. All of my victims are here. They are dead. Aren't they? Maybe I am dead and I am trying to bring the dead back to life. Is this the only way of bringing myself back to life? My victims are toying with me. If I am dead, they are going to do horrible things to me. Damn, it. Picking the wrong art genre is following me to my grave. Where is my dancing machine? I am feeling like dancing is the thing. We are all just going to forgive and forget and dance our way back into the land of the living. I am still looking into the eyes of the gallery. I am bowing to each and every one. I am hearing myself speaking.

"May I have this dance?"

The gallery is responding as one voice.

"Fool me once, shame on you. Fool me twice, shame on me."

Every middle finger is raised. I am, so to speak, fucked. I am also tiring of this dream and my thoughts are drifting away into some place dark and black. I am remembering it as sleep because on returning from this deep dark space, the buzzing is back.

The bee is sounding different. It is as though it is slowing down. Maybe the thing is tiring and soon falls dead from the air it is calling its home. Insects are not capable of living that long. Humans, if they are evasive enough, just wait them out; much like whatever is out there, in the unknown, is patiently waiting on our arrival.

There is a screeching sound. It is the sound of rubber hitting concrete. It is true. Gary and I are on a road trip. The buzzing is slower and slower. There is a jolt. There is slow movement. There are a few turns, another small lurch forward and then, silence. The plane's propellers are still and silent.

Moving my arms and legs is still impossible. My eyes are covered. Seeing is impossible. I am being carried. The legs on my gurney are collapsing into the horizontal position as I am being loaded into the ambulance. The back door is closing. The vehicle is moving away from the landing area. There is no siren. There is just silence. I am listening. I am not alone.

"Gary? Are you here? Is that your breathing?"

My brother's voice fills the silence.

"Yes, William. I came ahead to meet you. Remember that everything is going to be alright."

I am sobbing.

"I want to. I want to believe, but God what did I ever do to deserve this?"

I am feeling Gary's hand patting my chest.

"There, there calm down. Calling out His name really won't help."

The blackness is back and all I am hearing is, 'Road trip, road trip, road trip'.

Chapter Thirty-Seven

These events are things I am aware of only after my return from our road trip, a road trip that is more a trip for me than for Gary and me.

Gary is at my funeral home. It is very late in the evening. He is smoking cigarette after cigarette. Gary does not smoke. I, on the other hand, do smoke. Come to think of it, I am dying for a cigarette. He is standing in the morgue area. He is thinking out loud.

"Now would be a good time for conversation. What is the chance of a conversation in a place like this? Jack-shit-nothing is the chance. Well, it is time to get on with it. I'm not forgetting anything. I am sure of that. At least, I think I am sure."

Gary is humming to himself. It is close to Christmas and the tune just seems to fit his current situation. Gary's voice really is quite good. I am thinking that being there to hear him singing is something I am sad about missing.

"I'm making a list. I'm checking it twice. I know I am naughty and not very nice."

Gary is wearing gloves. He is wearing gloves not because he is worrying about prints. He is wearing gloves because it is colder than a Weiner dog's dick dragging down the streets of my neighborhood. Too, the electric is off due to another one of those Lake Erie storms our overdressed weather people are always talking about. I am admitting here that the women are really knock outs anymore. One time I am very drunk and end up standing on my head with my feet bracing me up against my bedroom wall. I am trying to look up this one female reporter's dress. It is one of those 'don't try this at home kids' moments. Seeing anything this way is out of the question. My advice is to just imagine them naked in your mind and be done with it. Every time I am watching the news and listening to the same thing over and over, I am thinking that I already know this shit. Just get to the late night stand up already. The very repetition of these talking heads is most likely responsible for me standing on my head trying to look up that female reporter's dress. Boredom is a driving force in all of our lives. Living with boredom is not my style. Oh, too, there are the car commercials. One car commercial follows another and another. I am living in Motor-Fucking-City for crying out loud. Give me a break. Sorry, I am off subject. It is just that the memories are coming back. Some memories mean something, but most don't mean shit.

Gary is inspecting my dancing machine. He is recalling watching me in the basement from the secret passageways winding underneath and through the mansion's false walls. He is remembering a few of my little inventions and is mesmerized by the way my machine is capable of mimicking human movement. He is thinking what I am often thinking. 'Is it possible to add feet and joints instead of hinges?' Great minds are always thinking alike.

Gary is thinking all of this as he is rolling my machine over to an end morgue body lockup. The lockup is on the top of two other lockups. Mostly, we are never higher than three. I am often thinking about this wasted space. It isn't like Detroit has a tourist season like Key West when things are always getting a little out of hand. Too, the crime rate in Detroit is temporarily down. Most of the dick-heads are done killing the other dick-heads and are waiting on new blood to start the cycle all over again. Gary is looking up at the top locker.

"Crap. This thing doesn't extend upwards. I'll have to get the roll rack and carry the fucker down to the table."

Gary is still talking to himself. The rack rolls very easily. Gary is placing the step-rack in position. He is one step up when the dam thing starts rolling.

"God damn it. God damn it. Get your head out of your ass and lock the wheels in place."

On his second attempt Gary is successful at getting to the top of the locker units, pulling out the body tray, draping the heavy green plastic bag containing the body over his shoulder and moving back down the moveable steps. Halfway down his back is beginning to itch and he is violently concentrating on getting down the steps before he is unable to stand the itching anymore. Gary is mentally addressing the corpse hanging over his shoulder. The corpse is not stiff, but it is not very bendable which is making the situation all that much more difficult.

"Don't suppose you might be able to scratch just underneath my right shoulder blade. Would, you? I know. It is a dumb question."

Gary is finally down from the upper body locker unit. My dancing table is in the down position, the bed position. The body from the locker is unceremoniously plopped onto the table. The rolling steps are returned to their original position against the opposite wall of the morgue room. Walking back over to the dancing machine Gary hops up on top of the body bag. He is hopping his ass along the corpse inside of the body bag and mashing down the body's contorted form into a somewhat flat form. This really is kind of funny from a mortician's point of view. What my brother is planning on doing makes the effort even more humorous. Anyway, with each bounce he is hearing a bone or two snap.

"Oh, I bet that hurts. That was a good one. I think I broke your dick on that one."

In all fairness to my dumb ass brother, there really is not a whole hell of a lot to do in Detroit to pass the time.

Gary is rolling the dancing table off of the elevator as it is stopping just outside my apartment's door. He is remembering something he has forgotten. The dancing machine is now in an upright position. Before going back down into the morgue Gary finds himself speaking to the bag full of dead flesh and bone.

"Now, don't go anywhere. I'll be right back. Shit, I'm starting to sound like little William."

The scalpel scissors from the morgue are where they always are. If nothing else, I am anal about my instruments. My instruments are more orderly and cleaner than most of the instruments doctors are using for their surgeries. Why the hell do you think so many people get sick when they go to the hospital? You don't see any of my patients coming back to life, do you? This is just a side note and something I think is really worth consideration the next time you are at the hospital. Gary quickly returns.

My bed coverings are pulled back, the body bag containing the corpse is laid on my bed. The scissors are for cutting the zipper away from the body bag. Gary is wearing a mask over his nose during this procedure. Some police are used to the smell and some are never used to the smell. Once the body bag's zipper is cut away it is rolled up and Gary puts it into his jacket pocket. Good, he is thinking. Everything is ready. Pulling the covers up over the body Gary is talking to himself again.

"I feel I owe you one big apology my friend, but this is for the good of my little brother. I am sorry about your partner, Bobby, and especially about having to burn your hat. William really loved that fucking hat of yours."

T.J. Plack's face is very well preserved considering the time it has been resting in the upper body locker in my morgue. Later, Gary is telling me how it looks as though the son-of-a-bitch isn't really dead, but just sleeping. My response is that this statement is a line for the funeral home. The mind is always playing tricks on you. You know. 'Oh, they have never looked better. One would think they are still alive'.

A small van is waiting in the vehicle room. My sports car is not there. The funeral home hearse is in the garage area. My special room items are in the back of the van and there is enough room for my dancing table. My big brother really is a very thoughtful person and the thought of me ever doubting him is always nearly bringing me to tears. He is forgetting my first piece of art, the one over my bed. This is forgivable, considering the pain-in-the ass that is his little brother.

The last thing on the agenda is the cremation oven. Setting it on full blast and leaving the door open, Gary momentarily warms himself before returning to the van and back out into the cold Detroit night. My bedroom is already in flames and the accelerants from a good friend of my brother are doing a wonderful job of sending Mr. T.J. Plack straight down into the fires of hell. Gary is always telling me to deal with professionals. What better friend for a job like this than a crooked retired fire fighter. Plack is or was a private investigator. I am sure he is going to hell for something a little amiss during one of his investigations.

The van containing my trophies and dancing table is moving down a Detroit side street when the sirens begin blaring in the distance. My funeral home is already nearing ashes. The buildings are close in this poor part of the city and the fire fighters are worrying more about the fire spreading than they are about the loss of one life. Gary is still humming his Christmas tune.

“I’m making a list. I’m checking it twice. I’m just another naughty little fucker in Detroit tonight.”

At least, this is the way I am remembering him telling me the story.

Chapter Thirty-Eight

(Painful Days)

Giving consideration to the pain my victims suffer is not my nature. If you are honest, you must admit that my victims suffer very little. A little twist of the scarf with a few minutes loss of breath and it is all over. If one is judging by time I do accept the argument that Gary's way is more humane. A quick bullet in the center of one's forehead is a kind of, 'now you're here, now you aren't' sort of thing. Gary's type of killing isn't art. It is skill and, properly executed, there is little if any pain involved. I know that you are thinking that using someone's blood for art is a little excessive, but they are already dead. What is the harm? There is no harm. Good artists often shock people. Can you imagine taking a piece of my art home and later discovering the color combinations are from Aunt Ellen's blood? I am thinking not all people are at odds with this approach. I am hearing some, especially relatives, applauding me for making the piece so personal. Still, I am the first one willing to admit that great things often require a certain amount of pain and suffering. This is just my opinion.

In my darkest hours, before knowing the truth of my life's new direction, I am suffering a great deal of pain. This, coupled with the fact that I am in and out of consciousness because of the drugs being administered, is taking its toll on both my mind and body. The only reason I am so lucid here is that these dark hours are over, I now understand the reason for them and they are quickly fading into dusty drawers of my mind's storage vault. The real upside of such an event is that one loses a great deal of weight. I am a real fat ass when arriving on that gurney at the airport some time ago. I.V. drips and liquid food is not capable of ever replacing a good steak, mashed potatoes drowning in gravy and a full bodied beer. During my confinement and procedure I am always thinking about real food. I am definitely surviving without it, but I am always thinking about good food. Too, I am always dreaming about making new art. It is most likely a good thing I do not, at this point, know about the destruction of my funeral home and my first impressionist piece hanging over my bed. Some things are just hard to give up. It is like a boy's first puppy. He does not like feeding and watering it and he kicks it from time to time, but there are always fond memories of the little shitter later on in the kid's life. Come to think of it, age is like a very slow bullet. It is the one thing that is capable of taking you down without people ever paying attention to the fact that they are dying. Maybe Gary's way of killing really is art. Could it be that it is just so fast that one does not have the time to be appreciating it? Is there a way to capture that instant, that moment when it is happening? Is there a way to be putting that instant on a canvas? I am thinking technology is the only way. I am envisioning a little camera of sorts sitting right there in the back of someone's skull. It is waiting on the pain and destruction and, at the very moment of, is capturing what only the victim is feeling. It is capturing it for you and me and the rest of the world. God, the possibilities are limitless. Let's get back to my pain, my situation during these dark hours of my life.

After the first procedure my finger-tips feel like they are burning, as if they are in touch with a hot frying pan. I am unable to tell you much more about this awful feeling other than saying that playing the piano is out of the question. I am holding my hands in front of my eyes and attempting to get a good view. My arms bend only at the elbow joints, the top of my chest is under restraint and my face is in some sort of mask. The mask is in place, but feeling it against my skin I am receiving a sensation of it floating on a thin layer of some sort of gel, most likely for keeping the skin underneath moisturized. Bending my fingers is not possible and my vision is restricted by the small openings in the mask that are serving as eye holes. I am seeing only the top half of my hands. They are bandaged and moving my finger joints is impossible. I am thinking that I am in another one of those dreams that are so real they seem like they are not a dream at all. Still, there is the pain, the real pain that is keeping me awake despite me being tired. The throbbing is there as well. It is keeping the pain company. I find myself trying to turn my hands over so that my fingers are pointing upward, but my restraints are not allowing it. At some point there is a strong pair of hands lifting up each arm and placing a pillow underneath my arms. This is allowing my fingertips to not be touching the mattress. I am grateful for this little gesture of kindness. I am thinking that being skinned alive is not something to be wishing on anyone. Quick death and quick art is the answer. It is all a matter of respect. I am not one to be advocating pain where it is possible to circumvent it and still achieve the same results. Do you know what I mean? I am humane like that. I am sure of this one little detail.

Most of my body waste is liquid and worrying about pissing is a thing of the past. I am just doing it and it is going away. I am thinking that some sort of medical bag is attached to me but am not a hundred percent sure of that. Trying to get answers is impossible. The mask over my face is making it impossible for me to communicate in any other form than undecipherable murmurs. Even so, distress is a tone more than a word and this is the reason my arms are placed in that position atop pillows.

Day by day the pain is going away and, in my opinion, I am on the mend. Becoming a little more lucid, I am trying to count the passing time. You know…first there is the counting of the seconds forming the minutes, adding the minutes together that are forming the hours and then adding the hours together that are forming the days. This is the theory. Making it to an hour is my best effort. This counting is also a way of taking my mind off of those itches that I am unable to scratch. Where is a fucking bed-bug when you need one? That is my question. Did you ever have an itch on your foot between the bottom of your foot and the inside sole of your shoe? My advice is to not try scratching inside your shoe while driving down the highway at seventy miles per hour. There are a few dead highway markers just outside of Detroit that are willing to testify that this is a dangerous practice. There is finally conversation at my bedside. I am grateful for this. Realizing just how loud silence is, in my opinion, cannot be comprehended without experiencing it first hand over long periods of time. When the sound of your heart and your own breathing is the only sound available to you, you find yourself longing for even the sound of Heavy Metal Music. I note quickly here that I hate that shit under normal circumstance. Anyway, I am finally hearing voices.

"How is he doing, nurse?"

"He is really doing quite well, under the circumstances. His brain waves are settled down, his heart rate is normal, urine flow is good. The solids are all gone from his bowels from the initial flush out."

"I know. I was here when you hit him with the first dose. I didn't know anyone could crap that much."

"That is why you are the doctor. It is worth a few extra years of study so you can leave the smelly stuff to us."

"You've been bitchy since the day I hired you."

"If this sort of thing keeps up, it won't get any better either."

I am hearing a chuckle. The chuckle is male. I am hearing a giggle. The giggle is female. My mind is racing. It is thinking that they might be considering fucking one another after my restraints are off and hands are unwrapped. My eyes are moving as far left or right as they can, considering the mask is still sitting on my face. I am thinking that the plastic contraption is sliding a little to the left because of the gel and am remembering some sort of syringe being placed near the upper left and right side from time to time, most likely for squirting more gel along my forehead and face line. I am trying to talk, but the words are still nothing more than a garbled sound. Their dialogue is continuing.

"It is time to take a look-see."

I am feeling my left arm being moved first. Next there is the sensation of cool fresh air, air-conditioned air, on my freshly exposed skin. Telling you just what a soothing feeling this is can't be put into words. I am feeling a pair of strong hands holding my hand. The grip is on the top of my hand and the palm of my hand. My hand is being twisted this way and that.

"They look very, very good. If the right one is a good, I may be upping my price to Interpol and the C.I.A."

"If they find out you are freelancing, you may need a little work done yourself."

"Don't be so pessimistic, my lovely. This is our way out. You do know that a rich family with this sort of specific need is our way out of this fucking furnace full of beans and rice."

I am lying right there, at least hallway lucid. I am thinking, 'Hey, I'm right here. Let me in on what the fuck is going on'. I am just a piece of meat and the talking continues. It is jibber this and jibber that. I am fixating on the bandages coming off of my right hand. Ahhhh, there is that feeling again. There is that cold air. I am thinking that freezing some of my future art may start up a whole new genre. No, it is too much trouble keeping art cold or frozen. I am thinking about those assholes that are always doing snow or ice art. Getting one little warm up above thirty-two degrees and your life's work is nothing more than mush in the sun.

"Everything is looking good. Tilt him up. I want to check his blood flow when he is near upright. I want a pulse count."

The next thing is a bright light in each of my eyes. I am feeling like someone is shining one of those big city spotlights into the back of my brain. My eyes are tearing.

"Good, good, we have good function all the way around."

After a little needle prick, darkness is next. I am out like the old proverbial light. Saying for sure is not possible, but this is what I am imagining taking place.

My straps are removed. I am stripped naked except for the mask and am washed down with a sponge. Just because this is my story, I am thinking I am being washed down by a beautiful blond nurse with size thirty-eight tits. There are two sponges. A sponge is attached to each of her breasts. She is dipping those things is a suds solution and allowing me to wring the sponges out when she is finished. The sponges are still attached to her. They are like wonderful squishy pasties you are allowed to play with, like a reward or something. I am getting an erection. Either that or I am upside down. How is one to tell in this situation?

The long and short of this whole recollection is that waking up is not as pleasant an experience. Remember that burning sensation in my fingers. It is now all over my face. Any muscle movement of my facial muscles at all is nearly unbearable. Screaming like one of my victims is not possible because of this fucking mask. No, I must be taking that last statement back. This is my thinking process. The mask is gone. These are bandages. I am beginning to breathe very heavily. My thinking process is that this is my attempt at bringing cool cold air into my lungs for helping put out the fire which is raging all over my face. There is a voice. I am hearing it off in the distance, most likely near my bedside, but still off in the distance.

"Give me calm, William. Give me calm. This is the last hurdle. I am going to give you something for the pain."

The needle prick is first. Darkness is next. Finally there is that place people always go before the doctor starts cutting. My last thought is, 'Who the fuck is going to ask me to count from ten backwards?"

The next thing I am remembering is being strapped into a chair. I am wearing a strait-jacket. Two faces are looking at me. One is the face of a nurse. Her tits are ok, but they don't approach a thirty-eight 'D' cup. I am guessing that having everything isn't always possible. Settling for the rest of my dream is acceptable. I am getting aroused again. It is amazing how horny one is capable of getting even under these extreme circumstances. Maybe it is just the medicine. Do you think it is just the medicine? My art is usually the only thing eliciting this type of response. The doctor isn't old and he isn't young. His breath is also terrible smelling. I contribute this to too many meals of road kill tacos. By now, I am guessing I am in Mexico somewhere. I am thinking I am a patient motherfucker and that I am going to kill the both of them just as soon as this strait-jacket is off. This thought is pushed aside by a soft voice coming from the other side of the room. Twisting my head as far as possible I am catching the glimpse of a third figure in the room. It is Gary. It is my big brother.

"I'm hoping you still love me after all of this, William."

There is silence in the room. I am mumbling again. Tears are welling up in my eyes. I am realizing that the burning sensation is gone from my face. I am hearing Gary's voice again.

"Come on, doctor. Let's have a look."

This is a special moment. Everyone who is ever under this type of stress, real or imagined, is always arriving at this moment. It is their complete and total mental breakdown. Breakdowns are born of three things. They are born of fear, pain and a total sense of helplessness. Only love is capable of bringing us back from the brink.

Gary is cradling me in his arms. He is kneeling beside my chair as I am feeling the bandages being removed one by one. I am feeling the cool air against the exposed skin of my face. Looking up, I am seeing the doctor and nurse nodding their approval. I am hearing the doctor's words first and Gary's words next. I am not sure if the doctor is talking to me or to Gary.

"This is a fucking piece of art, a fucking piece of art."

"Leave us alone, doctor. I'll deal with the rest."

Chapter Thirty-Nine

(Recovery)

The first part of my recovery is the mental. Don't be a smart-assed reader. I am just getting back to my normal self, as normal as that is for a person like me. I am not a new saint. I am not a newly repenting, Bible thumping believer. I am just returning to my normal self. There, I am saying it right up front and in your face. Those of you who are feeling the need are free to continue praying for my soul. I know some of you already are and I know some of you find yourself putting this book down a long time ago. It is no skin off of my back. Oh, I am forgetting. My missing skin is from my fingertips and face. Now, there is new skin taking the old skin's place. Frankly, the new skin is wrinkle free and I am looking ten years younger. I am thinking this cosmetic surgery thing isn't so bad after all. I am wondering what I might look like with tits or a bigger dick. Some women always want more than ten inches. Even standing up straight with the hardest of hardest boners I am only able to muster up a good eight inches. Men are always under so much pressure to please. Maybe getting tits and a pussy are possible, that way I can be fucking myself and eliminating the middle man. I am simply getting tired of being a sex symbol. My need is being loved for my mind. This is bullshit, bullshit and more bullshit. See my point, ladies? No, you probably aren't. If you are, you aren't admitting it. I know. I know. I'm nothing more than another chauvinistic pig. Ok, if that is the way you feel, I am good with it. All in all I am thinking my old wit and charm is returning. What do you think? I am even looking at the scarves the ladies are wearing while visiting their loved ones in the general area of this place. Scarves are big here south of the border. It also seems most of these people are always fucking in hammocks instead of beds. How does a person do that without getting twisted around and pulling either their dick or nuts off? There are just so many questions. Where is a person to begin? See? This is another question. Ok, I am done fucking with your mind. Talking more about my recovery is in order.

Gary is my rock. I am remembering him holding me until my crying is done. I am remembering him releasing the straps on my straight jacket and whispering into my ear.

“Now, I know you are a crazy little fucker. Let’s keep that our little secret until we can get out of this place and back home. Can we?”

At this point in my procedure, I am willing to promise anything that is capable of setting me free from my bonds and all of this forced immobility. I just want to scratch where I want to scratch and move the way I want to move. As the strait-jacket is loosening, it is as though I can breathe another gallon of air into my lungs. I am breathing deeply and the sudden rush of air is making me a little uneasy. Gary’s strong grip is steadying me in my chair.

“You feel like standing, William? Hold onto my shoulder if you do. I have your back, little brother.”

Gary having my back is a very touching immediate thought playing around in the back of my mind. I am thinking we can just be forgetting about that little crack about killing the motherfucker.

“I’m good, man. I’m good. Just walk me around a little so I can see if my joints are still working.”

After a few steps Gary’s voice is back in the conversation.

“Well, you aren’t squeaking. I’m thinking everything is coming back.”

We are moving in a slow and deliberate circle. Gary is on the outside of the circle and I am sort of leaning into him while moving my legs. Fifteen or twenty minutes later I am feeling like a marathon runner. Sweat is running down my face and I am physically exhausted.

"It's ok, William. It is going to take some time before your strength returns."

All of a sudden I am blurting out the obvious.

"Why, Gary? Why go to all this trouble? Why, not just kill me and be done with it?"

Gary is laying me back into my bed. For a time there is silence. Then, I am feeling his hand running through my hair and stroking the top of my head. Hearing his reply begins my crying all over again.

"It is because I love my little brother."

There is another silence from Gary. He is waiting for my crying to stop.

"Sorry about this, Gary. I am sure it is the medicine they have me on. I should be thinking about ripping your dick off right about now."

Looking into Gary's eyes I am seeing him smiling again. I am feeling myself smiling again. There is a little pain, but not all that much. This is a good sign.

"That is quite understandable, William. I'm wearing a cup over my dick. It is better to be prepared than to end up dickless."

"Don't make me laugh, prick. It hurts like a son-of-a-bitch."

After things are calm, Gary is again giving me instructions.

"I am going away for the night. I am coming back in the morning and we will be doing some more exercises. The quicker we get your strength back, the quicker we can both get out of here. Do you understand me, William?"

I am shaking my head in agreement.

"That is good. I am going to have them bring in some solid food for you. I want you to order what you want and don't go making a pain in the ass out of yourself. Turn on the television if you want. Just try not to fall on your face by getting up too quickly. It would be a shame to have to have this all done over again."

Gary is leaning over and placing a kiss on my cheek. This is a first. What the hell am I to be making of this? He loves me. That is all there is to it. Hearing the door locking behind him, I am well aware of the fact that I am not just yet totally free. The bonds are just a little looser.

Before there is a knock at my door and the entry of an orderly requesting my food order, I am laying back in the bed. I am twisting this way and that and am doing some of those Tony Little exercises. You know. Roll right, cross your leg over your other leg and then do it in the other direction with your left leg. My spine is popping like a lobster being cracked just before the butter is applied. God this is feeling good. A few times of this and I am lying flat on my back looking up at the ceiling. The ceiling is mirrored. Who the hell puts mirrors on the ceiling of a hospital room? More importantly, who the hell is that looking back at me?

Chapter Forty

Sometime during my darkest days, my brother is standing in front of my funeral home. He is watching the raging fire destroying everything I own. It is another cold night in Detroit and most of the homeless in my neighborhood are standing around watching. This is the closest thing to evening entertainment they get, other than the window televisions sets on display in the tiny Sears store just down the street.

Gary is unusually calm for such an event. He is watching the fire department; police department and local media go about their business. He is mentally judging their various performances. Gary is thinking he is grateful their response times are still in the toilet. This way there is plenty of time for the fire to get a good start. Besides, what is one more burned out building in this neck of the woods?

My brother is also holding a manila folder in his hands and leafing through its contents from time to time. He is shaking his head, looking at the folder and looking up at the fire. Eventually, Gary wanders over to the curb across the street. He is sitting on the curb with his head looking down at the roadway when he is patted on the back. Looking up Gary sees the young detective from the scene at the house just after Vickie's plunge over the railing to her death.

"I know it is hard to believe, brother. I am sorry to be the bearer of bad news."

Gary is looking into the young detective's eyes. In good acting style, my brother forces a few tears from his eyes just for affect.

"And you are sure of all of this?"

"We followed the paper trail on the one in Key West and that led us to the others."

"Any fingerprints or solid evidence or were you just picking him up for questioning?"

"There were finger prints everywhere in Key West. Hell there was more finger prints than trash in the dumpster area in that overpriced tourist trap they call Shipyard."

"I don't understand how you put it together. My brother has never been fingerprinted or arrested for anything that I am aware of."

There is a small explosion from the downstairs area of the funeral home as the fire is continuing to rage. Gary jumps and pulls himself to his feet. Some of the folder's contents spill out onto the ground. Bending over he is picking up the loose pieces of paper and photos of some of the victims as the detective continues."

"They have this gay police chief in Key West. Most don't think he is much of a chief and he spends more time hanging with the local politicians getting his picture taken, but he is damn good on details. It seems like your brother kept the victim's scarf and actually wore it down Duval Street. It was one of those gay color scarves. A couple of the local alternative lifestyle types remember this. William was pretty shit faced."

"Are you taking the word of a couple of fags?"

"I prefer the term alternate lifestyle."

"Yeah, and there is so much political correctness floating around we will be calling our asshole a waste ejection device next."

The fire is roaring and the firefighters are protecting nearby buildings more than they are trying to save my funeral home. Gary's last comment is capable of eliciting a small smile from the young detective. The cop goes on.

"The people at the hotel where you two were staying identified him coming in. I have to ask this, Gary. I'm apologizing ahead of time."

"Ask what?"

"What were you two doing in Key West and where were you during the hours listed in that report?"

"Everyone is suspect. I get it. I used to do this shit all the time myself. I just never thought I would be on the receiving end."

There is a long silence as both men stand in the cold and continue watching the fire burn. There are a few more minor explosions; the roof of the building begins collapsing while the fire fighters are pouring water into the center of the building while standing on top of a fire truck's extension ladder.

"One, I was drunk on my ass on the hotel sofa at the Pier House Hotel. I spent most of the evening at Bare Assets in the champagne room doing things you aren't supposed to do when you are a working cop. Two, William needed the vacation more than me. This thing with mother and the loss of our fortune really frosted his balls, but I never ever believed it could morph into something like you guys say it did."

"We know all of that, Gary. We also know your alibi is good. The only thing we don't understand is where William got all that money to pay for your property at the cabin and lake up north."

Gary is looking the young class one detective right in the eyes when answering this question.

"In hindsight, I would like to know that too. I don't know that much about his business, the funeral business. He just said he did a big one. I remember laughing about the big one part and joking about not knowing he went that way. That is about all I can say about that. I really don't have a good explanation. Since retirement I've just kind of been poking around, fishing, traveling a bit and in general just doing whatever I'm in the mood for. Frankly, retirement is pretty boring."

After a short pause, the young detective seems satisfied. Gary is thinking he couldn't figure out who was fucking who even if you put the dick and pussy right in front of him. Still, everyone needs to be starting somewhere and he did make the rank. Gary gives him credit for that much.

"Well, this all may be a mute issue anyway."

"And what is the reason for your line of thinking?"

"If there is a body upstairs in the bedroom..."

The detective does not continue. Gary's reply is a one word reply.

"Oh."

It is well into morning when the flames finally die and the embers of what is left of the funeral home begin losing their glow. The fire marshal is on the scene the whole time. The Mayor is very big on seeking out arson in this neck of the city. A big mansion can burn to the fucking ground for the money, but let a little man try to cash in and all hell breaks loose. Gary is lucky to have the near retiree on his side. The fire marshal is responsible for botching one case really big a few years before Gary's retirement and he owes Gary one. Gary keeps the whole fiasco under wraps because he sees himself in much the same shoes only wearing a different badge.

The smoke is still heavy when the fire marshal comes walking out of the ruins like some demon from the bowls of hell. It is a really eerie sight and Gary is momentarily seeing William's face under the fire helmet. Other than a few deliberate missteps resulting in the capture of some dirt bag, Gary is never really out of step with the letter of the law. This is not to say that he is never bending the intent, but all is well that ends well. Right now, he is nervous and is going over every step of his plan in his mind. What did I miss? Did I miss anything? Am I believable? Did I show too little emotion? Did I show too much emotion? Finally the fire marshal is standing toe to toe with Gary and the young detective. The two men are drinking coffee as the fire marshal is approaching. Gary is the first one to speak.

"Is there a body? Is my brother inside, Mac?"

Mac is looking at the detective. It is the fire marshal's way of playing it safe. He owes Gary, but he also is covering his own ass by looking for approval about answering Gary's question.

"It's alright, Mac. There is no harm or foul here. If there is a body and it is William's, none of the rest of this matters anyway."

Mac is sweaty and sooty from kicking around in the rubble of the funeral home. His hand is on Gary's shoulder as he is replying.

"You need to be making arrangements pending the coroner's final report, my friend."

"Shit" is all Gary is capable of replying. He is thinking, 'Don't overdo things'.

Gary and Mac are embracing when Gary is doing his best acting. His deep breathing is very convincing. The little bit about a family cursed for the last few years is also very convincing. Letting go of Mac and facing the young detective, Gary reaches the manila folder toward him.

"Here, I don't need this. If you need me, call. Please try to keep this out of the paper. Like you said, if he is dead it is over anyway. If I can help you anyway in the future, don't hesitate to call on me."

Gary's reference is not lost on the detective. Gary is a good one to have in your pocket. Baring anything surprising from the coroner's office, this case is closed. There is one last comment from my brother before he is seen driving into the early morning hours of the Detroit skyline heading north.

"I'm going to my cabin. I don't want to see the pieces brought out. If you don't mind, Randy, let me know the coroner's final ruling. There may be insurance or other small trust matters to deal with. I know William donated some funds to the local poor, even buried some without cost depending on their situation. This is why so much of this is a shock for me. When things settle, you and I need to sit down and look over all of this stuff. I really want to make sure you are right about this. I'm not second guessing you. Evidence is evidence, but this is my brother. You do understand?"

The detective is pleased to be called by his first name. It is a sign of respect. Randy is nodding his agreement with Gary's last request and is looking forward to picking his brain. Gary is a good poker player. The aging coroner is also at Gary's table...royal flush so to speak.

Chapter Forty-One

(My Mirror)

My mirror is not the liar. It is my face that is lying. I am beginning to accept this new image in front of me. I am beginning the process of being comfortable with this new image, waking in the morning and looking into the mirror as a new day is beginning. My old face is slowly fading into the background. It is easier, I expect, for me than for most. Even growing up, there are very few pictures of the family hanging on our mansion's walls. I do not regret this fact. It is just a fact.

The dream about my old face and my new face fighting with one another is happening less and less. I like this dream. It is entertaining. It is not a frightening dream. Imagine that you are in my dream. There are two faces on two horses. Neither face sports a body. The body is the prize and it is waiting on the sideline of the arena for the victor. The body is standing there with skull and brain exposed. It is waiting on its new face. The brain is thinking. You say, what is the brain thinking? The brain is thinking random thoughts like these.

I love my old face. It is with me so long. Why must I now be something different? Oh, right, that little incident in Key West is coming back to haunt me. It is such a stupid thing this old face does. Fingerprints, fingerprints are just a pain in the ass sometimes. Maybe it is the alcohol that is the thing at blame. What do you think, brain? You say you think I am just a dumb ass not capable of controlling my urges? Oh, fuck you. You are not possibly capable of understanding my art. My art is beyond your cerebral dumb ass. Now, I am ok with admitting that being a little drunk is also at fault. I am just not thinking straight at the time of this little infraction. Ok, ok, shut the fuck up. It isn't just a little infraction.

As I am talking to my old face, I am also hearing the snorting of the horses and the sound of their hooves scraping anxiously on the ground in anticipation of the charge. I glance up momentarily from my conversation with the old face living in the back of my brain and in this dream. The stadium is full of faces. The faces are floating just above their seat's headrest. I am wondering if this is a stadium full of old faces or a stadium full of new faces. My brain is whispering to me that someone's old face is another person's new face. It is saying that things are always being recycled and that this policy is good for the environment. Thinking about it this way pleases me. I am a closet tree-hugger at heart and hate the thought of things being wasted. Too, my old face is a very handsome face, if I do say so myself. This argument is a logical reason for accepting my new face and letting my old face slide away into oblivion…besides the obvious details about my fuck up in Key West. Can we get off of that subject? I am tired of hearing about Key West. I am, admittedly, fortunate having a brother like Gary. Gary's love for me allows him the strength to be watching me suffer during all of this madness. I don't like that word madness. I am going to strike that word from my vocabulary. Now, my new face is talking with my brain. The horse my new face is riding is even more anxious for this encounter to be over than my old face's steed. I think my old face is thinking it is a regular on the scene and that this new kid is about to get his ass kicked.

My new face is thinking. What is all the fuss about progress? The wrinkles on your old face are beginning to show anyway.

"Hey, I resent that", my old face shouts.

"Don't be getting your nickers in a twist, honey. The truth is the truth, no matter how you slice it."

My brain is thinking, 'Shit. Gary has given me a gay face.'

The new face continues its counter point in the back of my brain. It is talking about the real possibility of me being strapped to a gurney for a 'death drip' except for the devotion of my brother. The new face is saying that most brothers would opt for the drip and just get on with their lives. So, there is a little pain? That is nearly over. There are no scares. Knowing that this new face is not the one you are born with is something even a specialist may not be able to determine for sure. You, man, are fucking beautiful. Don't be worrying about that gay face thing. That is just your brain talking. Brains sometimes get in the way. Hell, rednecks are some of the happiest people on the face of the Earth. They don't know they're fucking up when they're fucking up. They are too busy having fun in this lifetime and not worrying about the next lifetime. Getting back to my point, some psychologists believe everyone is really gay and the battle for taking sides is going to go on forever. Why can't people just be both? I guess it is the same reason people aren't walking around with two faces. Do you understand what I mean? Accept me for what I am. Put that old face in the closet. It is like going both ways sexually. Only the ones needing to know need to know. I am also protecting your sorry ass from the executioner. Do you get my point?

By now the horse hooves are in full gallop and the crowd is screaming at the top of their lungs, wherever their lungs are at this particular moment in time. They are shouting encouragement for their own point of view.

"Keep the old face."

"Accept the new face."

"Keep the old face."

"Accept the new face."

Then, at the exact same time, I am seeing another figure standing next to my body by the sidelines. It is wearing a long white robe and only the fingertips are visible at the bottom the robe's long sleeves. The figure is pointing at me and slowly lifting its head. Its head is turning toward me. The prophet-like apparition is whispering into my brain at about the same place my ears usually occupy. Never mind about the two faces without bodies galloping along on a collision course. I am hearing a question.

"What if you are both? How do you know your old face is not hiding behind your new face? Does one every really know what is behind someone's eyes, behind someone's face? You two fighting one another are just a train wreck waiting to happening. Don't you think?"

Right before the oncoming faces collide, the robed figure is looking directly into my brain. It is waiting on an answer. Brains don't have eyes is what I am thinking, but the blind do learn to walk and function without sight. Maybe eyes are just a luxury and the brain knows something we do not know. Do you think this is possible? I am thinking that maybe this is the case. The floating faces above their seats in the arena are still shouting.

"Keep the old face."

"Accept the new face."

"Keep the old face."

"Accept the new face."

Then there is my epiphany. It is the figure in the white robe whispering into my brain, "You already have the new face. There is nothing to decide."

Sometimes things are just that simple. It is like the soldier losing a leg in war. It is what it is. My old face and my new face kiss and are one. The faces in the arena bounce away and out the arena exit doors. They are disappointed at not seeing blood.

My new face is rather noble looking. The nose is strong but not pointed or flat and it does not sit too close to my face like some boxer's noses do as a result of one too many poundings. I am thinking that my upper eye socket bones are a little closer to my brain than before. It may be an apparition because of my eyebrows. My eyebrows are not full and bushy as if they are trying to grown into the sides of my ears. I am getting a little older and beginning to notice little things like this. I am remembering someone telling me that some women are attracted to large full eyebrows and handlebar mustaches. I never even consider the mustache and the thought of both together remind me of something one takes by the legs and runs across the floor like a vacuum cleaner. Where did that come from? I hate eating across from someone with a mustache. I hate it even more when they are losing food in the brush and the wife goes looking for a loose piece of French fry or worse. Change the subject. Change the subject. This is a disturbing thought. Quit looking in the mirror. Quit thinking about your dreaming. Get on with your life, man. Gary is coming today. This is your last day in this adobe piece of shit hospital. You now understand the reason for all of this. Having someone love me this much, having someone go to these lengths is just something beyond words. I promise this face is a good face. It is a prisoner finding Christ, and not just for the sake of an early release.

Still, there is that old face haunting me. It is looking at me from behind my new face. I am wishing faces are more like dogs. You, know. Tell the thing to sit, give it a treat and everything is alright. Faces are not that way. They keep looking at you, even after they are gone.

There is a knock at the door. Gary is entering before there is enough time for answering the door.

"William? William? Where is William?"

I see my brother is smiling. His voice is such a welcomed sound.

"It is vacation time, William. I'm thinking someplace warm. What do you think?"

I reply after giving his question some consideration.

"Yes, I want to go someplace warm, but not Key West… anyplace but Key West."

My brother and I walk arm and arm out onto the hot concrete airstrip. The plane is old and bounces more than flies. For a moment I see us taking three seats; one for Gary, one for my new face and one for me. I am suddenly thinking about my art. It is at this juncture when my big brother begins telling me about my funeral home, about my death, my new beginning and a big surprise he is planning for me. I am suddenly moody and withdrawn.

"I hope it isn't like the last big surprise."

Gary pinches me on my new cheek as he is replying.

"You are a bit of a bitch this morning. Sit back and relax. This surprise is right up your alley. I love you, man."

I am holding onto this belief. It is all I have at the moment. Gary's carry-on bag is between his legs. I am watching him retrieving a bottle of scotch and two snifters lying on the top layer of his clothing. I am noticing we are the only two people on the plane. The other fourteen seats are empty. I am thinking that at least I am in a seat instead of strapped to a gurney. I am thinking about that old Janice Joplin line about, 'freedom being just another word for nothing left to lose'. Right now, I am thinking I am the freest person in the world. Three snifters of scotch later I am pulling back the bottle's label just to insure there isn't another brand's face hiding underneath.

Chapter Forty-Two

Gary and I are sitting on a little island in the Florida Keys. The place's name is Palm Island. Palm Island is a short boat ride from an area known as Little Torch. Palm Island is very exclusive and one pays from three to ten thousand dollars per night for the privilege of getting the island's surrounding sand between their toes. Our plane is sitting at the Marathon Airport, just north of us by about fifteen miles. There is a smaller island just off of Palm Island where many of the locals go to play. The name of this island is Picnic Island. It is little more than enough earth to walk about on for a few minutes while waiting on your dog to piss. It seems like everyone in Florida is obligated to the ownership of a pet or two. The local newscaster's pleas for blankets for the pets when temperature dip to below fifty five is something I find very amusing. Hell, up north, the pets get an outdoor pet house and bale of hay to keep warm. I'm guessing these tree huggers see things differently than I do. There are many interesting individuals among this group claiming Picnic Island and, in my opinion, are apt to be more interesting than the rich, stuffed-shirts surrounding Gary and me. Still, Gary affording this type of place is an item of suspicion. Being able to pay for my procedure is also a mystery and issue of concern. I prefer calling it a procedure. The word procedure sounds respectable. It is something one does because they are wise. A woman's face lift is vanity. See what I mean? My procedure is a clandestine purpose. Her facelift is someone throwing camouflage around her sagging tits. I guess one is capable of arguing that both have purpose. My feeling is that my procedure is a nobler endeavor. I am, in a sense, hiding a past. She is simply hiding from the future. This is sad. I believe having 'work done' is the highest form of insanity. Crazy people drive me nuts. Get my point?

The sun is about an hour away from setting. I am reclining on my lounger chair, watching the group of boats growing larger and larger that is anchoring just off Picnic Island. Gary and I are sipping our scotch on the rocks. Fuck these frou-frou island drinks with those little plastic palm trees in them. Drinking that crap is like downing liquid sugar. Too, that Jimmy Buffet guy can stick his margaritas and his songs where the sun doesn't shine. Hell, the john is even upstairs in that hole-in-the-wall on Duval Street in Key West he calls a night club. Parrott Heads, my ass. They are all just a bunch of pecker-heads wearing stupid hats and paying too much to drink. I know. Maybe a little 'work done', pecker head facial surgery, is in order so wearing those stupid hats is not a requirement when visiting the Keys. Can you imagine five thousand or so pecker heads all looking like pecker heads on this small island? Half of them are trying to put on lipstick and keep it from falling off their beaks. It could be more than fifty percent. This is, after all, Key West. I am laughing to myself and thinking what a hoot getting drunk some night and throwing bird seed at these assholes might be. No? That's right. My promise to Gary is to clean up my act. Even so, I'm thinking this idea isn't so bad. Is it? Despite the oddity of the population and its guests, giving this area credit for its sunsets is an easy thing to do. My concern is that in their haste to escape conformity, they are creating conformity of their own. After a while things just get to be the norm. This is when a guy like me is the odd one out. How am I expected to fit in? Answer that question.

There are about forty boats now anchoring off Picnic Island. My third scotch on the rocks is arriving by way of a busty, tanned blonde. She is bending down delivering my drink and I am watching the sun forcing its rays through her cleavage.

Gary is observing the other angle. The water is a little choppy and I am finding my view of her giving off the image of two large, firm breasts bounding across the ocean's top. Maybe this place is worth the price. Gary's voice enters my thoughts.

"So, you want some of that?"

"What?"

"Do you want the scotch lady? Everything is for sale out here."

"Naw, I have always just been, a breast man."

"Well, if you do, just let me know. This might be the last chance we get for any relaxation for a while."

I want to continue the conversation, eventually steering it in the direction of my concerns, but the scotch and beautiful surroundings are so embracing that I figure leaving the topic for a later hour is of little consequence. I am enjoying the moment. Perhaps, down deep inside, I am an islander at heart. Do you think this is possible? I think it is the scotch talking. My fucking lips are getting numb. Gary and I are both pretty well crocked. I follow up a little more on his question.

"Maybe, I will be later."

Gary's brain cells are already on hold and he is staring out into the clear blue-green water.

"Maybe, you will later what?"

"You know."

"Oh, yeah, I remember. I'll ask the service captain."

There are several boats that are rigged with side mounted grills. The smell of hamburger and brats is wafting toward our overpriced island. I am betting the same brats they are enjoying for a buck is fifteen or twenty dollars on this overpriced piece of real estate. I am hearing the tab tops on the beer cans and imagining the resulting sprits' sound spewing out a thin stream of beer that is mixing with the sun's light, creating a rainbow effect. I bet even some of the beer is gay in this area and one is required to tilt the can to one side before consuming. Am I a sarcastic bastard or, what?

I love dreams. Sometimes they are a sweeter reality than life itself. Dreams are the things allowing one to go places that the confines of some anal society say is not approachable. Sorry about the anal remark. It is just my sarcasm rearing its ugly head again. I am not really anti-gay. It is just that there is so much laughable material available to a jovial guy like myself. Too, I am the butch in the relationship. Don't ever say I am not the butch. This is a sure fire way of pissing me off. Understand I am not saying I am gay. I am saying that, if I were gay, this is the way I see things playing out. Never saying never is the best policy. That way one is covering all possible bases. I am sure your see my point. I love dreaming. I am drunk now and I am dreaming.

I am a shark. I am the biggest shark in the whole damn ocean. I am slithering through the water like some snake in a tropical forest. I am in search of my next meal, my next prey. Daring a glance into my penetrating, attitude-filled eyes is a quick recipe for disaster. My eyes are not reflecting a false bravado like those young poster freaks penetrating the heart of America. I am real. I am myself. I am a child of nature. My respect is born of nature and of years lumbering alone in the liquid belly of Mother Earth. Spitting out poster children with their hats on backwards is an afterthought for something as strong and powerful as I. You are not worth a second glance. I am after larger prey. Asking for respect is not my style. My respect is earned. My friends are few and the rest just swim away. Asking for love behind a false mask is not my way. Besides, love is secondary to survival. Hating is natural for me. It is like that old saying about 'swimming with the sharks'. If one is not naturally swimming with me, asking is a dangerous approach to be taking. But then, to be honest, my new face is a hiding place. Am I a little like you? Am I covering the truth of whom and what I am because liking society's boundaries is not my taste? Am I playing out in my art the anger and resentment thrust upon me at birth? Come on in, swim with me. Interesting and unseen things are coming my way.

The longer I live, the farther I go. The water is deeper and deeper. The depth of my soul is colder and colder because of the things surrounding me. I am losing. I am drowning in my own loneliness. Then, there is a strong and forceful wake beside me. I am in its shadow, staring into the blackness of its eyes, waiting to be consumed and wondering if mercy exists even at these depths. What is behind a set of eyes darker than mine? Suddenly I am pleading for its kindness. Yes, we are a lot alike…you and I. Gary's voice is near.

"Hey, dude, wake up. You're flipping around in you lounge chair like a fish."

I am back on the beach. The sun is down and it is night. The sky is dotted with more stars than I am capable of recalling on any ten nights put together above the Detroit skyline. The winds are picking up and the surf is lapping against the beach nearly reaching the bottom of our chairs.

"Come, on. Let's go in for the night. We will talk about things in the morning over breakfast. I want you sober and I want your undivided attention."

"You want my attention about what?"

I am looking into Gary's eyes. They are dark and serious. This is about business. It is about survival. It is not about love. The shark is out of the water and it is walking upright.

"We need to talk about the future, asshole. We are going home soon."

I sleep well, dreaming about my victims being fish wearing their different colored scarves. In the morning I am standing in the sand near the ocean's edge waiting for the scarves to come floating to the top of the water. Gary taps me on the shoulder around eight-thirty and I am in the shadow of someone larger than myself. It is someone I love. We are heading off to breakfast. I am thinking about reaching out and grasping his hand. Thinking better of it, I find myself refraining. Perhaps, I am not the butch after all.

Chapter Forty-Three

(Breakfast)

I am the kind of guy that orders scrambled eggs, bacon and toast when there are fish all around me. An omelet with any sort of fishy crap in it is just a waste of time. This is just my opinion. Eating fish is the sort of thing a guy does when he is trying to impress some woman he is expecting to be on top of in a few hours.

This is our last morning at the resort and my big brother is in a very serious state of mind. I am watching him walking to our table. He is carrying a manila envelope. 'Oh, my God', I am thinking. This is some serious shit. Then, again, maybe it isn't. I am into my third breakfast Bloody Mary. My promise about being good is a difficult one. Nothing is ever said about me not being able to drink. That big breasted waitress from yesterday on the beach is a real testament to my ability to keep a promise. I am remembering her hipping her way into my bedroom with some sort of fluffy looking boa constrictor thing around her neck. I am asking you right up front. Is that or is that not some sort of temptation for a person like me? I am reporting right here and now that sex with a willing partner is something I might relish again. I do not know her name, either. This is the way I like it. A no commitment relationship is the staple of any male's way of thinking. Why can't you women just get that? Thinking like a man and being equal to a man in every way is alright with me. My question is. If you get all the other benefits of being a man except the dick, isn't accepting our philosophy the next logical step? My brother, in all of his wisdom, believes they cut the dicks off of the dumb ones anyway. Now, don't be pissed at me. I am just telling you one of his many off-colored, chauvinistic jokes. It is like a woman saying she is always reeling her husband in to the right spot before getting a good fuck. Now, that hurts. Don't you agree? There is one other thing I am thinking about, too. Everyone is always calling someone sick because of the things they like doing during sex. I am thinking about a bumper sticker I once saw. It may not be about sex, but the message is the same. The bumper sticker reads, 'It isn't kinky after the first time'. Now, this is an in-your-face message. Anyway, I am about done with my third Bloody Mary and Gary is looking very serious this morning.

"Did you have fun last night?"

"I sure did. Thanks, big brother."

"Is she still alive?"

"I am happy to report that she is and, I would like to think, a very satisfied woman this morning."

"For what I paid for her to stop by, she would pretend to be happy with a limp pusher drinking Boone's Farm."

"I like my version better, Big B."

"What the hell is, Big B.?"

"It's short for Big Brother. I think it is an endearing term. I am thinking of calling you that from now on."

I think I see a little bit of a smile on Big B's lips, but being wrong is possible. God, I love a good Bloody Mary. I am wondering if its inventor is some guy who is a heavy drinker and the drink's name is in remembrance of his own little, violent, artistic slip. Know what I mean? Never having tasted blood I am not in the position to say if it is or is not good in a drink. Having a few drops of blood on me during my first foray into the world of canvas is not like drinking it, but this is definitely a way into a whole different world for a bartender leaning toward the macabre of the artistic world. Get rid of these thoughts.

Get rid of these thoughts. You are not that William anymore. Still, I am imagining a bar where every drink is reflective of some poor soul giving their life for its creation. I think this is a good idea. I mean, if you are going to kill someone, they are in need of some sort of remembrance, some sort of honor; maybe even a review in some underground magazine. Wine Spectator is this way. Why shouldn't artists of the macabre put out their own magazine? I am seeing it right now while I am chewing on my celery stalk waiting for Gary's follow-up comment. Let's see. How does one make an artery gimlet? Throwing in little pieces of extracted artery chopped into about one eighth inch sections for texture is the idea coming to mind. Maybe, impaling these little sections like, one does in a martini with olives is in order. I am feeling my creative senses again. Stop it. My mind is saying, 'Stop thinking like this'. Isn't it amazing how much thought is capable of rushing into your mind in just the few seconds between replies in conversations? No, it really isn't. I am remembering Gary interrogating people and how that ten or fifteen second pause seems like an eternity. It is enough time to bring a liar to a full sweat. I really like those interrogations. I love seeing the fear on their faces. Maybe this is why I love my art so much. Do you think this might be the reason and that it is a normal human reaction to the boredom and drivel we are facing in our day to day lives? I think so. I think this is the ticket. Gary's response is now interrupting my thoughts.

"Well, William, what say I start calling you Little W? Would you like that?"

"That is not respectful. I would also like to point out that is not true."

"That is not what I hear."

"Oh, shut up. Are you happy now, Gary, Gary, Gary?"

Gary is definitely smiling now. I understand Gary's point, but I am thinking about using that boa constrictor looking thing to strangle the waitress before leaving. She is probably spreading vicious rumors. I am not huge, but I am above average.

"Can we order coffee and get down to business?"

The envelope is full of papers and documents. It is my new identity. Traveling from Mexico by private plane into the United States is advantageous. Even right up to this point in time I am not thinking of these little details like passports, driver's license, bank account, savings account, social security number, picture identifications and on and on. It is really so easy to be a non-person. You just wipe the paperwork trail away. Building a new identity is something requiring time, patience, money and artists of the more shady kind. Mexico is the perfect Mecca for this type of art.

In short, I am now Jason Robert Whipple. What's up with that last name? Oh, yeah. I am an accountant. The name fits. Too, it is probably a payback for all the trouble my big brother is going through to keep me dead and out of harm's way with the police. I am still wondering why he is taking the trouble. He loves me. He loves me. He loves me. I am singing these three little sentences in the back of my mind while listening to my new instructions. The coffee is here. Thank God the coffee is here. A buzz before nine in the morning is a real ball buster. For the record, my balls are really big and I am imagining Gary saying, 'You don't fuck with your balls'. I am smiling.

"What the hell is so funny, Mr. Whipple?"

"What? Oh, nothing. Just thinking about something you might say. I am, Mr. Whipple. Aren't I?"

"You most certainly are. On the way home, I want you to go over this whole profile. You and I are going to create a new persona for this Mr. Whipple. You are going to live it like this is your name the day the doctor first slapped you on the ass. You got it?"

I am seeing that, 'Let me down and I will kick your ass look' in Gary's eyes.

"I've got it."

The plane is lifting off from the Marathon, Florida airport within an hour and a half of the completion of our breakfast.

I am burying myself in my new persona. "Should I be gay?" I am wiggling down the aisle. "What do you think, Big Brother? Should I be gay?"

"Be whatever the fuck you want to be, but what you were."

I am suddenly serious. I find myself asking. I need to ask.

"Gary, I am your brother. I will always be your brother. Tell me honestly. Do you still love me?"

I am pleased with Big B's response. I am keeping this name to myself as a little bit of personal endearment.

"Yes. Unfortunately, I do."

Chapter Forty-Four

I do not like flying. This is just me. My dislike of flying is not connected to any particular fear. I am not bothered because my father dies this way, flying. Everyone's number arrives out of the blue, suicide aside. It is the speed that bothers me. Everyone is in such a hurry this day and age. No one enjoys their wine. They just gulp it down like the next bottle is turning bad on them before their first glass is empty. Why are we always doing things in such a hurry? I am remembering our one servant back at the Sigrist mansion. Her job is keeping all of the kitchen supplies on hand and preparing for any upcoming big event. I am remembering this from when I am young, sitting in the basement creating things inside my own little dream world. This servant hurries to the store and, once there, ends up reading every damn label on everything she is intending to purchase. I am her company for a few trips and then put that shit on hold. I bring this up because it is the opposite of hurrying. Where is the middle ground? Why is everything so extreme with people? The last time I am with her on one of her journeys, I am sitting in the car watching the number of people who are arriving and going into the grocery after she is already in the store. Still, she is the last one out of the store. What is up with that? Read a magazine for Christ's sake. Imagine me killing someone too quickly, but not all the way. Imagine killing someone too slowly. Either you are not doing the job completely or you are taking the surprise out of the event. Just be yourself. See what I mean? One is asking for trouble by not taking the opportunity to savor what they are doing. I am not saying to be sloppy about things.

Pick the speed that is right for you and stay with it. This is all I am saying. Consistency is what makes writers great. They are always, day in and day out, practicing their trade until this artistic act is second nature. Writing becomes like pissing. The words just flow naturally. It is that way with killing, sex, shopping, praying, painting, playing the piano and sculpting and on and on. Doing whatever it is you do on a regular and methodical basis is what makes one what they are. How about being me? My new face is growing on me, literally and figuratively. My new persona is a work in progress, but it is getting there. I know the reasons for it and am adapting. So, shop slower, screw slower, drink your wine slower and appreciate the moments. There are so few of them to savor. Gary is looking at me, at my new face. I'm betting he likes this face better. He is the one responsible for picking it out.

"What are you looking at, Gary?"

"I'm looking at the new you, Mr. Whipple. You are adapting very well, not too fast and not too slowly. The doctor said that psychologically the procedure would be either a success or a bust. He said that there was no middle road and that I could tell by your reactions once all the stitching had settled in and pain had gone away. He said a few of his clients actually tried to pull their faces off trying to find themselves. People just identify with their appearances too much."

"How am I doing?"

"You are doing just fine. Underneath you are still the same old asshole I remember as my brother."

We are both chuckling as the plane is moving into Michigan airspace. Suddenly, we are hearing the Captain's voice over the loudspeaker.

"You guys might want to buckle up. We are hitting very bumpy weather and it looks like it will be lasting right through our landing process. Hit the head now and stay in your seats for the rest of the flight."

The little overhead speaker pings one more time and goes silent. Maybe, I am afraid of flying. Maybe, getting this fucking piece of tin with wings on the ground as quickly as possible is what I want most in life right now. I am wondering what it is like to be in the position signaling my father's last few moments of life. What is one supposed to do or say when they are realizing the end is near? Does one really have time to consider their end? Time is a funny thing. Even in very short moments it can seem so long, your life passing before your eyes and all of that shit.

Our plane is bouncing around like some Tonka Toy airplane being pushed over a washboard by some grubby little six year old bastard having a good time playing crash the airliner. My scotch is all over the crotch of my pants and the front of my seat. Where is a good prostitute when you need one? My dick tastes like a sixteen year old scotch right about now. If this infernal bouncing doesn't stop pretty soon, mixing that sixteen year old scotch with some of my own piss is a good possibility. There is lightning and thunder outside of my window. I see the lightning off in the distance and am hoping this asshole pilot is flying far enough away from it. That little ping is overhead again and I am hearing the pilot's voice.

"Grab your nuts, guys. We are going to shoot for the runway in about five minutes."

Gary and I are both looking into one another's eyes. Fear is a thing capable of being exchanged between glances without words ever being spoken. Gary is gripping the arms of his seat. I see him flipping the latch-swivel button on his seat. Pushing his seat with his feet the seat moves back into the face-forward aisle position. Given his police background, I am thinking he wants to see what might be killing him instead of it sneaking up from behind. Ok, I am getting the picture. My fucking dead father is doing his best to take us both out on the same runway where the remnants of his own nuts remain. I really do believe in ghosts fucking with the living. If Gary and I die in this landing,

I am going to kill my fucking father all over again. Not that I am responsible for killing him in the first place, but you know what I mean. I am hearing Gary's voice.

"Turn your seat around like mine, Mr. Whipple. You may have to put your head between your legs before this is all over. I would hate for you to fuck up that pretty face, given what I paid for the thing."

As I am flipping my own seat around, the plane drops quickly and lurches back upward again. I catch a glimpse of Gary's middle finger waving at me from across the aisle. Feeling the plane glide a little sideways while tilting its right wing up is very frightening. I am envisioning all my dead victims pulling on a series of different colored scarves tied together like a rope, trying to flip the plane over as it is coming in for its landing. The plane is experiencing a cross wind. I am remembering a film about cross winds I am once watching after a day of work at the funeral home. Why am I watching this documentary? Because it is the channel where my finger landed, just like the rest of you couch potatoes in the world find yourself doing every fucking boring day of your lives. Shit, shit, shit is pounding in the back of my brain. Why, is the crisis word always shit? Couldn't it be something like strawberry, ginger, and boobs or up yours'? No, on second thought, shit is the correct word.

The plane hits the runway so hard I am thinking the landing gears are near sticking themselves right up my ass, but we are down.

"You can't even kill us correctly, father. You're just a big fuckup."

"What?"

Gary is looking over at me from across the aisle. He is drinking directly from the scotch bottle.

"It's nothing, big brother. I'm just talking to myself."

"Want a swig?"

"I think I will. Mine is all over the front of my pants."

The bottle is coming toward me as Gary is making his last comment.

"You've got the walk down. Find a fag who likes scotch and you may get lucky before we get home."

The plane is at the gate and we are at a standstill. The pilot is sticking his head out of the cockpit.

"Welcome to Detroit, guys. Thanks for flying with me."

I see Gary handing the pilot an envelope full of cash. I am a little more reserved.

"You call that flying?"

The pilot is in response mode.

"You're on the ground, Mr. Whipple. So yes, I call that flying."

The man's point is well taken. Planes fall as fast as they fly. It is some sort of Newton shit, the apple going up and the apple coming down.

The seats of the limousine are comfortable. The bar is stocked. Detroit is cold and dreary. William, I mean, Mr. Whipple, is home. Gary is popping the top to two beers as the vehicle pulls out onto the highway.

"They have Bud Lite in a limousine"?

"I like Bud Lite. You have a problem with that, little brother?"

I understand that, other than in private, the little brother stuff is nearly over. Milking a last few comments is only normal.

"No, there is no problem. I do have one request, Big B."

Gary is smiling again.

"And what might that request be, little W'?

"Can we drive by where the funeral home used to be"?

Gary is considering my request for a moment or two. In his mind this request is a sign of closure. In my mind it is a memory of something I know I am going to miss very much. Picking up the limousine phone Gary instructs the driver.

"I don't see any harm. Sure we can."

The eyes in the rearview mirror of the limo are familiar. They are from my past. Johnny Murphy is looking back. He is looking for signs of the William he knows. His reply is simple.

"Yes, Mr. Sigrist. By the old funeral home site, it is. Is there anything else, sir'?

Gary is looking in my direction.

"Yeah, there is. Go through a McDonald's. I'm so hungry I could eat the McBurglar whole".

I see Gary is laughing. I understand the implications and respond before he can jab at me.

"Shut, up. Don't you say it. I know what you are thinking."

Being so close to someone, as I am to Gary, is like having a second skin; a second skin I am not shedding anytime soon. I am thinking this thought while snacking on McDonald's French fries. I like McDonald's fries. They are a simple little pleasure making life so much easier. They are like hot chocolate with graham crackers and many different colored scarves... comfortable, so very comfortable. It is good to be home.

Chapter Forty-Five

It is odd to be sleeping in mother's old room. I am sure this is Gary's idea of a gift and I think the thought is very sweet. I must say that the household staff is very thoughtful by their choice of décor and furniture. The bed with a new mattress and box springs and two night stands are all that remain of the original furnishings. The curtains are new and more masculine and there is now an electronic rod in place that one pushes for the curtains to open or close. The old wallpaper is down and walls are now a sandy beige color with a darker brown border running the center of the room. It is very tasteful. I like it very much. A dark mahogany colored desk is sitting facing the curtains so that I am able to look out into the garden area or close the curtains with the automatic curtain rod at my pleasure. A burgundy colored high back leather chair is with the desk. Maybe, I am thinking, this desk thing is a good idea. I am considering writing a book about my 'exploits' as William. This is to be under an alias name. Wouldn't that be a kick… writing a book people think is fiction, but is actually real? I think it is a great idea.

There is a small square table with two heavy, black, masculine chairs sitting to each side. I am sitting in one of these chairs as I am viewing the room where my mother dies, the room that is now my room. I am thinking, mother, mother, and mother, 'if only'. The 'if only' is that thought running in the back of every little boy's mind at some point in time, the one about making love to their mother. In my defense, my mother's presence and sexual appeal is as powerful as any woman living in my memory. Too,

I am not completely to blame for this feeling nor are any of my counterparts. This is an established Freudian thing in my way of thinking. It is not a perversion. Think about it. Mothers are dressing little boys like girls for many centuries and no one is thinking a thing about this practice. Too, the first thing thrust in your face is a breast. 'Tits and ass, tits and ass; all a girl needs are her tits and ass'. I love the play, *Chorus Line*. Throwing in a line about a little BJ from time to time and it is the perfect play. These are woman telling it like it is. No, this is not a perversion on a male's part. This is a response to conditioning. I think that it is very possible little girls covet their father's equipment as well. This is just frowned on more by woman because of the attention it takes away from their own relationships with their husbands. Call me crazy if you want. Oh, I am crazy. This I am accepting more and more each day. Still, I am comfortable in my new skin. Isn't that the point, being comfortable with who and what one is? I think so. We are not going to be arguing this point. Anyway, let's get back to my book idea. Isn't it just fucking great? Could it piss Gary off? I think, maybe. I am thinking about writing the thing, letting him read it before it is published and all. Especially, before I go accepting any interviews on Jay Leno or doing any book signings. My one desire is for Gary's happiness. I am already thinking about writing a second best-selling novel. Great artists are like this. They are on to the next project before the last project is finished. This book is going to be about a boy sleeping with the ghost of his mother. The sex might be really, really cold, but maybe not. How is one to know without trying it? Do you think this is a strange idea? Do you think this is a crazy idea? I give you strange, but artists are always pushing the creative envelope. I am remembering hearing this somewhere. As for crazy, only time is capable of answering that question. After all, Copernicus almost lost his balls while postulating that the world is round. Fuck all those religious thinking assholes. Now, there is one crazy group. Some even think there is only one position a couple ought to be using when screwing. That is a funny thought. Don't you think it is a funny thought? This is enough about sleeping with my mother or my mother's ghost. Loving one another is the main thing. Sleep with your cousin if you want. I really don't care. You should, however, expect your kids to be dumber than a mud fence. This is something I believe.

There is a knock at my bedroom door. I know it isn't breakfast because of leaving specific instructions not to bring breakfast to my room. I like wandering through the kitchen and getting reacquainted with the old staff again, as Mr. Whipple of course. My understanding is that Mr. Whipple is to be a regular at the mansion and part of the staff. He is to review the family finances and make specific investments as the family directs. Understanding how this is taking place is not yet clear to me. Gary simply indicates that all is soon to be clear and the end result is that of the Sigrist family being the Sigrist family once again. Only the controlling faces are to be different. Duh, the other ones are all dead is what I am thinking. 'A few more loose ends', is the way he is always answering me. Until then, I am to simply move about the mansion meeting people and to be looking over their shoulders. Answering the door, it is Gary's face I see.

"I've set out some wine, cheese, pate, and crackers down in the wine cellar. Are you up for a snack and a bottle of wine?"

I am somewhat apprehensive about being in the basement. This is my first return to my underworld and hiding place since all of, all of that other stuff. The first thing worth mentioning is that the steps down into the basement do not creek anymore. Part of the atmosphere for the place being haunted is gone. The steps are now covered over with carpet. The light leading down the steps is now a very ornate golden sconce-like fixture. On second glance I notice there is more than one of these light fixtures. They line the steps on either side, reaching all the way down into the basement and cellar area. The one lone light bulb at the top of the stairs is gone. Again, another ghostly piece of the basement's atmosphere is gone. I do, however, like the new look.

Gary is in front of me leading the way down into the basement. He is holding onto one of two brass railings, one on each side of the stairway. He is moving slowly and deliberately as if watching for ghosts of his own memories past. I am not remembering Gary ever being in the basement or cellar area, but what the hell do I know. It is possible he is sitting in one of the dark corners watching me at the very same time I am inventing, listening to the kitchen staff overhead and playing my own dark, melancholy mind games. When one is lost in their own world, the world around them often is a blur, a non-reality if you like. Think about the assholes that are always killing someone because 'God told me to do it'. That is crazy. It isn't about art or anything else. It is just plain crazy. Gary's first comment comes at the base of the stairs leading down into our past memories.

"Do you like it so far?"

"I'm thinking that I do, Gary. It is like anything else when you are a little kid."

"What do you mean, Mr. Whipple"?

"Things always look larger when you're a kid. They always look smaller when you are an adult returning home."

Gary is pensive for a moment. His reply is aimed at putting us back on a brother to brother level.

"Does that include the size of your dick?"

We are both laughing as we are taking the last step into the basement's interior. I am noticing that even the sound of my voice is different. I am thinking that the operation is the cause for this discrepancy. It is not. The ceiling is now tiled over with those sound absorption tiles and the beams, wiring, venting, pipes and cracks in the wood floor overhead are no longer visible. Flipping a switch at the bottom of the stairs Gary reveals new lighting overhead as well. It is soft lighting. His gaze is upon me when he is speaking again.

"You can come here to relax if you choose. I know there are a lot of memories here."

I am touched. Tears are beginning to well up in the sides of my eyes. All I think to do is jump on Gary like some big, fat, gay slug while giving him a hug.

"Ok, ok. Back away. You did something really nice for me with the title on the cabin and I just wanted to return the favor."

"I'm touched. I'm truly touched."

While backing away from my big brother, my glance is diverted over his right shoulder. I am looking into the inset area that is once the shelving space for many bottles of fine wine. It is where I am remembering my mother sitting in one of the two wicker chairs with an open bottle of cabernet, drinking directly from the bottle with her feet propping themselves delicately on a small round table in the middle of the space. This is the position she is in when I sneak my first glance up her dress. No underwear is what I am seeing. The rest of it I leave for your imagination. Even if writing my book is someday a reality, telling you everything is the worst thing a writer can be doing. Use your own imagination. It is more fun, more artistic that way.

"You've changed the cellar area?"

"I sure have. Come on over. Let's have some cheese, crackers and a bottle of that cabernet mom used to enjoy so much."

The cellar walls are now walls with wine shelving covering them, unlike the wobbly pieces of wood nailed hap-hazard together. It is a wonder so few bottles of wine were broken over the period of time I lived at the Sigrist mansion. I see by the dust covering some of the bottles that they are left over from my childhood. I watch Gary rubbing a pointer finger across one or two bottles as if in recollection of more memories of my past.

"It is true, I guess, that dust eventually covers our past. The important thing is the good stuff remaining behind."

"A fucking philosopher now, are we?"

"No. I'm just a brother looking back."

"Aren't you supposed to be addressing me as, Mr. Whipple?"

"Once that door up top closes, everything is sound proof. I like the idea of us being able to be our real selves from time to time. We have this place and the cabin. It is about all we can hope for."

I am circling the end of the bar, taking the seat behind the bar and watching as Gary is picking one of the four seats on the guest side of the bar.

"There used to be only two seats and a small table. Are we going to have guests down from time to time?"

"One never knows, William. I am actually expecting a guest very shortly, but that means you are Mr. Whipple again. Once that door up top opens, you are always Mr. Whipple. Can you live with that?"

I am about to answer yes to Gary's last question when the door to the top of the stairs opens in the middle of my reply. The stairway lights appear to be reflecting outward like some sort of fog against each side of the wall. The figure walking down the steps and through the fog is the figure of a woman. Her dress is tight, long and flowing. She seems to be floating rather than walking down the steps. I am swallowing a first piece of cheese and washing it down with a sip of Pine Ridge cabernet. My breathing is beginning to get heavy and my body is feeling hot all over. My wish is for something I want, but know down deep inside cannot be. I am thinking it, but do not verbalize the word. The word is bouncing around my mind at the speed of light. The word is landing against the inside corners of my skull like some heavy brick about to penetrate the one window of my burnt out funeral home…the one window still unbroken. I fear it is the one thing shattering my remaining hope. The problem is that I fear this is the end of my one reoccurring dream, my one wish. The truth is that 'wishing upon a star' is just a bunch of shit. I know this to be the truth. This vision is a self-fulfilling apparition stamping out the truth of what I know. It is like the parent who is finally forced into verbalizing the death of a missing child. It is all I can do to keep this word inside of my head. It is also all I can do to keep my eyes open. Closing them keeps the desire alive and the reality at bay.

"Mother, is that you?"

Chapter Forty-Six

(Not My Mother)

"Mr. Whipple, allow me to introduce you to my new bride. Marlene, this is Mr. Whipple. He is the numbers guy I was telling you about."

Swallowing anything down your wind-pipe, let alone alcohol, is very uncomfortable. Marlene is patting me lovingly on the back, trying to help me regain my composure. Gary is standing to one side probably thinking I am about to give up the ghost so to speak. I am a trooper and beg my way out of the situation.

"Sorry, I'm sorry. I was just about to say hello. Damn, if I haven't done this a time or two in the last few months. I may be in need of retooling, if you know what I mean."

"I've done it myself, Mr. Whipple. Don't think a thing about it. Just breathe deeply and you'll be getting your composure back in no time."

I am thinking I bet she does do it quite regularly, but it isn't alcohol she is always choking on. Gary has a slight smile on his face. It is not a full blown grin. He knows what I am thinking and is rubbing his crotch for affect. I am beginning to choke again. Seems we are close enough to be reading one another's thoughts, especially the dirty ones. I am thinking it goes back to my big brother pissing in the expensive flower vases in the upstairs bedroom hallways when he is staying at home. I appreciate unspoken humor more than you can imagine. Gary separates Marlene and me by offering her a glass of cabernet.

"Would you like to join us in some cheese and crackers and a glass of red, my dear?"

I am noticing a southern twang in Marlene's reply. I understand that Gary is capable of fucking anything female that moves, but I am getting the feeling this one is from the farm. She is from the farm on the fenced-in side of the property. This isn't right. This isn't Gary. Playing along is in order. I want to see her walking down the stairs again and not listening to her talking.

"That is a really good idea, sugar."

Its sugar, is it? Something is definitely not right. I am piling a hunk of cheese and pate on a cracker while listening to the cabernet falling into Marlene's glass. I love the sound of wine flowing into a proper wine glass. I am wondering if she normally is drinking Ripple out of a mason jar. I am thinking there must be a reason for Gary marrying this bitch. If there isn't, you are going to be my next piece of art. Marlene's next line is as big a kick in the ass as is the 'married' thing.

"I suppose Gary has told you I am Vickie's sister and am the heir to all of this. I would think Gary's motives were suspect except for the fact that we didn't know who each other was until later on in our relationship."

I am thinking 'in a pig's eye' and that Marlene is most likely unaware my big brother is a retiree from the Detroit Homicide Division. He is capable of finding a pasty on a cow's utter and figuring out why it is there...maybe to make the milking more enjoyable. I still am in possession of my sense of humor. Don't you think? After everything else and, now this, I am still in possession of my sense of humor. I just think this is fucking unbelievable and a testament to my own will to survive. What the hell is next? Maybe there are little piglets running around the mansion somewhere that Gary is planning on roasting with apples in their mouths. Eating a big one is no different than eating a bunch of little ones. Besides, witches are always saying the younger meat is the juiciest and most flavorful of all. Shit. I am having a flashback of my father and his trips to Thailand

and am imagining his preference. Was it little boys or little girls? Get your mind on track, William. I mean, Mr. Whipple. There is a plan here. I smell it already.

"Well, Marlene, Mr. Sigrist seems to have hit the lottery in both respects, a rich loving wife who is a good looker as well."

Marlene is blushing. This is going to be a walk in the park.

Chapter Forty-Seven

(I am my brother's keeper)

Do you know what it is like? I doubt it very much. Keeping my promise to mother is the most difficult thing in my life. I am there beside her before going to summon William to her deathbed. The secret we share is between mother, me and the man she really loves. Now, don't get me wrong. William's life is a tragic one and I understand that certain obligations come with family life. I must admit that I am always feeling things like, 'What about me'. Must the burden of others always be falling upon me? Isn't it enough that I am dealing with the lower end of humanity every day in my work? After a time, you just find yourself understanding that police work is babysitting. It is babysitting plain and simple with some of the babies packing heat. Normal babies just shit on you. My babies are the killing kind. I am glad my retirement is finally here, that there is time for writing this book. Everyone is a writer, you know. My wish is that, up to this point, you are convinced that the voice you are reading is the voice of William. Taking care of him so long, I am comfortable speaking for him. I assure you the conversations between William and me are verbatim from my memory. Taking literary license with the truth is not something I am willing to do. I do believe truth is the most powerful form of fiction. In my story however, what appears as fiction is indeed truth. Even though it is a different genre, I am glad to report that I am as great or greater an artist than my brother believes himself to be. I am also glad that Marlene and I truly love one another. This simplifies my quest for the family fortune even though it complicates my relationship with my half-brother. It is a fortune that I have earned. Still, my promise to my mother is haunting me.

"Gary, my son, take care of William."

I find myself replying that she is not to worry.

"Now, go fetch the child", she requests as a very sharp pain is shooting through her lower extremities.

You know the rest about what is happening when William and I are in mother's bedroom and she is passing through the final moments of her life. At some point in that experience I am thinking about some of the things I see over the years. I am remembering watching from behind one of the basement's many false walls. This is a little secret of my own that I stumble upon at a very young age, an age when I am thinking William's father is my father. William is sitting there like some basement rat waiting on something to kill. This is an appropriate thought considering the child's future. He is tinkering away. He is feeling sorry for himself. I am watching and wondering how his rebellion is going to manifest itself in his later life. Introducing the little fucker to Teddy is just my way of shedding a promise made under very trying circumstances. 'Why', I am asking myself, could he just not find his own way in life? It is just beyond me. I am pretty much a black and white sort of guy. All these different shades of gray are very confusing. That dancing machine and his art are another curve I completely miss. Being fucked up is one thing, but mentally dangling that far over the edge is not something I am expecting of my own half-brother.

I am remembering an encounter between mother and the one I am always calling the 'Black Witch'. She is older now and still part of the staff, still dressing in black and still sneaking down into the basement area to relive old memories of her and mother's affair. This is a memory where I lose a little respect for mother. I am watching as the two are sharing wine. William is not in the cellar on this particular day. I am watching as the second bottle of cabernet is uncorked, as the women are leaning closer and closer. Finally, there is a kiss. The 'Black Witch' is running her hands between mother's legs and, very shortly, they are both naked doing things to one another; things which only spying eyes are deserving of seeing. I am guilty about my desire to continue watching. I am guiltier of the fact that I am being aroused by this event, standing there behind my hidden wall with my own hidden erection.

My own justification for mother's activities is placed squarely upon my father's shoulders. I am thinking that he is always away, mostly out of the country looking for little children to fondle. I am young, but I am not stupid. Why should mother not have a few secret moments of her own? There is no reason in the world. This is my thinking. Besides, I like watching. I am willing to admit that I am a normal man sharing similar tastes with other normal men. This is my justification for watching.

There are other things I am seeing while roaming through the false walls of the mansion, this little maze of a playground that is all mine. It is my belief that these passageways are left over from the gangster years and are secret entrance and exit ways for various family members called to meetings by the overlords of any particular town ward. There are rumors about the Sigrist family. There are rumors about torture for information, organized crime connections during the time of the union movement and the Jimmy Hoffa spectacle. There are even rumors about Grandpa Pope's and Grandma Pope's death not really being an accident, whispers about Grandpa being the cut man during torture sessions in the little hidden rooms behind these very walls. I am imagining what it is like.

"So, Daren, is it going to be the hard way or the easy way?"

I am imagining the victim sweating profusely in this cold and damp environment. He is tied to a single steel folding chair. Grandpa Pope is hovering over him with a hook-blade knife in his hand. Daren is trying to be strong. His lips are quivering, giving away the fear that is pushing his blood faster and faster though his veins. Daren is silent until his first scream, until the first penetration of the hook-blade knife into one of his upper thighs. Grandpa Pope is relentless. He is not pulling the blade from Daren's leg. He is leaving it there. He is leaning in whispering to his victim in a very low and threatening voice.

"I really don't like this line of work, Daren. The truth is that we all choose sides. You are not on my side and you know something I need to know. Tell me what I need to know and I will quickly remove the knife. Don't tell me what I need to know and I will pull the blade all the way down your leg. You will never walk again, if you live at all."

I am remembering stories told by the servants about how only the most hard core do not talk, about how those who die are going to die anyway. They go to their graves with their secrets, most of them lying about information before their last breath. I am remembering dinner at the mansion and Grandpa Pope carrying most of the conversation. The conversation is usually about the changing face of the transportation industry and how the 'fucking unions' are ruining everything for families like ours. One of his comments is forever imbedded in my mind.

"I tell you right now. If you have it, a truck brought it."

I am remembering thinking, 'filled with the blood of others'.

This is one of the reasons I am, or was, a policeman. At some point in their lives all children, not just little boys, want to make a difference in the lives of others. They want this difference to be manifesting itself in a good way; then those fucking shades of gray begin creeping in as you are growing up. You realize you are just a baby sitter or a brother's keeper. This is not your choice. I believe most things in life are not by choice. Still, one is always striving to be the master of their own destiny.

I am standing here in my own private little world thinking all of these thoughts when there is a tap on my shoulder. It is John Murphy. It is my real father. The memory of me watching as he is making love to my mother is flooding back. My recollection is that this memory is more upsetting than that of my mother and the 'Black Witch'. Somehow, my voyeurism is repulsing in this setting. I am not an innocent child walking in on a mother and father. I am a sneaky little creep spying on a very private, though unholy moment. I am older now. Fuck the church. I believe in that old song line, 'If you can't love the one you want, love the one you are with'. I am, of course, now an adult and am seeing things a little differently.

"So son, are you wandering your secret memories again?"

I am pensive for a moment before replying.

"I'm sort of rewinding the tape and wondering how all of this will end, father."

"It will end as it should, boy."

"I know. I am just thinking that my planning should have been better and going this extra step would not be necessary."

"Love often gets in the way. Marlene was the wild card. Do you really love her, Gary?"

I am looking John Murphy squarely in the eyes while replying.

"I do."

"That being the case, there are things we must prepare. Some things end up being a tradeoff. It is just a fact of life."

"Father, can I asked a question of you?"

"Certainly, you can."

"Did you really love my mother?"

"I loved her more than life itself. We both knew the risks. You are standing here as testimony to that fact. I was crushed when she died, but she did leave me someone very special to love."

John Murphy, my father, and I embrace. The feeling is warm and sincere. I am watching as the aging figure, still very muscular in structure, is moving up a hidden staircase back into the main floor of the mansion. Moving through the sliding panel, I am again behind the newly remodeled wine tasting bar in the basement. A few minutes later I am hearing the door at the top of the basement steps opening. William, Mr. Whipple, is coming down the steps. I am thinking that knowing what I know

now, just a little earlier, means Mr. Whipple is not in existence, my marriage is secure and the family fortune is again in the rightful hands of its true owner. In my mind, this being the circumstance, Mr. Whipple is but the real remains of my dead half-brother in his apartment over his funeral home. Marlene is such a lucky woman. My love for her is so intense. Yes, there is the money. That is secondary. I understand where my father is coming from.

Sitting across from me Mr. Whipple is sipping from his glass of wine, a pinot noir this time. The wine is my choice. My tastes are mellowing. It is time for being me. William is holding his glass up and watching the wine's legs rolling down the inside of his glass. Out of nowhere there is a question falling from his lips.

"Is something bothering you, Gary?"

My answer is quick.

"No. I am just revisiting the past and thinking about the future."

William's smile is almost wicked. I understand that people like him can only put off their art so long.

"I've been thinking about the future too, big brother. How long before we do something about Marlene?"

My response is non-committal.

"Everything will be fine very soon."

I understand that my brother is correct. Waiting much longer is not an option. Another surprise like Vickie's sister, Marlene, is the last thing I need right now. I am thinking, 'Finish your book of memories. Write the last page before it is too late'. I am also thinking that William's mindset is bound to my wishes for only so long and that the threat of his art is always waiting in the wings. Keeping promises are bound by circumstances and certain limitations. Besides, there is always that Cane and Able thing from the Bible. My justification is stronger than that. Of this, I am sure. We finish our wine. I excuse myself. William is now alone with his own memories. Marlene is reclining on a long, golden-colored recliner sofa in our bedroom. The sofa is the type with just one high end and looks like a cushioned lounge chair. She is drinking some sort of sparkling water, watching her weight and all that sort of thing. As I am entering the room, she is up and immediately in my arms. I am fond of making love in the afternoon. Hopefully, no one is watching. I know that my father, John Murphy, is making plans of his own.

Chapter Forty-Eight

(A Conversation with Myself)

I am remembering my detective work before my retirement as a police officer. Being a loner makes me a very poor candidate for a partner. I am, as they say in police work, 'a piece of shit with eyes and good instincts' that is very good at his job. There are other phrases like prick, asshole, dick-head, and motherfucker and, my all-time favorite, 'man whore ass bitch' that come to mind. I do not know the origin of my favorite, but I am sure it is created especially for me by one of my loving brothers in blue. Anyway, most detectives need a partner. Partners are useful when doing the good-guy bad-guy thing as well as being handy when you know someone is going to get killed and you really don't want it to be you. A good example is convincing your partner to crawl into an open window to see who is inside, waiting on the gunfire and hoping he is still alive before going in to help out the poor bastard. My point is this. One develops his own alter persona for special occasions. I speak with mine to help convince myself that whatever stupid thing I am about to do is the not as stupid as the other stupid thing I am considering, the lesser of two evils so to speak. This thing I am planning with William, Mr. Whipple, is something that needs a replay in my mind. I am having the following conversation with myself. The first voice is mine. I am calling the second voice, 'man whore ass bitch'. As explained it is my favorite nickname.

"So, do you think I am doing the right thing? I, mean, especially considering me spending all that money for his new face. "

"Well, 'man whore ass bitch', you are the dumb ass that fell in love with Marlene. What the fuck is all that about?"

"I guess I've just been riding around life alone so long that I was subconsciously looking for a solid relationship, someone to love."

"William loves you, 'man whore ass bitch'."

"William is fucking crazy."

"Maybe, but he is the one the money will go to if he finds out you are the bastard son."

"That is a technical point, fuck-head. Besides, William was a fuck for money and security. Mother never loved his father. It had nothing to do with love."

"You could keep him around and split the money, but you would have to split the money. Too, you would never know when he might go out and do something stupid."

"You mean like kill someone."

"Art, 'man whore ass bitch', Williams calls it art."

"So, I need to carry through with the plan?"

"You love Marlene. Marlene loves you. Marlene has the money free and clear. Technically, William is already dead. Let me sum it up for you. You have one extra face in the equation that doesn't need to be here."

"True and I have been looking after the little whining fuck for his entire life."

"I tell you, man whore ass bitch, I was really surprised learning your mother was such a whore and, that thing with the black witch. What was that all about?"

"Don't go getting judgmental, mother-fucker. We both have a few kinky likes of our own."

"Right, I forgot. How about we just keep that between us?"

"Sounds like a plan."

"Don't suppose I could get you to do the rest of this for me?"

"Listen, 'man whore ass bitch', this is your bucket of shit. You have to be the one to clean it out. This time you crawl through your own fucking window. That last time didn't go so well for me."

"You know, I've been meaning to tell you. I really appreciate you talking to me after that little incident, you being dead and all. Most assholes aren't that forgiving."

"I appreciate the recognition. Is there anything thing else I can help you with, 'man whore ass bitch'?"

"Nope, there isn't. You've done great, as usual."

It is great having rationalization as a very close friend. Rationalization is one of the most important friends a person can have. How else is one to function within a society such as ours, one that is preaching so many different value directions? Too, one is able to listen or not listen at will. The trick in keeping this friendship is not allowing too many voices in on the conversation. The conversation is always about you, your question or questions and the responses of your good friend, 'rationalization'. Let too many voices into the conversation and you are just crazy. It is that simple. This is Mr. Whipple's real problem. He is taking advice from too many voices claiming to be his friend. Stick with what works. This is my philosophy. It is like that little incident about pissing in that expensive vase in the mansion. Rationalization says either piss in the vase or in your pants. I pick the vase. Any additional group conversation results in an unpleasant situation I am unwilling to accept. My relationship with my brother is at this point. My new information is all pointing in the same direction. At some point in time, William is going to come back to bite me on the ass. I am glad I am rational about life and am not like my brother, crazy. Here is one more example of why I think this way.

Pets are a good thing. They are loving companions. They are company for lonely and sometimes anti-social people. Hell, some of my murder cases involve wives and husbands killing one another over the custody of a pet dog or a cat. Now, don't get me wrong. For all of you animal lovers and tree huggers, 'animals are people, too'. I get your point. Still, pets sit around licking their asses and the like. Ok, ok I know your argument. Some people do this too, but no pun intended; they are sick fucks and don't have regular conversations with their friend, 'rationalization'. They are a lot like my brother William and are always in need of something to hold on to.

I am remembering a pet a girlfriend of mine once pulled from an alley in the dead of winter. She is carrying this thing into her bedroom right when I am at the ready, if you know what I mean. Making a long story short, I end up petting a pussy instead of getting any pussy. The irony of the whole thing is that the cat likes me better than my girlfriend. The only thing my girlfriend ends up doing is cleaning the shit out of the litter box, feeding and watering the fur-ball. To top it off, the cat is always whining at her for food and water. It wants what it wants when it wants it... that immediate gratification thing in action. To say the least, this does not go over very well. It literally costs me my relationship with this crazy bitch; I'm talking about the woman here. I go to visit. The cat comes out of hiding. I pet the thing while trying to get screwed. The cat lumbers back off into hiding. My girlfriend gets pissed off and I don't get fucked again. The irony is that I end up with the cat. My girlfriend is always complaining this all being my fault. I didn't want the fucking cat in the first place.

"I saved the little bitch. If all I am going to do is feed and water and clean up her shit, you might as well take her home."

Me, being me, and not being able to leave well enough alone, I let some asshole comment slip out.

"Well, you can always come over to my place to see her and do all of that other stuff."

My girlfriend quits calling after she drops off the cat and the key to my apartment one evening when I am out on patrol. My police buddies start calling me 'pussy lover' as an inside joke. I eventually get rid of the cat because of allergies, but my point is this. If you have something and it is not providing comfort and pleasure, why do all of these love everything-in-the-world crazies think it is your responsibility to suffer through being treated like a piece of shit so that thing is well taken care of? I just don't get it. If you are given every opportunity and keep fucking it up, the end result is your fault and not mine. I am to that point with my brother William. I just can't continue on like this and expect a life of my own. The case is closed. Thank you again, rationalization. These are my thoughts when a soft voice enters my mental ramblings.

"What are you thinking, lover? I'll give you a penny for your thoughts."

Marlene is standing behind me. She is rubbing the back of my neck. We are at my cabin for a little time away together and I am sitting on the end of my dock overlooking the lake. This is where I like doing a lot of my thinking.

"I'm thinking that I love you and that that really feels good."

Marlene continues rubbing my back for a period of time then sits beside of me. We are sitting in two tropical style wicker chairs with a small wicker table between them.

"Would you like me to make up some cheese, wine and crackers so we can nibble and watch the sun go down? It is a very lovely night tonight."

"That sounds good, baby. I'll help."

"No, you won't. You just sit right where you are. I'll take care of everything."

Marlene and I are into our second bottle of Pinot Noir. I like the lighter taste of the pinot over the cabernet. Marlene's taste is similar. Sorry, mother. This is just the way it is. The sun is setting in the distance and, but for knowing we are in upper Michigan; a few palm trees in my mind are making the sunset seem more like Key West. Marlene ends the evening conversation. The topic is unexpected.

"You know I love you, Gary. Do you really love me?"

"What would ever make you ask such a thing? Of course, I love you."

“Sometimes I worry that it is because of the money, that this is the only reason you stay with me.”

I am now facing Marlene. Never really considering this aspect of our relationship is making my friend, ‘rationalization’, look like an idiot. Men just believe women are lucky to have them, despite all of that disgusting stuff they do and want their wives to do as well.

“Marlene, it is true you control a fortune my family once owned. You need to understand two things. One, I didn’t know who you were when I fell in love with you. Two, I am not rich. Still, my retirement keeps me quite comfortably. I guess what I am saying is that I need you more than your money. My life was happy before we met. It is happier now than it has ever been. Besides, I’ve always made my own way.”

The sun loses its last rays against the face of the night sky. Marlene speaks one more time.

“I had my accountant destroy that pre-nuptial thing. I love you, baby. I want our life to be based on trust.”

Reaching over, Marlene’s hand finds mine. I squeeze her hand tightly. I do not reply. What can one say? This is not a rational act. It is an act of love. This is, however, all the more reason for the two faces of William Sigrist to be moving on. Calling John Murphy first thing in the morning is floating in the back of my mind. It is time to empty the litter box once and for all.

Chapter Forty-Nine

(The Chamber)

The servants are preparing the chamber. John Murphy is supervising every detail. Things must be just right. This is going to be a special occasion, an occasion topping off the Sigrist's family history like a cherry tops off an ice cream sundae. John Murphy is prancing around while giving orders, like twenty years of his youth are suddenly back. The servants, including the Black Witch, are all smiles. They are all thinking the same thing, 'We are going to be one again. After all of this time, we are going to be one again'. It is almost more than the group is capable of bearing.

For a moment, the Black Witch falls a little melancholy. She understands that her time is short, that she is ill and that soon her fate is the same as her lover, William's mother. Still, her thinking is that the two women are going to finally be together again. What better way to honor her than this final tribute? She is waiting for me. She is waiting to be in my arms again. She is so proud that her son, Gary, is willing to carry on the tradition of this great family's history. This event is worth the end of all of us. John Murphy is such a strong leader. Thinking these thoughts, the Black Witch is once again smiling and anticipating the event.

The Chamber is dusty from so many years of neglect. The walls are now restored and repainted and the figures of their faith are alive and bright with new colors. John Murphy is pleased. They are all pleased. John Murphy is facing the group. He is facing the driver, the butler, the runner, the cooks, the cleaners and the Black Witch. His fondness of the Black Witch is without question. They all know about those chamber hours with Mother Sigrist, the Black Witch and John Murphy. The memories of hours on end of passion still play like an old record in the back of their minds. But for the loss of their youth, all might be normal again. Still, there is one to carry on. This is the important thing. 'All our love for Gary' is the mantra of the day. 'Praise forever for Grandpa Pope', is the warm spot in all of their hearts. His financial trust keeps us alive to this point and now, what is rightfully ours is within reach. John Murphy speaks.

"I love you all. Now, do the rest."

The servants are fluttering around like bees in a hive. They are making final preparations. They are not making honey.

Chapter Fifty

Mr. Whipple is getting bored. He is wondering just how much longer he is to be an imprisoned man. He is thinking that his part in this deception is over. Isn't the ordeal of a new face, new fingerprints and a new life enough? What does one do to prove that he is worthy of being set completely free? This is what my younger brother is thinking. I am thinking not so much about his imprisonment as I am of his lust for his art coming full circle in the persona of his new identity, Mr. Whipple. Oh, it is true that he is able to wander about the mansion, take the Porsche out for a spin, but the requirement is that it always be in broad daylight and that he be home before the sun is down. I smile thinking this is the same thing vampires must do...just daylight instead of night. My smile is not one of laughter. It is one of resignation. Vampires, if you believe in such a thing, trade one thing for another. They trade the want for life with others in the light of day for immortality in the dark of night. My brother is thinking there are many types of prisoners. Some are confined within rooms, some within their own minds, some within the grasps of love for another that keeps them from fulfilling their own potential, some within a frail and useless body that is housing a brilliant mind and many in the grip of their own addictions; alcohol, sex, cult religion and the like. My point is that I know my brother is either cured or at the breaking point. Being a retired police officer I am the type that always wants to know the certainty of things.

I am alone at the mansion's basement bar. I am sipping on a cognac and staring blankly into the mirror on the opposite wall. I am thinking these thoughts while still trying to convince myself that the upcoming events are necessary. I know that they are, but it is still difficult for me. William and I are victims of our own history and are always leaning on one another for support. I am the strong one. He is the weak one. Together we are opposites. We are like a good marriage in that respect. At least, there is a bond and we are sounding boards for one another during life's travels. Marlene is the wild card. Sometimes a person's original plans take a detour we are not expecting. This is the case with William. That is why that proverbial 'plan B' is so important. I believe this. Too, I am very frustrated by the fact that there must be any upcoming event at all. Some of this is also my fault. Telling William that I am the one directing older men in the grasps of their young wives' talons toward him is not something worth mentioning. Telling him that it all starts with a higher up of mine figuring out William's first little accident in the funeral home is not worth mentioning. Telling him that this higher up is the first client I direct William's way haunts me for two reasons. It haunts me because of William's change and lust for these events and because I am the one sweeping up his loose ends. I am the one keeping him out of prison, or worse, from the end of a needle and a lethal dose of drugs. This is all history. Admitting to my younger brother, someone looking up to me that my meteoric promotion to Detective First Grade was not entirely accidental; is now a non-issue.

I am sitting here thinking all of this and realizing that some sort of deep-seeded attachment lives between the two of us. It is true we are only half-brothers. It is true this information is a surprise. It is true William and Marlene equal the wild cards. It is true that my father, John Murphy, is always there for me in the background. It is also true that, not knowing all this sooner is the reason I am in this pickle. It is true that most of these last years are lived in great frustration. There are a lot of ifs. What if the money is just left to us as the surviving heirs? What if this half-brother thing never surfaces its ugly head? What if William uses paint brushes for his art instead of squirt bottles full of blood?

What if? What if? What if? It is all just becoming too much. I am looking forward to this upcoming event only because these doubts are over once and for all. Still, I need to know. Like the psychiatrist putting the criminally insane back on the street, I need to know. Is William still William or is Mr. Whipple the new man? Is it as simple as giving someone a new face so they are capable of forgetting their past? Is a piece of shit like me who doesn't deserve the status of retired Detective, deserving of someone like Marlene? Will I ever be able to get off of this merry-go-round of doubt and just be happy? Is trusting anyone ever again possible? I am thinking these thoughts when there is a voice behind me. It is William's voice. He is sitting alone in the far corner of the basement. He is sitting against the same wall he sits against as a young child while looking between the overhead cracks in the flooring and into the upper kitchen area.

"It is strange. Do you know that?"

I am swinging my bar stool around while replying.

"Jesus Christ, you scared the shit out of me. What are you doing over there in the corner?"

"I am doing what you are doing. I am thinking and listening to your thoughts."

"Listening to my thoughts?"

"No, not really, but I would like to know what you're thinking. I don't remember seeing you alone with your silent company very many times. You were always out solving this or that crime."

"There is nothing to solve now. I'm retired. Besides, idle hands are the devil's workshop. What will our hands do with it? I am wondering if all this money will be good for either one of us."

"Other than what you've stuck in my pocket, I am seeing little of it. Wouldn't it be nice for us to be the ones handing the greenbacks out? Doesn't Marlene give you much of an allowance? I really don't think you want to be a kept man, Mr. Macho."

I see my little brother is becoming frustrated at being in the dark so long. I know the little devil is pushing on my psychic hot button. I approach the subject head on.

"Listen you little two-faced-piss-ant, no pun intended, you need to be giving your big brother a little more credit than that."

William is crouching back into the darkness of the far corner of the basement. He is sensitive to my feelings and is re-evaluating his comments. A minute or so passes and I hear movement. I am still facing where he is sitting and hiding in the basement corner. Turning my back on someone is not my style. Sitting facing the door in any public building is still a part of my training. I am pleased that people are buried looking up. It is easier to see who is trying to steal your jewelry or bones. William's face is pale white when it again appears from the depths of the blackness where he is now residing with his own thoughts and memories. His words are low, apologetic and pleading in nature.

"It is just that it has been so long. I am beginning to wonder who I am anymore. I am beginning to wonder if there really is a future for me."

"Well, William, there is a future for both of us. This Marlene thing is good for both of us. Come over here and have a snifter of cognac with me. Let's pretend we are at Burt's Bar and Grille again and that things are like they used to be. Hell, in a week or two, you will be able to build your own bar and grille, if that is really what you want."

William slides in next to me. His powdery looking face is a concern. I am beginning to believe that the transplant is going south. I do not mention this. I reach into my pocket and hand my little brother five thousand dollars.

"You need to get out and get some sun, William. The doctor says it is good for you in moderate amounts. If you aren't going to be walking the mansion grounds, maybe it is time to cut you lose a little. I will tell you straight up that, if you break your promise to me, I will personally fucking kill you with my bare hands."

I see a slight smile come across William's face. I am talking to him like when he is younger, like when he is fucking up and I am covering for the little bastard with my pretend father. William is a great receptor for what I am always calling, 'heart-break love'.

"You do love me. You do love me. You big old prick, you do love me. Now, what about Marlene? When are you going to do the deed?"

"Well", I say as I am sipping a little more cognac.

"The deed may not be necessary. That pre-nuptial thing might just be coming to an end real soon. Can you believe that? The girl is really in love with your stud brother."

I see William is thinking again. His eyes are fixating directly on mine and I know he is looking to catch me in a lie.

"It is our money. Isn't it?"

"Yes, it is."

I am leaning over toward William. My right hand is on his shoulder and I am pulling him up close to my face. I am whispering into his ear.

"The money is ours, William. It belongs to just you and me, but my thinking is that accidents are better than murder. No telling what might happen when we are fishing up at the lake in the spring."

"And you are willing to trust me, to set me free until then?"

"At some point you are either going to be grateful for what I have done for you or you are going to fuck it up. If you fuck it up, your new identity isn't going to reflect on the Sigrist family name. You have a choice to make, William. Only you can make that choice. Trust the one who has been with you all these years, the one who has stood up for you and the one who has killed for you. If none of that means anything to you and your art is all that really matter, go on out and start it all over again just don't expect me to be there to pick up the pieces this time.

Fuck, take up photography or something. Take up something a little less violent."

Now William is leaning in and whispering in my ear.

"That is a good idea, Big Brother. Can I take photographs of my art?"

My look is a dead giveaway. William is leaning back on the bar stool laughing like a hyena. He is slapping both of his knees with his hands and trying not to choke on his last swallow of cognac. Holding the glass up for another swig, the tears of laughter are beginning to roll from his eyes.

"I got you. I fucking got you. That's just a little payback for the fucking thing on the dock, where you jumped out of the water and I almost shit my pants."

The next thing I know William is hugging me. His embrace is strong and violent, but feeling his love for me is exasperating. He speaks again.

"I'll be good. I swear I'll be good. I just want two things from you."

"And, what might those two things be, William?"

"For one thing, I want this all to be over soon."

"And, what is the second thing?"

"If my face falls off, I want you to get me another one."

William is sobbing. He is sobbing like when he is a little boy and mother is calling him the 'two martini baby'. So much rage is inside of him. His emotions are up and down. One never knows what one is getting. It is not fair that I am the one sharing it with him. I am all the more intent on following through with John Murphy's and my plan.

"William, it will be over soon. It will be over this coming month. That is a promise I make to you from the bottom of my heart. As for your face, it doesn't even have to fall off. If you get tired of the one you have, we will just get you another. Shit, I've been thinking of a facelift myself. Mind you, it won't be quite as drastic as yours."

The cognac is taking its toll. We are both again laughing like madmen and our sounds are echoing through the false wall behind the bar, into the hidden hallways and chamber where most of my childhood still resides. It is a childhood full of memories of looking out from my own secret hiding place at this creature I am now sharing the night with. I am just, 'Gary'. William, even though he is not the wanted child, is something special. He is the topic of conversation. I am just a shadow behind the shadows. It is all about William. That is soon to end. John Murphy is more and more excited with each passing day. It is time for my father and me to receive our just rewards. Halloween is not that far away.

Chapter Fifty-One

(Three Musketeers)

William is being a very good boy. He is home on time and is as normal as I remember, this being an observation for debate in both his life and the life of our family. His moods are still present, but are not as drastic a shift as in the past. Marlene is out of her shell and is bonding with the staff quite nicely. Some of the servants are calling her, 'Sweet Lady'. I am pleased with this development. There are regular meal times now and, but for the lack of a father figure, Mr. Whipple, myself and Marlene take our meal at seven in the evening and drinks directly afterwards. I view myself as the father figure and sit at the head of the table. Mr. Whipple does not seem to mind. Marlene is very acceptable of Mr. Whipple being our guest at evening dinner and I am aware of several occasions where the two split a sandwich and drink for lunch in the kitchen area. Marlene does not bother the staff, making the quick lunch for her and Mr. Whipple herself. Dinner table conversation is light and often jovial. I am beginning to wonder just how many personalities my younger brother really has.

"Tell me, Mr. Whipple. Have you found anything outlandish during your auditing of the family books? Did Vickie waste it on anything worse than a truck load or two of cocaine?"

"No, ma'am, I am pleased to report that there is still enough money to get you and Mr. Sigrist through eternity together. The interest alone is more than most family fortunes. Mind you, I am not saying there wasn't a check here or there that might be suspicious, but overall I don't think Vickie did much more than do drugs, drink and...'.

Surprisingly, Marlene fills in William's unfinished comment.

"Didn't do much more than drugs, drink, and fuck? Is that what you were about to say?"

I see a slight apologetic smile on William's face. I enter the conversation.

"You can't blame a girl for the last vice. Can we, Marlene?"

"We definitely can't. I don't know where men get off thinking they are the only ones who enjoy sex. It is like that old saying about a, 'hard man being good to find'. Tell me, Mr. Whipple. Do you like sex?"

William's face is now in a full smile.

"Please, Marlene, don't fuck with me. Your husband is in the room. He will think we are having more than lunch together, ma'am."

"You couldn't handle this little lady, chump."

We are all laughing our asses off when the server walks in to tell us our drinks are in the main living room. Walking into the main living room, I am watching as William is stepping around the area where Vickie's body hits the floor the night she falls over the upper railing. I am also thinking that, if he is doing something other than having lunch with Marlene, killing both of them might be the right decision. I decide against it because of the prenuptial thing being canceled. There is no need in complicating things. Marlene loves me. I am sure. I am also sure that love and jealousy go hand in hand. This is a normal response. Isn't it? The conversation continues in the living room.

"How much longer is it going to be, Mr. Whipple?"

William is standing and leaning against the fireplace wall. His martini is on the fireplace mantel.

"What? How much longer is what going to be?"

"How much longer is your audit going to take? I assume you will want to get back home sometime soon, unless you like it better here than at home."

I watch as William is retrieving his martini from the fireplace shelf, taking an olive out with his fingertips, plopping it into his mouth and swallowing a little bit of the gin. He is turning toward me as he is swallowing the olive and gin and is beginning his reply.

"Oh, I don't know. How much longer do you think it will be, Mr. Sigrist?"

The sneaky little son-of-a-bitch is putting me on the spot. I know he is fishing for a response about our previous conversations regarding Marlene, the prenuptial and his total freedom.

"I'm thinking about a month longer and our friend here can be home."

Marlene's reply is a surprise.

"Do you like plays, Mr. Whipple?"

"Do I like plays?"

"Yes, do you like plays? My big handsome husband here doesn't like plays and I want to run over to Toronto so see The Phantom of the Opera. I hear it is the greatest thing since Fiddler on the Roof."

I know I am protecting my territory, but this is something I find attractive about Marlene. She is a very subtle at flirting and getting her own way. She is reeling me in like I am being reeled in by William that day on the dock up at the cabin. This time I am the one being controlled. My instinct is to protect my territory. She knows it. I know it and, worst of all, William knows it.

"Now, baby, I never said I did not like plays. What is up with that?"

"That's good. Maybe that was the other stud before I met you. I'll make the plans for all three of us to go. It will be our going away present for Mr. Whipple. Would you like to bring your wife, girlfriend or significant other? If not, it will just be the Three Musketeers."

"No, no and no. I am single, but I would like to go."

"Then it is settled. We are going to Toronto. I'll find a date for you. You will love her. 'Her' is, alright, isn't it?"

William is having great fun and his response is so quick I am unable to head off this invitation.

"Of course, a 'her' is fine. I've dated many lovely women in my time. I just haven't found the right one. Just when you think you have found one that appreciates things like fine silk scarves they end up being beer guzzling Bud Lite drinkers. Do you know what I mean?"

Marlene is giggling and I am starting to be put off by this whole conversation. This is the first time in my relationship with my younger brother where he is actually in control of a situation. Maybe, I am thinking, this is improvement or it is false security behind the mask of his new identity. Whatever it is, we are on our way to Toronto to see The Phantom of the Opera by Andrew Lloyd Weber. It isn't so much the play that is bothering me as it is wondering if William's 'her' guest is leaving Toronto alive. Marlene and I retire to our room for the evening. It is the first time since our marriage we do not make love. William is standing alone by the fireplace, second martini in hand, alone with his thoughts.

Chapter Fifty-Two

The Pantages Theatre in Toronto, Canada is like a brick and mortar soul always refusing to die. Its face, skin and coloring are constantly rotting away and the glitter of its gold paint and false marble walls fade gradually over the years. People, seeing their own reflection in the many restorations of this fabulous place, are in debt to this palace of the arts. It is a reflection of their dwindling physical self and I think this is why they are constantly restoring it to its original beauty. The theatre is a monument to their memory as much as it is a monument to the history of the art and creativity residing in this undying museum of Canada's past. In a way, as I sit here waiting for the curtain to rise on The Phantom of the Opera, I am thinking that it is a lot like me. I am the proud owner of a second face and a second chance in life. My immediate desire is to be forever like this theatre, where people are always picking up their mortar and brushes, using them in the process of restoring my shifting physical appearance to its original glory. If only one's mental state of mind might be forever young and happy, but 'if only' is a dream for artists much greater than me.

Places like this are their own art, even before the artists of particular disciplines take the stage to delight the crowd. I like the idea of being one's own art. My body, my very self is art. Never mind the body of work surrounding me and reflecting my life. These materials are only a snapshot of whom and what I really am. I am thinking that the problem with my art is that its end result is final and that my body of work is all that remains of my life. The life of this theatre is forever in the hearts and minds of everyone entering its doors. This is why its patrons are constantly digging it from its grave and jump-starting its heart again and again. Some things are lucky like that in life. I am thinking that my big brother is only my keeper and his fate is the same as mine, the same as all of us in the individual sense. Our life is timed with the sand running slower for some and faster for others, but the end result is always the same. Once we die we linger a little until the memories about us being held onto by others fade. It is then that we are truly gone. I want to be this theatre. I need to be this theatre. From reading the play's stage book I do not want to be the Phantom. His torture, his face, his fate is merely covered. Mine, though false, is whole and is sharing my pain and anguish with me. It is not ripped away by curious and uncaring meddlers, seeking the truth in my eyes. In this sense my destiny is my own and walking in the light of day is possible.

Even before the first raising of the curtain on this play I am sensing that this theatre is a kaleidoscope of emotions. It is more human than me. This is troubling. Still, this is fascinating. This theatre is the many souls of Canadian history turned inside out for the whole world to see. Its walls are holding all of a human's senses from the rich vibrant colors of red, green, gold and silver right down to its dark and secretive corners hanging like untold truths beyond the corners of your eye. I am not like this theatre. There are too many human truths living here for me to know. Suddenly, I am feeling small and insignificant. This theatre is a statement. It is a grand statement. I am just William, Mr. Whipple, a man with his new face who is missing his art so very much. I am a single man grasping for the last few pieces of his sanity, still not a member of any family. This is making me very angry. My date, her name is Alexis, is squeezing my arm as the play and its bombastic music begins. She is an escort from the area. Gary understands that a good fucking is more important than a new relationship. There are so many other issues in need of working out. She is wearing a bright multi colored scarf. The scarf is dripping with silver, gold, red, blue, yellow and a deep purple. The scarf's colors seem like they are reflecting the faces of all my past victims, my own pieces of individual art. The deep purple is so deep it is reminiscent of very dark blood, blood that is pure and clean and being made more vibrant in texture by it kissing the oxygen of its environment. I am feeling things inside of me living in the dark corners of my own human theatre, things on hold because of promises to my brother. How much longer? How much longer is this to go on before I am free to create again? I am a patient man. There is a limit to my patience. You understand that, right? The music is pounding. Alexis is gripping my arm so tightly her nails are digging into my skin. I am thinking of purple, wild sex after the play, returning home to finalize things, being consumed by all of these colors and souls surrounding me. The chandelier swings out over the audience and, momentarily, the living and the dead are all hanging onto it together. The play begins and, one by one, the living fall back into their seats witnessing history in the making.

Alexis Tong, what a conflict of terms. How a Chinese woman is named Alexis Tong is beyond me. We are sitting at Lime Ricky's on Yongue Street and are having a quick dinner after the play. Gary and Marlene are off by themselves. I am assuming they are already at The Sir Francis Drake screwing. Anyway, Alexis Tong and I are eating dinner and talking.

"Alexis, you seemed to be very moved by the play."

"I am moved by it every time, Mr. Whipple."

"Every time, how many times have you seen the play?"

"I've seen it about twenty times now and I still get goose bumps all over me."

"That's a lot of times to see one play. I would think a person might get bored."

"There are places I do get bored, but I am a working girl and one goes where the client wants to go."

"Does a girl also do everything the client wants to do?"

Alexis is looking at me from over her chocolate martini glass. There is a short silence. She is not offended. She understands that the ground rules must be set.

"Some things cost more than other things. I think, in that respect, you are a lucky man."

"I, am?" How am I a lucky man?"

"Gary is very generous. He must like you very much. Let's just say that, what he has paid gets you whatever you are in the mood for and I will be offended if you even offer a tip. I won't disappoint."

It is good that the ground rules are out of the way. They say Chinese and Japanese are tight naturally and that the sex is really exhilarating. I am looking forward to the night in bed with Alexis. My plan is to work her long and hard, so to speak.

"How in the world did you get your name, girl? It seems so at odds with your origin."

Alexis is very point blank with her answer.

"My father was black, had a big dick and my mother likes that sort of thing."

"She, likes?"

"Yes, she likes. Mother introduced me to the business and is still doing quite well in it herself. Some young kids like older woman with a little more experience. I am fortunate to have been tutored by one of the best. Mother and I are quite well off…sitting on a gold mine and all that sort of thing."

"Hopefully, you don't talk this much during sex."

"You don't have to worry my love. My mouth is usually full."

I am smiling. Alexis is smiling. The girl either enjoys her profession or is very good at pretending that she does.

"That's enough about me, Mr. Whipple. Do you care to tell me a little bit about yourself?"

I am thinking. What can it hurt? I am looking at that scarf again, how it drapes itself around her long professional neck. A time or two, I think I am actually seeing it tighten itself around her throat in anticipation of my hidden desires.

"There really isn't much to tell. I am an account. I am a damn good accountant. Oh, physically, I am ok with sports and all that shit. I did pretty well in college and am still in great physical condition, but I just like numbers. Numbers are not random like so many other things in life. I like order and I didn't relish the idea of getting my nuts pushed up into my throat while playing football or some other brain rocking sport. Right now, I am just doing some numbers crunching for Mr. Sigrist and his wife, Marlene."

"They seem like a very nice couple."

"Yeah, I guess. I just keep to myself and do my job. Coming along with them was just a fluke, a last minute business thing, and Mr. Sigrist's wife had to see this fucking play."

"You didn't like the play?"

"No, actually, I am very surprised. I loved the play. It says so much about love, tragedy, wants, desires and the intended and unintended cruelty of life. Sometimes I think life really is hell and nobody let us know when were checked in at birth."

Alexis is running her foot up my inside thigh and is massaging my groin with her foot. Her one shoe is off and, but for knowing better, I am thinking there is a hand under the table playing with my dick. Alexis speaks.

"What do you say we put all that heavy thinking stuff behind us and go on up to your room for a nightcap?"

"That's a good idea. I'll get the bill."

"There is no need for that. I've already slipped the waiter the money plus some. We are good to go."

The sex is out of this world. Our sweat is the lubricant giving us momentum and we go from one act, one position, to another. I am a natural or Alexis is making me look like a natural. I think my brain is even hard. After climax, I am checking the sheets to make sure it is really semen and not brain matter on the bed. I am watching as Alexis slithers off to the bathroom. Slither is the proper word. She moves like a cobra when she walks. One is hypnotized watching her performance, a performance right up to the end. This is the only thing negative about this woman and other women like her. Her work is her life and her life is a performance. In a way Alexis is her own art. Some of her work is less desirable than others. Isn't all art that way? I am glancing up a second time when she is coming back out of the bathroom. She is fully dressed and looking impeccable.

"You're dressed. Are you going someplace?"

"Look, honey. The deal is you get your rocks off and I am free to go. I have a couple of quick ones waiting in the wings, my mad money so to speak. A girl has to know when to stop at one martini. Two can get you in a hell of a lot of trouble. Bye, bye, now."

I am seeing red watching her slither out the hotel room door. She really is a snake. Is this my fault? Am I just a failure at everything? Is my performance that bad? No, my performance is great. This one is not art. This one is without feeling. She is nothing more than another little gold-digger feeding off the innocence of the world. I am thinking she is to be stopped. How dare her tell me my time is up. My time is up when I say my time is up. Gary is going to approve of this one. His money is not going to be squandered this way.

I am out of the bed and dressing on the run. The elevator is already moving down. I am racing down the stairs. I am into the lobby. Where is Alexis? I am on the sidewalk looking down the street. There is a voice behind me.

"May I help you with something, sir?"

I am breathing very rapidly.

"Yes, yes you can. My wife just left and forgot to take her scarf and glasses. She is blind as a bat trying to drive without them."

"What did the lady look like?"

My description is a dead giveaway.

"If it is the same lady she went down the side alley toward the back garage entrance."

"Thank you, man. Here, take this."

My twenty dollars feels comfortable in the doorman's palm as I am heading down the alley toward the back garage. I am in time to catch a glimpse of Alexis rounding the last corner and moving up the steps at entry door one. I am already out of breath, but my anger is pushing me on. The damn bitch is just like the rest of them. I am even having bad thoughts about my own mother fucking around. Money, money, is it always about nothing more than money? Gary is going to understand this one. Like the Phantom my new face is slipping a little more with each step up the stairwell. At the fourth floor I see the door closing. I am standing there panting and watching through the little glass window in the door. Alexis is walking directly across the aisle toward a red Miata sports car. I am thinking her ride is even small and deceitful. This is not a car. It is a fucking overpriced roller skate. Her keys are out and she is opening the door. This is my last chance. I am on her quickly. I slam her head against the top of the car. The scarf is in my hand. I put the scarf into my pocket. She is unconscious. This is not about art. It is about revenge for being treated like a fool. My new face is slipping farther and farther. I am William at this moment in time. There is nobody in the garage. There are no cameras that I am seeing. This is an afterthought that is overlooked in my rage. I am dragging Alexis back toward the fourth floor stair landing. A few seconds later she is over the railing. I am watching her plummet. Her landing is head first and very violent. The first floor landing is no longer gray. It is a deep purple, the color of Alexis' scarf that is residing comfortably in my pocket.

The next morning, upon waking, the purple scarf is over my face. I am relieved, rested and relaxed. Approaching the border certain fears are beginning to grab hold of me. The border crossing between Canada and the United States goes quickly. One more lost Chinese hooker is not a big deal. She is most likely having her toe tagged at this very moment. On the way back to the mansion, I am sleeping in the back of the car. My hand is in my pocket. It is caressing the multi-colored scarf with the deep purple accents. I am becoming aroused again. How much longer, like the Phantom, before this false face is off and I am William again? Gary is silent the whole way home. Marlene is asleep too. Her head is on Gary's shoulder as he is driving. She is snoring. Her snoring wakes me. I attempt conversation.

"Is that sound what you love so much about her?"

Gary is looking back in the car's rearview mirror. He is silent. I am wondering. Does he know? Does he know about last night? Does he approve? Or, is he going to kill me with his bare hands? I am thinking he knows and he approves. We do, after all, have plans of our own. Marlene is waiting in the wings. My big brother is the architect. I am the artist. I am sure of this. I am also sure that all Gary and I really have are one another. Suddenly, I am missing my dancing machine and the events of last evening are the farthest thing from my mind.

The car is entering the mansion's driveway around one in the afternoon. I am looking up the drive at the face of the Sigrist's home. Its windows are looking back much like Gary's eyes in the rear view mirror on hearing my question. No lights are on. Everything is dark. I find myself thanking Gary and Marlene for a wonderful time, and then hurrying off with my bag toward my room. Once I am in my room with my new trophy, my beautiful scarf is tucked away in the drawer beside my bed. My collection begins again. I am finally accepting of the fact that, no matter what face is in my mirror, I am still William.

Chapter Fifty-Three

(William's Time)

Father and I are in agreement. The Toronto incident will eventually lead to our doorstep. It is time for the termination of Mr. Whipple's services before any concrete trail about his real life is established. Halloween night is the target night anyway. It is but a week away. Now there is all the more reason and a sense of urgency. Buying a border guard's silence and clearance is not something one can be doing over and over again. My father, John Murphy, is conflicted. His long-standing promise to mother is to see William and me through thick and thin right up to the end. Though John Murphy is excited about the event, he is not excited about the deed. His promise to mother is the thing. He is trying to be rational about it.

"Oh, well, everyone must have something to carry to their graves. Otherwise it would be too peaceful of a sleep."

I am trying to be as supportive and understanding as possible. The truth is that I am ready for this to be over and for Marlene and me to be getting on with our lives. Too, father is up in age and needs the security of some semblance of peace of mind during his remaining years. The household staff is also aging. I am seeing a time when the mansion stands alone, empty and forgotten, while embracing its own secret soul. Traveling is on my mind, traveling to far off and exotic places.

"You know, father, William is sort of like a pet that becomes a burden. People buy all of those preconceived ideas that it is your responsibility to have one and to keep one safe from harm. Hell, part of our fortune, is built on our pet food section. Ask yourself. Do we have a pet?"

John Murphy replies without hesitation.

"No. I don't want one either. I never have and I never will. I remember you telling me about all those people walking around Key West with their dogs cleaning up pet shit as they went."

"That is my point. I know you promised mother, but there comes a time for hard choices. Besides, sacrificing one of our own for our faith is the highest testament for our followers. If we keep cleaning up William's shit, we'll be knee deep in it before it is over. I love you, dad. I've done things for you because of how much this promise to mother means to you. Honestly, the time for promises and guilt is over. We have ourselves to think about. William cannot be walked on a lease forever and, I believe, he is not capable of being trained. A new face does not mean what is underneath is not still the same. The Toronto incident just helps to confirm everything we both feared. There are too many fleas on William to keep him around. He is infecting all of us, our way of life."

"I understand, son. I just wish our original plan had worked. I really believed that if we immersed William in his desire for killing that he would outgrow the desire."

"That is wishful thinking, father. It is like the swinging sixties. Some psychologist believed that by swimming in sex and debaucheries one eventually finds it all blasé, moving on to some higher plane of existence. I'm here to tell you that as long as a man's dick can get hard, he is going to find something to fuck. William's 'art' is the same as fucking. It will eventually take us all down."

"I know. It is just that..."

I finish my father's sentence.

"You don't want to be the one to do it. Say no more. I will do it for you. If you want, don't even watch. Don't even attend the event. The bottom line is that we must confirm our faith for another year and this approach solves all of our problems."

Father is a loving man. This is a very difficult decision, but I finally see resignation and acceptance on his face regarding what is to follow. I also see tears in his eyes. I do not know if the tears are for William or are for a promise about to be broken. We are sitting in the secret chamber of the mansion. The concrete walls are thick and nothing but the sound of our breath is in the immediate range of our hearing.

"Would you like me to pour you a small dab of cognac, father. I think I will have one while finishing the preparations."

"No, Gary. I think I am going to take a walk around the grounds, just to clear my head."

I am alone in the chamber. William's scarves, the scarves of his victims, are all hanging along a thin wire at the back wall of the room. The wire is twisted tight around the two eyebolts on each side of the wall. I am amazed at how many scarves there are and, how together, they make something beautiful. I am thinking of a violent storm going away, leaving a beautiful rainbow behind. The problem is that I really know no one in possession of a pot of gold. The rainbow is nothing more than something beautiful and momentary, left behind because of Mother Nature's guilt at having brought so much destruction on so many innocent people.

William's dancing machine is in the center of the room. It really is a mechanical marvel and, but for actual moving joints, might mimic the human skeletal structure perfectly. This thing is more than a morgue table. It is the initial prototype of a mechanical person. It is like William is thinking, during its creation; build the frame and then the parts. I am thinking he is ahead of his time. I envision computer parts moving legs, arms and on and on. I understand this machine is, in so many ways, just a pipe dream for any resemblance of a flesh and blood relationship. College is William's greatest loss, even beyond that of any personal relationship. Great minds often love their work more than the people surrounding them. William, I think, is a great mind gone astray in a dark and lonely asteroid field of accidental collisions. He is now too far out there for saving. It is not his fault. It is just his fate."

John Murphy is not walking in the woods. He is sitting on the stone bench beside the family mausoleum on the other side of town. The cold and snow does not seem to be bothering him. If anything the cold is freezing the decision he and I make earlier, in a permanent place in his mind, so that it is not betrayed. He is waiting for mother's voice. He is waiting for forgiveness regarding what is about to take place. The winds are howling and whistling around the corner stones of the dead. Is this sound natural? Or, is this sound mother, screaming out her disappointment?

Mr. Whipple is sleeping. Soon, he is to be in a low state of suspended animation from drugs slipped into his drink. We are to drink together one last time. It is the least one brother can do for another. Watching him sleeping I am thinking it is not long until the 'two martini baby' is resting peacefully in the loving arms of the one unquestioning mother responsible for us all, the universe.

I am sliding the viewing panel of William's room silently back in place. I am thinking of Marlene. She is at the cabin preparing a comfortable place for us to rest after the big mansion party on Halloween night. Marlene is not a big party person. Still, being away from her for a number of days is frustrating. I am replaying her parting words over in my mind.

"Have your little party, baby. I'll be fine with my books. I'll be waiting with open arms. We are going to be together a long time. A little me time is a good thing. Enjoy your friends."

In this respect, Marlene is the exact opposite of Vickie. She is introspective, about books, about plays, about quiet time. She is the humanity often questioned in a life as a police officer. I am thinking it is a good thing we meet after my retirement, not while I am still on the beat. This is why so many police marriages fail. What one lives and what one sees are just too much in conflict. It is like my simple advice to my father, John, 'stepping in too much shit' changes your life. I am a lucky man. I still taste Marlene's last kiss. Getting to the cabin after the event is now all that is on my mind. I am torn by the fact that such a love is mine and not William's. William is the one needing unconditional love the most. I am now beyond offering it.

Chapter Fifty-Four

Vivian, the Black Witch, is busy putting the final touches on the chamber area. There is, however, a problem. It is the afternoon of Halloween and Mr. Whipple is missing.

"When is the last time anyone has seen him?"

"It was just early this morning, Mr. Sigrist", the kitchen aide, Reeves, replies.

"Have we checked the grounds?"

"John Murphy is doing that as we speak."

"What about the basement? He seems to like getting lost down there at the bar area."

Reeves, interjects, again.

"The last time anyone has seen Mr. Whipple was early this morning as he was passing through the kitchen with a bagel in one hand and a cup of coffee in the other."

I am furious and the staff knows it. My specific orders are to watch Mr. Whipple's movements and, if he is leaving the grounds, to immediately notify either me or John Murphy. I am in the middle of pulling a 'William' in the circular front part of the driveway. I am stamping my feet, jumping up and down, waving my arms and screaming at the top of my lungs.

"Shit. Shit. Shit. Shit."

My ears are catching another voice in the distance. The voice is coming from the garage area. It is the voice of Oscar, the family mechanic.

"Gary. Gary. A car is missing. It must have been taken before I got to work this morning."

Now, I am standing with my hands on my hips. I am looking down the driveway and toward the road. This is not happening again. It just can't be happening again, is what I am thinking. Stay calm. Get hold of yourself. William is impulsive, but he isn't crazy. Scratch that last thought. He is about as crazy as a dog with a flea up its ass. Ok, think man. Where is he going? What is your first move?

"Someone call John Murphy. There is no sense for him to be traipsing around in the woods if Mr. Whipple is in one of the vehicles."

"Yes, sir, I'm calling him. I'm calling John Murphy."

Vivian is punching father's number into her cell phone. This is the first time I am seeing the Black Witch nervous. Her hands are shaking violently. Oscar is just standing in the drive beside me. His arms are crossed, his head is tilting upwards and his appearance is that of a hound dog sniffing the wind for the scent of his prey. I am thinking this is just what I need, a hound dog standing on two legs sniffing the wind. Screaming into Oscar's face, I say.

"Go get a fucking car and let's go look for the little bastard."

I am dialing William's cell number. There is no answer. The crazy piece of shit is avoiding my call. I am going to rip his fucking head off the minute his beady little eyes meet mine. The chamber room's preparation is most likely for naught.

Out of the corner of my left eye I am seeing John Murphy lumbering out of the wooded area near the east side of the Mansion. He is noticing the cell phone in my hand.

"Is there an answer? Did he answer?"

I am looking into father's eyes. A response is not necessary. A second or two later the Mercedes sedan pulls to a stop in front of me. Oscar is driving. I am jumping into the front passenger's seat the same instant father is slamming the door to the back seating area. Oscar's foot slams the accelerator to the floor. The aging black pieces of tin and chrome is moving down the drive and belching smoke like some fairytale dragon with a bad case of heartburn. Just as we are nearing the end of the driveway another car is turning right. Oscar's instincts are very fast for a man of his age. A head on collision is prevented, but the shrubbery near the end of the street is demolished. As we are swerving to avoid a head on collision with the entering vehicle, Williams face is passing mine. He is smiling and leaning forward toward the windshield of the car he is driving.

"Drunk, I am thinking. The little mother fucker is already drunk at this hour of the day."

William's vehicle is now stopped in the center of a group of flowers lining the other side of the driveway. He is out of the car and is staggering back toward the three of us. John Murphy is anticipating my response and his hand is over the Mercedes' back passenger seat. His hand is gripping my shoulder so tightly it is nearly bringing tears to my eyes.

"Sit tight, son. Now is the time for patience, not a knee-jerk reaction. My guess is, right now, you and I will be drawing straws to see who gets to kill him."

I hear Oscar snickering as he is sitting in the driver's seat reviewing all the damage.

"You find this funny, Oscar?" father is asking.

Oscar is composing himself.

"No, I don't. I'm sorry, sir. I will go take Mr. Whipple under my arm before he falls flat on his face."

Father is still gripping my shoulder.

"Dad, I'm alright now. How about taking your hand off my shoulder?"

Father and I are standing near our car watching as William is being dragged off toward the mansion's front door. Father is placing his hand on my shoulder again. This time his touch is very gentle.

"Gary, go make sure your little brother is put to bed. Also, make sure he drinks a big glass of water. Do you understand?"

A few minutes later Oscar is on his way back to survey the damage, clean it up and do what he can with the yard before the guests begin arriving for tonight's Halloween party. I am watching William throwing up into his bedroom's toilet. Dry heaves are the worse. This is my opportunity.

"Get over here, dip shit. What was that all about?"

"I was starting to slip a little, just a little. Don't go getting all paranoid. I am better. I really am."

William is wiping the crud from his lips with the backside of one of his hands and is continuing his left handed apology.

"It was just time to clear the cobwebs out of my head, so to speak. I went cruising. I know. I know. Don't leave the fucking grounds without you. Here, kick me in the ass."

William is near his bed. He is leaning over with his ass pointing in my direction. I am seeing piss all over the crotch area of his pants and begin remembering various DUI cases from my street patrol years. I am convinced that this one drunk's urine is the reason for the back floorboards rotting out of my new patrol car. I am thinking about kicking William as hard as I can right in the ass, pushing his nuts all the way into his brain. The thought disappears as I am watching him falling face down on the bed. Reaching over and grabbing him by the back of his shirt collar and pulling upwards as hard as I can is the closest thing I can think of regarding my promise to rip his fucking head off with my bare hands. As I am rolling him over, he is reaching up wrapping both arms around my neck. The smell of his puke is just about all I can stand.

"I love you, big brother. William loves his big brother. We are going to be together right up until the end. You are my rock, man. You are my rock."

The glass of sparkling water on the nightstand is within reach. It is a little cloudy from the heavy sedative mixing in with the liquid.

"Drink this, dick. It will make you feel better."

William does not question me. He is holding the glass with both hands and, gulping the liquid down like some lost soul just in from the Death Valley Desert. Just after the last swallow there is a loud burp. Swinging William onto the bed in a stretched out position I am muttering to myself.

"If I didn't know Burt was dead and his place was burned out, I would swear you had been drinking with that fucked up Irish bastard all day long."

I am walking out of the bedroom door, hearing William's final comments before he passes out.

"Burt, good old Burt, I love Burt too, but I love my Gary better than Burt."

My father, John Murphy, is standing in the hallway next to the elevator. He is leaning on the same railing where Vickie plummets to her death.

"Interesting day, my boy, don't you think?"

I reply with a simple, "Yes".

Father and I stand there for a time without speaking a word. Then, for some unknown reason, I am asking him two questions.

"Father, did you push Vickie? Or, was it really just an accidental 'boo', like you said?"

Father is walking down the hallway as I am finishing my two-sentence inquisition.

"I'll see you below later tonight, son. Don't, worry about William. I will send Oscar for him."

I am peering over the railing, listening to father's footsteps going down the marble stairs. Just as his feet are hitting the hallway I see him looking up at me from below. He is standing in the exact spot where Vickie lands on the night of her death. One word echoes upward and grabs me by the throat.

"Boo!"

I am suddenly afraid of heights and hurry off in my own direction.

Chapter Fifty-Five

(The Deed)

I do not know this man we are dragging down the hallway toward the secret entrance into the chamber area. This is what I am telling myself. This is the rationalization keeping my conscious at bay. William is still heavily under the influence of the drug given him a few hours back. At that time it is my wish that, the combination of the drug and the amount of alcohol already in his system, is enough to kill him. It is not and he is destined to suffer more pain before being wrapped in the blanket of his own darkness. The time is eleven thirty-five in the evening and we are hurrying, attempting to beat the clock striking midnight. William's legs are like rubber and are flopping all around as John Murphy and I carry him on his last journey through the mansion's upper floor.

The party is already in full swing. Most of the party participants are at the mansion by nine P.M. at the latest. The food table in the main foyer is a thing of the past. A few crackers, a little caviar, ham and original style Triscuit crackers are all that remain on the food-stained white tablecloth that is covering a ten thousand dollar decorative table. The evening's guests are into the upper end liquor. They are waiting on our arrival just shortly after midnight. A few of the household servants are staying behind to ward off any 'free wanderers' wanting to hike though the mansion's many rooms and hallways.

As we are dragging William past one of the upper windows I glance quickly out into the night sky. Detroit is off in the distance, appearing to be lit up by small candles that are burning brightly throughout the city. I know that these are destructive fires from Halloween Night revelers, but there is a certain beauty to this scene that is looming so far off in the distance. I am remembering, as a little boy, standing on top of a small hill and looking out over all the campfires of the tents pitched randomly about the mountainside. It is like looking at a million lightening bugs being held captive in the jar of the world. I am thinking all of this in the blink of an eye. How quickly the mind is capable of running from its darker thoughts and into the arms of sweet memories, when a trying situation is requiring a steady course toward some singular purpose. My purpose is getting this evening over with and joining Marlene at my cabin a little farther north. I am thinking of the taste of cheese, wine and crackers and the feel of cool, early morning air laced with a light cleansing fog upon my face.

I am not as purposeful about this impending event as is my father, John Murphy, and the rest. I believe that getting from one day to the next is all that is possible for any member of the human race. The others believe there is something beyond the flesh and blood of our lives. I do not. I do bow to his will in this matter and am always secretly hoping father's death is before mine and that the gauntlet of his position in the group is passed to someone other than me. Being honest with myself and you, I am bound to admit that my involvement begins with need...a need for love and acceptance like any young child floating randomly upon the ocean of I life. The skills once in Grandpa Pope's hands and now, my father's, solicit much information that is useful solving this or that investigation during my police years. This is just a little more of that, 'the end justifying the means' thinking. I know down deep inside it is wrong. Still, what is really bad about a little torture? Aren't a few pieces of flesh, a tooth here or there, the loss of a finger or toe, being left with one eye worth the life of an innocent little girl buried alive along the farmer's back fence post line? Yes, it is true. The use of torture over my family's history means something different to them than it does to me. This is the point. I am not above it if the ending is a noble cause. Mankind is not perfect. That is why Gods are necessary. I am willing to give my father, John Murphy, his space. He is helping me. I am helping him. This is the long and short of all this Halloween Night bullshit currently taking place. The natives are restless one night a year. I think it is a very good deal, considering the consequences. Think about spring breakers around the country. They bring you money. They also bring you attitudes, filth, noise, drunkenness, and a sort of resentful acceptance of them. MasterCard and Visa smooth the way for new pulpits and police equipment. I am thinking we are all in bed with the Devil. I am thinking I am just another good person helping Satan clear the streets of all the trash left behind, these souls he is gathering up. Next year must be pristine for the new arrivals.

"Mmmmmm, what is happening?"

The tips of William's feet are bumping on the steps as we are moving down the secret passageway into the hidden basement chamber area.

"Nothing, champ. You came home drunk and we are just getting you ready for bed."

William's head is again bent over and his chin is resting on his chest. The chamber room is to the right of the last step. A circle of servants and believers are filling the wall area of the room. Their faces are covered and their heads are looking down. Their hooded robes are black. I am thinking, 'Ah, the bullshit effect'. I am also thinking that these are grown people playing a child's game once a year. Yet, I understand there are bankers, lawyers, politicians, blue-collar workers and our servants assembled here. A half dozen or so move a little forward into the room, allowing space for us to enter. Immediately they slide back into their position, completing the circle again.

William's dancing machine is in the center of the room. It is in an upright position. I am thinking it is true that our own creations are often the tools of our own destruction. The scarves of his victims are still hanging on the line against the top of the back wall of the chamber. The scarves are in stark contrast with the rest of the chamber's dark, molding and dying walls. I am thinking about my father's comment about needing new blood in the group. I am seeing one hooded figure leaning uneasily forward onto a four-legged walker. Candles are near the top of the ceiling. They are glowing ever so faintly as if fighting off their own death at the hands of the thinness and wetness of the air here in the mansion's belly. The shadows of the attendees are floating back and forth like stage effects in some cheap black and white horror movie. I am forcing my mind to be thinking of Marlene. This is all soon to be over and, all is well that ends well. My father, John Murphy and I, strap William onto his dancing machine. His lower legs are bound very tightly because of his condition. William is drooling down the front of his shirt, still stained from last night's vomit. I am looking at him as he is at this moment. He is a spring breaker. He is disgusting. He is in need of being swept up from the beach with all the other trash left behind from years of aimless and mindless wanderings. Father and I don the traditional 'scare me to death costumes' the others are wearing. We wait. We wait as William is hanging there all useless and disgusting. The clock is at eleven fifty-five. It is nearing the midnight hour. Things are happening quickly now. Another part of the circle separates. The members in the room are chanting. A figure is walking forward as the circle is becoming whole again. William is looking up. His eyes are barely open now. He speaks.

"Fuck, man, you need a shave."

The werewolf is there. His face is back, the one left for Vickie the night of her own Halloween Party. This party is different. The intended victim is different, but the end results are the same. Some prosper. Some die, all around the world for a faith older than time. The Sigrist family and their alliances are one. The wolf is leaning in; the costume is so real, I am wondering if this creature is not from Hell itself. The face of the wolf is within an inch or two of William's face. The believers are chanting louder and louder. The party above is louder and louder. Neither hears one another. They are worlds apart.

"Well, well, Mr. Two-faced, maybe I can count this one as a 'give me' for next year. "

The wolf is pulling on its gloves; the ones fitted with the large fish hooks in place of claws. The hooks are barely visible through the false fingertips because of all the hair cascading down the top knuckles of the outfit. I am desperately trying to stay logical. I am losing the battle. The costume is just so fucking real. The hands are in place. The costume is complete. William and the wolf are still face to face. The wolf is speaking again.

"It is a shame. I fuck most of my victims. This is a special situation. It is a family thing."

William is now nearing complete consciousness. I see him mentally trying to organize what he is seeing. I am thinking, 'get this over with'. The werewolf is circling the machine. He is whispering into William's ear.

"I love this invention of yours, William."

The creature taps his steel claws against the back of the machine up near William's right ear. The sound echoes through the chamber, clink, clink, and clink. The wolf is now in front of William. All of this is happening so quickly. With its arms up and outward the wolf asks.

"May I have this dance?"

The steel claws are quickly in William's upper back shoulder blade area. He is screaming in pain as the creature is turning him around and around while chanting.

"All hail, Satan. All hail, Satan and the fruits of his love."

The wolf's claws are tearing flesh from William's back as he is being spun around and around. The believers are chanting still louder. As quickly as an eye blinks, the creature is behind

William. His claws are in the center of my brother's chest near his heart. The werewolf is pulling the dancing machine down into its horizontal position. William's screams are now an anguished mummer of sorts. The wolf pulls his claws all the way down William's chest and yanks them out at about his waistline. William's whole body is trembling and his feet are flailing back and forth trying to run from his bindings. The wolf is moving around the room as if speaking to everyone in the chamber.

"Now is the time. Time is short. Take the flesh of this traitor and serve up the feast of your faith for another year."

The circle is moving forward. I am backing out of the room. No one is watching me. It seems a thousand daggers are in the air at once. William's last scream is bitter sweet. It is both agony and relief.

I am sitting near the fireplace. I am watching the servants and the believers streaming in from below one by one. My father, John Murphy, is working the crowd. I am sipping on a scotch trying to wake from my own dream. I am thinking that life is a dream and the best anyone of us can hope for is the erotica and pain of it being sweeter than William's end. I am hearing his last words over and over in my mind.

"Gary? Gary? Gary?"

I am not there this time. It is done.

A shoulder is next to me. It is my father.

"I know this was hard. It was for the security of us all. The wolf is very impressed with your offering."

Looking up I see our mechanic, Oscar, standing next to me. The wolf mask is in his hand. He speaks.

"Your offering was beyond your calling. Here, the mask is yours. I am the old blood. You are the new. Begin picking your flock."

Shortly, I am wandering through the crowd with another drink in hand. It is, I am told, what one does when they are the chosen one.

Chapter Fifty-Six

(Take Back)

Taking some things back is not an option. You're feeling guilty as hell, but your guilt is internal. Guilt is nothing more than a learned response to one's upbringing. For me to be feeling this guilt is really wrong. This is what I am telling myself. After all, some societies wipe away murder by forgiving the perpetrator and accepting 'blood money' as compensation. Is this really any different from my situation with my younger brother, William? I guess one might argue that I am the one receiving the money. Still, I feel this is a technical item. The world is better off without the little bastard. God only knows that the murder rate around the Detroit area is immediately lower. In that light, my receiving compensation is the right thing. I am sort of a bounty hunter. His rationalization is his art…I should say was. Mine is, like I say, that I am a sort of bounty hunter. Am I starting to sound like him? The little son-of-a-bitch is trying to haunt me from his grave. If he is, I am going to kill him all over again in his afterlife. Fucking with me beyond the grave is not something I am willing to put up with. You do understand?

The next morning is calm. The servants are going about the mansion putting everything back in order, as if nothing is out of the ordinary. How many people are like us? I am thinking about this. Up until last night, our history and my involvement is more or less a game. It is a grown-up's game. It is like me wandering through the secret passages of the mansion as a child. I am watching John Murphy, before knowing he is my father, putting his pointer finger up to his lips and blowing that 'secret sound'. You know the one, 'shhhhhhhhh'.

"This is our secret, Gary. Only you and I know this secret. Can you keep this secret with me?"

For some reason I am unable to explain, I do keep the secret. It is something making me special. All little boys are in need of being special; all children for that matter are in need of being special. That little brat, William, is not the only child with needs. I am, at this moment, remembering the resentment always lingering in the back of my mind for the little prick. Oh, I am always hearing things like, 'He is your little brother', and 'Watch out for the little one, today ', 'Mommy is depending on you to look after William while I'm out. The list goes on and on. I am bitter about this time in my life. I am bitter now; even knowing he is dead and off my plate of things to do. Do you think this makes me an evil person? I don't. I think it makes me a realistic person. It isn't like he does not have every chance in the world for changing himself. Hell, the new face thing is beyond the call of duty. There is no way you can argue that point with me. Is there? Hell, no, there isn't. So, just shut the fuck up.

I am tired. It is the middle of the day and I am tired. This 'all hail the big shit head' stuff is very tiring. I am glad it is going to happen only one time a year. I am supposed to be thinking about next year already. Who the hell does that, kill someone one night and then start making plans for next year's big event? These fuckers do. My family is just plain fucked up. I understand some crack-head freaking out and claiming God made him do this or that. I get it. Don't you? The asshole is just out and out crazy. This stuff is different. My families' dark history is not something I want to deal with year after year. Ok, I killed my little brother, but the whiney little dipstick forced me into it. I am backing out of this whole thing now that my goal is met. Other than my father, servants and locals are the ones making up our group. Shit, I forgot. Some of those locals are very high up the food chain. I am having a hard time understanding this. Do you understand it? The 'money' is my conclusion. It is the money. Rush is always saying, 'follow the money'. I think I am right. Don't you? Following the fucking money is all one must do. So, here is my thinking.

The mob tortures a few people, maybe a cop or two. The cops are soon returning the favor. Soon it is a game of who is holding out the longest and who is screaming the loudest. Sounds like some out-of-control church where people are always running up and down the back of the pews screaming at the top of their lungs in a language no one understands. This sounds like controlling the crazies to me. If anyone who is anyone is playing, the rest of us don't have a chance. Shut up and let me finish. I don't give a fuck about your degree in psychology. I know how these things work. I am remembering it from my days as a cop, a cop on the shit streets of this shit city named Detroit. You pay to play and if you don't pay, forget about playing. I think that makes perfect sense. Maybe, it doesn't. Crap, I am really tired. Am I starting to sound like, William? I've already asked you that. Haven't I? Nerve ends make you tired. You can sleep twenty-four hours, but unexpected stress makes you tired. Try looking at the end of a gun every fucking day of your life for twenty years and then you might just fucking understand. I doubt it. Your mother probably screwed her way into millions. Hell, maybe William is the answer. I'm helping out a real artist who is doing something that is really important, getting all those dark hearts in mini-skirts off the fucking streets. I'm calling that guy in Mexico, Dr. Whatever. I'm betting he is capable of putting the little creep back together. No, check that. Billy's ashes are already stinking up an already stinking Detroit skyline. The little fucker is probably falling onto the roof of the mansion right now. What goes around comes around, doesn't it? Someone is touching me. Who is touching me?

"Gary?"

"Oscar? What is it, Oscar?"

"The servants have changed and turned back the bed in William's old room. Everything is clean right down to a new mattress and boxed-springs."

Oscar, the Werewolf, is really a leathery-faced figure. I am thinking he might do the werewolf thing next year without a mask. This is, however, my gig now. I am forgetting this little detail for an instant or two. I am surveying the man up close and personal. His hands are long. The tops of his hands are showing very prominent veins, as if the skin is just stretching itself over blood vessels and bone. I am remembering my dead mother being very embarrassed at a late afternoon tea when my little shit-head brother asks one of the older women in attendance a child's question.

"Do you have skeleton hands?"

I am leaning against the wall watching. My 'I don't give a shit look' is planted firmly on my face.

"Why, no sweetheart, I don't. Your hands just get this way as you get a little older."

I am looking into the old woman's eyes. She is thinking about ripping William's face off right, there and then. Inside I am laughing like a son-of-a-bitch. I am waiting for William's reply about never wanting to get old. This is when I see mother yanking William up by his arm and out the kitchen doorway, at the same time apologizing for her 'two martini baby'. I think this is the moment when I realize I am, like many of my friends, looking for a way out...a way out of this house, this city and this state. Oscar is speaking again. Leaving one's past is possible. Drowning out your past calling you home is not possible. This is my conclusion.

"Your father is very proud."

Oscar's skeleton like hand is lying firmly on my right shoulder. The feeling is like being gripped by the hand of the Devil.

"John wants you to rest up and take evening dinner with him. He says to tell you that he knows you are the master of the house now, but would still like you to do him this one last favor."

"Why, one last favor?"

I see Oscar is thinking a moment and choosing his words to my question very carefully.

"Gary, certain things must be decided so that none of us are a burden on one another. True, the wealth is enough for everyone. It is true also that that wealth is rightly yours and only one thing is standing in the way right now. The hard part is done. I'm sure John Murphy will want to talk about our next move, whether it is tactful or direct?"

"What do you mean, tactful or direct"?

Again, Oscar is silent for a moment or two before replying.

"The family's attorney is a very understanding person. He is also very pleased you are now the head of the Covenant. You two shared a drink last night after the event. Strong willed and a good fit for the future is what he is calling you. Still, there is the issue about Marlene."

I am offended.

"There is no issue with Marlene. The prenuptial is a thing of the past."

"And you know this how?"

"Marlene says so. That is how."

"I know your feelings for her. We all know your feelings for her, but this is not what we are being told. The paperwork is still in place."

I am taken back by this announcement. Oscar is walking down the corridor and I am hearing his last words as he is leaving.

"Please join your father for dinner tonight. Blind love is dangerous love, Master. Dinner is at eight. Your place at the head of the table will be waiting."

'Master', I like the sound of my new title. I am tired. I am thinking that there is now more worth considering than one relationship between two people, one of those people being the recipient of a lottery so to speak. Damn Vickie, and all of those like her. I am beginning to appreciate William's art more and more. I really am sorry William gives himself up for the good of the group. I really am guilty as shit about the whole thing. Still, there are no take backs. It is what it is. Sorry about that, little brother. I rest today. I dine with father tonight. I travel to my cabin up north tomorrow. Marlene and I are going to see eye to eye on this issue or there is going to be hell to pay. She promises me destruction of the prenuptial. A promise is a promise. Am I right?

I sleep easily, but for an occasional different colored scarf floating through my dreams. My last thought is of Grandpa Pope and William sitting together on that stone bench by our family mausoleum. Grandpa Pope is trying to put the whole thing in perspective.

"William, you must understand. It was for the good of the family name."

William's head is down. The Detroit night air is cold and my little brother's ghostly white lungs are filling with the dirty pollution of the surrounding automotive factories. William is not ready to be speaking to me in my dreams. He is still very pissed off over the events of Halloween night.

"My asshole brother isn't even worth haunting."

Grandpa Pope's laugh is loud and shrill. One might be mistaking it for the whistle of one of the area's automotive plants signaling quitting time.

"I like your point of view, son. The fact is that something haunts everyone."

William is pouting. He is somber. He is like a developing storm waiting to rip open the calm of an evening sky.

Chapter Fifty-Seven

Under the circumstances, staying mad at Marlene is not possible. We are riding back to the mansion together. The weather outside is cold and crisp, but the sky is blue…not a cloud overhead. This is very unusual for the Detroit area. Marlene is sitting silently next to me. I am not going to be bringing up her not answering her cell phone. Reception is bad around the cabin. Relaxing is the whole point. Marlene is looking very relaxed. I know just how tense it is when one is trying to fit into the Sigrist family lifestyle. Marlene is a simple girl. She is now a simple girl controlling great wealth and I am thinking that things are going to be fine. I am glad we are able to communicate the way we do. She is the first person where my words are not necessary for my meaning to be clear; just a look is enough. This bond does not even exist between me and my brother. Well, for sure it does not now exist. That is a whole different topic. Isn't it?

Oscar is a great mechanic. This old BMW is zipping along like it is fresh off the showroom floor. The car is a nineteen eighty-five. It has character. It says, as it is rolling down the highway, '*I am something special. I am carrying special people to a special place. I am an old, beautiful and strong vehicle that is full of knowledge. Knowing how to get from point 'A' to point 'B' in the most fashionable, stylish and discreet way is part of my heritage. I am not like all of those new plastic siblings claiming to be an automobile. Hell, most of them are incapable of deciding what they want to be. I mean, tell me. What the hell is a 'crossover'? Is that a straight car that is now gay? There is even a car on the drawing boards with something under the hood being called a compressor. Is that for young want-to-be cars that can't get it up anymore? Is that the automobile world's answer to Viagra? God, don't get me going on what is being called a sports car this day and age. I am thinking they look at some girl's big ass, put it into steel form, then chop it off for the rear of the car and stretch the car's front end so it looks like the dick is ahead of the pussy. I mean, just how embarrassing is that? Talk about getting the cart before the horse. I guess I am just from the old school and still believe the dick should be doing the pushing and not the other way around. Know what I mean? I am immediately offering my apologies all around to the girls who want to be boys and the boys who want to be girls. This is why the automobile industry is so fucked up. Think about the Mini Cooper for Christ's sake. Fucking in that thing, unless you are a midget, is impossible. I am not above admitting that a few of the new cars possess a little of what it takes to get things going. The rumble of an eight cylinder Mustang vibrating a guy's nuts is something that gets a conversation going and you can't tell me the girl doesn't like the feel too. The secret to a good car is that it does possess something for both, but doesn't try to dominate the sexual divide.'*

'Too, I breathe in all this shit in the air coming from these other want-to-be cars and spit it out like mucus from a bad head cold. Those little gender benders are always having their little purifier filters changed. Feeling downright gay is the result. Imagine, you humans, walking down the street with a tampon sticking out of your nose to help purify your system. Now, do you understand why I feel the way I do about new cars? The only way the industry is getting anywhere close to getting it right is by creating retro cars…cars just like me. I am a steel, loud, don't give a fuck, sleek, shiny, comfortable bed on wheels trimmed in chrome and capable of being fixed by a real mechanic instead of some little new wave jerk who is always sticking a probe up my ass or down my throat. I am asking you

point blank. Do you get my point? If not, stay off of my leather seating. Now back to Gary and Marlene. They are driving me back toward the mansion. Besides, we all know, this is what Gary is thinking at the moment. He is lost in the experience of throttling up a stud like me while in the company of one foxy lady. I am preparing her. I like Gary; his brother…not so much. I don't have to worry about little Willie anymore. Do, I? Going through all of that mumbo-jumbo is a waste of time. Putting him behind me and letting me slip out of gear and, well, a fucking, whining-assed problem is solved. If it looks like an accident and waddles like an accident, it must be an accident. Am I right? One of those little plastic look-a-like versions of me would go off running for another probe up their ass or down their throat. Hell, I would be hitting the opposite gear and running over the little fucker again. They just are not making cars like me anymore. Anyway, my problems are not that important. The stabilization of the Sigrist fortune is what is important, especially if I am to be around to have my rusting fenders and other parts repaired. I like being an historical vehicle. I am sort of like a handlebar mustache, out of place and in your face.'

The following is the conversation Gary is having with himself as he is driving back toward the mansion with Marlene sitting quietly at his side.

—

I am really glad that father understands my desire to give Marlene a little more time. I am sure that her promise regarding the prenuptial is good and that no deceit is intended. Father is well aware of my love for this woman and frankly, the shoe being on the other foot; I might be thinking the same way initially. Father's response to me is direct. I see myself in him, the way he carries himself and the way his logic moves in circles until the final option is a given. Politics is his missed calling, but I am wondering if some of those in the White House are like us; worshipping their own faiths in the hidden bowels of our country's main symbol of freedom. This is probably not that farfetched. Everyone knows that the United States is host to the 'great Satan' anyway. I am comfortable with this thought, especially now being a participant and knowing the ranks and status of many of those in the covenant. I am still uncomfortable with this Warlock and Witch thing. The violence one night a year is a small price to pay, especially if someone is deserving of killing. It is not like we are going out and scooping up some innocent person off the street just for the gratification of the act. Do you understand my thinking? My thinking is more refined than my late brother, William's. Watching as the little prick is hiding behind his urge for killing while calling it art is just warped. I do admit that it is with purpose in the beginning. I also admit that I am responsible for helping him along a little while he is struggling for his place in life. Still, how the hell am I to know he is enjoying it so much? I am listening if there is an answer out there for that question. Go, ahead. Speak up. That is what I thought. You do get my point. Down deep inside you are all a little like me, only on different levels. Like I am saying, father's response is both expected and appreciated.

"Love is blind, son. It really doesn't matter what that love is. It can be love of someone or love of something. Sometimes we must just let things run their course. You have given a great sacrifice in offering up William. I want you to know we are not monsters, just believers. Still you are committed to the possible task at hand if this prenuptial thing is not resolved in the very near future."

"I am, father. It will be by my own hand."

"The covenant's decision is a wise one. You are a fine leader and you and yours will be the new backbone of the next generation. Protecting the Sigrist legacy is protecting the world, so to speak."

"Some might say a world of darkness and sin, father."

"People are afraid of the dark only if they fear to step out and walk in it. Light, too bright, blinds one's perspective of things. This is why the Master fell from on high. He is powerful and inquisitive. He is loving and savage. He admits these things openly and rewards those walking with him. He does not pretend these things do not exist in the name of this or that. Every time I read The Canterbury tales I want to puke."

"At any rate I appreciate your patience. We will see."

"Yes, son, we will see."

Our dinner is lamb and it is especially good. Father likes eating lamb as often as possible. It is a constant reminder of the biblical reference and a source of humor. I am thinking about him putting the first fork full in his mouth. His is cackling like a child in joy over some secret only he understands and is finding humorous.

"Mmmmmmm, this is so fucking god damn good. I'm thinking of washing it down with a martini or two just so He knows what the fires of hell taste like."

With a martini under my own belt and a feeling of reprieve regarding my love, Marlene, I am off to the cabin. She is still not answering her cell phone. It is probably the weather or the fact that she just doesn't give a shit. Most women are like that. It is, 'leave a message' or it isn't worth my time. This is odd coming from a gender that is usually flapping their gums fast enough and long enough to keep a hovercraft in the sky for weeks.

On arriving at the cabin I am surprised to see Marlene sitting alone at the end of the dock in one of the wooden chairs. She is bundled up and intently gazing out across the lake. An open bottle of red wine is beside of her. Being the wine snob that I am I am thinking the stuff is probably too cold to be drinking and needs bringing inside so that its aroma and texture can be fully appreciated. There is a second glass sitting next to the wine bottle. It is as though she is expecting me, even without the cell phone call. We are spiritually attached. I am thinking that, with time, Marlene is a good addition to the covenant. I am also thinking that this prenuptial thing is on the back burner for the evening. I am horny as hell and looking to get my rocks off. Either that or my dick is frozen from this fucking nor-eastern weather coming off of the Great Lakes.

"I'm home, baby. I love you."

Marlene is stoically quiet. This is not her personality, but everyone is not cut out for a life of solitude. She is from the big city and it is understandable that relaxing among the hustle and bustle of sounds and sights without people around is a great deal different from my cabin here in the northern Michigan woods. Marlene is not a tree hugger and her idea of a tree's value is directly related to the wood's grain in a piece of fine furniture. I sense some distress at being away from people.

"We are going home, my love. Thank you for your understanding these last few days. You are the best catch ever from this little lake in no man's land."

Scooping Marlene up in my arms like I am carrying her over the threshold again, my legs move wearily toward the BMW again. If she is not happy here, I am not happy here. We are going home. During the ride I am remembering reaching out and feeling her skin. Hypothermia is a funny thing. Her flesh is a little blue, but it is warming. I am pleased with this development.

It is very early in the morning as the BMW is moving up the lane toward the mansion's many gazing window-eyes. I feel like the whole Sigrist family tree is watching, is lying in wait and judging if this is a proper woman for me to be bringing home. I am remembering that time I am caught fucking one of the local girls on the kitchen preparation table. You trip up on one little indiscretion and you are suspect for the rest of your fucking life. Do you know what I mean? Let's be honest. It is a meat table I am remembering. It is my opinion that some of the meat we put in our mouths taste a whole lot worse than pussy. Enough said. Now I am laughing like I am remembering my father's laugh at eating lamb and drinking martinis. He is such a wonderful father. He is going to know what to do now. I am sure of it. Finally the BMW is sitting in front of the mansion's front entrance. I am exhausted, leaning forward on the horn. It is blowing constantly. I am also crying.

"Oh, fuck. Be warm my love. Please be warm. Where the hell are you father? I need you father. Someone please help me."

Oscar is running from the garage area. He is limping, lumbering and running at the same time. The lights to the mansion are coming on. My father, John Murphy, is the first one out of the mansion door. He is being followed by the Black Witch. Shortly other servants in various degrees of dress are close behind.

"What is it, Master Gary? What the hell is going on?"

I am still leaning forward on the car's horn and the sound is surely waking up Grandpa Pope and the others at the family crypt. I am sobbing. I am pouring my heart out. This is not the way it is supposed to be. I am home and my make-believe world is over. Oscar's hand is grabbing my hair.

"Sir, sit up. You are going to wake the fucking dead."

This is about the same time I am remembering my father opening the passenger's door. Marlene is falling sideways and out onto the cold snow covered asphalt driveway. My father is looking at Oscar and is cradling Marlene's upper torso in his arms.

"That's a bad choice of words, Oscar. It looks like the girl has been dead for a couple of days now."

I am remembering John Murphy pulling the note from the knife that is sticking through Marlene's heart. He is reading it aloud.

"Gary, I know how much we love each other. I also know you are attached to Marlene. It is unfair that you are the one who must do the deed. I am, at present, a little drunk. I hope you understand and see this for what it is. It is not art. It is a gift to you from someone who loves you beyond words. Besides I am finally taking your advice and growing a pair."

The note is signed, 'William, alias, Mr. Whipple'. There is a little smiley face under the signature. The smile is upside down.

Those standing around are silent. One or two are scurrying back with a blanket. Marlene's body is unceremoniously scooped up and carried toward the garage. I am wishing for the brightest light in the universe. Only blindness is capable of taking my hurt away. John Murphy is leading me toward my bedroom. He is the last to speak.

"So that is where the little bastard was."

Chapter Fifty-Eight

I am sitting on a bench across the street from the Sigrist Mansion. It is a place so full of memories I do not know where to start. Most of my memories are very dark and frightening ones, except for a few small kindnesses given freely from the hearts of this or that staff member. The Black Witch is one of these servants. She is definitely different, but is also kind at heart. Because of her kindness I forgive her that little sexual transgression with my mother. Mother, like me at the time, is only reaching out for love. By this time, I am sure the Black Witch is also dead. I am thinking about writing a book about all of this someday, but my time is short. My state-provided therapist means well and I like her. She is the first woman I bond with, if you know what I mean. Anyway, I am thinking about writing that book. I know this is not going to happen, but it is surely a best seller. I am sure of this. It is my age that is hampering this suggested project. Living to be seventy-nine is the last thing to ever be entering my mind.

Writing is like sex. Too much of it and the whole act is just repetition without gratification. I know that people still have sex. I do not know that people are still reading. Some are barely understandable when speaking. This fact is recognizable even without a college education, something I never experience. I am sure that reading is beyond their educational training, the system being what it is. Hell, the teachers are fucking the students instead of teaching them how to read. The three 'R's'... reading,' riting' and 'rithmatic'...are now snorting, drinking and fucking. I am ok with things changing, but we are overboard and the ship is sinking. My life is overboard, too. It is overboard for a very long time. I suppose my comment about the current state of our educational profession is unfair. One is capable of learning to live underwater. I am proof of that fact. Maybe, there is hope. Maybe, writing that book is in my future. One's life span is a secretive sort of thing, given no unforeseen medical circumstances. There is always hope. This is what I am always telling myself.

It is a sunny day and the winds are calm. The air is pure today. I know this by living on the streets for so long. My lungs are like a walking weather filter. Walking is another topic. I do a lot of walking now. You are not allowed in the shelter before seven at night and leaving before seven in the morning is a requirement for maintaining your residency status. I understand. The staff's job is hard enough, cleaning up all that puke and filth from the night before, without having all of us in the way. I do not like being around the others. They are always telling me their own stories. What the fuck do I care? I am a private sort of person. This is an odd statement considering I am thinking about writing that book. I am thinking about writing it a few days before I die. This way listening to all of the criticism and analysis is something I do not have to endure. I am sure you understand. If not, fuck you. I am at that age, somewhere between sixty and death, where speaking my mind is both expected and somewhat of a requirement. It is like continuing to drive that old car, the one that is technically historical, right into the grave with you. Why buy a new one? They are overpriced, shitty looking, without character and made of plastic. Honestly, I might buy one, but buying takes money and this is something I am without. Still, I am living. I am living for a very long time and I am thinking about writing a book. There is something to be said for this. The hardest part for me about writing a book is in a conversation I am remembering with my therapist, Zoe. I like the name Zoe. Maybe you don't. Fuck you if you don't. This is just my opinion. Here is the conversation I am remembering.

"You think I should write a book?"

"Why wouldn't you write a book, Gary?"

"Only people in college write books and this is after years of training on how to write."

"This is not true. Many of our greatest writers never went to college. Writing was a social thing."

"I don't understand?"

"Pretend you are back in earlier times."

I am listening to Zoe and I am pretending. I like pretending. It is a big part of my life and takes me away from some place I do not want to be. I am no longer pretending I am not homeless. I am homeless so long that homelessness seems like my home. Do you understand what I am saying? You probably don't, but I really don't give a shit. This is my story and I am telling it the way I want to tell it. If you don't understand just fucking stop reading, right now. I'm sorry. I don't mean for those last few lines to be creeping in. I get a few 'take-backs' anytime I am socializing. It is a good rule, especially for someone my age. I am pretending and listening to Zoe, my therapist. I am picturing myself in a black suit and top hat in front of a roaring fire in a dimly lit room. I have those hand warmer things on that are not quite gloves. I am holding an ink pen with a big feather sticking out of its top end. I am leaning over a writing desk, the type where the top flips open for storing your important manuscripts. All these types of desks are really good for is letting everything on top slide to the floor when you are trying to retrieve something you have forgotten from inside the thing. I hate this style of fucking desk, but it is appropriate for the time I am dreaming about. I am pretending Zoe and I are husband and wife. She is my rock and inspiration. Zoe helps erase the memory of my dear departed wife, Marlene. The only thing I love more than my writing is wrapping my arms around my Zoe at night and falling into a comfortable sleep, a sleep without dreams. I am thinking about how pretending to kill William during a satanic ritual is my attempt at killing the memory of my past. The problem is that

I am basically a coward. Despite everything, I like living. I am thinking about how my new pretend face fails to cover what I am seeing daily in my own mirror. Ok Zoe, I am with you. I am pretending. Go on.

"Back then, Gary, writing was a social event. People gathered once a week or more to share their stories. Mary Shelly's book, Frankenstein, was born this way. Everyone in the group would give their thoughts on the other person's work. It was a great way for people to express themselves. It was even therapeutic given the times they were all living in. I think you should write a book. Even if you don't share the book, write it for yourself. I think this might be helpful."

There is a long silence. Zoe is waiting for my response. Sometimes a pause is a very effective tool. The truth is that my therapy is now so many years in the making that I am capable of out-pausing the best of them. I know this is frustrating to Zoe. It pleases me to no end. I am in control of something. If not my life, I am in control of my therapist. I am also not thinking about killing her. I am thinking about loving her. This is a good thing. At this late juncture in my life, I am making great progress.

This is the conversation I am remembering as I am sitting on this bench across from the Sigrist Mansion. These last few thoughts are about the book I might write, if I were to write a book. The book is about a little boy. His name is Gary. Gary's father is a very bad man and is taking advantage of Gary, sexually. Gary's mother is looking the other way. Gary is creating a little brother in the deepest and darkest corners of his own mind. Gary is keeping his little brother safe, but is failing time and time again. Gary's little brother is doing horrible things. It is not Gary doing these things. This is what Gary is telling himself. Gary is a detective in his pretend world. He is helping others. He is not his fucked up little brother. I am trying to explain myself through my therapy in the form of this book. Forgive me if some things are a little confusing. Gary's life is confusing and separating what is real and what is not real is the reason I am writing this book. Too, does it matter if Vickie is dead for real or only dead in my mind? She is still dead to me. Accepting the fact that these events are real in my mind is very important for your enjoyment and understanding of my story. Gary and William is one person. Is this so hard to believe? I say it is not. Fuck you if you are thinking along different lines. This is, after all, my story, my life and my book. I am writing it and ending it as I see fit. Sorry about that last 'fuck you' comment. I am trying to get better. Too, I love Zoe. I think I love Zoe more than Gary. She is something real. She is something warm. She is something capable of being touched and loved in the real world. Now that I am thinking about it, Zoe is a big part of my story. I know having her is not possible. This is a good thing. I am finally accepting the reality of disappointments being able to make one a better person. I hope the plot is acceptable. Keep in mind I do not possess a college education. This is all I am asking. My book is entitled, <u>Little Brother</u>. It begins.

Gary wants a little brother. It is something to love. It is something to take care of and keep out of harm's way. Gary wants to be a hero. All little boys like the idea of being a hero. A policeman is a good idea because protecting everyone is possible. At least in Gary's mind it is possible. Gary is sitting alone in the basement of his big old house. Gary is pretending to be his little brother. His little brother's name is William. Gary likes the name William. Gary's little brother is very smart, very creative, but very reclusive. His little brother, the one in his mind, is making things while he is sitting alone there in the basement.

One day there is something happening to Gary's little brother when Gary is not around. Thank God, at least in Gary's mind, this thing is not happening to him. His little brother's father comes into the basement looking for William.

"William, why are you alone here in this dark and dusty, old basement?"

"I am waiting on mother."

"Why are you waiting on your mother?"

Gary's little brother is tentative. He is afraid of his father, but he is more afraid of the games he and his father are always playing.

"I don't want to play with you today, father."

"Well, G.W., I am the father and you really don't get to make that choice."

G.W. is father's little nickname for his boy toy. Gary William Sigrist is feeling his father's sweaty, smelly old body again, even in the mansion's cold and dusty basement. He is feeling the pain again. His father is breathing very heavily. William knows it is about over. The breathing is the key. He is learning to just give in and listen for the breathing. William is wishing his big brother were here to see what father is doing to him. William is wishing his mother were here, too. William is hearing the breathing getting quicker and louder. There are footsteps on the basement stairs. William's head is bending back and he is seeing his mother coming down the steps. His mother is stopping. Why is she stopping? She is turning around and going back up the steps. Why is she going back up the steps? Don't you see what father is doing? The breathing is stopped. There is a heavy sigh and then release. It is over for another day. William is watching his father going back up the basement steps. He is thinking about another place to hide, a place impossible to find. Is there such a place? William is thinking perhaps it is inside of his mind. This is where he is hiding his hate. This is where he is hiding his hate for all the monsters roaming the mansion and always looking the other way. William is thinking this is the answer, his hiding place deep inside his mind. This hiding place can change…being whatever William wants it to be at any given time. Why, not? Don't think it and it isn't real. Doesn't this make sense? William is in need of his own world. Gary is not always around protecting him. Expecting this is unfair. Gary's life is Gary's life and William is capable of understanding this. He loves Gary. Gary is not like William's mother. Gary is the one walking down the steps and not walking back up the steps pretending not to see. William hates women.

The years move on. William's love for Gary is growing. A therapist might say that they are one. It is that old advice about needing to love yourself before you are able to love someone else. Sadly, Gary is arriving at the conclusion that William is beyond saving and that too much damage is done. Perhaps a new face is needed; perhaps a new life; perhaps a story about two boys who are one being overlooked by a society charged with the responsibility of looking after them. Perhaps it is as simple as a mixed up order at a fast food restaurant. Just saying you are sorry is, enough. Gary and William, the same little boy, are hearing it all the time.

Lashing out is understandable. William is trying very hard to please his big brother, but is always failing. William always needs his art, his final hiding place away from all his pain and guilt. His art is his retaliation for the hand life is dealing him. Parts of this story being true and some not being true are also understandable. This is what writing and therapy is all about. Ask Zoe, my therapist. The killings are my burden, my secret, and are in part why this story is being written so close to the time of my death. Don't be too judgmental. I am trying. Don't want to disappoint my big brother or fail at the art of written expression. I think I like writing. Paintings are just too hard to carry around from place to place. A funeral home is a good idea. Too bad this is just part of my story. Too bad my shopping cart isn't really a dancing machine, like the one in my mind and in my funeral home. I am getting better. The hate for women is subsiding. It is probably my age. Thinking about killing Zoe is difficult. I like her. I love her. Loving a woman is a very good sign about how my therapy is going. I am hoping Zoe does not say something to piss me off. You already know that I love her. I can't imagine Zoe ever pissing me off. This memory and age thing is beginning to get on my nerves. This writing my story is in need of being done quickly, before I am forgetting what I am writing about. I desperately want to be this thing other people are calling normal before my death.

Gary, my older brother, likes the scarves in my shopping cart. Gary is always complimenting me about my eye for color. My only disappointment about my big brother is he not figuring out a way to keep my new face from falling off. Looking at my real self in the mirror is very frightening. There I go again, falling back into my pretend world. I am Gary. God damn it. I am Gary. Quit bringing William into the equation. Zoe is going to get pissed off. Thinking back I am of the conclusion that my release is through my art as my father's release was through me. Still, mother should not be walking back up the steps.

I am sorry I am wandering and getting away from the story line…the book I am writing. It is the way it is when you are my age. Anyway, the cops are here. I must leave you now. We must pick up this train of thought later.

"There he is, Hank. He is just sitting there on that bench again."

"I know. How many times do we have to arrest this asshole before he understands he can't be doing this? The home owners are really starting to get pissed at the department."

"We can only do what we can do, Hank. Until the city takes a stand on the homeless issue, this is going to go on and on."

"What is his story?"

"Says he was rich once and that this place was his home. Visions of grandeur coupled with a little too much wine, if you ask me."

"Did you ever get any specifics out of him, family and all that sort of thing?"

"You can't keep the fucker on track long enough. His identification does say Sigrist and the Sigrist family did live here. That's been a long time ago."

"Wouldn't it be a kick in the ass if he was telling the truth?"

"Look at him, partner. Whatever his story is, it is too late now to be hoping for a brighter future."

I hear the police cruiser doors close as the two officers are approaching me. I know what they are thinking when they are pulling up next to me. I am sorry to be such a bother, but I am what I am. Maybe Gary is going to show up this time and kick their asses for continually hassling me. Oh, no, that is not going to happen. Zoe is right about Gary and I being the same person. Accepting this fact is central to me getting better. I am not talking about my art with Zoe. Patient-client privilege or not, I am not taking this chance. Be nice to Hank and Ron. They are very nice policemen.

Hank is sitting next to me on the bench. Ron is looking through my shopping cart, my dancing machine. That is fine with me. There is no blood on it. Changing shopping carts from time to time is part of my method of operation. Burning my victim's belongs in different burn barrels around town is a pain in the ass. I do believe that a portable crematorium might be a big seller, even a lucrative business venture. These little deceptions of mine are necessary. They are necessary for protecting my art, the art of a fucking genius. This whole art thing is just so complicated. I am sure that it isn't because of never going to college. A genius operates on a whole different level. Someone like me is always laughing at the need for some stupid college education. Colleges are no more than document treadmills. Am I right? It is getting cold. I hope they are burning bodies tonight. Leaning against that outside wall is a sure fire way of keeping warm. That's funny, 'sure fire'. Get it? There is to be no flipping out tonight. I'm going to be co-operative with these two nice police officers. Besides, Gary is probably watching me right now. I hate disappointing my big brother. Fuck, there it is again. I am Gary. I am sorry, Zoe. I am going to get this right. I promise you that I am going to get this right, even if it kills me.

"Gary, you have to stop this. If you don't we will have to say something to the shelter and you know what that means," advises one of the police officers.

"Yeah, I'm on the street twenty-four hours instead of twelve."

Officer Hank is frustrated. I am sorry about this.

"What in the hell is so important about this particular spot in the city, Gary? There are a thousand benches in this city. Most of them have a hell of a lot better view than that of an old mansion in bad need of repair. Why can't you just go someplace else? Make our jobs a little easier and help yourself at the same time."

These are difficult questions to answer. To answer them my book needs completing. Maybe Hank and Ron are readers. Maybe writing my life's story with all of its hidden secrets about my art and my pretend little brother, William, is a good idea. Maybe this is the only way of killing the Werewolf forever. Did I say that I really like my therapist, Zoe? I am sure that I did. Suddenly all these memories are coming back. I am sitting on the bench with Officer Hank next to me. I am crying. I am a little boy again. This is very embarrassing. Officer Hank's arm is around me. It is not like when my father is putting his arm around me. Hank's arm is full of understanding and love.

"Come on, Gary. Things are going to get better. I am sure of it."

"I'll go and I won't come back. Just don't take me to jail."

"Do you promise?"

"I promise. My word is good."

I am pushing my dancing machine down the sidewalk toward the other side of town, the side of town where my funeral home is in ashes. That it is never really my funeral home is not important, that I am the one leaning against the back crematorium wall to stay warm and that parts of this story are true and parts are not aren't' important. Maybe I accidentally burnt the place down and maybe I didn't. A lot of things are really confusing for me right now. I am thinking there is a bench where my funeral home's ashes reside. Perhaps it is a safe bench where the world passes me by unseen, where all of my realness and make believe come together making me whole and comfortable with what remains of my life, a twisted life with a make believe brother and make believe monsters that continually haunt those who have caused me so much pain. The only thing I know for sure that, is real, is the fact that my soul is living somewhere between a broken heart and a troubled mind. I am thinking about my relatives. I am thinking about opportunities missed. I am thinking about my mother's dying words.

"Don't worry about it. Boys will be boys."

I know she understands my second face. I know she understands that by protecting a pretend little brother I am protecting myself. I know that his face is in need of falling by the wayside, while facing the reality of my past. One cannot hide from their father forever. There is no other reason for her saying, "Boys will be boys". This is all about father and me. It is not about William and me.

The damn right wheel on this shopping cart is beginning to wobble. It is time to get another one. I don't want it going off in the wrong direction when I am not paying attention. I'm trying to remember what color Zoe's eyes are, what color scarf she might like. There is a voice in the back of my mind. It wants my attention. I answer without thinking.

"William? Is that you?"

Previous books by Frank J. Basham

BUCKET OF STRANGERS

SPILLED WORDS,
a collection of poetry

Awards & Publications

National Poetry Review

Pegasus Magazine

Florence B. Allen Literary Award (The Ohio State University)

Ian F. Howell Memorial Award

Honorable Mention, Great American Poetry Contest

Outstanding English Achievement Award (The Ohio State University)

Watch for Frank J. Basham's upcoming books.

DUST

Bad memories are like dust coming back again and again, constantly falling onto the tabletop of your mind. I am Louise. It is a simple name; my past, not so much. Living with my memories is a given. Judging me for what I might have been and not for what I have become is all that I ask. This is my story.

Often I think of all these grains of sand squishing up between my toes as I jog along the beach. I like the sand. It is not so easy a victim of some horrific crime, illness or manmade calamity. Sand is pliable and resilient. Each piece of sand is an entity in and of itself. It is working in a community of smaller parts, parts that comprise the whole. Drop a foot into sand and, as you are running away, it is busy folding back onto itself and becoming whole again. It is sad that life is not like sand. Life is random. This is true. Looking at the big picture, one understands that life is more tightly compacted than sand. Life is not as fluid. Life is not as forgiving and, in the hands of some, is easily turned into an outright hell for all of those experiencing its touch. Yes, it is sad that life is not more like sand.